MASTER OF STARLIGHT

MASTER OF STARLIGHT

KEITH SHORT

Matador
9 Priory Business Park,
Wistow Road, Kibworth Beauchamp,
Leicestershire. LE8 0RX
Tel: 0116 279 2299
Email: books@troubador.co.uk
Web: www.troubador.co.uk/matador
Twitter: @matadorbooks

ISBN 978 1838590 406

British Library Cataloguing in Publication Data.
A catalogue record for this book is available from the British Library.

Typeset in 11pt Sabon MT by Troubador Publishing Ltd, Leicester, UK

Matador is an imprint of Troubador Publishing Ltd

PROLOGUE
London 2060

'I can't wait to get in there, Gunther. I gather it's going to take at least three hours to get around these exhibits. What are we waiting for?'

'Hold on, young man, there's plenty of time for all that. I'd just like to take this in before we start the tour. The story behind this statue is even more fascinating than the one we're going to see inside the museum, you realise?'

'No, I *don't* realise. Come on, let's go. This was *your* idea for a day out, after all. I can't believe it all started here and we've made all this progress since the third decade of the millennium. Don't you find that fascinating? Aren't you excited? Why are we waiting?'

'Just indulge an old man. Come, sit by me for a while.' He tapped the Chesterfield's green padded upholstery and, once the frustrated youngster joined him, he pointed up to the statue in front of them.

Together with the sparse seating arrangements that surrounded it, it was the only feature in the entrance hall of the magnificent old building. 'You can see what a powerful man he was in the physical sense. And despite what the science historians would have you believe, he was a great man in every other sense. He had vision and he held his nerve. He *backed the man*, as Oppenheimer would have said.'

'I don't know about that. Rumour has it he made his money from the sex trade and other shady enterprises.'

Gunther shrugged his shoulders and laughed. 'Maybe he did. Who knows? But if it wasn't for him committing his fortune to what was a fading dream for others, we'd still be reliant on the old thermal reactors. And you also have to remember, we were still burning coal and gas to produce our electricity in those days.'

The young man gestured towards the plaque on the podium beneath the statue. 'He must have been self-opinionated to have his statue inscribed with that.'

'It was Leon Dabrowski himself who commissioned the statue and composed that testimony. In one way, you see, Vladimir Chekhov really *was* the father of nuclear fusion power. And the true history isn't inside that museum over there. It began just a few miles from where we are now. Fate can intervene from the most unlikely corner …'

PART 1 – London 1990

STARLIGHT LOST

CHAPTER 1

Routine day over, feet up in front of mindless television and a relaxing cup of tea. Nothing life changing about that, she thought as she hung her nurse's coat at the end of the row of empty pegs. Changing her life was something she could well do with but, at the same time, something she couldn't bear to contemplate tonight. In fact, the prospect of a quiet evening at home made her sigh inwardly and smile, as if she'd just settled into a hot bath full of bubbles for the first time. But first there were routine checks to be made. She stared at the closed door at the end of the corridor and the trepidation slowly rising in her gut swilled away any thoughts of contentment. It would take only a few moments to cross her living room floor to the kitchen and seconds to check that the door to the outside was locked. But until she could be sure, she couldn't relax. Nerves jangling and heartbeat rising, Jean Douglas opened her living room door – and threw her hands to the sides of her head.

'Robert!'

He was comatose on his back, his eyes staring through their liquid glaze to whatever it was he saw beyond her. A dirty spoon and saucer, a ripped-open plastic bag and a cigarette lighter – scattered among the discarded garments to either side. The leather belt he used as a tourniquet hung loose around his upper arm and, on his emaciated lower arm, a hypodermic needle dangled from one of his barely visible veins. Jean started sobbing. She'd seen it all before, but it was usually outside in the shed or in the yard, not in her living room, for God's sake. Deep down, she always knew it would come to this one day. But that didn't prevent the shock and the anger that came with it. Inside her home – her precious home. She had to scream.

'You bastard! You lousy, useless smack-head! How could you do this in *my* house?' Snorting with anger, she bent down hands on knees and snarled into his ear, 'You and that sister of yours don't pay a single penny for the privilege of living here. You even have me borrowing from the bank to pay your court fines and keep you in those stinking rags you wear. And God knows what you're doing with the food in my cupboards. You're not eating it, that's for sure. Do you hear me?'

But Robert wasn't listening. She could tell he was incapable of that. And even if he heard her ranting, what would he care? Jean was already weary from her long day at work. Now, exhausted from her futile tirade, she sank to her knees and looked at the debris surrounding her. Robert's head rolled to one side. Powerless to do anything, she could only watch as bright yellow bile oozed from his open mouth and pooled on the carpet.

4

Numb with despair, her head dropped into her hands. *Can't go on any more.* But she had to keep going, she told herself. What else could she do? *I still love him.* Resigning herself yet again to her thankless task as a mother, she did what she always did – at least this time there was no need to haul his limp and withered body back into the house. She carefully removed the needle from his arm and summoned up the strength to lift her nineteen-year-old son on to the settee. She sniffed as she wiped away the tears of agony with the back of her hand, picked up the spoon and lighter and began her ritual clear-up once again.

Jean hadn't seen Robert for three days. Nothing unusual about that and there was little point in worrying. They say that drug addicts possess a natural ability for survival; they always know where they can find shelter among other users – another fix if they're lucky. Robert had even apologised before he left, said he wouldn't fix at home again if he could keep his house key. She couldn't trust him, of course. But this evening she had a reassuring feeling inside that she was returning home to an empty and peaceful house. She closed the front door behind her and removed her coat. What was that clunking noise? She stood still and listened. *There it is again.* It was coming from upstairs. *Oh God, he's in the bedroom.* She threw her coat to the floor and scurried up the stairs two at a time. *This is the last time. He's getting no more chances.* She burst through the bedroom door and stopped dead.

'Mary! What are you doing?'

Her daughter – in bed with a stranger? And what a filthy mess. The stench of stale alcohol and sour body odour made her want to vomit. She covered her mouth and nose as the scruffy middle-aged man threw back the sheets to reveal his nakedness and brazenly walked towards her. He smiled at her, displaying his uneven black teeth as if proud of them. 'You all right, love?' he said, showing no shame as he stepped into his urine-stained Y-fronts.

Jean turned towards Mary in bewilderment. *Why?* she tried to say, but the pointless question wouldn't leave her mouth. Mary reached across to the bedside table for her cigarettes and lighter, eased herself up on the pillow and lit a cigarette. Her daughter's breasts, reddened with scratches from the pawing they'd no doubt just received, the filthy assailant who was responsible perched at the foot of the bed and nonchalantly pulling on his socks – it was all too much.

'You dirty slut! *My* bed, *my* bedroom. You didn't even have the decency to use your own.'

'My own bed wasn't big enough, Ma,' Mary said, as if deliberately goading her mother. 'But don't worry, I've left you some money over there on your dresser. My minder doesn't know about this one.'

'Take the bastard down to the park next time!' Jean screamed. She turned towards her daughter's client. 'And I've seen better than that on a chipmunk. The only swelling *you'll* get down there is with the clap. Now get out of my house before I call the police.'

The man finished dressing as if he couldn't care less, slung his grubby jacket over his shoulder and shoved an unlit cigarette into the corner of his mouth. As he squeezed his way through the doorway, he glared down and muttered into Jean's face.

'Cow!'

She closed her eyes and grimaced at the smell of his foetid nicotine breath and the vile sensation of him brushing against her breasts. She wasn't going to budge one inch until he left the house.

The sound of the closing front door was the signal for the house to become tranquil once more. For a moment, the beautiful and effervescent schoolgirl she knew a year ago smiled at her from the bed. Captivated by her innocence, she felt her motherly love and wanted to hug her baby girl – bring her back home for good. She looked again at her ruined daughter – dishevelled hair, running mascara, a cigarette smouldering in her trembling hand. She was weeping.

'I'm sorry, Ma.'

Was there love buried behind those tearful eyes? She had to believe there was. It was all she had left to cling to in this miserable life.

'I'm sorry too.' But nothing they could say would bring that love to the surface. What was happening to her little princess? She shook her head in resignation – there was little point in starting another row. 'Just change the sheets before you go, will you?'

Worn and defeated, Jean went downstairs to the kitchen where she paced about aimlessly. How much more of this mental torture could she endure? The vicious circle her daughter was trapped in – work the streets, pay the pimp, snort the coke, work the streets – wasn't Mary's fault, she tried to tell herself. It was

Robert who made that deal with local pimps. Her son had an incurable illness that held no respect for family values or middle-class status; he'd even prostitute his own sister for his next fix. She started to cry. The front door slammed. How could Mary leave the house like that, without even saying goodbye? Like she always did when she reached the end of her tether, Jean sat down at the kitchen table with her head in her hands – and cried some more.

Jean was a community nurse in Camden Town but didn't work Saturdays. This was the day she visited her local library – a place where she could hide from Robert and Mary, a secure shelter from her life of misery. But today, as she sloped along on her traditional pilgrimage, the scraps of joy she usually gleaned from her trip to the library were absent from her heart. The morning was overcast and depressing, but that wasn't the reason for her hunched gait; it was the weight of her problems pressing down on her petite frame. And how self-conscious she felt today without her neatly pressed nurse's uniform. She wouldn't normally think about what she looked like but today the awareness was lodged in her mind like a jagged shard of metal – she was dishevelled. She'd never let herself become grubby, of course; she was too proud for that. She washed her long auburn hair with regularity, even if she couldn't be bothered to groom it. She'd let it dry naturally, leaving it bedraggled and unmanageable, but at least it was always clean and fresh smelling. She rarely looked in a mirror nowadays; if she did, she'd see how the grey strands were multiplying at pace, ageing her. Not yet forty, she'd already stopped looking after herself. Why should she bother about her appearance when there was no special man in her life? George had left a long time ago and she'd been glad to get rid of the evil bastard. Would anyone ever love her again?

As she entered the old red-brick Victorian building, she bowed her head to hide her face, conscious as always of the prudish gazes of the librarians looking down on her as if she was some kind of homeless tramp. But at least they'd come to accept her presence. They even spoke to her sometimes and, to her consternation, today was one such occasion.

'Here again, are we?'

She didn't look up; with her eyes swollen from perpetual crying, she was too embarrassed.

The reference section exuded its usual calm stillness. She peered around at the familiar volumes on art and science. Normally, she'd lift the books unaided from the upper shelves, lug a pile of them across to her favourite table and study their diagrams and glossy photographs until closing time. But today she hadn't the energy, the desire. She stroked her hand down the binding of a book entitled *Cezanne Composition*. One of her favourites, but maybe not today. She left the grand old hall, helped herself to a bundle of magazines and newspapers from the wall racks in the foyer, and found a free armchair. *Welcome to the Nineties* was the title on the front of one of the magazines. The headline's optimism sent her into despair over her reprobate offspring – they were throwing their lives away in front of her eyes. She hated

9

Mary for what she was doing, cringed at the thought of those grimy old men defiling her daughter's body one after another. In fact, she was beginning to despise both of her children. There was a fleeting thought of suicide, but she forced it from her mind. After all, she loved her children, didn't she? And she wouldn't want them to be left with the bother of organising her funeral. *How can you love and hate someone at the same time?* How could her children tear her in half like this? Browsing through today's newspapers, she found concentration difficult. She turned the pages with no obvious purpose, until she came across a discreet advert in the Vacancies section of the *London Evening Standard.*

In need of a caring mother, contact my father.

She was intrigued. Given her dire family circumstances, there was a poignant note of irony in the wording and she couldn't even be sure she was looking at a job advert until she read the small print. *Wow!* That was almost three times her current salary. This must be some rich father. But that wasn't all. The job – a nanny – required someone to live in. Here was her opportunity to get away from her family problems. She'd be better placed to support Robert and Mary financially and at the same time she'd no longer have to put up with their degenerate behaviour. She could feel herself trembling with excitement. There'd no doubt be many applicants and despite her own impressive nursing qualifications, most of them would be better qualified and more experienced than her. It was a long shot but what did she have to lose? *Life couldn't get any worse, could it?*

CHAPTER 2

Oleg Malkin bowed his head against the hammering rain. The sudden and unexpected downpour flattened his thick black hair and fogged his spectacles as he waited patiently for the approaching cortège. He shivered as the water from the drenched collar of his black woollen overcoat trickled down the back of his neck, yet he had no choice but to remain in this dignified position – he had to show his respect for the occupants of the lead car which was easing to a halt in front of him. Maintaining his sombre expression, he pondered the irony of the car's luxury marque as he opened the rear door of the black Bentley. *How emblematic of the English ruling classes to ride in such a vehicle.* The passengers stepped out and Malkin's head remained bowed as Vladimir Chekhov and his personal bodyguard passed him by without a word and laboured their way to the edge of the six-foot-deep rectangular hole – the final resting place of the *pakhan*.

There were less than twenty mourners at this funeral, with no children among them. Close acquaintances of the Chekhov family lined the grave alongside invited senior members of the *bratva*, waiting to show their respect to their outgoing and incoming leaders. At the arrival of the chief mourner, Malkin sensed the wave of relief within their ranks but could see that Chekhov was already looking around impatiently for the officiating minister. At last, the Russian Orthodox priest emerged from his shelter under a nearby acer and took his place at the head of the grave. He took a whole minute to study those who had gathered, as if he was reading everyone's private thoughts, before finally nodding his approval to the closest pall bearer. The coffin was lowered, the priest rattled out his incantations without once looking up from his prayer book and after ten minutes, it was all over. He solemnly shook Chekhov's hand, acknowledged the rest of the mourners and left the Highgate cemetery. A thankless duty – and executed with no compassion whatsoever.

He caught the eye of Illyich Slomensky, the Chekhov *bratva*'s most experienced brigadier, who'd been watching this terse burial service a few paces back from the others. Slomensky acknowledged him with a stern nod but Malkin could never read this old warrior. He'd been at the bedside with Slomensky a week earlier and listened as he informed the old *pakhan* that the *bratva* was becoming a laughing stock. He'd suggested that he, Illyich Slomensky, was the right man to whip it all back into shape before the whole organisation collapsed around their ears. But Anatoly Chekhov was too tired and too ill to take much notice of his brigadier's counsel and by then it was clear he no longer cared.

The ceremony over, it was no surprise to see Vladimir Chekhov conversing with Slomensky before he left. After all, Slomensky was a long-standing loyal comrade of Chekhov's father, working for him for over forty years and heading up his various brigades for the past two decades. For five minutes, he studied the two men sitting out of earshot on the remembrance bench under the old acer, leaning within touching distance to exchange their words in private. At one point he was sure that Slomensky pointed briefly in his direction. A cold electrical spasm welled in his stomach – was that responsive turn of Chekhov's head aimed towards him?

No one dared to leave the cemetery during this time. The mourners huddled together in tight groups to gain what little warmth and protection from the rain they could. The gravediggers watched from a distance, waiting in the incessant rain for the opportunity to complete their job.

'So, that's Vladimir Chekhov?' Malkin heard one of them say.

Up to now, Chekhov's courtesies had consisted of little more than brief murmurs. Even as he prepared to leave, all he seemed to offer his fellow mourners was an empty thank you or a condescending handshake here and there. At last, his new *pakhan* marched towards the car. *Thank God, we can all go home.* But, to Malkin's surprise, Chekhov's final words were for him.

'My father's office, nine thirty tomorrow morning.'

Taken aback, Malkin could do little else but stand speechless and gawp as he opened the car door. *Why me? I'm only the bookkeeper.* Could this unexpected invitation be a turning point in his life?

Two in the morning, wide awake and mind racing, it was becoming a losing battle. There would be little sleep for Malkin tonight. *What sort of man is he?* Would Vladimir Chekhov, like his ruthless father before him, sweep aside those who stood in his way? Would he ever go as far as his father by having them killed if it suited his purpose? He rolled in his bed with unrest. *How much does he know about me?* Did Chekhov already know that his father's bookkeeper was a pacifist, a hater of violence, working in a violent and merciless environment? Would he consider him suitable for such a role? *Is it only me he's seeing today?* What about Slomensky – was he going to offer the old brigadier his job? That would make sense, he conceded. It would remove Slomensky's fading talent from the front line and provide Chekhov with a right-hand man who had decades of valuable field experience. The aggravating questions swirled around his head as he turned over and back again, trying to dispel the heat from his body. But the sheets were like hotplates and his overheated skin was becoming sore. Anatoly Chekhov always knew of his bookkeeper's abhorrence of violence. Malkin was only twenty-two when the old *pakhan* discovered his pacifism. And, to this day, he couldn't remember what he'd been doing down in the lower basement when he stumbled across the scene.

Sarco was bound naked to a little wooden chair. His cheeks were red, obviously from the hard slapping he must have just received from Anatoly Chekhov's security officer.

'Ah, Oleg, glad you could come,' Chekhov said as he grabbed Sarco by the hair and violently shook his head. 'We simply cannot tolerate treachery like this. Would you agree, Karlov?' The security officer pulled his leather glove up tight and nodded his agreement with a sardonic smile. 'What do you think his punishment should be, bookkeeper? After all, you found the anomaly in his return, you discovered that he must have pocketed the majority of the money.' He looked Sarco in the eye and added another slap to the previous barrage. 'Money, which by now has been squandered on the whores provided by our rivals, no doubt? What shall we do with him, Oleg?'

Malkin remained silent – it was up to Chekhov what to do next. Chekhov hissed through gritted teeth into Sarco's face, tilted the hapless prisoner's head back using a single finger under the chin and struck his face with the palm of his hand. Sarco's nose broke with a sharp snap. He groaned as his head fell forward on to his chest and the blood from his crushed nose streamed down his torso into his groin.

'I can see you're having trouble deciding, bookkeeper. Well, let me make your mind up for you.' Chekhov nodded to Karlov, who pulled a pistol from the inside pocket of his jacket and offered it to Malkin.

With reluctance, Malkin took the gun by the handle and turned towards his *pakhan*, urging him with despairing eyes to stop this violence. *Please don't make me do this.*

'Go ahead, Oleg. Shoot the bastard.'

Sarco looked up at Chekhov with a dazed expression. He broke down and cried for mercy. 'Please – spare me!' The blood from Sarco's nose spattered off his lips. 'I'm sorry, I'll find the money and return it, you have my word.'

'Too late for all that and your word isn't worth the shit in your pants. Look at him, Oleg, he's pissed himself like a dog. You need to put this filthy animal out of his misery. It's all he deserves.'

Malkin put the gun to Sarco's temple and his hand began to shake. 'I can't do it.'

'Do you want to be next in the chair, bookkeeper? Just man up, for God's sake, and get on with it.'

There was no choice, the threat to kill him was real. His own punishment would be carried out there and then if he refused his *pakhan*'s order; they had no mercy, no scruples, these people. He squeezed the trigger with his trembling hand. Although he was squeezing with all his strength, the trigger wouldn't move.

Sarco was shaking and started sobbing again. 'Please – don't!'

What am I doing here? 'I can't!'

'Just fucking do it!' Chekhov yelled.

With one last effort, Malkin overcame the psychological stiffness in the trigger and the gun went off in his hand – with a loud click. Sarco grimaced and screamed out. Chekhov and Karlov burst into coarse laughter, hollering deep belly laughs as they fell about each other and as Chekhov leered into Sarco's blubbering face.

Rubbing the tears of laughter from his eyes, Chekhov eased the pistol from Malkin's hand and passed it back to Karlov, who was still chuckling away to himself. 'Come, my humble bookkeeper, we have important financial matters to discuss, you and I.' He placed his arm around his shoulders and turned him towards the door.

The ear-splitting gunshot sent an echo ringing around the cellar. Malkin lurched to one side. The arm around him tightened like an instantly applied tourniquet and prevented him from falling. Chekhov spoke softly into his ear. 'Don't look back, Oleg. Never look back on a decision.'

The ringing in his ears persisted as his tortuous thoughts were disrupted by his bedside alarm. The alarm's red digits were flashing, telling him it was seven o'clock, and he felt an icy cold. How could that be, when he'd been so hot during the night? *Oh God, the sheets are drenched in urine.* He breathed a sigh of relief as he realised it was the sweat from his body evaporating in the cool morning air that poured in through the open window. The thought of his forthcoming meeting with Anatoly Chekhov's son sent a surge of fear through his body and he began to shiver. Would he be like his father? *What will he do with me?*

'The *pakhan* will see you now, Mr Malkin.'

The uniformed Russian opened the grand eight-foot-high door and Malkin strode with confidence towards the mahogany period desk behind which Vladimir Chekhov sat perusing a document. He'd steeled himself for this moment, arrived determined to show he was the epitome of self-assurance. However, before he could bid his new *pakhan* a good morning, he was cut short. Without looking up and with faultless timing, Chekhov gestured towards the single chair in front of the desk.

'Take a seat, Malkin.'

'Thank you, sir,' he said, wondering whether he was about to be praised or reprimanded.

Chekhov removed and folded his spectacles, looked up from his reading and smiled. 'Thank you for coming.' The smile left Chekhov's face. 'Now, to business.'

He's just like his father.

'I spoke many times with my father in the weeks before he died,' Chekhov said, in a deep and eloquent English accent. 'He spoke highly of you.'

'I'm very grateful, sir. Your father looked after me well.' He'd heard much about Chekhov's powerful personality but hadn't expected this to be matched by his physical presence. Muscular frame bulging from his open-neck shirt, spiky blond hair shorn flat, he could have been one of Russia's top field athletes. It was time to grovel. 'Now that he's no longer with us, how can I be of assistance, Mr Chekhov? Is there anything you want me to do for the *bratva*?'

'I can do things for myself, Malkin. That is why I am a successful man. I make good decisions and part of the reason for that is my ability to judge character. I can tell at a glance, for example, why my father trusted you.' Chekhov replaced his reading glasses and turned the pages of the document in front of him. 'I've been looking over his accounts and I see you've done a thorough job under what were difficult circumstances. But I need you to explain to me why you think the *bratva*'s finances are in such a state. Only one brigade within the whole *bratva* is maintaining a steady income stream, the rest are showing a continuing monthly decline. Given the scale of his operation, he should surely have made more money than this?'

He felt the heat as Chekhov continued to study him. The untraceable offshore accounts included some in his own name. *Oh shit! Have Chekhov's own accountants looked at these figures?* He could tell his cheeks were turning red, as they always did when he came under stress. 'I have to agree with your findings, Mr Chekhov. The books *do* show a poor turnover during this past year. But I can only record the money I collect in person from the brigadiers. Once they've handed it over, I enter it in the books then store it in the safe until it can be capitalised into our legitimate cash operations. Bars and restaurants, refurbishments of private dwellings, all of it receipted by reputable companies.'

'Yes, yes, I have no doubt you are doing a fine job laundering the money. But if Slomensky's brigade can retain profitability, why can't the others?' Chekhov leaned forward and spoke in a soft but menacing tone. 'Do you think they were withholding cash from you?'

It was Anatoly Chekhov in those intelligent grey eyes. And he'd seen, close up, Anatoly Chekhov's vicious retribution for any brigadier who concealed money. He swallowed hard. 'Sir, your father would no doubt have informed you about the difficulties we were encountering. The brigades were performing badly in the field and our warriors were being intimidated by other organisations of *mafiya* origin.' Glancing up and seeing no obvious sign of offence in Chekhov, he continued with eyes averted. 'We were losing men and giving up estate. I saw it all happening on paper but I was powerless to stop it.

All I could do was give your father my opinion. But I'm your father's bookkeeper, I have no authority over the manner in which his brigades operate.'

'No authority!' Chekhov barked. 'But you were the *pakhan*'s right-hand man. You were responsible for advising him, not just offering vague opinions. What were you doing to prevent this happening?'

Malkin recoiled at Chekhov's stark demonstration of how he could make a man shake with fear. And he was afraid now – afraid for his job, afraid for his future, for his life even. None of this was his fault. He merely provided an administrative interface. All he'd done was cream off a bit of the money that the brigadiers were already dipping into. 'I did inform him that we were operating under significant risk of a meltdown, but your father deliberately chose to ignore the warning signs. He—'

Chekhov held up his hand to stop him. 'Are you suggesting he was incompetent? Let me tell you, my father built this organisation in a country that was foreign to him. He recruited well and, until he fell ill, he had the unreserved loyalty of every warrior and every brigadier. They respected him because he'd been out on the streets alongside them, shed blood with them and if they were wounded, he would always care for them.'

This imposing man was beginning to show the first signs of distress. Everyone was aware that not only had Vladimir Chekhov recently lost a father but, less than two months ago, his wife Natalia died giving birth to their first child. And with this thought came the first strains of pity.

'But I accept that my father could be a fool at times,' Chekhov continued, in a calmer voice. 'He was of the old ways. And yes, I suppose you are right, Malkin. You were merely his bookkeeper. You had his respect but he wouldn't give you his authority. That's how it was always going to work in an organisation like his.'

Chekhov stood and turned his back on him. He seemed to be gazing upwards as if to admire the stately room's fine ceiling coving. Was he looking towards the heavens for inspiration – or was he hiding his sorrow? Considering this devastation in Chekhov's life, how could he even contemplate setting about an analysis of his father's business – so soon and with such poise? His new *pakhan* was to be admired, not feared.

'This organisation is a mess,' Chekhov growled; he turned and leaned on the desk. 'Which is why I'm going to make some profound changes,' he calmly said, before sitting back in his huge chair. 'As someone who has been close to him, I want you to tell me this – what is your personal opinion of my father's current organisation? Take your time and think about your answer. And please be so good as to continue in English. You speak the language well and that pleases me. We are based in Western Europe now and we need to speak their languages well.'

The question threw Malkin. After all, he'd only that morning resigned himself to the golden bullet. He couldn't possibly have been invited here today to brief a powerful oligarch on how to run a business. *Have I got this wrong?*

'Well?' Chekhov asked again, clearly feeling that he'd allowed sufficient thinking time. 'You did ask me if you could be of assistance. What is my father's organisation really like?'

Their gazes locked and it seemed like minutes before Malkin could summon the gumption to step into the silence. 'As you suggest, Mr Chekhov, your father's organisation *is* in disarray. But we can correct these issues. I've thought about these matters at length and I have ideas I wish to discuss.'

'Then tell me of them,' Chekhov said, with a mixture of resignation and cynicism.

This was an unexpected opportunity. *I must be assertive, just like Chekhov.* 'We need to urgently address the narcotics business. Turnover in this area is high but my analysis shows that the gains are outweighed by risk of disruption from rival organisations. My view is we should terminate all drug dealing activities, shed unwanted personnel ... I've studied our arms dealing operation ... I've developed a business plan in the area of political extortion ...' He continued with his proposals for twenty minutes, systematically covering each business area in turn. There was no interruption and he was encouraged throughout by Chekhov's body language. He was playing the right chords – a symphony hitherto unheard but apparently wonderful music to Vladimir Chekhov's ears. At the end of his uninterrupted presentation, he could see that Chekhov was staring at him poker faced. *Oh God, have I said the wrong things?*

Chekhov pursed his lips and nodded his satisfaction. He got out of his seat and gave Malkin a friendly wag of the finger. 'I'm delighted with everything you've said. You and I think along the same lines, Malkin. You

22

know, I even tried to persuade my father to steer his organisation in a similar direction. Like you, I consider the *mafiya* concept to be suitable for use in our current lines of business. The military-style structure works well and there is nothing wrong with making money from activities the authorities traditionally consider to be illegal. However, times have changed. We need to provide more sophisticated services that people cannot avail themselves of elsewhere – and for which they will pay well.'

'You speak wisely, sir,' he said, hoping Chekhov wouldn't consider this to be patronising, 'but this will require a vast overhaul of our personnel. Most of the brigadiers contribute little to our day-to-day operations and their warriors are out of control.'

'The brigadiers have become soft, Malkin. But their time is over. We no longer need their flabby supervision and the ineffective violence of their warriors. Only the best will be retained, those who understand much more than how to handle themselves in a fight. We will indeed continue to bleed the finances of the greedy pigs who wallow in this city's excrement, but we no longer need to bleed their bodies. The days of leaving our enemies crippled on the streets are gone.'

Having said his piece, Chekhov's demeanour switched yet again. His ferocity subsided and once more he came across as the kind fatherly figure. He smiled and placed his arm around Malkin as if he were his only son. 'Oleg Malkin, I want you to stay on as my bookkeeper and reorganise this *bratva*'s internal structure. You will start to implement these changes at once.'

Chekhov's squeeze almost crushed him. It reminded him of the many times Chekhov's father had embraced him like that. As it did on those occasions, the embrace told him he was to be taken under Chekhov's wing. But this time it also contained a subliminal warning – *don't fuck with me.*

'That is all for now,' Chekhov declared, releasing his hold and inspecting his Rolex chronometer. 'I leave for Monte Carlo this afternoon. We'll speak in two days' time.'

Malkin bowed his head. Not so much in relief or in respect for his new *pakhan*, it was more about hiding the pleasure that now flushed his face. He'd just taken the first big step towards his dream of becoming rich.

CHAPTER 3

J ean scrunched her way up the long gravel drive. When she reached the top of the steps leading up to the Highgate mansion's main entrance, she paused to collect her thoughts. Three preliminary interviews in three separate hotels, each progressively more challenging, each requiring a supreme effort to hold herself together and mask her destroyed confidence and lack of self-esteem. By the end of so many aptitude tests, her confidence was coming back and the money she'd borrowed to buy new clothes and smarten her appearance had proved to be a good investment; she felt so much better in herself. And now here she was, standing outside the London home of one of the world's richest men – on the shortlist for his final selection. 'Jean Douglas,' she announced on the intercom.

She took a step back, peered up towards the grey sky and counted the storeys in the building's ornate façade. There were five as far as she could make out, six including the roof space. So, this was Goldhurst. Some place – it set her nerves jangling. The glass door opened to reveal a smart young man in his mid-twenties. With his brass-buckled uniform and pillbox cap, he looked like an old-fashioned bellboy from a Mayfair hotel. 'Come this way, Madam Douglas,' he said, in what sounded to her like a Russian accent.

The mansion's entrance hall, a vast atrium providing bright natural light, had a welcoming feel to it, yet the female receptionists paid little attention as Jean and her guide clacked their way towards the lift. Inside the lift, Bellboy smiled at her as he reached for the control buttons and, to her surprise, the lift set off on a slow downwards journey into the basement. It was the best part of a minute before the lift came to a halt. The door opened and they stepped out into a wide modernist corridor with pale marble flooring and hidden lighting. She stopped to take it all in – and almost collapsed with shock. The walls were adorned with the paintings of Van Gogh, Renoir, Cezanne. There was a huge Monet that she wasn't familiar with. In fact, she didn't recognise any of the works on display but from her browsing of art books over many years, she could identify the unique styles of these Impressionist masters. And from what she'd seen so far of this magnificent building, they had to be genuine. *Priceless?*

She was torn from her spell as Bellboy took hold of her forearm and, as if they were going to be late, hurried her past the paintings. Perhaps she'd get the opportunity to saunter along this beautiful corridor and savour these works of art after the interview? *Oh God, the interview.*

At the end of the corridor, they stopped outside a large wooden door and Bellboy knocked twice. He turned the shiny brass knob at the door's centre and the great door rumbled open. 'Wait here, please.'

Jean tried to compose herself by taking a few deep breaths and straightening her blouse, while Bellboy went into the room. She heard him say something she didn't understand, only to be reprimanded in English.

'You should never enter before a lady. Off with you.'

Bellboy came out of the room with his head bowed in contrition and looking embarrassed. 'My apologies, Madam Douglas.' He took her hand and led her forward a step. 'You may go in now,' he said, then scuttled away along the corridor.

Jean found herself peering into a cavernous high-ceilinged chamber which reminded her of the entrance to a cathedral. The room was sparsely furnished with a single desk and two chairs; across the polished wooden floor stood a giant of a man in his thirties. He smiled at her as she walked slowly towards him.

His handshake was warm and firm. 'Please be seated, Madam Douglas. I am Vladimir Chekhov,' he said, before sitting down himself on what looked to Jean like a king's throne. It was going to be a one-to-one interview. With a straight back and hands crossed on her lap, she waited nervously in the captain's chair for his questions. *How many other candidates today?*

'My team has done all that is necessary regarding preparation for this interview and I have your CV,' Chekhov said, indicating with his open palm the single sheet of paper at the centre of the otherwise empty desktop.

She braced herself and tried to appear confident by smiling at him, but Chekhov ignored her and continued in his matter-of-fact fashion.

'I have but one question for you,' he said, rubbing his smooth chin as if composing the question for the first time. 'Do you think you could ever replace Abram's mother? Abram is my beautiful four-month-old son and, as you have no doubt already been told, my wife died bringing him into this world.'

Her intuition told her that it all came down to the answer to this question. 'Sir,' she said, 'I'd look after your baby son as if he were my own. I'd nurture him, I'd teach him whatever you want me to teach him,' she paused to muster as much assertiveness as she could find, 'but the answer to your question is – *no*, I could never replace Abram's mother.'

Chekhov smiled, took his reading glasses from his inner jacket pocket and picked up her CV. He glanced at it, but she could see he wasn't reading the words. He placed the piece of paper back on the desk and dismissively slid it to one side. Returning the glasses to his pocket, he leaned back in his huge chair, tapped his lips with the top of his steepled fingers and studied her from across the period desk. 'I would like you to start the job by the end of the week. I'll take care of whatever is necessary to discharge you from your current position and make arrangements for your monthly remuneration to be transferred into a bank account of your choice.'

She was stunned. Was he really offering her the job? She felt like blurting out *That's fantastic, you won't regret this*, but bit her lip. *Mustn't throw it away at this last hurdle.* 'Thank you, sir,' was the only feeble response she could manage.

Chekhov looked at his watch and was by now appearing to lose interest. 'My house manager, Mr Malkin, will show you around your personal quarters before you leave. Good day, Madam Douglas.'

Chekhov must have been a man with enormous influence. The day after Jean's interview, the health centre manager informed her of the decision to release her and, three days later, here she was – working for a Russian oligarch in what must be Highgate's finest mansion. There'd been no redundancy payment, but she'd signed a contract with Chekhov that dwarfed her district nurse's salary and promised eyewatering bonuses based on her performance in the role of nanny. She said nothing to Robert and Mary about her plans; she simply left a short note on the kitchen table explaining that she'd changed her job. They took her for granted and it would probably be a week or more before they realised that she was gone. Even then, would they bother trying to find her? They could continue to live for nothing, although the house would no doubt degenerate into a hovel within days. *And what do I care? They live in my house and I'm still supporting them.*

By contrast, the Chekhov household was run with efficiency and style. There were forty or so household staff providing support to Chekhov's *bratva*, as it was known. She had no idea what the *bratva* did or what sort of family business they all supported. All she could gather was that the business was in the services sector and organised in a similar manner to the military. Her charge, Abram Vladimir Chekhov, was the only bloodline family member in permanent residence following the demise of his grandfather, Anatoly Chekhov – the old *pakhan* as they all called him. Abram was a little gem. Despite what she'd said at her interview, she became his new mother instantly and settled back into the role of motherhood as if she'd never left that phase of her life. Abram's father, Vladimir, had a suite at Goldhurst but rarely used it. If Vladimir Chekhov visited his London residence, it was for meetings at the Russian Embassy, she'd been told. And to see Abram, of course.

At first, she wasn't allowed to leave the mansion with Abram. However, with external grounds of over three acres and an underground complex the size of Buckingham Palace, there were plenty of places for them to explore. The iceberg house, as it was apparently known locally, included a huge nursery dedicated to Abram. Its construction had begun the moment Natalia Chekhov discovered her pregnancy, and the rooms included a mathematics suite and a language laboratory for when Abram became old enough to require specialist teachers. Her bond with Abram was becoming stronger by the day. He was happy and never demanding, though like any baby he would always let you know when he was hungry. God willing, he'd never become like Robert. But Robert wasn't brought up in an environment like this. *He never had a chance with a father like his.* When she thought of her own children, she felt guilty about her new-found happiness with Abram and everything else at Goldhurst. But it wasn't her fault her children had turned out as they did, was it? She still loved them, but she couldn't live her life like that anymore. She was happy now, wasn't she? And that was down to the beautiful little boy she cradled in her arms and the lovely place in which she'd come to live.

From the lounge of her private quarters, Jean could look out through the tall bay window over Hampstead Heath and beyond, and take in whatever the day presented in the way of weather and mood. Inside this room, she felt smug in her own surroundings, safe from everything and everyone in the world outside. But this evening, she disregarded the magnificent view. Abram was wide awake and she was cooing him and watching him cackle with glee as she played 'This Little Piggy' on his bare toes. Her own children were tiny like this once. She would recite the same rhymes as she did now and she would cuddle them like she cuddled Abram. She studied the beautiful child in her arms and stroked his forehead. He was just like Robert at that age. Abram smiled at her and the tears cascaded down her cheeks. *How could Robert and Mary have turned out like they did?* It had to be their father.

'Stupid bitch! Can't you stop that kid from crying?'

'Babies cry, George. He's hungry, I'm sure that's all it is.'

'Well, feed the little bastard.'

George was back from the pub and she felt sick with worry. She carried Robert through to the kitchen where she'd left his milk bottle. The milk was still lukewarm; he hadn't taken any at all when she tried to feed him fifteen minutes earlier – and he had a temperature. She'd try again; it was all she could do to protect them both from George's temper. 'Come on, sweetheart. Be a good boy now.' *Please take it, son, please don't cry.* But Robert pushed the teat away from his mouth and continued his wailing. His eyes screwed up tight and his face turned red as if about to explode. His screams became louder and more piercing as he squirmed in his mother's arms, rejecting her desperate attempts to cosset him. *He's in pain, I need to call a doctor.*

'Here, give him to me, I'll fix him.' George startled her as he snatched the defenceless baby from her arms. She followed him back into the living room and watched in horror as he threw Robert into the cot like a rag doll. 'Get to sleep, you little brat!'

'No, George, please. He's not well.'

'Not well? Maybe he'll die and leave us all better off.'

This time, he'd pushed her too far. 'He's your son, for God's sake – an innocent little child.' She launched herself at him with every ounce of her strength, scratching at his face and swinging a wild punch that missed his head. She flailed with her fists but she was getting nowhere – George had her by the throat and was holding her at arm's length with ease, despite his inebriated state. With his free hand, he wiped the blood from his cheek and studied it. His drunken eyes turned dark with anger.

'That's it, you bitch!' he shouted, as the back of his hand swiped her face.

She'd brought this on herself with her uncharacteristic outburst, hadn't she? She provided no resistance as she took her punishment; it would have been futile anyway.

Curling into a ball she gritted her teeth and closed her eyes, relieved that George was venting his anger on her and not on their son. Robert echoed his mother's squeals throughout her whipping with the buckled end of his father's belt. Perhaps this was the moment his tiny brain started to form its subliminal life-shaping programme?

She heard the key turning in the door and gasped as Vladimir Chekhov appeared in her room. *Doesn't he have the courtesy to knock?* She gathered herself – after all, she'd always have to be grateful for the position he'd given her. 'Sir, this is a pleasant surprise.'

'Ah, there you are, my little warrior.' Chekhov plucked Abram from Jean's arms without acknowledging her presence. Like the inexperienced father he was, he swung him through the air and jiggled him up and down until the baby threw up over his white linen jacket. 'Forgive the intrusion, Madam Douglas,' he said, as he handed Abram back to her, 'I have a meeting with the Russian Consul this evening and I wished to see my son while I was over here. How are you getting on with him?' He made a despairing attempt to wipe the sick from his sleeve with a silk pocket handkerchief and Jean had to supress her laughter.

'We're getting along fine, aren't we, little man?' she said, fingering Abram's cheek.

'Yes, I can see you're bonding well.'

Discarding the sodden handkerchief, Chekhov took a small object from his jacket pocket and Jean could see it was a tiny mobile phone. Some of her friends who were better off than her possessed mobile phones but she'd never been able to afford one. Robert had a mobile phone but it was much larger than the one Chekhov was now showing her.

'This is the latest technology, not yet available on the wider market,' he explained. 'There is no external aerial and it fits easily into a purse. You must charge it every day.' He produced a bulky charger from another pocket. 'I'll call you whenever I wish to check on Abram's welfare, so you must keep it close to your person at all times. If Abram is ever in danger, you can contact me by pressing this button.' He pressed the *contact* button on the phone's keypad and Jean heard a ring-tone coming from somewhere within Chekhov's jacket. 'But you need to be aware that the phone has been adapted so you can call no other person.'

He was giving her a phone? Was this really to check on his son or was he keeping track of her? *Why would he do this?*

'Abram is precious to me. He is my sole heir and I wish him to be brought up correctly, here in England. I want someone there for him every day, someone who can provide the devotion of a mother. You will recall your aptitude tests, Madam Douglas? My psychologists chose *you* from over a hundred candidates. And you gave me the exact answer I wanted at our face-to-face interview. That is why I've employed you and why I'm asking you to look after my cherished son. He means everything to me. I want you to protect him with your life.'

I'll do that. Like I did for Robert and Mary.

Jean was in her third week. It would be another week before they allowed her to set foot outside the grounds of Goldhurst with Abram, but the mansion still offered what seemed to her like endless new places to visit and her days were full and satisfying. If Abram looked like he wanted to play, she would take him into the gardens at the back of the house or into his nursery if the weather was inclement. If he was sleeping, she would wheel his buggy to the library that was being assembled and see what new books appeared on the shelves. They were gradually allowing her more freedom – yet she couldn't shake off the uncanny feeling that she was constantly being watched.

'What shall we do today, Abram?' Jean said as she tickled the baby under the chin. Abram giggled and she gently poked his tummy. 'I know, let's go down to the lower basement and see those marvellous paintings. Do you fancy that?' She tickled him again and he whimpered. 'Oh well, you'll just have to lump it, grumpy drawers. I've been dying to take a good look around down there.'

The lift's downward journey seemed endless – there were so many more levels than in the upper storeys. The lift finally stopped and the door opened, but this wasn't the corridor she'd been expecting. And who were these people?

'Where are you going?' asked a tall thin man as he stepped inside the lift.

'I was trying to get to the corridor with the Impressionist paintings on the walls.' The half-dozen younger men who entered the lift behind him were smirking. To her horror, one of them adjusted a pistol in its holder under his coat. She spotted another slip a knuckle-duster off his fingers and into his jacket pocket.

The thin man scowled in turn at those who'd made such clumsy attempts at concealing their weapons; he had to be their leader.

'Has no one told you? You're not allowed down here with the baby.'

He's Russian. 'I thought I was free to go anywhere in the building, as long as it wasn't marked as private.' She summoned her courage. 'I'm Abram's nanny and I don't yet know many of Mr Chekhov's staff. Can I ask who you all are?'

The thin man smiled, but she could tell it was contrived. 'Forgive me, madam, my name is Brigadier Slomensky and I report directly to the *pakhan*. These are some of my men and I *do* know who you are. With respect, you shouldn't be wandering around in these lower levels unaccompanied. You should be restricting yourself to the baby's nursery areas.' Slomensky pressed the button and the lift ascended. 'I'll have a word with the bookkeeper,' he said, with contempt in his voice. 'And I'll take you and the child back to your quarters, if you don't mind.'

She submitted to Slomensky without question; she was the newbie here and although she didn't like his rudeness, she'd need to find out how important he was before she could stand up to him. Back inside her private quarters, she fretted and mulled over what she'd just observed. Were these men really part of Chekhov's organisation? *I suppose an oligarch needs to protect himself with armed security – but knuckledusters?* And who was this bookkeeper Slomensky referred to?

CHAPTER 4

After several weeks of internal reorganisation, Malkin was finally ready to deal with Slomensky. Malkin was only the bookkeeper but sitting in this chair of power made him feel indestructible. He feared no man, not even the scowling old brigadier who was sitting in the captain's chair in front of him, waiting to be told why he'd been summoned. And he'd planned carefully for this interview – just like Chekhov would have done.

'Tell me, Comrade Slomensky, what do *you* think of our current organisation?'

Slomensky looked surprised by the opening question but launched into his response with a gusto worthy of the old men of the Kremlin. The organisation was black shit and just as soft. His fellow brigadiers spent their time cavorting in the wine bars and fornicating with the painted English slags who hung around in them. They neglected their jobs, their warriors and their duty to the *pakhan*. His own brigade alone ensured the profitability of the *bratva*. He was the only brigadier to continue to uphold the *mafiya* tradition.

Malkin had to agree with everything Slomensky was telling him. The organisation had fallen apart as a result of Anatoly Chekhov's deteriorating health. He'd watched it happen himself, standing by helplessly as the *bratva*'s warriors ran amok with their extortions and thuggery and the brigadiers failed to exercise control – they themselves no longer being accountable to a higher authority. They'd all been too busy enjoying the comfortable lifestyle that London offered, funded by the money they'd pilfered from their own *pakhan*.

'The young upstarts I have to put up with in our current organisation,' Slomensky went on, clearly aiming the remark at Malkin himself, 'they're not of the old tradition. They don't appreciate our objectives and they don't lead by example.'

Slomensky obviously considered himself superior to the other brigadiers of the Chekhov *bratva*. The bastard was even mocking his comrades behind their backs and belittling him at the same time. But he had to remain calm in the face of such a slur – that was what Vladimir Chekhov would do in this situation.

'None of them have earned the badge of *Vor*,' Slomensky said, snarling. 'When was the last time one of our warriors was made up to Thief in Law? I can tell you that Anatoly Chekhov personally conveyed this honour on me following my regular demonstration of outstanding leadership.'

Although he was boasting, once again Malkin had to agree with him. The old brigadier was to be admired for his achievements. He was entitled to be proud of that star he would no doubt have tattooed on his shoulder, the badge of the Thief. He was a made-man of the *mafiya*, a follower of the code of the *Vor*. But Slomensky was old school and didn't fit the new organisation – they had to get back to the business in hand. 'Dear comrade, please stop,' he said, holding his hand up like Chekhov would have done. 'These traditions you refer to are no longer what we need in our organisation. This is what our new *pakhan* wishes to address with all haste.' He gave a condescending smile to the embittered old man.

Slomensky ignored him and continued his tirade. 'This extravagant house you all live in. This is not how we would have behaved in the days of old. We worked hard, we pursued our quarry, we made our money. But we redistributed it, fed it back into the brigades. We didn't pay for pantry maids and butlers and swimming pools. Why did our *pakhan* feel the need to do this?'

I've heard enough. 'Comrade! It was not our beloved old *pakhan* who set this up. It was Vladimir Chekhov, our new *pakhan* – Anatoly's son. *He* put up the money. *He* arranged for the engineers to build our magnificent subterranean complex. He also paid the many fines for road closures and noise pollution during the construction period.' He sat forward in his chair and lowered his voice. 'We'll always make our living outside the law, but we no longer want to be *seen* as corrupt. We want to be respectable in the eyes of the police, the law courts and everyone else.' He was asserting his new authority and he could tell he was getting the upper hand; Chekhov would surely have been proud of him. 'Have you never realised this, comrade? Well, realise it now.'

Slomensky was staring down at the polished wooden floor. Like the rest of this magnificent chamber, it was an expensive refurbishment in the style of a period long vanished and the old brigadier wouldn't like that one bit. *He must be seething with rage. What would Vladimir Chekhov do in this situation? I know.* He stood up, turned his back and gazed up at the ceiling. After a deliberate pause, he returned to his chair to find Slomensky goggling in astonishment.

'Comrade, it has given Vladimir Chekhov immense pleasure to do all of this in the heart of his father's domain. This deeply located sanctum provided his father with a place to plan his business and execute his key decisions. You realise, of course, that the authorities have always been aware of the nature of our business, but Vladimir Chekhov provided the cover his father needed for all these years, that air of respectability. This is, after all, just the UK residence of a rich Russian family.' Slomensky clearly begrudged the way in which the organisation was changing and this counselling would no doubt leave him devastated. The fearless warrior of old was a broken man. It was time to pounce. 'My dear comrade, you're looking tired. You've served our *pakhan* well in your time. You gave him your absolute loyalty and devotion for all those years and I can tell you that both he and his son have appreciated this. But there are to be changes. You've completed your service, comrade. Anatoly Chekhov is at rest, God bless his soul. His son has taken over and you have our permission to retire.'

Slomensky squirmed in his chair. Malkin could see that his implication of familiarity with Vladimir

Chekhov galled the old man. The old brigadier's white bloodless knuckles gripped the chair's curved arms while his face reddened with the increasing pressure of blood in his head. He was in a state of shock; now was the moment to deliver the final blow and finish the job.

'You can walk away with dignity and pride, Illyich Slomensky. Feel secure in the knowledge that our *bratva* is in good hands with Vladimir Chekhov at its head. Enjoy your retirement, comrade. We'll provide you with ample funds to do so.'

CHAPTER 5

t was several weeks before Jean had her first proper discussion with the house manager, Mr Malkin. It confirmed her first impression of him from her interview day: he was an affable and courteous man. He asked how she'd settled in and answered her many questions, constantly smiling and bowing his head. He suggested she start swimming lessons with Abram. 'It's Mr Chekhov's idea,' he told her. She was concerned about this at first; why hadn't Chekhov mentioned this to her himself? It seemed so premature for a young baby to be in a swimming pool. But they must know what they're doing. They continued chatting for an hour and, at the end of their discussion, Mr Malkin casually mentioned that he'd arrange the first swimming lesson for the next day. She went to bed feeling content that evening; she'd already earned their trust. But she wasn't sure about the swimming; it niggled away at her into the early hours.

When she arrived at the spa with Abram and the duty bodyguard, she was met by a fifty-something woman who introduced herself as Lidia Leonova. Lidia was a fierce-looking Ukrainian with the build of a shot-putter, cropped and bleached hair and a manly gait. She explained that she was due to retire soon. Perhaps this was to be her last job at Goldhurst – Abram's swimming instructor?

'I'll go and change. Back in a jiffy.'

'I will hold the baby while you get ready. Yes?'

When Jean returned from the changing room, Lidia was already in the pool, bouncing up and down with Abram so that on each landing he dipped in and out of the water up to his waist. 'See how he loves water,' she said, as Abram cackled with glee. 'He is going to be a good swimmer, I think.' At that, Lidia tilted Abram face down on the water and let him go. He sank beneath the surface and slithered forward and downwards.

What's she playing at? The helpless baby was going to continue his involuntary surface dive and glide towards the bottom of the pool until he was several metres out of reach. Jean dived into the pool but before she could reach him, Lidia scooped Abram out of the water, raised him over her head in one smooth motion and restarted her bouncing-dipping game. Her feelings a mixture of relief and embarrassment, Jean said nothing – although she secretly wanted to throttle Lidia.

She left the rest of the swimming lesson to Lidia, who'd obviously done this before. After half an hour, Lidia declared that it was enough for Abram's first day and asked Jean to bring him back at the same time tomorrow. 'I will not be here later in the week. You must make sure he has time in the pool every day but no swimming without me.'

The daily swimming lessons continued. Each morning, a different bodyguard turned up and accompanied them to the spa. And each day they'd be met by a different female attendant. But unless it was Lidia supervising the session, Jean would never let go of Abram and the bodyguard and staff member would monitor her every movement. The day's combination of bodyguard and staff member seemed to be random, except for the days when Lidia attended. On those occasions, they were always accompanied by the same bodyguard. Whenever Jean saw him outside the spa, they'd greet each other with a silent nod. *There's Lidia's minder*, she'd think.

Abram was becoming more confident in the water; Lidia was bringing him on in leaps and bounds – literally. And her own confidence and well-being were improving by the day. She missed her job as a community nurse but she'd adapted well to her new role. Her servile existence was constrained within the bounds of this mansion but, compared to her home life with Robert and Mary, this was freedom beyond her wildest dreams.

Jean's probationary period was complete. Once a week, she was permitted to leave Abram with one of the female attendants for a few hours and take a stroll, go shopping, do whatever she liked within reason. She missed Abram on those days but there was a sense of relief in her freedom from round-the-clock household security. Today was her own time; she put to one side her concerns over the organisation she worked for and started to savour her solitary ramble. Here at Hampstead Heath, she enjoyed her liberty among other walkers and cyclists and relished listening to the banter of the office workers as they wolfed their packed lunches.

It was warm on the Heath today. She breathed in the scent of cut grass blended with the smells wafting from London's traffic and the moisture from the Heath's evaporating ponds. This was a fantastic day for taking in the capital's unique atmosphere; she felt like a new person – until she met Robert.

He appeared from nowhere and walked by her side, his steps tramping in unison with hers. 'Hello, Mum. How you keeping?'

She was startled. Her first reaction was to look at his eyes and see if she could tell what sort of state he was in. His eyes were glazed over but at least he appeared lucid. 'Nice to see you, Robert,' she said, without conviction. It was no surprise to find Robert in these parts; the Heath could turn into a foreboding place during the dark hours and she was sure this was where he bought his gear. But what was he doing here during the daytime? *He's found out where I live and he's been following me.*

'Well, it's nice to see you too, Mum. You haven't visited us for a while.'

She was trembling – in the company of her own son. 'You got the note I left you about my new job?' she asked, without looking at him. 'I told you, it's live-in and I won't be coming home as often. But the household bills are still being paid.' She forced a smile. 'I thought you and Mary would be pleased about having the run of the place.' *No change there.*

'Well that's kind of you, Mum. But there *are* expenses associated with running a house, aren't there?' Robert's demeanour changed. He grabbed her upper arm from behind and forced her along the path.

She tried to convince herself this wasn't happening, but she knew what Robert was capable of and fear welled up inside her. She had to placate him. *Don't panic, he's handled you like this before.* 'Take it easy, Robert, no need to rush around the place. Tell me how you and Mary are getting on.'

'Just get a fucking march on!' he shouted, ignoring the startled looks of picnickers to either side of the path. 'You and me have business to do.' They must have looked so unnatural as he trooped her forward. The passers-by stared at them but there was madness in Robert's eyes and one after another they averted their gazes. He pulled her towards him and hissed so loudly that she could feel his spit in her ear. 'Don't look back at them. Keep walking.'

'Where are we going?' she asked but received no answer. Robert steered her out of the park and headed towards a nearby cashpoint. 'You're hurting me, Robert.' She felt the tears rolling down her cheeks – tears of pain, tears of sadness. What had she done to deserve this? She'd brought him into this world, that's what she'd done. And he'd turned into a monster like his father. A monster on hard drugs in this case. She could see no remorse in her son for the physical distress he caused her as he twisted her arm up her back and demanded she withdrew two hundred pounds. He tightened his grip as she tried to squirm free, making it appear to onlookers that he was supporting her, helping this poor lady with today's modern technology. Robert was clever when it came to such matters.

She took the money from the cashpoint and handed it over. When Robert finished counting the ten-pound notes, he licked two of his fingers and prodded them against her lips, forcing her head back. It was the first kiss from him for as long as she could remember. 'Thank you, Mother. Now just fuck off back to your life without us,' he said, before merging into the passing crowd. Robert vanished, and so did her money.

It was a bad dream. The warm day now felt cold and she was frozen to the spot where he'd left her. It wasn't Robert's profanities or his contempt for his own mother that hurt her most. It was the *without us*. How could he refer to *us* when he'd stripped his own sister of her dignity, used her as currency? She meant nothing to him. *We both mean nothing to him*. The heist was brutal and impersonal, leaving her aware of the mental prison from which there was no escape. Worse still was the realisation that she'd lost all maternal feeling for her son. And there was something else bothering her. She felt as if someone had been watching this encounter with Robert – following her every movement. Perhaps it was someone from the Chekhov household, seeing what she gets up to on her day off? *Why didn't they help me?*

Abram looks ready for his swimming lesson this morning. It's as if he knows where he's going. The child was showing signs of real intelligence. And Lidia's minder was the perfect gentleman – politely opening doors for her, nudging Abram's tummy like a gentle giant. Yet he looked distinctly edgy today. She was beginning to feel nervous herself as she watched him hold the door open to allow two big men into the lift. As the door closed, the three men cast anxious looks at each other. Why didn't they start the lift? She raised an eyebrow at Abram's bodyguard.

'Going down – yes? The swimming baths? Is it something I've said?'

The answer came from one of the others. 'Madam Douglas, before we make our descent to the pool, we have a matter of extreme importance to discuss with you. This baby you have with you, he must be taken away. This is not a good place for him to be brought up. You must help him to escape from Goldhurst and we will pay you one hundred thousand pounds for your assistance.'

'What? You'd have me kidnap Chekhov's only son? For money? You must be mad. He's asked me to look after this child and that's what I do.' She looked him straight in the eye and at the same time pointed to the bodyguard. 'And he's looking after the both of us.' She turned to Lidia's minder for support. 'They lay one finger on this child, we tell Chekhov, right?'

The bodyguard shrugged his shoulders and raised his hands. 'I think you need to listen to them,' he said, 'and we should also discuss this with Lidia.'

All three men studied her. Those people she'd met in the lift only two weeks ago – they came across as mobsters. But they were on Chekhov's side, weren't they? And these people in the lift now – they wanted her to take Abram away from Chekhov? It was confusing.

Like a civil war within a criminal organisation and with Chekhov at the head of it. Was Chekhov a gangster himself? Whoever he was, he'd entrusted her with his son and she had responsibilities. Terrified, she stared into the distance beyond the claustrophobia of the lift, pulling Abram close and resting her chin on top of his little head. She'd protect him with her life if she had to. But who was she protecting him from? Who were the good guys and who were the bad guys? The lift descended in silence.

By the time she reached the changing rooms, Jean's head was reeling.

'I see our offer tempts you, Madam Douglas,' said Lidia Leonova. 'You must admit, one hundred thousand pounds is a lot of money, but you must also understand that you have no choice.'

Jean was mortified. Lidia had been so friendly during her swimming coaching. Yet here they were facing each other in the swimming pool changing room having a conversation like this. Twenty thousand now and the rest on delivering the baby to a predetermined rendezvous in the countryside. It was a life-changing fortune they were offering.

'Why are you doing this?'

'Matters you wouldn't understand. But you must by now be aware of the nature of Chekhov's business.'

Jean lowered her head and nodded her acknowledgement. From what she could make out, there were many others involved in this scheme but Lidia offered no names. She could understand why she was their ideal choice to take the lead in such a kidnapping; as Abram's

49

nanny, she was the only member of household staff who was occasionally allowed near him without bodyguards in close attendance. *And I'm the one to carry the can if this plan fails.*

'Why are you putting me in this position?'

'You put yourself in this position the moment you accepted his job. Chekhov has specific requirements. He's not interested in the usual agency workers or nannies with experience. He appointed you because of the efforts you make for your son and daughter. We know how they were abused as children by your drunken husband.'

But that was years ago. How did they manage to unearth all that in the time between her response to the advert and her interview with Chekhov?

'This is crazy. I'm responsible for Abram. Chekhov would find out and stop us before we left Highgate.'

Lidia responded with an icy glare. 'Crazy, yes. But we have our reasons. You're involved in our plan now and if you inform on us, there would be dire consequences for you and your family.'

'I can't do it.'

'Despite the troubles you have with your son and daughter, I imagine their elimination would still concern you. If you refuse to do what we say, we'll have one of your children killed. Maybe the daughter – you've lost the son to heroin already.'

The words cut like a cold blade. Lidia was right – Robert was no longer hers, yet she was still trapped by him. And Mary, for all the trouble she'd given her, was still her precious daughter. This way, she'd save the lives of her children. But who would care for them? And what about Abram, what would she be doing to him? These were dangerous people she was dealing with and she could tell they wouldn't wait for an answer. But how could she meet their demands without destroying those she loved? She was in a dreadful predicament, devoid of any clear option.

'Is there some other way?'

'I've already told you, there is no choice. You must be ready for when we need you.' Showing no emotion, Lidia stood up to leave. 'One of my comrades will discuss the details in the coming days.'

Jean sat frozen to the bench with the baby in her arms. Lidia left with the guards. This was a different person from the one who'd given the swimming lessons. In the eerie silence of the deserted changing room, she looked down at Abram's tiny form and wept. *How I've misjudged her.*

CHAPTER 6

Malkin eased himself on to the *pakhan*'s chair and waited. At seven o'clock, four tiny LEDs on the false desk drawer came to life, the signal that Chekhov was calling the *pakhan*'s office. He pushed the button next to the cycling red dot display and, from the centre of the desk, a flat-screen monitor motored upward and clicked into position. The screen came to life and Vladimir Chekhov greeted his bookkeeper from the main office of his luxury yacht.

'Good morning, Malkin, I hope you are well.'

'Yes, thank you, sir. I'm ready with my report.' The aquarium at Chekhov's back provided an amusing backcloth – King Neptune with laundered deck wear, on his throne and surrounded by his minnows.

He started his report. 'We've informed everybody of the outcome. Some of those who've been severed from the organisation will behave as if nothing has happened, I'm afraid. They're likely to continue to steal and deal in drugs or street prostitution, but I assure you there'll be no link between their continuing petty crimes and our *bratva*. In fact, with no line of command, I'd expect them to be devoured by the mobs in no time at all.'

Chekhov nodded his approval.

'This first stage of the reorganisation will result in our drug dealing operation being removed in its entirety. The brigadier responsible has agreed to be pensioned off. Navalov could always go it alone once he has his money, of course, but I judge him to be wiser than that. Removal of this business activity will in turn leave our security staff more time to develop their contacts …'

He could tell he'd implemented his *pakhan*'s instructions well. A potential money-spinning activity would be lost but there'd no longer be conflict with rival drug mobs. No longer would extreme violence blight their lives. Permissible arms dealing, covert political extortion … his report was clearly meeting with approval. Those police officers and high-ranking government officials were firmly in Chekhov's sights.

'… removal of our street prostitution operation will leave the remaining resource in this area free to concentrate on our more sophisticated call-girl service. I've already identified two further suitable properties which, with your agreement, we can purchase and refurbish within six months. We'll need to discuss recruitment plans in this area, of course. High-class *Olgas* don't just fall off trees.'

'I'll leave that to you,' Chekhov interjected, for the first time. 'I suggest you appoint a first-class director and let him find his own stock. Let me know what the business will require in the way of my consultation with the judges and police authorities. I take it you understand my meaning?'

'Of course.'

'Indulge yourself in this side of the business, Malkin. I trust you.' Leaning forward in his chair, Chekhov abruptly changed the agenda. 'What about Slomensky? How did he take it?'

'Not well, sir. We may need to watch him for a while.'

Chekhov nodded. 'I agree. I'll take whatever action I deem to be necessary if events transpire to my displeasure. Keep me informed.'

Slomensky's devoted service to Chekhov's father was to be admired, yet his redundancy was inevitable. Malkin's one concern was that any aggressive response could potentially result in the old brigadier's elimination, an undeserved fate for one so principled. With his hatred of ruthless gangland killings, he'd have to give some thought to an alternative means of dealing with Slomensky, should he become a nuisance to Chekhov.

'Overall, we're making good progress. I'm confident that we'll soon have a streamlined and legitimate-looking organisation, one that's more akin to your other international enterprises.'

'I am well pleased,' Chekhov said, leaning back from the camera to expose a burst of background colour from his tropical fish tank. 'We'll speak again on these matters in a few days' time when I'm in London on business.' The screen went blank and the video-conferencing equipment wound itself back into the desk.

Malkin breathed a sigh of relief. He was on his way.

CHAPTER 7

Jean opened her door and admitted the two brawny men. The taller of the two was familiar to her; he was the one who'd confirmed the date and time and now he was to help her smuggle Abram out of Goldhurst. It made her shiver.

'Come with us,' he said casually in his Russian accent.

She checked the corridor in both directions. 'Where are the bodyguards?'

No answer.

She picked up Abram and forced back the pangs of guilt – he would never remember this night; he'd emerge one day into another world. *I can only pray for a happy future for this beautiful child.* As instructed, she'd packed no spare clothing or bedding and no baby food. She wrapped him in a single blanket, taking care not to wake him. 'I'm ready.'

They made their way to the main kitchen, avoiding the reception area. One of the men, the shorter of the two, switched on his torch to illuminate their route past the ovens then disappeared back into the house. Jean and the tall man waited by the open door. Why was the rear exit not alarmed and why were there no garden lights of any sort? They must have arranged a power cut for this side of the house. Even the street lamps were switched off.

After five minutes, they stepped outside into near-darkness. The light pollution from the distant city centre was just enough to enable her to make out the first few feet of the garden path; with the baby in her arms, she followed her guide as he set off towards the bottom of the garden. It was slow progress, each step chosen to avoid snapping a twig or crunching one of the many snails. Halfway along the path, a light came on in an upper storey room, covering the garden in an eerie glow. Her guide held up his hand as a signal to stop. She froze, her heart pumping so loud she thought it would give them away. After a few moments, the garden descended into darkness once more. 'Let's go,' the guide whispered.

They picked their way to the end of the garden, where they came across a solid metal door in a nine-foot-high brick wall. The guide spoke to the door – in Russian. A few seconds later, the door started to open.

'How did—?'

'Quiet,' came the whispered voice from the other side of the wall. The faint background light was insufficient for her to make out the man who appeared through the open door, but she reasoned it had to be the shorter of her two guides. He must have left the building by the main reception, made his way to the rear of the garden and unlocked the door from the other side. 'Follow me,' the shorter man said as they left the grounds of Goldhurst. His torchlight was dim and she could barely make out the pavement in front of them; she'd have to remain within touching distance – make sure she didn't stray off the edge of the kerb. Holding the sleeping Abram against her cheek, she followed him for five minutes until they reached a parked car. The moment they stopped, the street lights came on. *They've timed this to perfection.*

'You've memorised the route?'

'Yes.' She squeezed Abram without thinking. The baby gurgled but didn't wake up.

'They'll be waiting for you at the agreed time,' the man said as he handed her the key to the Ford Escort. His parting look said, *Get this right.* She pursed her lips and gave him a single nod; there would be dire consequences for both of them if she didn't.

She surveyed her deserted surroundings, illuminated now by neon street lights, and realised she didn't have to drive past the front of the house. *They've set this up well.* She started the engine and turned to make one last check. Abram was asleep under his blanket in the crude plastic box they'd strapped to the rear seat. 'Say goodbye to your life of luxury, little man. No going back now, my love,' she whispered, as she drove off into the unknown.

The impulse was strengthening by the mile; she could resist it no longer. The tyres squealed as she whipped the car around the bend and left the main road. She drove for a mile along a dark lane, reached a layby and pulled on to the little patch of rough tarmac. With an irrepressible sigh of relief, she switched off the car's headlights and engine and opened the window. There was a stillness out here in the countryside; it allowed her to hear the whispered little gurgling sounds coming from Abram's box on the back seat. *He's fine.* She rubbed her hands across tired eyes, leaned her head back in the seat and took in a deep breath of fresh, soothing night air. She opened the glovebox, prised out the large brown Jiffy bag and tipped the contents on to the passenger seat. It was all there – the twenty thousand pounds advance with which they'd bought her trust and a false passport in the name of Eva Clarkson. Who was Eva Clarkson, she wondered? *I suppose I'm Eva Clarkson now.*

The rendezvous wasn't far. There was ample time to reach the derelict farmhouse where they'd be waiting for her. Once she handed over the baby, they'd drive her to one of the East Anglian fishing ports where she'd be smuggled on to a fishing boat, transferred at sea and subsequently met at Ostend harbour – how many times had she been through that scenario in her head? And the extra money she was to receive at the farmhouse tonight would give her a flying start in her new life. It was a good plan, if you could call kidnapping good. But her tumultuous thoughts during the car journey through Essex had left severe doubts cascading through her mind. *I've stepped over the precipice. It's not for the money – my children are under threat. If I deliver Abram, my children are safe and I'm free to start a new life – a life without my children. Then what happens? Chekhov is the head of a ruthless criminal organisation; he could pay the ransom then hunt us all down like dogs. And what about Abram? He deserves his inheritance, but he'd*

be inheriting a life of violent crime. Can I let him do
that? And what if Chekhov doesn't meet the kidnappers'
demands? God knows what would happen then. I could
call Chekhov, let him know his son is safe and agree to
meet him. But would he trust me or would he have me
killed anyway? Either way, my own children are dead if I
do that. If I were to just disappear with Abram ...

There was no right answer, no way out of this cruel
dilemma. Percolating through her confused thoughts,
there was fear. The fear of them coming after her. And
if *they* didn't catch her, Chekhov would. She started the
engine.

Five o'clock in the morning, thirty minutes beyond
their specified rendezvous time. She drove with fierce
resolve along the M11, leaving Essex in her wake. Her
collaborators would know something was wrong by
now, but what reason would they have for imagining her
driving north? Had Chekhov discovered that Abram was
missing? Where would he start looking? He'd no doubt
want to find them before the police did, yet he'd have no
choice but to cooperate with the authorities if he wanted
security to be tightened at airports and ferry ports.
His searches would be like an all-consuming monster
emerging from the centre of London. She glanced in
her wing mirror; great spiralling tentacles were already
bearing down on her car. She began to shiver and closed
the car window. She'd make her trail impossible to follow,
think like they would think, then do something different.
But they'd be thinking like that themselves, wouldn't
they? It was a game of chess and she was playing against

the devil's disciples. On pure instinct she headed east towards Chelmsford.

Abram was sleeping but Jean knew he'd be hungry soon. Her leg of the abduction was planned as a short trip and he wouldn't have needed food and clothing until they reached the farmhouse. She parked the car down a tight alley at the edge of the town centre and waited. At nine thirty, she locked the car, headed into town on foot and bought a range of camouflage in the form of hoody, scarves and sunglasses; Abram's camouflage was a pretty pink baby dress. At the high-street chemist, she bought rusks, baby milk and a feeding bottle, together with a week's supply of nappies and wipes. Finally, she bought a large rucksack into which she packed the rest of her purchases and set off back to where she'd left the car.

Abram was always going to be safe in the locked car. But this didn't prevent her sigh of relief when she returned to find no police surrounding the car and Abram still inside – screaming his lungs out. She drove out of town and found a quiet lane where she could feed and change him. As the baby on her lap sucked at the cold milk, his first meal of the day, she began to work out her next move.

After driving for two hours, she pulled into a car park in the market town of March in Cambridgeshire. The morning newspapers on sale at the entrance to the supermarket carried no front-page headlines about the missing son of a billionaire. Hopefully, that meant they weren't reported missing yet. Her collaborators in the kidnapping were bound to be starting their own searches and there was no way *they* would be going to the police or the press; their obvious strategy would be to look for the hire car while making sure they avoided being tracked down by Chekhov. She'd have to find another car. Or maybe change her mode of transport? Either way, she had to keep moving. She bought herself a bottle of fruit juice and stole an unattended buggy from outside the supermarket. *Hardly national news*, she told herself. After abandoning her car and dropping the keys into a drain, she set off towards the railway station pushing Abram in the buggy. In the rucksack on her back, she carried their worldly possessions; it didn't seem like much, volume-wise, but it did include her blocks of twenty-pound notes. At the station, she bought a one-way ticket and boarded the 14.16 train to Newcastle-upon-Tyne. She had no idea what she'd do when she reached the city; she was running blind but running in the right direction – away from London.

CHAPTER 8

Malkin sprang from his chair in surprise as Vladimir Chekhov stormed into the incident centre. After disturbing Chekhov's breakfast in Monte Carlo with news of the kidnapping, he hadn't expected him to complete the journey to Highgate in such a short time. The communications facility wasn't yet ready. *Shit, I thought I had at least another hour.*

Chekhov beckoned his bookkeeper. 'Malkin, over here at once.'

At the table in the corner of the hall, Malkin began to run through the brief he'd prepared, out of earshot of the computer science officers who were busy making their final connections to the local area network.

'What have you done with them?' Chekhov asked.

Malkin knew he was referring to the three staff members who'd been apprehended earlier that morning, within a couple of hours of Chekhov setting his personal security officers loose. 'Leonova is dead. She didn't survive the interrogation by Abram's bodyguards.' His stomach turned at the thought of her battered corpse. 'Two are still alive, but they're in a bad way in the cells.'

'Imbeciles! The bodyguards had no right to take matters into their own hands like that. Now I can't extract any useful information using skilled interrogators of my own.'

He was dealing with the real Chekhov here, the man who made on-the-spot decisions that affected people's lives. There'd be no altruism today, no father figure other than one who was seeking revenge. 'They panicked once your security officers handed them over, sir. They assumed you'd hold them responsible and they feared for their lives. I promise you, I gave no instruction for them to do what they did.'

'I'll deal with them later. How many more perpetrators are there?'

'We have the names of four current staff – all of them missing. Some of those we laid off may also be involved – we have warriors looking for them. We don't yet know who organised it at the top. We extracted nothing from the three we've interrogated so far. I'm convinced they don't know.'

Chekhov was calmer now. 'From this moment, all brigadiers, all security staff, everyone in the London organisation, will have a reporting line through you. This debacle must never be repeated in my absence. From now on, you are to take over my role as *pakhan* whenever I'm not here.'

That could be most of the time. Amid the building tension in the incident centre, Malkin was thrilled by what Chekhov was telling him but at the same time astonished that he wasn't laying any of the blame on his shoulders. *And I thought I was in serious trouble.*

'*You* will be responsible for directing my day-to-day operations,' Chekhov continued, 'and *I* will tell you how I want this doing. Anyone acting on his own initiative must have your explicit approval. Anyone who makes a serious error of judgement outside the scope of my instructions will be severely dealt with. I will not have an incident like this again.'

'*Pakhan*,' a young computer science officer said with excitement, 'we've located the nanny. I have her on my monitor.'

Chekhov abandoned his motivational talk and bolted across the hall. Feeling delighted with his elevated status, Malkin followed him to the CSO's desk. On his monitor screen, the CSO pointed them to the small red disc flashing on and off as it moved northwards up the map of Yorkshire.

'She's on a train heading north for Newcastle,' the young officer explained. 'The tracker whose code you provided is giving a weak signal but we've managed to lock into it.'

The clever bastard. How did he manage to plant a tracker on the nanny?

Chekhov turned to Malkin. 'You are in charge, Malkin. Make a start on mobilising our security resources, while I start to call in my favours. Don't let me down.'

Clearly puzzled by his *pakhan*'s delegation, the CSO looked at them both in turn, then spoke to Malkin. 'Can you see what's happening? The train has stopped at Sheffield.'

'Shall we contact the Yorkshire police forces, sir?' Malkin asked of Chekhov.

'We have no choice. We can't get our own men up there in time to cover every station. That's why I need to call my contacts in high places, get them to instruct the authorities to mobilise their resources in the north. You must coordinate our internal activities. Come on, man, get on with it. Use my helicopters – they are yours to direct. Intercept her before the police find her, if you can.' The voice of the hitherto calm and collected Chekhov was breaking. 'Make sure no harm comes to my son. And take the nanny alive.'

Malkin's nerves were rattling, but he managed to quell his thoughts on the potential consequences of failure. He felt an excitement like never before. This was his first serious operational task for the *bratva*. The resources he now controlled were considerable, not only as a response team but as a potential source of huge income in the future. It was everything he wanted.

CHAPTER 9

At each station, Jean took careful note of everyone who entered her carriage. As the train left Nottingham, the vacated seats around her filled with babbling youths. That was good; it would draw any would-be snooper's attention. Two middle-aged men boarded the train at Sheffield; she looked out of the window to avoid their scrutiny as they passed down the carriage. At Leeds, the youths left the train and a man in his thirties took up the adjacent seat across the aisle. He opened his newspaper and her heart rose into her mouth. The front page of the *Yorkshire Evening Post* featured an overblown old passport photograph of her that she'd supplied with her CV at the time of her job interview. She'd changed a lot since the photograph was taken, so why would anyone want to link the newspaper article with her and the baby girl she was travelling with? She may look a bit old to be travelling with such a young baby but was there anything unusual about a grandmother travelling alone with a grandchild? *Close your eyes, relax.* With the help of breathing exercises, she convinced herself that she'd successfully merged into the daily commuter ranks.

Sudden loud beats from helicopter blades stimulated keen interest inside the carriage. Several passengers strained against the windows to get a view of the helicopter's underside, describing every detail to those in the carriage who couldn't see. The pilot was flying parallel with the train and at close range. 'What's he doing?' the woman in the seat in front remarked. 'Why's he flying so bloody close? It's not the police, you know.'

The chopper moved forward a couple of carriages but Jean could still hear its throbbing blades. The ticket inspector arrived in the carriage. She fumbled in her handbag for her ticket and recoiled in horror as she realised what was happening. *Chekhov's bloody mobile phone.* She should have left it hidden back at the mansion. She'd been lucky to get this far undetected; Chekhov must have only just discovered what was going on. The voice over the tannoy announced that the train was approaching Darlington. Would they be waiting on the platform ready to board the train? Would it be the police? Chekhov's men? Surely not her collaborators – they wouldn't risk showing their faces. She showed the inspector her ticket and, once the sliding door at the rear of the carriage closed behind him, she picked up Abram and the rucksack containing their belongings and left the carriage by the front door. As the train commenced its deceleration, she checked that no one was watching and slipped into the lavatory, locking the door behind her. She placed Abram on the toilet seat lid. He smiled up at her, a trusting smile like a baby would give to his mother.

She blew out her breath in resignation. 'Sorry about this, little man. So sorry.'

This guy is perfect – long hair, headband, he's even got a rucksack like mine. Glad I put the bandana on. If I walk out next to him, they'll think we're together. Smile at him. Great, he's smiling back. Get closer to him. Done it, we're out.

Jean studied the helicopter from the far end of the street as it hovered menacingly over the old Victorian clock tower. A loud noise, more beating blades, a second helicopter flew high overhead without stopping. *Here comes another one.* What were they doing? From a distance, she heard a whistle and the sound from the engine as the power was revved up. Another whistle was the signal for the original helicopter to take off vertically. A third helicopter turned and flew towards the rear end of the train. A squirming movement against her spine caused her to shiver. The train's aerial escort moved off.

She watched the first of the police officers leave the station, mount his motorbike and ride off. He was followed by a horde of plain-clothed and uniformed personnel. They piled into cars and screeched away. *Give it half an hour before going back into the station, it has to be clear by then. Buy a ticket to somewhere on the coast.*

The Anchor was a rough-looking, down-at-heel establishment close to the gates of Hartlepool's Fish Quay. Jean knew little about this town but from a casual conversation on the branch line train, she discovered it still had a working fishing port that would offer her the chance to escape England. It was early evening and a cackle of bar chat and laughter was drifting out through the open window of the tap room; she studied the handwritten *Vacancies* sign sellotaped to the back of the entrance door's glazed panel – it looked recent enough to be meaningful. She took a deep breath, entered the pub and marched confidently across the bare floorboards to the ancient wooden bar. The room was full of scruffy characters conversing in strong northern accents; would they think she was a new prostitute on the patch? Thankfully, they paid her scant attention.

'Hello. What can I do for you, pet?'

The middle-aged woman behind the bar was exactly what Jean expected for the landlady of such a pub – dyed black curly hair, thick make-up, heavy gypsy-like jewellery and an authority beyond that of a barmaid. The way Mary was going, this could be her in twenty years' time.

'You have a room?' she asked, praying that Abram wouldn't wake up and hoping that the background clatter in the room would be enough to drown his crying if he did.

'Well, a matter of fact we do, pet. But you're dead lucky, you know, I've just had a cancellation. The room's yours for twenty quid a night if you want it. Do you want to see it?'

'No. That's fine, I'll take it. I'm only staying for one night.' She felt Abram move against her back. Once again, she willed him not to start screaming at this awkward moment.

'Do you want a drink before you go up?'

'I'm really tired. I've travelled a long way down from Scotland,' she lied, mentally urging the landlady to get on with it.

'All right, pet. I'll show you up to your room. It'll be cash in advance. OK?' Turning around, she shouted across to a middle-aged man, 'Jim, can you look after the bar for a couple of minutes, son?'

The room was spartan with its floral wallpaper worn in places. The floor was covered in old brown canvas and sloped at one edge. If the bedding was clean, this would do. She handed the landlady twenty pounds and her babble finally stopped. When she could no longer hear her footsteps on the stairs, she removed Abram from the rucksack; he was rubbing his closed eyes, going to wake up any minute. She boiled the kettle and made up a bottle of his powdered milk; hopefully, he'd take his feed and go back to sleep for a while. She'd have to risk leaving him in bed for an hour or so while she located the red-light district. It had to be somewhere close.

It was a balmy evening but the anxiety in Jean's stomach made her shiver. Ten o'clock. Most of the punters would be drunk by now and easy prey for the ladies of the night. She was a lone wolf in a forest full of wild and hungry wolves; they would come for her first. *Here we go*. The scrawny young girl emerged from the shadows and slowly approached her. 'What are you doing here?'

'I need to talk to you.'

The scantily clad creature challenged her again. 'You're a cop, aren't you? You can always smell rozzers, even above the stink of the fish.'

'I'm not a police officer.'

'Well, if you're not a cop, you're going to have to be one of us then, aren't you? And we don't take kindly to competition. If we find you're working for a fuckin pimp, we'll cut your tits off, right. We work for ourselves here.'

'Aye, and we look after each other, don't we, hun?' said a voice from the shadows.

Jean was taken aback at the sight of the older woman as she stepped out into the street light. She had to be in her sixties – her gaunt, worn face no doubt the result of many years on the game.

'We always stick together if there's any trouble. Safety in numbers, they say. And it's two on to one now, isn't it?' The old pro put her arm around the shoulder of her younger colleague. 'You having trouble, pet?'

'Dunno yet,' the younger girl replied, 'she's just turned up from nowhere. I still think she's a rozzer, though. Let's have a look in her bag.'

Before the young girl could grab her shoulder bag, Jean took a step back and raised both hands in protest. 'Look, I can promise you, I'm not a cop and I don't do your line of work. I just need your help with something really important and I'm willing to pay.' She'd stuck her head above the parapet, she realised; how would these girls react to a strange woman on their streets, especially one with money. They were both shameless, lacking in decorum, and the younger one reminded her a bit of Mary, a madam in every sense and not yet turned twenty.

'Hark at this posh hussy,' the young girl said with a sneer, seeking her colleague's support with a sideways glance. 'Why aren't you going to the cops for your help, then?'

'Because I wouldn't want the police involved. Look, I need to know where I can find a foreign fisherman who'd be willing to take me to Belgium or Holland, anywhere over there. I'm trying to get away from someone who's going to hurt me if I stay in this country.'

The older woman was taking the bait; looking for a chance to make an easy bob or two, no doubt. 'There's a pub at the other end of Northgate, where the Dutchies drink,' the old pro said. 'Leave it with me and I'll see you back here in an hour. But it's fifty quid each for something like this, isn't it, pet?' she said, prompting her colleague.

The younger girl affirmed the bid. 'Aye, at least that. I don't suppose you've got any tabs, have you?'

Jean accepted their offer but told them she didn't smoke. 'Back in an hour. Bring him with you.' She needed to lighten the mood, get them on her side. 'And no rozzers or the deal's off.'

The prostitutes laughed at her joke. 'She can't be such a bad lass, after all,' Jean heard the younger girl say, as they disappeared into the night.

Six o'clock in the morning and still dark. Jean left the sleeping pub. Abram was already weighing heavy on shoulders still sore from yesterday. She crossed the empty street and slipped through the Fish Quay's old wrought-iron gates, open in readiness for the morning's fish market. The first of the fishermen were transferring their catch; they paid her little attention as they slid their trays of fresh-smelling cod from the quayside into the covered market. She felt as if she'd been lugging Abram around like that since yesterday afternoon.

She soon located the trawler that was to provide their passage to freedom. She'd been told that the boat would be moored close to the ice house and how she could find that by following the smell of ammonia. There was only one boat at the quayside next to the ice house. The rusting old tub bobbed gently on the oily water; it hardly looked seaworthy but what did she know? 'Here we go, Abram,' she said as she attempted her next step into their future.

'Hoy, what's this then?' The Dutch skipper stopped her with his calloused hand as she tried to climb aboard his trawler. 'You say nothing last night about bringing a kid.'

Abram was awake in the rucksack, evidently enjoying his latest adventure. The sack's flap was folded back and the wispy strands of hair on his exposed little head were fluttering in the mild breeze. 'Look, she's my daughter. And if her father finds us, he'll kill us both. She has to come with me.' There was no way she could have mentioned Abram the previous evening. If the prostitutes watched TV when they weren't working, there was always a chance they'd recognise what was going on and try for the ransom that Chekhov would no doubt be offering.

The skipper sucked on his pipe and rubbed his bristled chin. 'I do this for you,' he eventually said, 'but I have to charge an extra thousand pounds.'

'I've already paid you two thousand. Surely that's enough?'

The skipper dolefully shook his head.

'OK, but there's no more,' Jean said as she handed over the additional fee and let him see he was taking almost everything she had left in her handbag. There was no way he was going to search her underwear, where the rest of her money was hidden.

Taking her by one hand and tickling Abram under the chin with the other, the skipper helped them down to the trawler's deck. 'Welcome aboard my boat, madam.' He winked at her as he said to Abram, 'And you also, young lady.'

Jean shook her head and smiled inwardly. They hadn't fooled him.

First light was appearing on the eastern horizon as the trawler pulled out of the harbour into Tees Bay. The water was calm and the boat chugged away steadily; they had a tough journey ahead and the potentially perilous sea crossing was only the first leg, but Jean was beginning to feel she was in good hands. The skipper seemed genuine; there was a kindness in those deep eyes, but she also detected his sadness as he brushed the grey matted curls to the side of his face. He told her how he'd fallen on hard times – ageing fishing tackle, poor catches, debts with the port authorities – the money she'd given him would be put to good use. She was helping a man in his hour of need and he was helping her to escape this cruel life; they needed each other right now. The skeleton crew spoke little English and, from their mannerisms, she guessed their conversations were riddled with profanities, but they seemed like honest men. Before setting off, one of them even tucked Abram into a spare bed so he could get to sleep before they reached the open sea. *We'll be OK, I'm sure.*

After devouring a breakfast of tinned sausages and baked beans, her first hot meal for two days, Jean went up to the deck and walked to the stern where the wheeling gulls were following the boat. Exhausted, she leaned on the deck rail breathing in the smells of fresh sea air and stale fish and reflected on the past thirty-six hours. At Darlington station she'd spotted them with ease. Chekhov no doubt had men boarding the train further up the line at York and Durham. With luck, they'd have tracked her all the way to Newcastle before they found the abandoned buggy with the mobile phone in its pouch. Only then would they have realised she'd given them the slip.

The gentle breeze invigorated her and cleared her mind. What was she was leaving behind in England and what would life hold for her in another country? Vladimir Chekhov had picked her from the gutter and set her on her feet; how was she repaying him? Chekhov may be a mobster, but he'd done nothing to deserve the father's anxiety he must be suffering at this moment. And what about Abram? That innocent little boy had a birthright beyond anyone's wildest dreams, yet he would never know his real father. She tried to convince herself that she'd rescued him from a life of crime. From her encounters in the lift and Lidia confirming the nature of the organisation's business, her actions were justified, weren't they? But would Chekhov pine forever for his son? It was that final thought that disturbed her most as she turned away from the strengthening wind and went below to check on Abram.

A swell was developing and the trawler started to roll. She could feel the soft thumps as the boat's bow penetrated each wave. Tears in her eyes, she looked down at the sleeping child. The maternal love she felt for her own children at that age, she felt for Abram now. He was so peaceful, blissfully ignorant of both the life ahead and the life he was leaving behind. She'd chosen to abandon her own babies and, as she lay down next to him, she began to wonder whether all this was about Abram replacing them. *There's no going back now, little man.*

CHAPTER 10

Malkin stood alone in his darkened office. Only the soft blue emergency lighting illuminated the cavernous room; he found it relaxing, it helped him to think.

The nanny had disappeared off the radar with Chekhov's son, as he'd predicted. His intuition told him she wouldn't be able to bring herself to hand over the baby and, although it was a huge gamble, he'd judged her reaction well – beaten Chekhov at his own game. He'd even managed to convince Chekhov that the failure to track her down wasn't his fault. He'd have to extend his private searches, of course – make sure there'd be no comeback. And he'd have to replace the scapegoats within his organisation. He paced the floor of the old *pakhan*'s office. *I'm going to get away with this.*

Slomensky would never know that he'd been indirectly acting on his behalf and he found that satisfying. His selection of the retired Slomensky to manage the kidnapping plot was a stroke of genius, the choice inspired by Chekhov's own astute decision to get rid of his most successful brigadier and move his organisation in a different direction. Slomensky was no longer an issue; he'd been put away where no one would ever find him. But what about his three aides who were still on the run? How much were they aware of the seeds that he and Lidia Leonova covertly planted?

Oh, Lidia, what have you done? He shook his head in sorrow. She was meant to disappear with a chunk of the money he'd made available for bribing the nanny. She must have succumbed to temptation, become greedy and stayed on for the ransom money – the jackpot. And what about the two who'd been hospitalised by the bodyguards? If they showed signs of recovery, how would he deal with that? He shuddered at the thought of their brutal treatment – that hadn't been his intention. *There's no way I could have them killed.*

With luck, Chekhov would soon stand down their resource-sapping search for his son and leave matters in the hands of the police; then he could return to the task in hand. There was much to be done but he was satisfied that the *bratva* was on the right track, progressively ridding itself of the extreme violence associated with the *mafiya*. Those he'd laid off should offer no threat if they decided to go it alone. *Let them squabble among the rest of the low life.*

Above all, Abram Chekhov was gone. He'd never see the inside of this room, Malkin thought, as he sat down. Chekhov's son no longer offered a potential future threat to his momentous plans. He, the humble bookkeeper, would be the one who developed this *bratva* into an organisation worth many billions, with most of the money going into his own bank accounts. He'd be the one who sat at its head and he'd be untouchable.

The tiny red LEDs lit up and performed their dance. Malkin raised the terminal and leaned back, smug in his *pakhan*'s chair. *I'm the one in charge now.*

PART 2 – Europe 2020

RISING STAR

CHAPTER II

The bedside alarm warbled at 6 a.m. Magda stirred but didn't wake. She seemed immune to this particular tone, so Leon always selected it when she stayed overnight. Careful not to disturb her, Leon slid out of bed, pulled on his dressing gown and sneaked into the kitchen to order himself a coffee. Rubbing the sleep away with his free hand, he walked barefooted into the lounge and looked down from the window of his Krakow apartment to the swirling grey river below. *Time flows like that.* He pondered the aggressive Russian takeover of the research facility; difficult to believe that was almost two years ago. He'd never forget the dazed looks around the site the day the collaborating institutes from the United States and Japan made the announcement and the shock that followed as the new owners ruthlessly culled the research team within their first month – careers swept away like leaves with a broom. He'd been one of the lucky ones. A theoretical physics postdoc on secondment, he was amazed when they asked him to head up their technical programme.

He still shook his head in disbelief whenever he thought of it.

Today should be routine, he told himself as he set down his empty mug, dropped back on to his leather couch and glanced at his watch. His watch alarm signalled six thirty and he spoke out to the empty space that surrounded him.

'Leon.'

'Good morning, Leon,' said the Melomet in its soothing female voice. 'You have one call waiting.'

The wall in front of him came to life and the young man sitting behind the desk smiled at him. 'Good morning, Dr Dabrowski.'

'On time, as always, Dr Schroeder.' He rubbed his eyes once more as he greeted his project manager. 'What news?' he asked with a suppressed yawn.

'Very good news, Leon. The stellerator behaved like a dream last night. No glitches, no breaks, no faulty starts. We achieved max plasma density on the first run with a temperature over one-twenty million.'

'Great stuff, Gunther.' He sat up and moved forward in his seat. 'How many more runs did you manage?'

'Two more. One at a similar field strength to the first run. The old dear seems to enjoy running with the settings you've selected.'

Leon laughed. 'And your final run?'

'You're not going to like this. We ignored the next two of your scheduled runs and went straight for Test 18.'

'You did what?' He jumped to his feet and started pacing in front of the couch. 'What the hell were you

84

playing at, Gunther? Without the parameter adjustments from those runs you skipped, you were taking a huge risk. You, more than anyone, know the damage you could have caused to the containment. You could have set the programme back two years. You could have—'

'Steady on, Leon. We obviously *didn't* damage the stellerator, did we? Do you think I'd be sitting here reporting results this morning if we did that? No, the final run last night was a resounding success. And guess what?' He could see that Schroeder was speaking with an excitement he could no longer contain. 'On Test 18, the plasma held steady for a full forty-five minutes before we decided to switch off. The heat we were dispersing would have incinerated the district.'

This was astonishing. Still in shock, Leon tried to force a laugh at the joke. The results were fantastic but Gunther's gung-ho attitude in his absence was exasperating. And why, oh why, had he chosen this weekend to be absent from the Greifswald laboratory? After all those years of research and development, this was meant to be just another set of routine tests at the Wendelstein-7X − more terabytes of data for the theorists to analyse in the weeks to come, a couple of scientific papers maybe. There was no need for his presence as programme director. And now he'd missed a significant breakthrough. His eyes widened and he gave out a long hollow whistle. 'But that means—'

'Yes, it means we have the technology for a commercial fusion reactor. We could start the design tomorrow.'

'I'll call an urgent stakeholder meeting in London for the end of the week,' Leon said. 'That gives us two days to get our presentations together. It's burning the midnight oil again, I'm afraid.'

'No problem, Leon. I've already existed on four hours sleep a night for the past week. You know I'm an adrenalin junkie when it comes to this.'

'See you there, Gunther. Leon out.'

The video-wall returned to its sleepy grey silence. Leon punched the air in delight. *I'll wake Magda and tell her the good news*. On second thoughts, did he really fancy a theoretical grilling from one of Poland's brightest mathematical talents at this time in the morning? *Perhaps I'll wait till we've finished making love*.

At the main entrance to Goldhurst, a converted mansion in the Highgate area of London, three casually dressed young men stood around like contract office workers arriving for their first day of work. While they waited for the scan to clear them, Leon Dabrowski mulled over the corporate names on the brass plaques attached to the mansion's old wall. There was only going to be one company operating from this building on his next visit, he decided, as he studied the shiny new plaque for Fusion Ltd. How he hated that bland name the Russians chose. But there was nothing uninspiring about Fusion's achievements since their takeover and that was largely down to him and his two colleagues beside him. And, he had to admit, to Chekhov's money. Who would have believed this two years ago? Here he was, at the tender age of thirty, heading up the scientific delegation at the most important commercial meeting in the history of nuclear fusion. How would they be received by these city types? The glass entrance door slid open; they were going to find out soon, he thought as Fusion's head receptionist greeted them in a barely discernible Russian accent. 'Welcome to Goldhurst, gentlemen. Please come this way.'

They followed her to Fusion's head office, striding past the reception desk without a challenge, and made their way to the conference centre. 'Drs Dabrowski, Schroeder and Kaminsky,' the receptionist announced as the men from the research site filed into the stately room and took up the three remaining places at the conference table. Leon found himself in the seat next to Roman Slavic, Fusion's chief executive officer, who looked as if all his birthdays fell today. No wonder, Leon thought.

'Welcome, gentlemen, welcome.' Slavic shook Leon's hand vigorously. 'This is splendid news. Just wonderful. I won't go around the table for introductions,' he said, as he gesticulated towards the business delegates. 'We basically have Mr Chekhov's legal and financial representatives with us today. You may recognise some of their ugly faces?' There was polite laughter from the suited assembly. 'Mr Chekhov sends his apologies but once we have full agreement on the veracity of the costs, you and I will fly out to see him, Leon.'

Vladimir Chekhov's absence was no surprise to Leon. It never ceased to amaze him how Chekhov could consider, almost at a whim, spending an almighty chunk of his fortune on a technical project he couldn't possibly understand. And he hadn't paid a single visit to the site since the takeover. Surely, he should have attended a meeting like this, even if he just joined them by video conference. Chekhov must be the supreme gambler. *He must understand probability and risk as well as I do.*

'Are you ready with the first agenda item, Dr Dabrowski?' Slavic said, impatiently tapping the table and still grinning.

What, no coffee? The scientific world had taken over half a century to get to this point. *And look what we've got.* This should have been nothing less than a three-day conference attended by the world's leading figures in nuclear power generation. At least the chairman of the meeting was trying to introduce a modicum of formality into this momentous occasion. He had to be thankful for that.

'Yes, we're ready to go. I'm sure you all know my project manager, Dr Gunther Schroeder. Gunther was the test controller for the latest stellerator runs and he's going to take us through the technical background.'

With his audience gripped in a tense silence, Schroeder ran through his presentation, assisted by the sonic screen that was set up to match his voice pattern. No complex physics, no equations – he presented the bare facts about the significance of the latest results from the Wendelstein-7X experimental reactor.

Gunther was communicating at precisely the level they'd agreed and Leon could see that the accountants were impressed with this part of his delegation's presentation; there'd be money in this for them. The solicitors seemed to have dropped their usual superior attitude as well; he had to stop himself laughing when he spotted their little group nodding and shaking heads in unison as they tapped away at their wafer-boards. And the contrast in dress codes across the table was comical – suits versus casuals – he couldn't prevent the impulsive little smile and shake of his own head.

Pawel Kaminsky followed with a presentation on software protection and data security. The security of their data was vitally important to Chekhov, who'd even insisted on his own staff being involved in the functional design specification for the software. Kaminsky explained how he had personally transported the data from each experimental run on a wafer-zip and Chekhov's refusal to use electronic means of data transfer in order to avoid hacking. The city bods were losing interest at this stage, but Slavic was still smiling and that was all that mattered.

It was Leon's turn. This was why they were here, after all – to justify the financial funding and intellectual property control requirements for the next phase. Their eyes were glued to his sonic screen; *don't drop any pins, anybody*. Ten minutes in, he could tell he was getting through to them – speaking their language. They were happy, but how would they react at the end of his presentation when he dropped the astronomical figures on them like an atomic bomb? He didn't get that far.

He was in mid-sentence when the unexpected torpedo hit. The door to the conference room swung open and a short, rotund man with slicked-back grey hair and round-rimmed spectacles marched up to the table.

'Mr Chekhov would like to speak with you via his private video link, Slavic. It's urgent.'

That's going to wipe the grin off Slavic's face, Leon thought, pocketing his hands to prevent himself from decking this little idiot.

A nervous-looking Slavic rose from his chair like a schoolboy summoned to the headmaster's office. 'I do apologise, ladies and gentlemen. Please carry on without me. Miss Lermontov, would you be kind enough to take the chair until I return?' He fumbled with the papers on the table in front of him and ended up with half of them on the floor.

Leon ruefully shook his head as he helped Slavic to retrieve his briefing notes. Slavic needed to get himself into the twenty-first century. *He should have used a wafer-board*. He looked across the room at the intruder responsible for wrecking his presentation. The man was staring at him, studying him as if he wanted to say 'I know you, don't I?' But he was sure they hadn't met. And now he'd finished disrupting this meeting – why didn't he leave? *This little joker could spell trouble*.

Slavic finally shuffled his papers straight and, with no further acknowledgement of Leon or anyone else at the meeting, set off to face Chekhov. To Leon's relief, the diminutive man turned away and followed him out of the room, slamming the door behind him.

'Who was that?' Leon asked, after they were gone.

'That's Oleg Malkin,' one of the accountants said. 'He's the building's facilities manager. Reports directly to Chekhov, I believe.'

'Well, he's a rude little man.'

Miss Lermontov placed her wafer-board on the table and put her head in her hands; she clearly had no desire to continue in Slavic's absence. Stony-faced delegates looked across the table at each other like condemned criminals awaiting the gallows. The depressing silence around the table was only broken by the occasional nervous tapping of a pen. Had Chekhov decided to pull the plug? This shambolic apology for what should have been a world-changing scientific symposium was becoming soul destroying. *Maybe Magda can get me a job as a theorist?*

Slavic returned to the meeting after fifteen minutes. To Leon's surprise, he was smiling.

'My apologies, ladies and gentlemen. But I'm delighted to tell you that the break in our proceedings was good news for all of us. Our chairman, Vladimir Chekhov, has agreed a budget of one billion euros to design the world's first commercial fusion reactor. He intends to franchise the design to the Chinese and the Koreans and following that – well, I'll leave you to consider the possibilities yourselves. This is a major step into the worldwide introduction of nuclear fusion power.'

The delegates looked at each other in stunned bewilderment. Slavic started to clap his hands slowly. One after the other, the rest of them followed his lead and joined in the applause. The clapping gathered pace and volume, smiles mushroomed on faces and laughter and cheering broke out like water from a burst dam. They'd won the super-lottery and the commercial world was at their mercy.

Amid the backslapping and the congratulatory handshakes, Leon was left wondering how this could have happened. *How has Chekhov come up with exactly the same figure as my own?*

Later that day, in the basement complex below Fusion's headquarters, Alexei Rodin made a secret transatlantic video call from the security centre annexe.

'It's true, I tell you. They've had a massive breakthrough on the German research site. Chekhov has really hit the jackpot here.'

'How did you find out?'

'Through Malkin. He couldn't contain himself. Chekhov will lose all interest in his brothel estate now and that will leave Malkin free to expand his Eight Over Nine project without Chekhov knowing what's going on.'

'This represents a fantastic opportunity for us. We could have access to Fusion's data within days of them receiving it from Greifswald. We'd be back in the race and, personally, I'd be laughing at Chekhov behind his back. What a sucker he's going to feel when he finds out we're building our own plant using his design data.'

'There are going to be substantial costs associated with procurement and delivery. You do realise that? If my own people ever found out I was involved in this, I'd be dead within the day. They'd normally expect to be the benefactors of such industrial espionage and they don't take kindly to traitors.'

'Don't worry, buddy. You'll be well compensated.'

'And you do realise there will be significant setting up costs. We've yet to find a way of accessing the stellerator data.'

'Sure, sure. Don't worry about the money. And I understand why there's no point in us trying to intercept the manual data transfer from Greifswald. We're putting a lot of faith in you, Rodin. I trust you'll come up with a way to break through Goldhurst's IT security screen. Let me know if you need any technical help.'

'There *will* be obstacles to setting up the supply chain other than technical ones.'

'Such as?'

'I was thinking of Leon Dabrowski, the project's scientific head. From what I hear, he's extremely bright and focused on his work. If he decides to spend more of his time at Fusion's London HQ, it's not going to be easy to deceive him.'

'I see what you mean. Have you any ideas how to deal with that?'

'I have. I intend to make sure he has other matters to think about. He's going to get one almighty shock when I completely disrupt his personal life. Believe me, within the month, Leon Dabrowski is going to have little interest in Fusion.'

'OK, I'll leave the details in your hands. Look forward to working with you, Rodin. Have a nice day.'

CHAPTER 12

'Have a good day, Leon,' said the Melomet. The screen went blank. Leon rubbed his tired eyes with cupped hands then collapsed back in his chair. The video conference with his London design office had been everything he'd hoped for. The latest results were consistent with their underpinning calculations; the data from Test 23 were already downloaded to portable memory, ready for Kaminsky to personally carry over to London, and they could press on with confidence in the detailed design of the reactor. Poor Kaminsky. He must already be sick of the sight of Chekhov's private jet. But that didn't matter to Chekhov, as long as the databanks were filling up at a rate that kept the design teams occupied around the clock. This was going to be one superb nuclear fusion reactor, with a power density beyond the wildest expectations of research scientists.

But there was a downside. Two years ago, after a meeting like today's, his secretary would have already booked his flights and hotel for the next international conference on nuclear fusion. Back in those days, they could look forward to announcing their results to the world. But all that changed after the summer's stellerator runs; he now worked for a commercial behemoth whose technology was top secret. And the Greifswald site wasn't the same anymore. With the tightened security, it took him fifteen minutes to get from the gatehouse to his office even though he was Fusion's chief scientist, known to every security officer on the site. There were armed guards around the perimeter, security barriers everywhere, even the cleaning staff must feel as if they were being scanned to death every day.

At this stage of the programme, it seemed strange that Gunther Schroeder spent all his time in London, headhunting for the new design team. Why Slavic wanted him on recruitment rather than working on the experimental programme was beyond Leon. He never seemed to overlap with his right-hand man nowadays. And that didn't feel right. 'I don't know what you're up to in England,' he said to his good friend during one of their rare informal chats. 'I can never get hold of you outside our formal video conferencing. Are you sure you haven't got a girlfriend tucked away somewhere?'

'I don't need one,' Gunther replied. 'I've already got one back in Germany – she's called Wendelstein. Just make sure you look after the old girl while I'm away and let me know how she is at our next video meeting.'

Leon was used to working long hours as a research scientist, yet he was struggling to get to grips with this punishing new regime. He and his team were living and eating on the hoof and late-night video conferencing was the norm. Today's intense technical meeting on plasma physics had left his exhausted brain spinning with vivid images. *Helium nuclei drifting in a molten sea at the centre of a new-born star. Huge gravitational forces fusing them together. Enormous binding energy releases. Starlight.* He needed a break soon or he'd crack.

He saw little of Magda these days. But this weekend would be different. He'd cut himself off from Fusion and spend the whole weekend with her, back in Poland. *She's more precious to me than any of this.* The images of the burning sun gave way to thoughts of Magda and he drifted back to their halcyon days as undergraduates in Krakow.

It was the summer of 2010 and today was finals day. They walked slowly along the side of the river and stopped under the shade of the old tree. As one of the most gifted mathematicians to pass through the Jagiellonian University, Magda would no doubt sail through her final paper this afternoon. He couldn't even be bothered to think about his own exam on a warm day like today.

'What are you going to do after you get your double first, my clever Leon Dabrowski?'

'Oh, I already have that planned, my equally clever Magda Tomala. I'm starting a doctorate in nuclear fusion theory at the Krakow Institute of Nuclear Physics. How about you?'

'Well, I think there has to be a more elegant solution to Fermat's Last Theorem than the one Andrew Wiles produced. I may just have a go at that,' she said, laughing.

'Trouble with that is, if I'm successful in my research, I'll earn a googolplex of money. Whereas, if you crack Fermat, the world won't give a *plink*.'

'Won't give a *plink*!' she screamed, raising her eyebrows. 'You've been reading Abramov's latest papers on group theory, have you? Should stick to your own field, physics boy.' She knelt beside him on the grass. 'So, when you've earned all the euros in the universe, what are you going to do?' she asked with a mocking grin.

'I'll use the money to fund my next brilliant project,' he replied, pushing his tongue into his cheek. 'You see, it's like this, Magda Tomala. When I look into your eyes, I imagine those billions of neurons moving around that network in your head. And if your brain can decipher their tiny electrical signals, then so can mine. I'd like to develop a way of reading your thoughts – that's what I'm going to do.'

'Ah, well I have you there, Leon Dabrowski. You see, when I look into *your* eyes, I can already read your mind. And I see that you love me every bit as much as I love you.'

They stared at each other in silence. She was a burning sun whose crushing pressure he could no longer resist – he held her in his arms, fusing with its brilliance. They kissed for the first time as lovers.

If only Magda could work alongside him, they'd make a great team. But their objectives differed, driven by their respective missions in life. One day they would marry – he was sure of that. But in the meantime, while they were at the peak of their intellectual powers, they were compelled to seek their own destinies apart from one another. The excitement from the project was his adrenalin – it drove him on relentlessly. But the weekend couldn't come soon enough.

CHAPTER 13

Magda quietly closed the bedroom door behind her.

'It's good of you to do this for us, Magda. I know how busy you are,' said Szymon Dabrowski as he got out of his chair on the upper landing. She was a smart girl and he valued her opinion.

'I do worry about her, Szymon. Is she always like this lately?'

He couldn't prevent the tears from streaming down his cheeks. 'Yes, and I don't know what to do about it. She sometimes doesn't even know who I am. But it's not so much what she's forgotten. It's her obsession with two children who don't exist.'

'I'm as confused as you are. She claims Leon has an older brother and sister and they're both dead. Worse than that, she insists she's at fault over their deaths. She has to be hallucinating.'

He took a deep breath and pulled himself together. 'I've looked up the symptoms of dementia and there *is* one form that can cause the victim to hallucinate.

They see people who aren't there. It's called Lewy Body Dementia. But LBD affects the ability to move, a bit like Parkinson's disease, whereas Lynne is perfectly mobile. Leon was three when I first met her and there can't have been any other kin. She would have registered them when she became a Polish citizen. Come on, let's go downstairs.'

Magda ran her hand down his arm. 'Listen, Szymon. She's getting close to the point where she has to be moved into a home. She needs to be looked after by professional care-workers and you need to return to your job at the bank. There, I've said it. Leon was going to discuss this with you. He's accepted that he's losing her and you have to do the same. I'm so sorry.'

Szymon dropped his head. He was already in mourning. He'd been with Lynne for twenty-five years and loved her from the day they met.

It was Christmas 1994. The snow was falling and the Stare Miasto was busier than usual this Christmas Eve. Resplendent in their seasonal livery, the horse-driven carriages lined up one behind the other alongside the awnings – the glistening beasts, steam snorting from their noses, tapping the ice with their hooves as if keen to summon their next customers. Szymon Dabrowski disliked this time of year; it reminded him of the crash in which his wife died those many Christmases ago. But Christmas Eve was different. He would always show his Christian respect and, after mass at his local Catholic church, he'd walk the two kilometres to the city centre and join in the festivities with as much enthusiasm as he could muster. That perfect gift to mankind, two millennia ago, had left this part of the world devout. And free, despite the monstrous attempts of the Nazis during World War Two. For these reasons, he felt obliged to give thanks and come to Krakow's main square to share in the traditional seasonal spirit.

From his seat in the warm little kiosk bar, he had a perfect view of the carriages, the impressive tower and the giant fir tree with its blazing white lights. The heavier-than-usual snowfalls seemed to have enhanced the square's festive ambience and for the first time in as long as he could remember, his spirits started to rise. He'd try his utmost to enjoy Christmas this year, he decided.

As he sipped at his hot mulled wine, he couldn't help but notice the lady with the small boy in the street outside. She was arguing with the carriage driver at the front of the rank. Or perhaps pleading with him. On impulse, he left his drink and the warmth of the heaters and, tightening his woollen scarf, he stepped out into the cold night air.

'Can I be of assistance, madam?'

'Oh, don't worry yourself. I'm just trying to explain to my son how the inflated prices at this time of year are extortionate. At the age of three, he has no concept of money.'

Szymon looked at the carriage driver, who raised his eyebrows in return.

'Maybe I can help. Why don't we share a carriage and the costs become reasonable once more? In fact, I quite fancy a spin around the square myself.' He looked down at the boy. 'What do you say, young man?'

'His name is Leon. If you're sure you don't mind, we'll pay our way of course.'

'Nice to meet you, Leon. My name is Szymon.' Like a true little gentleman, the small child reached up and shook the hand on offer.

'And I'm Lynne,' she said, shaking his hand and presenting him with a warm smile.

Thick blankets wrapped over their knees, they pulled their scarves over their faces against the wind and tightened their hats to protect themselves from the falling snow – Lynne and Leon in their woollen bobbles and Szymon in his Cossack's hat. 'Yah!' the driver shouted. The hooves clattered, the carriage pulled away to the jingling sound of bells and the wheels crunched over compacted ice. As they passed by the arches, the delicious smells of traditional Polish food wafted across from the Christmas market – it reminded Szymon of how he used to feel about Christmas when Naomi was alive. Three circuits they got for their money and as they started their second tour, he found himself willing the driver to slow down so he could savour it all for longer. He didn't want the exhilaration to end.

Lynne was first to speak. 'That's a greatcoat you're wearing. I didn't realise people still wore them.'

'They're deceptively warm. Evidently there was a resurgence of the fashion in the nineteen seventies. But now it's all these modern lightweight padded jackets.' He nipped the sleeve of Lynne's duvet coat and shook his head in mock derision.

She laughed.

'You're English?' Szymon asked.

'Yes. My accent must be so obvious. You live here?'

'Have done for many years.'

At the end of the ride, Lynne shook his hand again. 'Thank you, Szymon. I enjoyed that.'

'I enjoyed it too, Mummy,' Leon chipped in. 'Can we go for some hot lemonade? Can Szymon join us?'

'Oh, I don't think—'

'I think that's a splendid idea, young man,' Szymon interrupted, 'and that's an amazing command of Polish for a three-year-old.'

'He's actually three and a half. But I have to agree, he's advanced for his age – except when it comes to the value of money.' She gave Leon a wry smile and the boy looked up and chuckled at Szymon.

Back in the kiosk, they managed to find seats near one of the big gas heaters. After ordering their drinks, they took off the outer layers of their clothing and started to thaw out in front of the welcoming yellow glow.

'Will you play me at Stone, Scissors and Paper, please?' Leon asked.

'Does the lad know this game?'

Lynne gave a knowing look and nodded. 'He's good at it.'

Over several rounds, Szymon won just two. He couldn't believe what he was seeing. 'One, two, three, go.' He'd make a sudden scissors sign with two fingers and at the same time, Leon would pull out a fist representing stone. 'Stone wins,' Leon would say excitedly, 'another point to me.' They played on. It was a simple game but one of strategy and bluff. The youngster seemed to have an almost telepathic awareness. Statistically this was possible, but perhaps the boy was a child genius.

He turned to Lynne. 'He's so clever that he can even …' Despite the drift of warm air from the nearby heater, Szymon froze. He could tell that all this time she'd been watching *him* and not the game. He sensed the admiration in her eyes. It was as vibrant as the butterflies he felt in his stomach. Szymon never stopped mourning following his tragic loss. He was resigned to being a widower for the rest of his life – until this magical moment on Christmas Eve.

Now, she'd been taken from him. He'd done nothing to deserve such a punishment. But Alzheimer's disease doesn't distinguish the good from the bad, the haves from the have-nots. It starts by taking one prisoner and gradually cripples until family and loved ones become victims themselves. *This unstoppable disease destroys everything in its wake.*

'Szymon, are you all right?' Magda said, snapping him out of his thoughts.

Szymon stirred the coffee. 'So how is Leon's big project?' he asked, deliberately changing the subject.

'He tells me it's going well. But he's often in Germany or England and with all that's going on in my own research group, we have precious little time together. In fact, for the first time in months, we're going to spend this coming weekend in Krakow. A whole weekend together, would you believe? If you can get someone to look after Lynne, perhaps you could join us for dinner down the square.'

'I can't, Magda. I have to stay here. Have a lovely weekend and make sure he comes to visit his mother.'

'We'll both come to see her, Szymon. I promise.'

CHAPTER 14

Converted from sixteenth-century stone catacombs, the Keller Klub off Krakow's main square bustled with young people on a Saturday night. Leon and Magda arrived at the club's subterranean bar as two women were leaving their barstools. 'May we?' Magda asked the trendy thirty-somethings, before they disappeared into the annexe where the band was just starting to play.

'Timed to perfection,' Leon quipped.

'Perfection is what I'm about, my love.'

Leon sighed. 'It's so nice to relax. I can feel the batteries recharging already.'

They touched fingers and smiled into each other's eyes. They talked of sweet nothings over a background of soft jazz and flickering candles. Magda took occasional sips through the ice and sliced orange at the top of her tall glass of Henry. Leon took his time over three small bottles of Tyskie beer.

The ambience in the bar was becoming more vibrant, the conversations growing louder and mirthful – a tangible vivacity filled the catacombs. Magda laughed. 'You're not getting a bit tipsy, are you?'

He loved it when Magda laughed like that. But he wasn't drunk at all – euphoric, he would call it. He felt himself wobble on the stool. 'Oops, not used to this,' he joked as he excused himself.

When he returned to the bar, their stools were occupied by a well-dressed couple of about his own age. 'I was sitting here with my girlfriend a few moments ago. Did you see where she went?'

The couple looked at each other in surprise. 'Sorry, friend, there was nobody in the seats when we arrived. Would you like them back?'

'Don't worry,' he said, looking around the room, 'we'll find somewhere else.'

The bar heaved and he could feel its humidity rising. Every seat was taken and new arrivals were pouring into the annexe. Perhaps Magda was in there – she loved her music. *I'll take a look.* The jazz trio was in full swing with foot-tapping music. He leaned against the old stone archway and scrutinised the throng of young people who were crammed against the walls and jostling to get the best view. *Where is she?*

He trotted up the stone staircase to look outside in the square. Perhaps she'd come up for fresh air? The night air was cool and the gentle breeze cleared the stuffiness from his head. A group of smokers chatted in their little huddle. They hadn't noticed anyone of Magda's description. Concerned, he returned to the bar and enquired around the tables.

'A good-looking blonde girl, my age. Did you see her leave?'

A shrug of shoulders from a disinterested group of male students.

'Excuse me, I'm looking for my girlfriend. We were sat at the bar about fifteen minutes earlier.'

'Sorry, we've just arrived.'

Nothing from the bar staff; most of them were too busy to bother with him.

Concern became anxiety. Magda wouldn't just go off like that. He was about to ask a female customer to check the ladies' toilet for him, when he noticed a middle-aged couple staring at him from a table at the back of the room. Perhaps *they* knew something.

'There *was* someone. Over there.' The man pointed. 'She was drunk, slumped between two men. She couldn't walk and they had to slide her feet along the floor. I saw them help her towards the far staircase. It's at the end of that corridor and it leads up to the rear courtyard. Perhaps she's outside sobering up?'

'Thanks. I'll check it out.'

They must have been mistaken, Magda didn't drink. A cold sweat came over him. Half an hour since he last saw her, nothing to go on, he ran up the stairs three at a time. The back of the building was deserted. He searched the whole club again, three more times, bumping into folk, stumbling into tables. Anxiety turned to panic.

'Hey! You take care where you're treading, my friend.'

He checked the front entrance again. Nothing. Where was she?

Call her.

Not available.

Call Szymon.

'She hasn't contacted me. Are you OK, Leon?'

He checked again at the bar.

'Sorry, sir. I can't imagine what you're talking about. Perhaps you had a tiff?'

'Not really.'

Call the police.

'Yes, sir. If you'd like to come down to the station and provide some details.'

Leon caught sight of a man at the far end of the room who seemed to be staring at him. The man averted his gaze, slid off the bar stool and left the club. Exhausted and distraught, Leon sat down on the stool he'd vacated.

Where did she go?

This was his second visit to the Keller Klub since Saturday evening. As for the first visit, Leon arrived early before the bar became too busy. Different staff at work tonight and at last he'd found one who might be able to help.

'Yes, I remember the girl. I noticed how elegant and well-dressed she was.'

The butterflies in Leon's stomach took flight and his hopes rose with them.

'OK, let's talk about it. I'm Leon. What's your name?'

'I'm Zena. Are you a cop?'

Zena was a tiny girl, twenty perhaps, and seemed to have an ideal personality for this line of work. *Let's hope she's observant.* 'No, I'm not a cop,' he said, trying to reassure her. 'How was she dressed? Do you remember?'

'I do. She wore a smart white blouse and a short black waistcoat. I'd die for a waistcoat like that, I would. Never going to afford one though, not on my wages.'

'Did you see what happened to her?'

'Something odd happened. I saw it from that end of the bar —' she pointed '— where I was working.'

'What did you see, Zena?'

'These two guys left with her and I thought I saw her stagger a bit. That's what was odd. She hadn't been drinking alcohol as far as I could remember. And like I say, she was so elegant and ladylike while she sat at the bar. But all sorts can happen on a busy night. I thought nothing of it and decided not to get involved.'

'The men you saw, did you know them?'

'I know one of them by sight. He always comes in on jazz nights. A bit of all right, actually. Don't know his name though. The other one, I've never seen before.'

'You've been helpful, Zena. Look, if this guy comes in again, can you call me? Here's my card. I promise you, I'm not the police.'

At last, the prospect of meeting someone who assisted Magda that evening. *Surely, he must have some idea about what happened to her.*

To Leon's delight, Zena came up trumps at the very next jazz night, a day later. He rushed down to the club to meet her *bit of all right*.

'She was your bird, was she? A good-looker that one. But she was in a right state.'

'Can you tell me everything you remember? It's important.'

'Something wrong, mate? I don't want to get involved in any marital spats.'

'No, there's no issue for you. It's just that I haven't seen her since that night. She's gone missing.'

'Well, she was fine when I left her.'

'You left her? You said she was in a bad state, why did you leave her?'

'We took her up to the courtyard. The other dude, he said it was all right for me to go. He'd look after her. Seemed like a decent guy, so I just came back down to the music.'

'This other man, did you know him?'

'Never seen him before in my life, mate. But he did have the decency to come back and tell me she was OK and that he'd ordered her a cab. Then he left. Listen, if you're worried, why don't we go to the police? I'd be happy to talk to them if you want. But I've already told you everything I know.'

'No, that won't be necessary. Thanks anyway, you've been very helpful.' *Looks like a long night for me, trawling around the taxi firms.*

CHAPTER 15

The bedroom was large and opulent. The soft white lighting created shadows that merged and unravelled in time with the throbbing pain behind her eyes. This had to be a dream. But dreams were about places you knew, weren't they? Or if you've never been in the place before, its dimensions were vague and distorted. *I can see every detail*. This place was real.

'Good morning, Ana.'

The voice sounded real enough. A male voice, not as intoxicating as the female voice of the Melomet but almost as reassuring.

'Who are you?'

'Who I am is not important. We're going to look after you from now, Ana. You will have a life of bliss.'

'I'm not Ana!'

Raising her voice made the pain in Magda's head worse. 'What am I doing here?'

'All in good time. But for now, you need sleep. Someone will come along and give you something. Goodnight, Ana.'

'Wait, don't go. At least tell me how I got here.'

'You came by helicopter.'

Her mind, like her eyes, began to focus. The beat of whirling blades, a dark human shadow – the sting of the hypodermic needle made her feel warm, she remembered. There were others on board – a bleak atmosphere of panic and fear among them. Russian voices trying to calm them down. Did they crash?

'The others, who were they? What happened to them?'

'They came to no harm, Ana.' The voice was beside her now. 'Don't worry about them.'

'I'm not Ana. What are you doing to me?'

'All in good time.' The last thing she heard him say as she felt the cold fluid enter her vein.

She woke to the echo of approaching footsteps. The soft bed was now a hard table to which her limp body was stuck and she could do nothing but watch as the man in a white lab coat slid the hypodermic into her forearm.

'Where is this place?'

'I can't tell you,' he said, checking the monitors to her side and shaking his head in apparent disappointment.

She recalled the vivid flash of light. A light of such intensity would have burned out her retinas; it must have been generated inside her head. And what about the classical music? She could see no audio speakers; that had to be inside her head too. The thought that they'd tampered with her mind sent her into a tailspin of panic.

'What do you want with me?'

'We're preparing you for your new life, Ana,' came a distant voice.

More than one of them. Her final thought as she drifted back into her dreamworld.

She stood alone in a scorching desert and looked into the sky. The lengthy equation she'd assembled spanned five long rows – hieroglyphics to the non-mathematical but mesmerising against the backcloth of electric blue. She added and deleted until she had perfection, stepped back and admired her work. Into her dreamscape came the helicopters. The noise was deafening but she couldn't see them. Their beating blades blew the first symbol out of the sky and it fluttered down to earth, turning to dust in the desert sand. Line by line they dismantled her beautiful creation. Mathematical symbols fell like autumn leaves until the sky was empty. Empty, except for that brilliant fusion reactor they called the sun.

'Leon!' she cried aloud. 'Where are you, Leon?'

Magda came to in a room that was warm with a smell of fresh paint. She rubbed the crusted sleep from her eyes, rolled down the sleeve of her pyjama top and eased herself out of the bed. Standing was difficult but she soon got the hang of it and started to totter around her new environment. In the bathroom, she found a towelling gown and soft slippers in her size; without thinking, she put them on and set off to explore. State-of-the-art kitchen, expensive furniture – this place was impressive. *Why no windows?* No pictures or any other forms of wall art, everything was decorated white. *A door to the outside?* That was white too. No lock, no door handle, she tried pushing it. Nothing happened.

'Door open!'

No response.

'Magda!'

Still no response.

No Melomet, she decided. She was trapped until someone chose to let her out.

In the open-plan living and dining area, she poured a glass of drinking water from the filter-tap and gulped it down greedily; it tasted good in her dry mouth. She refilled, set the glass down on the coffee table and slumped into the sumptuous armchair. *I'm hungry – when will they feed me?* She'd come from an obscure world with strange voices. Why had they put her in a place like this? *So many questions, no one to answer.*

As if she'd rubbed a magic lamp, the door chimes tinkled and the section of wall above the entrance came to life. There was a lobby on the other side of that door. The overhead view on the screen revealed the top of a man's head. Jet-black hair and muscular torso beneath – he'd found her.

'Leon!'

She rushed to the door and tried to open it with her fingernails. In frustration, she banged at it with her clenched fists until they ached.

'Leon! I'm in here. Can you hear me?'

The door opened.

In the lobby, a young man stood smiling. She threw her arms wide, inviting him to hug her. 'Leon …' Her voice tailed off to a deflated moan, her arms flopped by her sides and her head sunk on to her chin. Her visitor strode jauntily into the apartment and the door closed behind him.

'What do you think of it?' he said, opening his arms and spinning around on the spot like a ballet dancer.

'Who are you?' she asked, making no attempt to conceal her disappointment.

'I am Sergei, your personal training instructor,' he replied, snapping to attention.

Disappointment turned to anger. 'Well, PTI Sergei, I don't recall joining a health spa. Just tell me what I'm doing here.'

'All in good time, Ana. Today is about introductions. I'm sure we're going to get along fine.'

He was Russian. His English was good, but he spoke with those hints of accent and diction that can never be shaken off.

'You must be hungry,' he said.

'I am. I'm starving.'

'I'll arrange for a meal to be sent down to you. You'll be impressed, I promise.'

Sent down, he said. So how far was up? She could tell there was little point in pursuing him for answers. Besides, she could think no further than food at the moment.

'Goodbye, Ana. I'll come back in the morning, at around eight. You'll find suitable clothing for exercise in your bedroom.'

That was his introduction? She wanted to scream at him, tell him she wasn't Ana. But she had no energy. There'd be a better time for asking questions. *And then I'll squeeze the blood out of him – whoever he is.*

The following morning, Sergei turned up on time and let himself into her apartment. Magda was dressed in a Lycra suit, sweatband and trainers – ready for whatever Sergei had in mind but feeling a tad ridiculous. 'Before we go, PTI Sergei, there are a few things I'd like to talk about. This place, and—'

'No time for that, Ana, we have a tight schedule.'

The gym was located two levels down from her apartment, at the end of a short corridor.

'Where is everybody?'

'This is it,' he answered as he set the treadmill's inclination, 'booked exclusively to us for the next hour.'

'And the next clients are?'

Sergei chortled and shook his head as he continued to adjust the machine's programme. This was a case of doing as she was told until she could figure out what was going on.

She followed Sergei's instructions to the letter throughout the thirty-minute workout. The session was easy, although her laboured breathing and long recovery times left her both surprised and disappointed. *Thought I was fitter than that*. When the session was over, her attention returned to her predicament, yet there was an underlying feeling of euphoria that she couldn't explain. For a moment, she even felt pleased to be here. *They must have drugged me.*

'Sergei, you're going to have to tell me what this is all about. You can't hold out on me any longer. I deserve—'

'All in good time, Ana.'

CHAPTER 16

Leon watched in silence as the police sergeant nonchalantly scanned through his scribbled notes.

'When was the last time you saw her, Dr Dabrowski?'

'Saturday evening.'

'And it's now Wednesday. What makes you think she's missing?'

'She failed to show up yesterday at an important Jagiellonian seminar. I've tried contacting her, but no answer.'

'Could she be ill? Have you tried contacting her parents?'

'Foster parents, actually – both dead. Look, officer, I've spent the last twenty-four hours retracing every possible lead and trawling the video-net. She's a mature woman, a prominent professor. She's a professional. You get that?'

'Calm down, sir. We have a procedure to go through. Do you know how many missing persons we have on our books?'

'No, but I doubt you have any like this one. She's well known, revered by her colleagues. You need to understand that.'

'Sorry, young man,' the police sergeant said, with contempt. 'I don't know her at all. She may be important in academic circles, but she's no celebrity. She isn't a pop star or a sports personality, is she? With respect, she's hardly a household name.'

'And she's not one of your run-of-the-mill vulnerable persons, as you call them. What are you intending to do about it? It's out of character. I'm frantic with worry.'

'Maybe you're right,' the sergeant conceded, sitting up and at last making the effort to look interested. 'How about this? We'll contact the broadcast companies, see if we can get a public appeal out. Now, if you'll just speak into this wafer-board, we'll take some details.'

Leon stood up in a rage, incensed by this petty bureaucrat. 'I want your help on this!' he yelled, kicking his chair in frustration. The chair rebounded off the wall to his side and clattered against the sergeant's desk. 'I'll be back tomorrow. And I want to see some progress.' His head boiling like a kettle, he pointed his finger at the sergeant. 'And *you* had better be here in person, officer.'

The inspector seemed to be genuinely interested in the case. At least he was more enthusiastic than that useless sergeant he'd met last week.

'Her disappearance is well publicised. We've had another five potential sightings in the past week, spread throughout the whole of Europe. We've tracked down every friend, every associate, all visitors to her university faculty, everyone we can think of. We're doing all we can.'

Leon wasn't impressed. 'Tell me something I don't know. Don't you think I've already done that myself?'

'We're putting out feelers in the Immigration Departments throughout Western Europe.'

'Why are you doing that?'

The inspector got out of his seat and paced back and forth. 'I want you to consider the following possibility, Dr Dabrowski. It's not a pleasant thought, but we have to look at all potential outcomes.'

Leon knew he was about to be told something he wasn't going to like.

'Back in the nineteen nineties, there was a spate of abductions by Eastern European gangs. Attractive young girls from Western Europe, most of them English travelling abroad alone or in pairs, were taken by these gangs while holidaying in cities like Paris, Berlin, Brussels. They were used mercilessly as prostitutes in countries like Turkey and Russia. Those who were lucky ended up in the harems of rich Arabs. Those who weren't so lucky ... well, I won't go into that. This sex trafficking as it came to be known was eventually dealt with by the police authorities and all but snuffed out.' He sat back into his seat and sighed. 'But, sad to say, it's begun to re-emerge. This time the flow is from east to west, from Eastern Europe.'

'I don't know anything about sex trafficking. You're not suggesting Magda is caught up in it, are you? She's far too clever to be duped by people like that.'

'It's just a possibility, Dr Dabrowski. In my opinion, it's our best line of enquiry so far.'

The words were cutting. If they were shifting their efforts into this type of investigation, there had to be good reason. The thought of Magda in the hands of depraved monsters like that was unbearable. He couldn't wait for the police – he'd have to look into this himself. But where did he start?

The doorbell chimes jolted Leon from his drunken sleep.

'Magda?'

He fumbled for his wafer and called up his entrance security camera. The image of a hefty grey-haired man standing in the corridor outside his apartment appeared on the screen. He deflated like a balloon.

'Who are you?'

The man offered up his identification to the camera. 'My name is Leonid Pavel. I'm from the Police Department in Warsaw. I need to speak with you urgently.'

'What's a Russian doing working for the Polish police?'

'Russian in name only. My parents. Can I come in?'

'Depends what it's about.'

Pavel looked around the corridor, before whispering, 'Magda Tomala.'

'Open, door!' Leon shouted, desperate for any news.

'Security lock off,' the Melomet replied.

He studied the big man at the opposite end of his couch. He was well-groomed and clean-shaven, but his dark grey suit was grubby and worn to a shine in places. *Archetypal police detective.*

'I realise this is somewhat unusual but once I've explained, you'll appreciate why I've had to come to your home in person.'

Can I trust him?

'I'm the head of a new *Policja* Department in Warsaw responsible for dealing with sex trafficking cartels. I believe you're aware, from discussions with my colleagues in Krakow, that this is a serious crime which is growing in this country.'

Leon's heart came up into his mouth. If they visited you in person it was bad news, wasn't it? 'Are you going to tell me you have news of Magda?'

'Not exactly. We still don't know what happened to her. However, we've recently made something of a breakthrough, which I'd like to discuss with you in confidence. But this is sensitive. You must not disclose the nature of our discussion to anyone. Not even to the Krakow *Policja*. Do you accept this, Dr Dabrowski?'

'I'm promising nothing until I know where Magda is.'

Pavel scowled. 'You're a professional man. Highly respected, I understand. On that basis, I'll continue. But please bear in mind, a breach of security in this area could cost lives. You *do* appreciate that?'

He was referring to Magda's life. Leon nodded.

'We recently apprehended two members of a particularly active cartel. They work throughout Poland. We interrogated them with the assistance of truth drugs and they revealed that they often operate in Krakow. But I was surprised to hear how little they knew about the cartel for which they work. Modern police methods are effective, believe me, so we have to accept that their ignorance was genuine. However, we did manage to elicit *some* valuable information.'

'I'm listening, but I can't see how this involves me.'

'Please bear with me, Dr Dabrowski. I'll tell you what we know. We know they drug their victims and transport them in a van to the outskirts of Berlin. There, they hand them over to German nationals. But we could extract no names. They did, however, reveal that, from their idle chat during handovers, at least one of the destinations for these unfortunate girls is London. In fact, putting this together with evidence from elsewhere, we believe this is where most of the abducted Polish nationals end up.'

'Are you saying you think Magda might be in London?'

'We can't be sure, but there's a good chance. We did try to elicit information about the girls they abducted, but they were vague. Their descriptions were all similar, except for hair colour. And they didn't know the names of any of the bars from which the girls were taken. They pick them up at a predetermined time and location, often abandoned in a collapsed state.'

The thought of Magda lying unconscious in some dirty side street, waiting to be picked up by some perverted criminal. Leon felt sick.

'We've since been in close touch with our counterparts in London. They admit they have a growing problem with prostitution. The number of brothels run by professional criminals is increasing. They also confirm they have a lot of Polish girls working in the sex trade. They—'

Leon stood up. 'Just a minute. I've listened to everything you've had to say, but I'm learning nothing new. I'm glad you've caught a couple of these pond dwellers. But what has this all got to do with me?'

'Dr Dabrowski, will you please sit down? I was coming to that. Please be patient.'

Simmering, Leon reluctantly did as he was asked.

'The secret service in London has agents planted around the patch,' Pavel continued, 'and they have a name – Alexei Rodin. They believe that Rodin is some sort of overlord for many of the Russian brothels. But they tell us he's elusive. No one knows what he looks like or where he's based.'

'Surely, it's just a matter of time before MI5, or whoever is dealing with this, finds this man?'

Pavel gave a cynical laugh. 'Yes, MI5 are increasing their resource to take this on. But between you and me, it's a slow process and I don't think they have any real incentive. For whatever reason, they're not interested in tracking down Alexei Rodin. An easy life, bribery and corruption, politics – who knows? But rest assured, unless *we* do something, no one else is going to. And that is where you come in.'

This was becoming more confusing by the minute. 'What on earth can I do?'

'You can walk into any of their brothels as a client, for a start.'

'What?'

'Yes, Dr Dabrowski, you can pose as a … punter, I believe is the English term. We can hardly do that ourselves. It would cut straight across British police operations, maybe even cause a political furore between our countries. As it stands, the crime is on their patch but the victims are our nationals – stalemate. You, on the other hand, spend legitimate time in London. You're perfectly placed to enquire into the identity and whereabouts of this *Pimpernel*. No one in his right mind would imagine a man in your position being involved in such a covert operation.'

'I'm to have a new career as a spy for my country, is that what you're saying?'

'Call it that if you like. We'll help you as much as we can, of course. For example, we can tell you everything we know about Rodin. We don't have any physical description of him, but our forensic psychologists tell us he's going to be a powerful and assertive person. Someone his underlings will fear.'

'But why me?'

'Many reasons. Because you're intelligent and good at solving complex problems. Because our analysts advise us that if we found Rodin's lair, we could blow his operation wide open without any political ramifications. Because, Dr Dabrowski, our analysts also tell us that if you find Alexei Rodin, you'll find Magda Tomala.'

CHAPTER 17

Magda's training, which by now included swimming in an Olympic-size pool, was becoming longer and more intense by the day. After two weeks, she was training so hard that by the time she finished her evening meal, all she could do was drag her weary body into the bedroom and collapse into bed. But they weren't going to fool her; this schedule was designed to soak up her energy and smother her ardour for questions. They may be draining her body but they weren't going to stifle her creative mind; for a start, this complex had to be far more extensive than the areas she was restricted to. She soaked up as much information as she could during each trip with Sergei. She studied her surroundings, looked for anything new and began to construct a model of the place in her head. After all, she was a prisoner and she'd have to start thinking about her options for escape.

Another week passed and Magda's mood began to fluctuate. Some days she would use every minute of her thinking time to plan her escape. Then there were the bad days when she would mope about and hate herself for making such poor use of her intellect. On those days, her thoughts turned to Leon. The prospect of being reunited with Leon gave her strength and steeled her resolve. She would sit in her chair, imagining he was in the room with her and hold fictitious conversations. The thought of being cooped up in this apartment twenty-four hours a day was unbearable, she would tell him. But compliance meant privileges and she'd have to go along with whatever ruse they presented. *I'm not going to give in to these bastards though, Leon – whoever they are.*

After a month of frustration, Magda reluctantly accepted her daily routine; yet she would never let them kill her determination to escape.

'What delights do you have in store for me today, PTI Sergei?'

'No training today, Ana. I'm going to show you more of the complex.'

Her heart beat faster. At last, she was about to see the world beyond her limited existence of training, eating and sleeping. As she followed Sergei to the elevator, her eyes were drawn to his pert buttocks. *What's happening to me?* Sergei turned and smiled as if he knew what she was thinking. That ubiquitous smile, and those eyes … she mentally shook her head. How were they doing this to her? *He's my gaoler, for God's sake.*

As usual, Sergei operated the elevator from the wafer he kept in a pocket at the rear of his shorts. And as Magda always did, she mentally counted the seconds as they descended; when the elevator stopped, they were at least three levels below where he normally took her. Another corridor, another room, another opportunity to extend her mental model. Sergei opened the door. 'We call it the black drum,' he said.

Every surface was matt black and the circular floor and ceiling were lit by thousands of pin-prick white lights.

'Go ahead, Ana. Step inside. But take your trainers off first.'

Magda took a single step into the room and stopped. The floor beneath her foot undulated gently and the tiny floor lights rippled as the wave she'd created slowly crossed the room. Reflections from the ceiling. 'Water below?'

'A low viscosity gel under a rubber surface. Try moving on it.'

She marched on the spot. 'The waves? They've been damped?'

'The pressure of the gel automatically adjusts in response to the movements of your feet.'

'You're impressing me, Leon.'

'Leon?'

For a moment, she'd lost her focus. 'What is this place, Sergei?'

He ignored her question. 'Feel the wall.'

Her hand left an impression which slowly disappeared. 'Astronaut foam?'

'Something like that.'

She walked around the perimeter, sliding her hand along the wall. The warm soft surface beneath her feet felt good and the desire to run became overwhelming. *Do it*. She bolted like a racehorse from the stalls. Feeling as light as a feather and running within inches of the wall boosted her adrenalin flow and the burden of being a prisoner lifted from her shoulders. There was no angling of her body, yet in her mind she was running a tight cambered bend. *Go faster*. She accelerated until she was running flat out. The virtual wind from her pace swept her hair back and she squealed with delight. She could hear Sergei shouting from the other side of the room through the megaphone he'd formed with his hands.

'Run to me!'

She turned through ninety degrees and cut across the floor towards him. Five metres from where he was standing, she impulsively launched herself into a swimming pool dive and landed at his feet. It felt like hitting feather pillows, yet the surface under her panting chest was now firm.

Sergei helped her to her feet. 'You enjoyed that?'

She gasped for breath. 'It felt like ... almost sexual.'

'Glad you feel that way. One more thing to show you.' Sergei tapped his wafer and a double bed-sized cylinder rose silently out of the floor in the centre of the room. At the height of a metre, it came to a stop with a melodic jingling sound.

'What's that for?'

'For whatever you like, Ana,' he said, grinning suggestively. 'Go over and sit on it, see what it feels like.'

Magda walked over to the podium and sat on its edge. It felt hard at first, like a table. As she leaned back on her elbows, soft undulations seemed to spring from everywhere; they played at the back of her thighs and sent ripples of pleasure up and down her hamstrings. Adjusting her position generated more waves and she felt moist between her legs; this was more than just the sweat from her running efforts. Her thighs slowly moved apart and she couldn't stop them. She looked across at Sergei. The subtle changes of lighting created moving shadows across his face, yet his eyes were transfixed. He was leering at her. He started laughing. She could hear the raucous bellow of sadism and perversion and fear curdled in her stomach. This wasn't the gentle Sergei she knew. He walked towards her. His eyes were glazed over and menacing and he clenched and opened his fists. *My God, he's going to rape me.*

'Don't worry, Ana, I won't hurt you.'

'Stay away from me, you bastard.'

'It's *meant* to make you feel like that.'

'Let me out of here!'

Sergei leaned over her and pressed his hands down on the surface to either side of her hips. A deep hollow appeared under each hand as he leaned forward and eased down his torso until he almost touched her intimately. He slowly pushed himself away as if doing a press-up then flipped himself back upright. The surface under Magda felt firm once more. *He's switched it off.*

'You can get up now, Ana.'

The kind smile was back. The predatory animal was gone.

'Sergei, please take me back to my quarters,' she said calmly, as the weight of oppression returned.

CHAPTER 18

Leon settled down at his London hotel room table and spread the papers that Leonid Pavel had provided. He'd found it surprisingly easy to persuade Roman Slavic that he should join Gunther at London HQ. This would be the best use of his time during the long gap between stellerator runs; he could add momentum to the process of getting the design teams under way. He couldn't remember the last time he'd pored over paperwork like this. Proofreading of scientific papers was always done on a sonic screen nowadays. But the Warsaw *Policja* considered it too risky to allow sensitive files to flash around the net outside their control or reside on a single wafer-device. And who was going to mug a scientist for his paperwork? Nevertheless, he'd received strict instructions to destroy the whole file once he'd committed it to memory.

There were over a hundred establishments on the lists they sent him. One hundred addresses for him to memorise, one hundred records – albeit scanty ones. He could do that easily, of course, but it could take him up to six months to pay them all a visit. He'd need to prioritise. Other than defining the locations of the brothels, the records didn't tell him a lot. The dataset was consistent in one respect, though – most of the brothels were Russian-owned. And from Pavel's estimates of how many girls worked at each location, he could see that Magda was going to be hidden within a pool of thousands. But that wasn't the issue for Pavel; his problem was that Alexei Rodin could be based at any of these establishments, maybe even flitting between them to stay ahead of the game. Rodin was the proverbial needle in a haystack. With the information locked in his head, Leon shredded the file and started to formulate the plan for his first visit.

'Welcome to our club, Leon. I hope you don't mind me referring to you by your first name. Client confidentiality of course. I'm Stephan. We spoke over the Melomet video-net.'

'I have the five hundred pounds you asked for, Stephan. Cash, of course.'

'Ah, most grateful.' Stephan bowed his head as he accepted the sheaf of plastic notes and tucked it into his desk drawer. 'You do realise, of course, once you've viewed our catalogue this money is non-returnable?'

'Yes, I understand. And I pay in advance for any girl I select, plus a monthly membership fee if I decide to come back.'

'Precisely. Now, I'm going to give you this,' he said, producing a wafer from his desk drawer. 'It has no voice control. Security reasons, you understand? You scroll down the list like this.' He slid his finger up and down the small screen. 'And when you wish to view one of our ladies, you select the hologram and control it by circling your thumb like this. See?' He used his thumb to rotate the image. 'Do you have any experience with life-size holographic image manipulation?'

'Just a bit,' Leon replied, tongue in cheek.

'Then we're ready. Someone from security will show you the way to your private viewing room.'

'You have much in the way of personnel security?'

'You've seen them in our reception area.'

'What, those scantily clad girls who welcomed me at the entrance? I thought they were your—'

'Our ladies of pleasure? No, they're part of our security team. Deceptive, isn't it? But believe me, those girls can handle themselves. Any funny business would be dealt with very quickly. But don't worry, Leon. Since we opened this establishment, their skills have never once been required. We entertain only exclusive clients. Think of it as an insurance policy, if you like.'

Exclusive, my oath – stinking rich, he means.

The elevator dropped down a single floor level. Leon stepped out into a brightly lit square room with a circular pedestal at its centre. 'Enjoy your viewing, sir,' the young woman said before leaving. The elevator door closed behind her and the lights in the room dimmed.

He sat down in the only chair and the wafer in his hand came to life. At the touch of its screen, the holographic image of the first girl appeared. She was naked, with her back to him, hands by her sides and legs akimbo. Slim, about five and a half feet tall, pale skin and permed red hair – she looked real. This was sophisticated equipment, no expense spared. He rotated the image until the girl faced him.

'Good day. My name is Margot and my fee is five hundred pounds per hour.'

Leon turned cold. He imagined some pervert viewing an image of Magda like this, getting himself into an aroused state and deciding she was the one for him. He felt sick to the stomach but forced himself to continue. This was going to be a painful process.

He scanned the catalogue as quickly as he could, moving on as soon as it became obvious that it wasn't an image of Magda in front of him. All of them were beautiful women – tall, petite, slim, curvaceous, of various ethnic origins – no doubt selected to appeal to a wide range of client tastes. But none held any attraction for him. They were prostitutes, he kept telling himself. And the stock could include Magda. He had to scan to the end.

Image number forty-four struck an immediate chord. He studied the back of the girl's body and his adrenalin flowed. The curve of her spine, her elegantly-boned shoulders – it could be her. Her hair was dark brown and cut to a medium bob. But that would have been easy to arrange if they wanted to change her style. With bated breath, he rotated the image, longing to see his love's face again, praying that he'd found her before she'd been abused. His heart sank. This wasn't Magda.

'Thank you,' Leon said, as he handed the wafer back to Stephan, 'I've seen everything. You have no others, I take it?'

'If you've viewed the whole catalogue, you've seen them all. None to your liking?'

'I'd just like to take my time, go away and think about it, Alexei.'

'Alexei?'

'Sorry, my mistake.' *He knows him, but that's not Rodin.*

After a month, recruitment was complete. Out of Fusion's technical lead team, only Kaminsky remained at Greifswald, with Gunther assisting Leon at the London design office, under the watchful eye of Slavic. Hopefully, Slavic wasn't watching *too* carefully, otherwise he'd notice the enhanced levels of stress and tiredness in his face in comparison with those of his colleague. He had to admit that Gunther was bearing up well under the pressure and he expected nothing less from his right-hand man. Then, Gunther didn't have to follow his day's work with an evening crawl through yet another batch of brothels in a relentless search for Rodin. Sure, he was building up data in parallel with Pavel's surveillance team, yet there was no sign of Rodin and Pavel was becoming more anxious by the day. It all meant that he was no closer to finding Magda. And that was all he really cared about.

The door to his office flew open. Schroeder wore the scowl of a man who'd just had his Ferrari stolen as he covered the ground between the door and his desk in record time. What was irritating Gunther? And how had he managed to persuade his secretary to open the locked door? He'd have to have a word with her.

'Yes, Gunther, what can I do for you?'

'I need your advice. We're having problems with the hydrodynamic analysis for the heat removal systems.'

'What do you want me to do about it? You have experienced engineers, don't you? You're telling me they aren't capable of solving this – they have computers, don't they?'

'It's a serious problem, Leon. It's holding up the licence applications for three UK power plant proposals. I thought you ought to know about it.'

'Gunther, if there's something you're not sure about on the plasma physics side, I'll help. But don't come in here with run-of-the mill problems like that. What do you want me to do? Send them all back to university to repeat their hydrodynamics courses? For God's sake, man. I'm not their wet nurse.'

'Actually, I didn't come in for a solution, Leon. I came for a reaction. And you've just given me exactly the one I expected. I'm worried about you – you're not yourself.'

'Look, Gunther, I'm busy. Is there anything else?'

'That's just the point, I reckon you're not busy at all. You sneak in early morning and lock the door behind you. And as far as I'm aware, you're never at the office after six. You may as well get rid of that little girl out front. Replace her with a voice recording: "Sorry, he's busy, can Dr Schroeder be of any help?" But I don't know what you're doing, so how the hell can I cover for you?'

'It's your job, isn't it? Finger on the pulse and all that? You know more about the design detail than I do. Just deal with it.' He realised he was raising his voice; his own heat removal system was boiling over.

'But it's *you* they all want to speak to. We have a problem with the design of the emergency heat exchangers, it's *you* the licensing authorities want to hear the story from. *You* they believe when you tell them not to worry and that everything's fine. Slavic tries to get hold of you and you're not answering your calls. He comes to your office and you're "not in" – the other stock answer we get from your secretary. And when you aren't here, Leon, where are you? Not back in Germany at the Wendelstein-7X, I've checked that. Who are you hiding from?'

Leon put his head in his hands and sighed. 'You're right about one thing, Gunther. I'm feeling stressed at the moment. This business with Magda is getting to me.'

'Ah, that's what this is all about. But it's been a long time and it's in the hands of the police, isn't it?'

He could do without this. 'What are you suggesting?'

'Look, my friend.' Gunther looked dismayed. 'And that's what we are – friends, not just work colleagues. If I could help, I would. But I can do nothing to bring her back. And you can do no more yourself, so leave it with the police. Take a look in the mirror – you may convince yourself you need a break. Go away and sort yourself out. Come clean and I'll take over while you have a sabbatical. But never forget, Leon, we're going to need you back some day – focused and ready. It's mankind's biggest step forward since flight and you're the driving force.'

'Perhaps you're right. I'm tired. I'll go back to the hotel and sleep on it. Talk to you again in the morning.' But Leon had no intention of doing anything of the sort.

Although he was weary at the thought of it, he had other plans for the evening.

'Have you been here before, sir?' the madame enquired.

'No. I'm a bit nervous about it. I wonder if you could just run through the procedure with me before I make up my mind?'

'Aw, that's cute that is, love. Guess that will be OK, though. Have you ever used a lady in this way?'

'Never.'

She beckoned over the security guard. 'Me and this young man are going to have a little chat in private. Can you ask one of the senior girls to take over the desk for a while? We'll use room four, so can you post someone on the outside?' She turned to Leon. 'No offence, young man, but we can't take chances, you understand. What's your name by the way?'

'Leon.'

'Hi, Leon. I'm Mary.'

Room four was what Leon always imagined an old-fashioned brothel to look like, a high-ceilinged room with no windows and a tacky candelabra. The room was painted in garish shades of red; there was a huge bed with lots of silk bedding and far too many pillows.

Mary sat on the edge of the bed and tapped the bedcovers to her side. 'Come on, Leon. Don't be shy, sit next to me.'

Her black gorgon-like hair bobbled as she tilted her head back and he could smell her Yves Saint Laurent perfume. It was the perfume his mother always used.

In fact, apart from her hair and the extra weight she carried, the madame reminded him a bit of his mother.

'Now tell me, what is it you're looking for? And don't be shy. I *am* a woman of the world, you know. Otherwise I wouldn't be here.' She laughed at her little joke.

'Well, first of all, can I ask you about your set-up here? Are you the owner?'

Mary laughed again. 'Good God! No! That would be Dimitri Byelov, that would. Why do you ask?'

'Oh, I just like to understand the set-up of any business I deal with. Do you know a man called Alexei Rodin?'

She gave him a puzzled look. 'Can't say I do, love. Sounds Russian to me and we have so many Russians associated with this establishment. I can't claim to know a quarter of their names. So, tell me, what is it you like? Want to see a catalogue of our ladies? We have several nationalities.'

She was avoiding his question. *Sorry, Pavel, I did ask. My turn now.* Without answering her, he took the wafer from his jacket pocket, tapped at the screen and handed the pocket-sized computer to Mary. 'Have you ever seen this woman?' he said, pointing at Magda in the middle of the photograph.

Mary took the wafer in both hands and studied the photograph. Her hands began to tremble and the wafer fluttered between her fingers like a playing card.

'Mary, what's the matter?'

Her eyes filled with tears. 'She looks like my mother.'

'Don't be ridiculous, she's younger than you.'

'No, this one,' she pointed at the photograph, 'standing to the right of the blonde girl. She reminds me of my mother and we just let her ...' She crumbled into a fit of sobbing.

Her reaction startled him. The security guard burst into the room. Leon threw both of his arms up in surrender. 'Hold on, friend, I've done nothing.'

'Get out, bastard!' the Russian guard yelled. He turned towards Mary. 'Has he harmed you?'

Still crying, she shook her head. 'No, he hasn't. Just let him go.' She turned towards Leon. 'Just think yourself lucky. Byelov's not here.' She pointed towards the door, her bowed head still shaking.

Leon was in a panic. What must this look like? *Get out of here, fast*. He snatched the wafer from the madame's hand and bolted for the door like a man possessed.

'Let him go,' he heard Mary say again to the security guard, as he fled down the corridor. 'He won't be back.'

At eight thirty in the morning, the entrance hall of the Fusion Ltd central design office was like a busy railway station. Visitors queued at the check-in desk to pick up electronic identity tags, their tickets for the day's journey. Their hosts poured into the area in their droves, like passengers alighting from an incoming train. But no one was allowed on the 'platform' unaccompanied, and there were security officers everywhere.

As Leon dragged his exhausted body into work, he told himself never again to come in late like this. The hustle and bustle were not for him; he preferred the peaceful welcome of the night shift receptionist at six in the morning and the courteous bows from Fusion's skeleton security team. He was still suffering from the shock and trauma of the previous evening's encounter. Almost getting his head kicked in by the brothel's security, the madame a neurotic lunatic – what was all that about?

He cut through the throng funnelling towards the elevator, hoping there was no one from Greifswald who'd spot him and try and butter up to him. At least his pasty complexion and sunken black eyes would make him difficult to recognise. He veered away from the lead team's private elevator entrance at the last moment; he needed a strong coffee before he faced Gunther. The vending recess was the last post in the entrance hall; the corridor beyond was never used. 'Black coffee, strong, no sugar,' he commanded. Thirty seconds later, a small hatch door slid open and a steaming mug of coffee appeared. He took a sip and it made him feel at ease. At that moment, a robed figure floated past – a young Arab in his late teens, followed by three broad-shouldered men in black western-style suits. The group paid no attention to him, other than a casual glance from the man at the tail end of the boy's cohort. *Bodyguards. Wonder where they're going.*

He waited a few seconds before stepping into the hall, just in time to see the last of the bodyguards disappear around the corner at the end of the deserted corridor. Curiosity aroused, he set down his drink and trotted along the corridor after them. This was uncharted territory. He'd always presumed this part of the building to be an artefact of the past, leading to nowhere of interest. Fusion was the only company with a nameplate at the entrance nowadays; they'd taken over the whole building to accommodate their army of scientists, engineers and support staff and this remote end of the ground floor would contain nothing but storage cupboards.

He turned the corner and stopped. *Nothing?* Another corridor leading to a dead end – no doors, no windows – even the glass roof of the atrium didn't extend this far. *Where have they disappeared to?* He shook his head as he accepted the painful truth – he was seeing things. He'd been functioning under huge stress for these past few weeks, but never for one moment imagined it would come to this.

'You look terrible, Leon.'

'Bad night.'

'You've thought over my suggestion?'

'Sure, Gunther, I've thought about it.' But Leon's thoughts were on the Middle Eastern group marching through the concourse. There may be franchises in the pipeline for a number of foreign states, but Bahrain and Kuwait weren't among them. Were the Arab boy and his entourage real or was his mind playing tricks? Either way, Gunther was offering sound advice. 'You're right, I do need a break.'

'Thank the stars for that.' Schroeder breathed an audible sigh of relief. 'I can explain to everyone that you're ill. A stress-related illness, perhaps.'

'You mean tell them I've had a breakdown?'

'Well, I didn't mean—'

'I'll go for that.' *I need to take him into my confidence.* 'Sit down, Gunther. There's something I have to tell you.' He explained how he'd been trawling London's Russian-

140

owned brothels, looking for Magda. It was occupying his every evening and draining him. The scale of his task, his experiences to date – he poured it out, chapter and verse. But he said nothing about his work with the Polish authorities or their quest to track down Alexei Rodin – the man he held responsible for separating him from the love of his life.

Schroeder raised his eyebrows and whistled. 'How can you be sure she's here? Where's your information coming from?'

'Let's just say it's a scientist's hunch. You know what I mean – don't just accept what others tell you, think outside the box. Oh, she's here all right. And at the moment, I feel I want to tear the whole of their seedy underworld apart to find her. But we scientists don't work like that, do we? We collect data, we analyse, we model and we test our theories. And that's what I'm going to do, Gunther. I'm going to find out everything about their organisation, analyse their strengths and look for their weaknesses. I'm going to bring them down. If it takes me the rest of my life, I'll find her.'

'But think about this, Leon. Slavic isn't just going to hand you a sicknote and tell you to come back when you feel better. Then there's the little matter of sensitive commercial data. Other than Kaminsky, only you and I have full access to the data from the stellerator programme, now that Chekhov has classified it as top secret. Slavic can review it, of course, but without us he hasn't a clue what it means in terms of progress towards full commercial viability.'

'And if I'm running loose, I'm a security threat. Is that what you're saying?'

'You're going to have to go deep underground, Leon. How are you going to do that?' They sat in silence for a while, contemplating the enormous significance of the plan. 'I'm not sure when we'll see each other again. I'll miss you, Leon.'

He thought his friend was going to cry. 'The first thing I have to do is find a hideaway and change my wafer-set. And you, my friend, if you're going to be Fusion's chief scientist, you're going to have to get a haircut and start coming into work in something more appropriate than bomber jacket and jeans.'

They both laughed. Leon couldn't remember the last time he'd laughed. *Probably the last time I was with Magda.*

CHAPTER 19

Alexei Rodin looked troubled, not as cocksure as normal, and Malkin wanted to know why.

'What is it you want to discuss? And why the face to face?'

'This is highly confidential. We can't afford a security breach.'

Malkin shrugged his shoulders and gave a *so what* look. The *pakhan*'s central office, in which they sat, was the securest location within Goldhurst, wasn't it?

Rodin leaned forward and spoke in a low and serious voice. 'Someone is going around every brothel in London trying to find a particular girl. He never actually reveals who she is, he just shows the manager her photograph.'

Another *so what* look. 'This sort of thing can be irritating, I agree. But I wouldn't read too much into it. Can I see the photo?'

'He never leaves one. And that's not all. He's making enquiries about our operation.'

'Do you think it's the police? After all, we're not exactly one hundred per cent legitimate.'

'No, it's not the law. In fact, I've found out who he is. You'll probably know him.' This was becoming interesting. 'His name is Leon Dabrowski. I believe he's the chief scientist for Fusion.'

Malkin sat back in his chair and gave a silent whistle. Why would one of the world's leading nuclear scientists want to get himself involved in the sex industry? 'Yes, I *do* know him. He's a brilliant young man. But there's something about him that prickles me and I can't quite fathom out what it is.' He smiled again at his colleague. 'You've done the right thing coming to see me. I'm grateful.'

'I just thought you ought to know about this. After all, we wouldn't want Dabrowski to find out what was going on, would we? I could deal with it if you want me to. I suggest we—'

Malkin shook his head vigorously. 'No, no, no. I don't want any loose cannon security staff hounding him like a pack of dogs. Leave it with me and I'll take a closer look. You have more important matters to attend to.'

As soon as his young manager left the office, Malkin laid his wafer on the table. 'Malkin,' he said firmly.

'Good day, Mr Malkin,' said the Melomet. 'What can I do for you?'

'Get me Ivan Kuzmin from security.'

While his security officer was carrying out his investigations in Poland, Oleg Malkin achieved little in the business sense. He spent his daytime hours in the *pakhan*'s office, searching the internet for information on Leon Dabrowski. He hardly slept and would often get up in the dead of night and wander around the deserted lower corridors; he had a bad feeling about this. After an absence of almost two weeks, Ivan Kuzmin finally returned to Goldhurst.

'Good day, Kuzmin. Sit down. Let me know everything you've found.'

'Good day, sir,' Kuzmin replied, placing his ring binder on the desk and opening it at the first page.

The young man looked confident. And he'd had the good sense to turn out smart for a meeting with his superior. In fact, with his chiselled face and typical security officer haircut, he reminded him of a younger, slimmer version of Vladimir Chekhov. The file contained a sheaf about a centimetre thick. Malkin settled himself down for a long meeting. But he knew there'd be little wasted time this afternoon – Kuzmin had an outstanding ability to crystallise facts and draw focused conclusions.

'Dr Leon Dabrowski has an impeccable CV,' Kuzmin looked up from his file, 'which does not include regular visits to brothels.' He returned to the file and continued in his polished quick-fire style. 'He was an exceptional student and after gaining a double first in physics and mathematics, he commenced research in nuclear fusion.'

'Yes, yes, I know all this.' Malkin was already getting impatient. 'And he was good at sport, could have been a professional footballer and so on. Just tell me something I don't already know.'

Kuzmin carried on unfazed. Not one to be easily harassed by a superior, thought Malkin.

'As far as I could make out, there were no suspicious extra-curricular activities in his life. As you must appreciate, it's not unusual for someone of his intellectual capacity to be approached by the Polish secret service, or even the KGB. But I could find nothing like that.'

'His family, anything unusual there?'

'His father is Szymon Dabrowski, a wealthy self-made Polish banker as honest and dependable as they come. Stepfather, actually. He married Lynne, an English immigrant, when her son, the subject of our investigations, was four years old.' Kuzmin abandoned his file. For the first time, there was enthusiasm in his voice. 'This starts to get more interesting. I've searched the records and found that Eva Lynne Clarkson registered herself and the six-month-old Leon in Poznan, Poland. The papers show Leon's father Andrew Clarkson as deceased. I went online and trawled the British births, deaths and marriages records and found the marriage certificate of Andrew Joseph Clarkson to one Eva Lynne Jones.'

Malkin shuffled in his chair. He could tell from Kuzmin's body language there was more to come.

'Here the trail fragments,' Kuzmin continued. 'I could find nothing further on this particular Andrew Clarkson – no record of his purported death. As for Lynne, I did find something most interesting.' He paused and shook his head as if puzzled. 'The only Eva Lynne Jones I could find in the records died in the nineteen eighties at the age of twenty. She was cremated in Camden Town, not too far from where we are now. I could find no other relevant correlations.'

Malkin was beginning to feel nervous. 'Surely the Polish authorities would have discovered this? They'd have checked her background for such anomalies.'

'They wouldn't have been interested. It was easy to register in Poland in those days. The European Union was on the verge of a massive increase in east to west migration and anyone arriving in Poland from the opposite direction would have been welcome to stay, especially if they had money. I can't say whether that was the case with Leon Dabrowski's mother. By the way, it may not be significant, but Lynne Dabrowski is suffering from Alzheimer's disease.'

'I'd like a little more time to study this myself. Your file, if you please.'

Kuzmin handed over the results of two weeks' work. 'I would draw your attention to one further issue,' he said. 'It perhaps isn't important. But Leon Dabrowski's girlfriend, Magda Tomala, an outstanding Polish mathematician, has mysteriously disappeared. You'll find the relevant police records in the file.'

So that's what Dabrowski's up to. 'Thank you, Kuzmin. You've been very thorough. Anything else?' Malkin's neck was becoming hot and he opened the collar of his shirt.

'There is. It may not be significant but, on my return from Poland, I discover that a member of Fusion's technical lead team, Dr Gunther Schroeder, has been downloading visitor records from the admin computers.'

'Why the hell would he want to do that?'

'I don't know. He could be looking for a specific name. He may have spotted someone around the offices who shouldn't be there, a known competitor perhaps. One of my men picked this up from browsing through our routine security checks and I thought I should let you know.'

'You did the right thing, Kuzmin, as always. You may leave now.' But Malkin's thoughts weren't about Schroeder downloading visitor records. He broke into a cold sweat at the realisation that his plans could soon be in tatters. And, what was worse, his life could even be at risk.

Oh, God! Leon Dabrowski is Abram Chekhov.

Malkin's head felt like a boiler about to burst under pressure. He could almost feel the steam coming out of his ears. The results of Kuzmin's investigations were shocking, but his own research in the days that followed showed that the situation was worse than he feared.

'You mean to say we've abducted and incarcerated one of the world's most prominent mathematicians. And what's worse, we've fucked about with her mind and it hasn't worked. She's not responded properly to her conditioning and now we don't know how she's going to react. She's a fucking loose cannon.'

As always, Rodin remained the epitome of calmness. 'It was an accident, nothing more. Tomala was simply trawled up with a recent batch of recruits. I hadn't realised who she was. May I ask how you came to discover this?'

'Good question, Rodin,' Malkin said sarcastically. '*You* provided the information yourself. You told me that one of the world's most prominent nuclear physicists was looking for her and I've since looked through your database records and worked out she's down there in Eight Over Nine. Magda Tomala – Ana to you – is Leon Dabrowski's fucking girlfriend. So, where does this leave us? Well, I'll tell you. We've forcibly separated two of the world's most intelligent people. Interpol will no doubt be looking for Magda Tomala by now. Meanwhile she's probably setting about a quantitative analysis of our operation while her boyfriend has lost interest in Vladimir Chekhov's fucking nuclear power company.' He knew he was shouting loudly and probably glowing red by now, but this state of affairs was just insufferable. 'It's a fucking time bomb!'

'We could repeat the n-flash?'

'Too risky.'

'We could possibly have her … eliminated?'

Malkin glared at his director. He abhorred killings of any sort. No way was he going back to those hideous *mafiya* days. He needed to think this through.

'I'm not going to have her killed.'

'Our only other option is to keep her down there and keep her occupied. It's working so far but it's going to be a huge drain on our resources.'

'Just fucking do it.'

CHAPTER 20

Five weeks after going into hiding, Leon was receiving regular visits from Leonid Pavel. Pavel travelled to London on scheduled flights and they met on different days of the week at varying locations around the capital, avoiding a regular routine that could get them noticed. He was pleased that today's progress meeting was in the penthouse apartment the Warsaw *Policja* rented for him. With its gated entrance and Melomet-operated alarm system, he felt safe. Leon greeted Pavel with a warm grin.

'I'm glad I've managed to persuade you to adopt our team disguise.'

Pavel seemed in no mood for frivolities. 'I'll have you know I've had some explaining to do back in Poland. But I have to agree, your idea to blend in with this rapidly expanding subculture is a good one. Who would think of looking for Leon Dabrowski, the nuclear physicist, among this extrovert lot?'

'Exactly. They got the idea from the northern soul scene that sprang up in the UK last century. "Why not identify with classical music in the same manner?" some upper-class bod said three years ago. And his zany style choice for attending classical concerts went viral.'

'Yes, yes, and the next thing we have is dozens of bespoke *Classico* venues springing up in the big cities.' Pavel was clearly grumpy. 'It offers the perfect cover for us. Let's get down to the business I've come over to discuss, shall we?'

'Hundreds of venues, actually. And your estimate for the number of brothels is equally understated. There are more brothels than your list provides.'

Pavel gave Leon a stern look. 'And your point is?'

Pavel's haircut was so funny. But he'd agreed it was important that he looked no different from the other *Classicos* who lived in this part of the city. 'I mean to say, you need to reconsider getting some of your men inside these establishments. I can't visit them all myself.'

'You know we can't do that. If they were discovered to be Polish police operatives, there'd be a diplomatic war. MI5 must have men in there, of course, but I reckon they're more interested in dipping their wicks than exposing illegal practices like sex trafficking. You have to keep going. I'll reinforce the surveillance teams if you think that would help.'

'It's going to be better than nothing, but the ground we need to cover requires at least three times what you have at the moment.'

Pavel threw up his hands, clearly frustrated. 'You know that's not possible.'

'I'm only telling you the facts,' said Leon, apologising with an open armed shrug.

'But what I can suggest is we start using our satellite surveillance system. We recently put a satellite into geo-stationary orbit over London and you'd be amazed at the resolution. I was going to discuss this later, but seeing as you raise the subject of surveillance—'

Leon opened his eyes wide. 'How does it work?'

'Ha! I thought you'd be keen. The data will come directly into our computers in Poland and we'll forward an encrypted version to you by secure link. You can carry out your analysis in the luxury of your own apartment.'

'This is a change of heart, isn't it? I thought you people were neurotic about transmitting data like that?'

'Actually, the software security is very good in this case. And who's going to be interested in just another set of satellite surveillance photographs? MI5 wouldn't be bothered if they stumbled on activities like this, as long as we weren't literally treading on their toes inside the brothels. And I doubt whether Rodin's lot would even think of looking. It would be up to you to request scan coordinates in advance and we'd need to set up a third-party means of doing that. For the foreseeable future, this will be the main task of the new system. I'll sort out the approvals when I get back.'

This was good news. His visits to the sex-for-money underworld were becoming physically and mentally draining. 'Sounds great to me. When do we get it?'

'Sooner than you think. Our technicians are carrying out trials as we speak. We can install your monitoring software as soon as they've finished their soak tests. But we need to keep the ground surveillance and the personal visits going. Speaking of which, I've read the report you provided to Schumann. How many of these brothels do you think are run by Rodin?'

'About a dozen, by my reckoning. But we still have a lot of potential Rodin-operated houses to visit. They aren't hard to spot once you're inside. They're leagues above the rest in terms of opulence and clientele.'

'OK, let's go for them with our limited ground resources. In the meantime, I'll be in touch about the satellite data.'

And I'll go and collect my own data.

Leon studied Gunther Schroeder as he walked through the front door of Classico Lounge. Gunther looked straight at him but didn't acknowledge him. He laughed to himself as his friend continued to survey the rest of the bustling bar. Satisfied that he hadn't been picked out of the crowd, he waved to catch his attention.

Schroeder came across to his table. 'What the—?'

'Yes, it *is* me. How are things with you, Gunther?'

'Well, *I'm* fine. But, what about *you*? What are you doing in a place like this? And ... you haven't joined them, have you?'

'No, not joined the *Classico* fraternity,' he grinned at him, 'just merging with them. They provide me with great cover. I like to think I could walk out of the bar, straight past you, without you noticing.' He rubbed his shaved head and scratched the four days of growth on his chin. 'You like the stubble?'

'Yes, it suits you. And those ludicrous braces. You're well disguised if that's what you mean. I wouldn't have recognised you if you'd stopped me in the street and asked me how the stellerator runs were panning out.'

'Thanks, Gunther. I'm pleased about that. I reckon some of the brothel security staff have been checking me over, so I thought I'd get a new image. In fact, the Russians are beginning to see *Classicos* as a lucrative source of clientele. Money talks. Did you manage to get the data?'

'Yes,' Gunther replied, dropping him the wafer-zip.

Leon mouthed silently to the barmaid. *Two*, he indicated with his fingers. She brought them two small beers.

'The zip file contains everything you specified. Damien downloaded three months' worth of desk check-ins, security pass requests, entrance door scan data, video footage, everything. I've also downloaded the pattern recognition software you asked for. I can't imagine for one moment what you're going to do with this lot.'

Leon ignored his implied question. 'Are you sure no one detected what you and Damien were doing?'

'Don't worry. Damien knows the admin security system inside out and I had no problem getting the download out of Goldhurst. There are certain privileges that come with rank. Glad you didn't ask me for stellerator data, though – that might have been a little bit tougher.'

'Ah, I was just coming to that.'

They both laughed, although Leon didn't feel much like laughing nowadays.

'Are you going to tell me what you plan to do with Fusion's visitor records?'

'Not even sure myself. Let's just say it's a nosy scientist's intuitive investigation. There's something niggling me about that place.'

Schroeder seemed concerned. 'You look healthier than when I last saw you, Leon. But are you really OK? Are you getting anywhere with all this surveillance stuff?'

'Don't worry about me, I'm fine. I've recruited a few private agents to assist me. They're doing most of my groundwork. And I'm just about to take delivery of a fancy bit of computer technology to help with my analysis. Main thing is I feel in control.' Most of what he told Gunther was true, so there were no guilty feelings. He just forgot to mention that the private agents he referred to were the Polish secret police and his new computer system was a sophisticated device that could stream data from their state-of-the-art satellite surveillance system.

'Where are you living?'

'Best you don't know, Gunther. What about our project? Are we winning?'

'We're getting there, but progress isn't good enough for Chekhov. Slavic has become head slave driver and I'm his taskmaster. The guys are pulling out all the stops, but I wouldn't be surprised if we soon had a mutiny on our hands at this rate.'

'I presume Slavic has noticed that I've gone missing? And Chekhov himself – what does *he* think of all this?'

'I explained to Slavic at the outset that you needed a lengthy break before you cracked under the strain. He thinks you're in a private health farm somewhere. He's not happy about it, of course. He's without his key man at a critical stage in the project. But I think I'm providing him with enough support to cover for your absence. As for Chekhov, he's always asking why you're never at the video conferences. We've appeased him by telling him you're too busy with vital work. I must admit, Slavic looks uncomfortable every time he asks – he daren't tell Chekhov the truth. And I don't think Chekhov believes us for one … are you listening, Leon?'

Leon was listening, but not digesting what he was being told. He'd just spotted Pavel's right-hand man, Schumann. The *Policja* agent indicated, with a flick of the eyes, that he was to get rid of his acquaintance.

Schroeder continued, 'I'm not sure how long we can keep this charade going. At some stage, we're going to have to explain—'

'Sorry, Gunther. I *am* interested, but something has just come up. I'm sure you'll understand.' He could see that Schroeder knew better than to turn around and look at whoever had diverted his attention.

'I get you, Leon,' he said, with concern in his eyes. 'You take care. You know how to get in touch with me.'

'I haven't forgotten the hidden code. And I'm pleased to see you've trimmed your hair. It makes you look more dignified.'

'Can't say the same for you, bonehead.'

'I suggest we go through to the music lounge, Mahler?' the agent said, using the *Classico* nickname that Leon adopted as part of his cover.

He shook the hand of his contact. 'Fine by me, Schumann.'

The string quartet in the centre of the room was playing Schubert's *Trout Symphony*. They found a free booth and swiped their wafers to register their presence as members.

'Who was that?' asked Schumann.

'Don't worry, he's a work colleague of mine. We can trust him. Anything to report?'

'Lots. You're sure we can discuss such matters in this place?'

'I've told you, Schumann, I've looked into this in fine detail. Believe me, this latest *Classico* craze provides us with perfect cover. Its membership is expanding exponentially and they've become accepted in all walks of society. Like being a hippy in the sixties. Where they gather, how they dress, their music – it's just fashion. And money is the only prerequisite for being accepted into this extrovert society. Trust me, no one is going to be looking for us among a bunch of socialite dandies.'

'How can we be sure MI5 aren't doing the same thing?'

'Why should they? Besides, even if they're in the next booth they can't overhear what we're saying, thanks to the phase de-synchroniser we've just activated. Every booth enjoys the music in isolation.'

'OK, I trust your judgement.' Schumann leaned closer to Leon and whispered, 'There's a brothel in Highgate we've been observing for twenty-four seven, as you call it. And we've collected some interesting data.'

'It has to be one of Rodin's if it's in that area. Close to where I work?'

'Yes. We've focused on the higher end of the market, as you recommended. It *is* likely to be one of his and, as you suggest, it's about a mile from where you used to work.'

The implication that they no longer considered him to be employed by Fusion was galling and Leon had to bite his tongue. 'What have you come up with?'

'We've reviewed the video logs and identified who is using this establishment. They seem to have a regular group of clients, all of them wealthy as far as we can make out. The place is popular with a few *Classicos*, I might add.'

'Surprise, surprise.' Leon smirked.

Schumann remained straight-faced. 'Nothing surprising in all that,' he added solemnly. 'But we've detected anomalies. A close analysis of comings and goings indicates that clients leaving the place are not always the same as those who went in. So where have they come from? And what happened to those who never came back out?'

'Disguised? Preventing the press from discovering their perverted habits?' *Come on, Schumann, have a little worldly nous, will you.*

'Not as simple as that. We have excellent analysis software and I can confirm that these are different people. Some stay overnight and we pick them out the next day. But there are some going missing and some appearing from nowhere. I can also confirm that, over the period of a week, the numbers don't necessarily add up. It can't just be about a change of clothing or the shaving of a beard.'

'What sort of numbers are we talking about?'

'Not high. Three or four anomalies each week, perhaps. The average footfall of a typical brothel is around fifty clients a day. As you say, it's big money.'

'OK, I reckon what you've got is statistically significant. There has to be something odd going on and we need to apply the same sort of surveillance to other brothels in the Rodin fleet. I've mapped a dozen or so potential establishments across the capital for when I get access to your satellite data. When you get the map, I suggest you select one you haven't already surveyed and get your men in situ ASAP.'

'I already have your map. Same place next week?'

'I'll be here, Schumann.'

'Goodbye, Mahler.'

And in the meantime, I'll just sit back and think about all this. Leon leaned back with his hands behind his head. *Listen to the Schubert and think.*

CHAPTER 21

'Take your places, ladies.'

The six girls arranged themselves symmetrically around the circumference of the cylindrical podium. Like the petals of a daisy, heads almost touching at the flower's centre and bare feet resting on the black rubber floor, they shuffled themselves into position and opened their legs wide apart. The floor's tiny ripples settled and the room became still.

Satisfied with his preparations, the sexual fantasy designer left the black drum.

'Well, what we got us here today, cowboy?' the burley Texan said as he entered the chamber with his colleague. 'And that floor feels real good on the feet. What do yeh reckon, Joe?'

'Well, I reckon we got ourselves a nice little set of doggies, Clem. Howdy gals. Meet yeh ringmasters. We're out for a good time and I hope yeh ain't gonna disappoint us.' He turned to his partner. 'Now, what was them rules of yours again?'

'Well, yeh see, I'm a gonna start with number one. And at the same time, you're gonna start with that one opposite, number four. When I say go, we each gotta give 'em six good thrusts. An' I mean proper ones, no cheatin'. When yeh done six, yeh can move to the next one and yeh do the same again. The idea is we chase each other's butts clockwise and if yeh get caught up or yeh jack out, then yeh lose. Ten thousand bucks, y'agree?'

'Well, I say we start right now.'

'Not before we inspect one of these little doggies.' He made for the girl nearest to him and pushed his hand up her tiny skirt, grabbing at her naked womanhood. She stifled a squeal and gave him a forced smile.

'Yeh like that, do yeh? Well, yeh gonna really love this little rodeo of ours.' He spanked hard at her bare thigh, leaving a red weal in the shape of his hand. Despite the tears of pain, she smiled again, as if she'd enjoyed his vicious slap. 'Are yeh gonna have a little test of one of them doggies yourself, partner, before we get this show on the road?'

'I reckon ah might just do that, Clem.'

Joe stepped forward towards the girl of his choice. The tiny girl blew out a breath and started hyperventilating. Fear in her eyes, she catapulted from the bed and ran towards the door.

'No, not me. I'm not doing this.'

Joe ran after her. 'Now, yeh come right back, yeh little whore. Yeh ain't gonna spoil the fun like that, are yeh?'

The rest of the girls remained motionless – the flower still formed, but with one petal missing.

'Get her, Joe. I'll go this way and we'll round the doggie up.' Half crouching, they lumbered their fat frames towards the trapped creature, each of them instinctively holding an arm to one side as if they were carrying lassoes.

The girl dashed around the room's perimeter, screaming. She dipped as Clem tried to grab her and bolted across the room like a whippet. The two men, perspiring and snorting like horses, reformed their pincer movement. Again, she managed to escape their clutches. She ducked and weaved like a rabbit, avoiding their flailing attempts to catch her, screaming all the time. Joe managed to get within a few feet and dived at the terrified girl. He missed her by inches and hit the floor. He got up, laughed and wiped his mouth as if he'd filled it with dirt.

The door opened. Two security guards rushed in and bundled the men over. One of the guards grabbed the girl and slung her over his shoulder. The two cowboys sluggishly got up and, out of rodeo habit, dusted themselves down.

'Yaw Russian bastards. We was just havin' ourselves some fun, weren't we, Clem?'

'Sorry about that, sir. You'd better come with us, gentlemen. Girls, out. Now!'

'This is a serious aberration.'

'It's under control. We've managed to placate the Texans. After that shambolic fantasy, they wanted their money back and even threatened to spread slanderous information about us among their influential colleagues.

In the end, we managed to persuade them to try another fantasy.'

'And?'

'It went well – they were delighted. We kept the rodeo theme but used some of our heftier girls as wild cattle. And they still managed their private bet. This time it was who could stay on a bucking and thrashing fat whore the longest. They came out shattered but happy. I think they may even come back.'

Malkin nodded his approval. 'You've done well to retrieve the situation. Splendid insight of yours to employ big beautiful women.'

'I must admit, I was beginning to wonder whether we'd ever use them. We processed six through n-flash and retaining them on our books could have been a financial liability. Anyway, they've earned their keep.'

'Good. But this whole episode leaves me with a much greater concern. The girl who panicked.'

'Gina.'

'What went wrong?'

'Two of our psychiatrists interviewed her and agreed that her mind is shot. She's of no further use to us.'

'The other girls – they were in the same situation. What about them?'

'All OK. They're still under our control. One of them was assaulted by one of the clients. She hadn't expected anything like that and it upset her at the time, but she sees it as part of the job now.'

'I think we need to consider providing better protection for our girls. We shouldn't be doing sadism or anything like that. It could lead to all sorts of trouble and we don't want any damage to our valuable stock. Set up a workshop with the sexual fantasy designers.' Malkin was dreading the next part of the discussion. 'That leaves us with Gina. What do you propose for her?'

'We need to dispose of her.'

'I won't have her killed.'

'That would have been my preferred solution. But you're the boss and I've given further thought to this. Gina is a nervous wreck. She hasn't a clue where she is and, even if she comprehended what was going on, she's incapable of explaining herself. Believe me, the best interrogation in the world would just come up with gibberish from that one.'

'What are you suggesting?'

'I'm suggesting we dump her. Fill her full of dope and leave her in the park on a dark night. She's bound to be picked up by a smack-head or some sleazy whoremaster. Her survival would be down to herself, not our responsibility.'

'OK, arrange it, Rodin.'

Mary could see that the girl was trembling. How could a prostitute be so timid? 'Come in, sweetheart. I'm not going to harm you.'

She sat on the bed next to Mary and bowed her head. Her lank hair fell in front of her face and Mary could see it hadn't been washed for days. The girl twisted her fingers together, as if solving an invisible Chinese puzzle.

'Has someone hurt you, my darling?'

She shook her head.

'Don't worry, you're safe now. I'm going to look after you. I look after all the girls. You'll have your own room and there'll be no need to work the streets anymore.' She brushed the girl's hair back with her hand and lifted her chin with her finger. 'Hey, come on, don't cry. You're still a beautiful lady. A shower and change will make the world of difference, you'll feel so much better. And we'll get you a hot meal. Would you like that?'

The girl nodded and showed a hint of a smile.

Mary embraced her. 'So,' she said, sitting up and patting her own thighs with both hands, 'one of my security staff finds you wandering alone in the park, no handbag, no coat, looking like a lost cat. Did someone assault you?'

'No,' the girl whispered.

'Were you working in those parts?'

'No, not there. In the Fantasyworld.'

'In the what?'

'I had a good job. Lived in a real palace, I did. Along with the other girls.'

Must be one of Rodin's. 'How long were you there?'

'Don't really know.'

'And what happened, sweetheart?'

'Don't properly remember. I think they've finished with me. All I remember is going to bed one night and next thing, someone brings me here.'

'The other girls, what were they like? Did you get to know them?'

'I knew all their names. We didn't get too many chances to talk, though. But I know most of them were foreign. I could tell by their accents.'

165

Eastern European, no doubt. 'Were you mistreated?'

'No, I don't think so. Most of the men were kind. But it's all a bit of a blur. I used to feel … sort of funny. Every day.'

'Well, we'll have to put that right, won't we. What's your name?'

'I've forgotten. But they called me Gina in the Fantasyworld.'

CHAPTER 22

Sergei was normally easy-going and friendly – harmless, affable even. But he could change his mood like a chameleon changes colour. The more Magda tried to find out where and why she was incarcerated, the more jovial and evasive he became. Then occasionally, she'd do something to trigger his dark side – and that would seriously unnerve her. Was he capable of physical abuse, she wondered? She'd have to watch him and be ready for anything. Like, where was he taking her today?

As they stepped into the elevator, Sergei turned his back on Magda. *He doesn't want me to see where we're going.* The elevator went up. *Accelerate, decelerate, constant speed for less than a second. Easy calculation.* They were two levels above her quarters. Her heart skipped a beat; would she get sight of the outside world? The elevator door opened to reveal a long corridor with no daylight. Disappointment.

Sergei took her hand, walked her to a door at the end of the corridor and they entered the room without knocking.

It was a refectory with a group of five women dining at the only table. As soon as the diners saw Sergei and Magda, they stopped eating and turned their chairs to face them. *I've never seen synchronised table etiquette before.*

'Come on, Ana. Meet your team.'

The women were all young – and outstandingly beautiful. As she approached them, she could see they were studying her, each of them with the same vacant expression – they were expecting her. At least there were others living in this place.

'Let me introduce you,' Sergei said. 'This is Abi.'

The nearest girl rose from her chair, curtseyed and offered her hand. 'Pleased to meet you, Ana. I look forward to working with you.'

The next girl jumped up at the sound of her name, like a squaddie responding to her sergeant. 'Pleased to meet you, Ana. I look forward to working with you.'

Sergei introduced each girl in turn and each time she was greeted with the same response – same words, same choreographed courtesy, but never a smile.

With the introductions complete, all Magda could say was a weak and condescending 'Hello.' She turned away from the girls. 'Can we go, Sergei?'

'Yes. We're finished.'

'Goodbye, Ana,' the girls said in unison. Magda glanced back to see them returning to their meals as if there'd been no intrusion. She gave Sergei her daggers look but said nothing.

Back in her quarters, clenched fists on hips and shaking inside, she squared up to him. 'What the hell was that?'

'I've just introduced you to your team. When you finish your induction, you'll be looking after them.'

She was a geyser about to erupt. 'My team? What sort of team – a football team? How many other teams have you got down here?'

'Calm down, Ana. They're the same as you. But you have to complete your training first.'

'Same as me?' she shouted. 'You mean you class me alongside those bimbos? They were a bunch of zombies. They—'

A dark shadow appeared across Sergei's face. Her anger turned to fear.

'Ana, I suggest you accept the position of authority you're being offered. Otherwise, you *will* be one of them. A team leader's role means privileges. You wouldn't have to do the things they're going to do.'

Oh God! I think I know what he means.

'And you still have to pass the selection process.'

'The what?'

'You'll need to compete with other girls for the team leader role.'

Magda laughed out loud. 'You mean someone's going to interview me. Well, you've made my day, Sergei. I look forward to that. Bring on the panel.'

'Not an interview, Ana. It's a race. It's what you've been training for.'

The elevator outside Magda's quarters started its descent. After two days of fierce training to exhaustion, followed by two days of relaxation, Magda felt as fit as she'd ever been in her life.

'Are you ready for this, Ana?'

'I'm nervous. Do I have to do it?'

Sergei patted her on the back. 'You're in good shape. I expect you to do well.'

When the elevator stopped, she instinctively knew they were on the level at which the black drum was located.

'I thought we were heading for an athletics track.'

She sauntered head down towards the elevator door; this was just another of Sergei's ruses. Sergei stopped her with a hand against her chest; she looked up to see he was smiling and pointing to her rear. She turned and found herself looking out through an opening on the opposite side of the elevator.

'What's this?'

'It's a monopod,' Sergei said. 'Go on, strap yourself in.' He indicated the row of four empty bucket seats. Two of the facing seats were already occupied. The man smiled at her; the woman, a tiny Filipino about her own age, showed no interest. *Nervous before the race?*

The monopod accelerated and Magda counted the seconds until they reached steady speed. She listened to the faint swish from what she presumed to be a monorail and mentally timed another minute. Her heart was pumping faster. They had to be over two kilometres from their starting point. That would surely be way beyond the bounds of her subterranean prison? *A chance to escape?*

When they reached their destination, Sergei pushed open the swing door that faced them on the platform and Magda and her travel colleagues entered the indoor arena. The vast hall had a six-lane running track at its centre and was totally enclosed with no windows; a single white panel lit the roof where she'd hoped to see skylights. Her heart sank. Thinking about it, she hadn't noticed any elevation during their journey; they were probably still deep underground. She studied the layout of the stadium as they walked around its perimeter. The only additional exit was a wide double swing door behind the main stand. Over the door was a sign – 'Warm-Up Area'. There was no escape from this place – no option but to get on with the race.

Ah well, here goes.

The rest of her competitors were already into their drills, striding along the warm-up area's six-lane straight, encouraged by their vociferous coaches. Magda started her own preparations. For fifteen minutes, she followed Sergei's instructions, gradually easing herself into the zone – that zombie-like state where she'd be primed for action and the world outside the race meant nothing.

'Five minutes, ladies,' the marshal called out. 'Assemble outside the door as soon as you're ready, please.'

She followed her competitors into the arena. The crowd in the stand began to applaud. *Where did they appear from?*

Stripping off her tracksuit and crouching to tie her running spikes, she surveyed the spectators. At one end of the stand she could make out a small cluster of Arabs – some traditionally dressed, others in western suits. The central seats were occupied by Chinese, chattering into their wafers and nodding vigorously among themselves.

A few isolated spectators were scattered throughout the rest of the seating.

'What's going on?' she asked Sergei, tipping her head up to indicate that she was referring to the Chinese group.

'Gambling.'

'You mean, they're betting on the outcome of this race?'

'Big bets. But don't let it concern you. Just do your best.'

'Do my best?' *If I don't do well in this race, I become a piece of meat.* She shook her head and slowly walked towards her mark.

'Eight hundred metres, ladies. Four laps of the track,' the starter announced. 'Break after the cones at fifty.' A tense silence fell over the arena. 'To your marks!'

On the B of the bang.

The starter's gun cracked. Magda snapped out along lane two. The spectators erupted into applause. *Hard as you can, first five seconds are free.* By thirty metres, she'd eased alongside the girl in lane three and settled into her steady pace. The break at fifty metres was hair-raising as all six girls attempted to funnel into the two inner lanes at once. The spectators cheered wildly at their animal-like jostling for position. Magda rode the pushing and elbowing well and even managed to give herself room on the outside. She looked up to the front of the field. The tiny Filipino was flying around the second bend, way ahead of the pack. *She's going too fast.*

The adrenalin disappeared and by the end of the first lap, she was running relaxed. After the second lap, she was leading the chasing pack with two girls in front of her. *Don't go yet*. End of the third lap – the bell. The two in front kicked and opened up a gap of ten metres. She wanted to accelerate but resisted the urge. *Wind them in, they'll come back to me*. Final back straight, approaching the camber with one hundred metres to go – the two girls in front were fading and the three behind were losing touch. Final bend – *stay in lane one, don't run wide*.

She entered the home straight. Thirty metres out, she hit the invisible tub of treacle and her world went into slow motion; she was deaf yet she knew the spectators would be shouting themselves hoarse. Twenty metres out – the girl in front wobbled to the side. *Her legs have gone*. Her stride shortened as lead weights materialised on her ankles. But Dinky-tot was slowing too. *Go for her*. Ten metres to go – she could almost touch her. With a huge last effort, Magda lurched across the track into the lane to her right, took one final torturous step and lunged towards the finish line. She caught a movement from the corner of her eye. It was Dinky-tot collapsing on to the track.

Magda's limp upper body hit the track's rubberised surface. The echoing roar of the spectators blasted her senses. Her head swimming, her chest heaving for breath, she slowly moved her hand across the track and touched the hand of the prostrate little girl to her side. Sweat streaming down her face and panting hard, Dinky-tot raised her chin from the floor and forced a smile. With the remnants of her strength, Magda nodded back to her. 'Well done, champion.'

'Third place, with a time of two minutes, twenty-two point six seconds, Heidi!'

There was polite applause from the spectators as the third-placed girl stepped up to receive her medal. The young Arab dignitary presented her with the bronze medal, stepped back and applauded her himself.

'In second place, after a magnificent run and with a time of two minutes, twenty-one point two seconds, Ana!'

Magda stepped on to the podium. The Arab boy placed the silver medal around her neck and smiled at her. He rubbed his hand sensuously down the side of her thigh before nodding his approval and joining the crowd in their applause. Who the hell did he think he was? She wanted to take a swipe at him but knew better than to do that.

'And in first place, with a time of two minutes, twenty-one point one seconds, the eight hundred metre champion is – Chloe!'

The Chinese went wild – even those who'd lost their bets, Magda imagined. She joined in with their applause, no thoughts of the dire circumstances that had taken over her life – until she noticed what was happening in front of her.

He must be sixteen, if that. The young Arab took the hand of the petite girl with the gold medal around her neck and assisted her down from the podium. To Magda's horror, he ran his free hand across the girl's breasts and unzipped her tracksuit top. As if expecting this, Chloe removed her top for him. Magda noticed that the stand had fallen silent. She looked across at the

Chinese group, who uttered a soft cacophony of groans and gave each other surprised looks. To them, this was obviously an unexpected bonus.

The boy grabbed Chloe's hand, whisked her to the high jump area and sat her at the edge of the landing mat. She bowed her head like an obedient concubine as he removed his robes. Knees together and hands in prayer on her lap, she offered no resistance as he pushed her shoulders and her torso dropped back on to the canvas.

Magda was transfixed, powerless to move. She could only wait like the others to see what would unfold next within this bizarre tableau. She glanced towards Sergei. He was frozen like the rest of them. *Why doesn't he do something?*

The young Arab lifted Chloe's feet off the floor and slipped off her tracksuit bottoms and Lycra running knickers. The spectators gasped as the boy's loincloth dropped to the floor and he spread the girl's legs apart with his hands. The crowd's reaction caused Magda to look up again towards the stand. A man three rows back from the Chinese contingent was staring at her; he had to be the only person in the arena with no interest in what was going on in the high jump area. 'You don't scare me,' she mouthed at him with venom.

The boy mounted Chloe. Magda could no longer bring herself to watch this depraved act. 'Get me out of here, Sergei.' He gave no response. 'I mean now!'

They sat alone in the monopod, waiting for it to start. Magda broke the silence. 'I want to ask you something, Sergei. And I want the truth.'

'I think I know what it is, Ana. What would have happened if you'd have won?'

'Well?'

'I didn't give you any chance of winning, before the start. There were some fit girls in that field, most of them with running experience, and they've been training for longer than you. But I underestimated your willpower. The odds against you were enormous, by the way. Anyone backing you for a place today will be a rich man.'

'Stop beating about the bush. Tell me what would have happened if I'd won that race.'

'You would have resisted him, of course, and I would have stopped his bodyguards from becoming involved. It would have—'

'Stopped them! Are you stupid? They looked like serious heavies to me.' She felt the blood rush to her head.

Sergei stared at her with fire in his eyes. 'I'm telling you, I would have stopped them.'

'This is some sick fantasy world for super-rich perverts and gamblers. And I'm to become part of it.' She unbelted herself from the seat. 'You bastard!' she yelled, flailing blows at his head. But Sergei obviously knew how to protect himself. He was even laughing behind the arms he used as his shield.

She refused to speak again for the duration of the journey. Did Sergei think this was one big laugh? Or was he a sadist? Either way, he'd looked into her eyes like never before – and it scared her. She was calm by the time they reached her quarters, but there was no getting away from her fate. *That's it, I'm to be used as a prostitute. Well, we'll see about that.*

CHAPTER 23

'Where are we going, Sergei? Why aren't we dressed for training?'

Sergei offered no answer. The elevator descended into the depths of the complex. She hadn't been this far down before. *What's up with Sergei today?* The elevator door opened.

The corridor was long and littered with marvellous paintings. *Wow!* At the end of the corridor, they stopped outside an enormous wooden door. Sergei opened it with his wafer. With no explanation, he eased her forward and the door closed behind her, leaving her inside a cavernous room.

'Good morning, Professor Tomala,' said the slim, elegant man behind the desk. She recognised him as the spectator who'd been studying her after yesterday's race. 'Please take a seat.'

'You know who I am?'

'Yes. You are a mathematician from the Jagiellonian Institute in Poland. An extremely competent one, I'm led to believe. I am Alexei Rodin.'

There was a distinct femininity in his soft voice. Who was he? 'What am I doing here, Rodin? And I don't want any bullshit. Why am I a prisoner in this bizarre underworld?'

'A mistake, simple as that. It was our mistake.'

'Come on, I need more than that. You've taken away my freedom. You've drugged me. You make me take part in a ludicrous race in front of gambling addicts and God knows who else. What are you up to?'

'I'll be straight with you, professor. We've assembled a cast of beautiful young ladies who are being trained to entertain important clients of ours. Think of this place as a wonderful holiday destination for the rich and affluent.'

'You mean you run an upmarket brothel. And I'm to be a part of it? Not on your life. I hereby reject your offer, so can I go now?'

'Ha! I appreciate your sense of humour, but it's not as simple as that. As I said, incorporating you into our organisation was a mistake. Our ... talent scouts, let's call them, were unaware of who they were recruiting. I'm afraid we can't let you go. You know too much and this whole set-up is highly confidential. Our clients insist on that, you understand.'

'I understand your perverse logic, if that's what you mean. But you're holding these girls against their will.'

'Not quite. They come to like it after a while. They adapt to their new environment.'

'You mean you brainwash them into wanting to live underground. Well not me, Mr Rodin, whoever you are. I'd like to see the stars again and walk through a forest and take a tram to the city centre. I don't even know where in the world I am, but I want out.'

'You don't seem to understand. We have no option but to retain you for the rest of your life. The risks and financial implications of your release would be unacceptable to our organisation. I'm sorry about that, but you'll just have to come to terms with it. You are here for good. But rest assured, in your case I've decided you will not be part of the entertainment staff. We'll respect your status in the society you left. We'll even let you indulge yourself in your mathematical research and I'll provide you with a computer in support of that. My advice is to accept it and make the best of it. Enjoy your new life.'

Magda was in shock. But there was no way she was going to give in to him. 'The answer is no. You can't keep me here against my will. People are looking for me right now and when they find out I'm being held prisoner, they'll have your guts.'

'And my response is this – you're staying. And if you attempt to escape, your boyfriend and his family will be killed. This discussion is over, professor. I'll have you conducted back to your quarters.'

Magda felt defeated. Her situation was worse than she'd imagined – and why hadn't Rodin been concerned about them looking for her? She could continue to work on her escape strategy, of course, but it would have to be foolproof. She'd play along with their little games, offer them her full compliance while she searched for a weakness in their set-up. At least they weren't going to drag her into their sordid world of prostitution. She had to be thankful for that.

Her thoughts were disrupted by a scuffling sound from the lobby. Couldn't be Sergei, he'd escorted her back to her quarters thirty minutes earlier.

The doorbell tinkled and after fifteen seconds the door opened itself as usual.

'Good day. I am Jakob. I have your computer.'

The grey old man wheeled his trolley straight past her. Magda had to laugh. 'What's that? Have you been raiding skips at the back of the Science Museum?' At least Rodin had kept his promise and provided a computer. But what an antique.

Jakob looked at her with a blank expression. 'Where do you want me to install it?'

'Over there.' She pointed to a recess at the back of her lounge.

Jakob wheeled the bulky trolley through to the anteroom and connected the equipment to the mains.

'A keyboard?' she said, feigning surprise. 'And a mouse connected by wire.'

Her sarcasm seemed to go straight over the top of his head. 'Yes, and you have many input-output devices,' he said, pointing towards the old-fashioned disk drive. He picked half a dozen memory sticks from a tray and held them out in the palm of his hand.

'Wow, that's impressive,' she said sarcastically, before spotting a bank of modern input-output sockets on the side of the computer's monitor. *Those may come in useful.*

'Yes, good system.'

Typical Russian sense of humour, she mused. *He doesn't have one.*

With an expressionless face, Jakob continued to connect the individual components of the ancient system.

'Are you an android, Jakob?'

No answer. He obviously didn't understand the question.

She swivelled back and forth in her armchair and watched dispassionately as the old computer technician worked in silence. After fifteen minutes, he gave himself a satisfied nod and stepped back to admire the workstation he'd created.

'I give demonstration.'

'Ooh, I'm looking forward to that. Show me the voice control first, would you?'

'No voice control,' he said, shaking his head. 'Conventional input-output. You will—'

'OK, OK. Just take me through the software you've provided.' *My God, where did they get him from?* She'd already decided there was no way they'd provide her with any form of communication to the outside world. No Cloud access, no Melomet; it was a stand-alone system in every sense. At least they wouldn't be able to monitor her activities with this lot. She watched closely as Jakob navigated through the system software and the installed apps, making a mental note of any programme she'd need to inspect in more detail. There were a few useful maths algorithms, but they were well short of what she needed. *Obviously trying to limit me.* At least the computer's memory size was nowhere near as stingy as she first feared.

181

'And we have provided games. Look, you find them here.'

'My God, some of these were written decades ago.' *Dungeons and Dragons*, as old as the hills, but maybe she could deconstruct it and use it as the basis of her model.

Jakob ignored her remark and pressed on. 'You like me to show how mathematics programs work?'

'No thank you, Jakob. I'll work that out myself. It will give me something to do.'

'Oh? I thought perhaps you—'

'Goodbye, Jakob!'

She waited until he let himself out; at least the old fossil knew how to operate a wafer. She studied once more the heap of junk they'd provided. What an insult; it was like someone buying Leon *The Big Picture Book of Physics*. She sat down and scanned through the preloaded software. This was all she was getting. *Better than nothing, I suppose. Now I need to get some data.*

It was a week after her interview with Rodin before Sergei turned up again. 'We're going for a swim today, Ana,' he said. 'You need to catch up on your fitness training.'

This was her opportunity. 'I'll be with you in a moment, Sergei. I'll just get changed.' She went into the bedroom.

'Don't be long,' she heard him shout. 'The pool is only free for an hour.'

'Can you come through, Sergei? Something I want to show you.'

Sergei came into the room and stopped dead as soon as he saw her.

'What do you think? I haven't worn this one yet. Not too revealing, is it?' One foot on the floor, the other on the bed, her sleek red all-in-one swim suit was having the effect she'd hoped for – this was going to work. 'Fancied a change. The shiny black one makes me feel so unsexy.' She tilted her head back in a sensuous laugh.

'Well, I—'

'Oh, stop mumbling. Come and help me with my zip,' she said, turning her back on him. His touch tickled. She spun around, pulled him against her chest and fell backwards with him on to the bed. With Sergei on top of her, she clamped him in a vice-like grip between her arms and legs and clasped her lips across his mouth. As she relaxed her hold, Sergei responded with a passionate kiss. She'd gone past the point of abort now – the recent memory from the black drum filled her senses. *Don't panic.* She rubbed her hands across his back and caressed his buttocks; he was swelling between her legs. *Please stop.*

With a sudden jolt, Sergei appeared to come to his senses. He tore himself free and backed away from the bed. 'We can't do this,' he gasped as he wiped his lips with the back of his hand.

Magda disguised her relief and, like a guilty schoolgirl, offered her apology. 'You're right, we shouldn't. And it's my fault, not yours.'

'Well, let's just pretend it didn't happen and no harm is done.' He stood upright and straightened his T-shirt. 'I think we'll give the swim a miss for today,' he said, sweeping back the fringe from over his eyes.

'I'm sorry, Sergei. I don't know what came over me. I've been cooped up for so long. A woman has needs, you know.'

'Leave it at that, shall we? It won't happen again.' Sergei left the bedroom.

Magda's heart was racing and the adrenalin pumped through her veins. *Got it!* She sat on the end of the bed, listening to Sergei's footsteps as he made his way through the lounge. As soon as she heard the whirring of the exit door's motor, she jumped up and rushed to the anteroom. *Thirty seconds, a minute max.* It would be tight but the computer was set up ready – including the wafer-reader she'd been surprised to find among Jakob's box of spares.

The front door clicked into its closed position – the sign that he'd reached the elevator door. *He's on his way back.* She finished off at the keyboard.

The doorbell chimed. Fifteen seconds later, the door opened.

'Ana!' he shouted. 'Are you decent?'

'Yes, I'm just about to change.'

Sergei entered her bedroom for the second time that morning. Magda was rummaging through her wardrobe, still in her swimsuit.

'Don't worry, Sergei, there'll be no repeat. You've forgotten something?' She could see his face was taut with trepidation.

'Yes, I just … ah, there it is. Must have slipped out while we were—'

'Oh, your wafer – mustn't go without that,' she said with feigned surprise as he picked it from the crumpled bed sheet.

Sergei seemed quiet and less jovial since the episode in her bedroom. The way he looked at her nowadays was a bizarre mix of disgust and longing.

'You're looking a little forlorn today, Sergei,' she said as they wallowed together in the jacuzzi. 'Don't you enjoy my company anymore?'

'I'm fine. What training do you fancy this afternoon?'

She tapped his shoulder in admonishment. 'Don't change the subject. Look, we've known each other for months and I'm going nowhere soon. I'm just interested in who I have for company. You don't let me mix with the other inmates, so, what about *you*, my gaoler? Tell me about yourself.'

'You know I don't like being referred to like that. But I see no harm in talking about myself. What do you want to know? Within reason, of course.'

'How did you end up in a place like this, for starters? Do you like your job?'

'One question at a time, please.' His muscular torso relaxed as he eased himself back on his elbows. 'I was in the Russian nuclear submarine fleet at the time and, while I was on shore leave, I was approached by someone who told me he was a former submariner himself. He explained how psychological profiles like ours were ideally suited to a fledgling company in the leisure industry that was owned by a rich Russian cartel. If I was successful in my assessment, they'd buy me out of my navy commission and install me in a fantastic job with a salary many times what I was earning in the navy. So, here I am.'

'You mean they were looking for someone who didn't mind being stuck down here for years? That makes you no better off than I am – you're a prisoner just the same.'

'Not quite. But you're right in one sense. I signed a contract for ten years. After that, I intend to retire on the pension they've promised. My plan is to complete the contract then go back to St Petersburg, my home city.'

'How do you know they'll honour their side of the bargain? And don't you want your freedom before that?'

'It's the choice I made. But coming to another question of yours – yes, I do like my job. Look around you. How many others can say they're being paid a fortune to work in an environment like this?'

'But you're not enjoying it at the moment – am I right?'

'Well, I *was* happy. That was before I met you. I have to admit, I'm finding this special assignment a strain.'

'It's nice to be considered a special assignment,' she said, trying to lighten the mood, 'but I'm not a strain, am I? When have I not done as I've been told?'

'It's not like that. It's just that ... Change the subject, shall we? Let's just say discussing our relationship is out of bounds.'

She held his gaze until he couldn't look into her eyes anymore. *So, that's it.* He was falling for her and putting himself in a difficult position. She could live with that.

'OK, we'll change the subject, but on one condition. You need to admit that you know what's going on. I'm not stupid. Even with my limited exposure to other girls, I can see there's been some serious manipulation of their minds. You're brainwashing them, aren't you?'

Sergei looked around the spa as if expecting someone. 'OK, you're right,' he whispered. 'I don't know how they do it. But whatever it is, it didn't work on you.'

I don't believe him. 'You realise that what they're doing is wrong? They're taking away our free will.'

'They're providing contentment. You're all well looked after and you live in what is effectively a five-star hotel.'

'But these girls are sex slaves living in a brothel, made to pander to the perverted desires of strangers. What about the families and loved ones they've been torn away from? What about *my* loved ones?' She forced herself to calm down. So far, he'd been responsive to her own amateurish brainwashing. Charm the pants off him, she told herself, realising that it may literally have to come to that at some stage.

'Are there follow-up drugs to supplement this process?'

'Yes.'

'And have they given these drugs to me?'

'Yes, I'm sorry to say. But they stopped once they realised they were having little effect.'

'How did they administer them?'

'By injection at first, while you slept. When they realised your resistance was strong, they put extra drugs in your food.'

'And you knew all along?'

He nodded his head. 'Yes,' he said dolefully.

She could tell Sergei's resolve was weakening but she restrained herself through five minutes of poignant silence before breaking the impasse. 'You're a lovely man, Sergei. I can't deny that.' She rubbed her hand down his arm. 'I've always wanted to see where you live down here. Even more so, now I know it's to be your home for ten years. Would you ever be able to show me?'

He scratched his chin. 'I suppose there's no harm, given our respective long-term situations. Actually, it's not down here at all. I live on the ground floor.'

CHAPTER 24

'**G**ood evening, sir. How can we be of help?'

'Do you have a catalogue of your girls?'

'Yes, of course. Any particular requirements? I can show you who's available.' Mary opened her ring binder. She could see Gina out of the corner of her eye, frantically waving a newspaper about, trying to catch her attention. Mary ignored her, the clients always had to come first. 'See anyone you like, sir?'

Gina kept on waving. Her gesticulations were becoming more animated. 'Look at this,' she mouthed across the reception area.

Not now, Gina. 'I'm busy!' Mary hissed back. 'Sorry, sir. What was that again?'

'This one. *She* looks interesting …'

Once her client disappeared down the corridor with his purchase, Mary turned her attention to Gina. 'Now, Gina. You're obviously bursting to tell me something.'

Beside herself with excitement, Gina started rambling and stuttering. 'Look at this photo, in today's newspaper. This is Ana, from the Fantasyworld. It's definitely her, I tell you. Do you remember me telling you about the Fantasyworld? Well, this girl was going to be my team leader. And it says she's a university professor who disappeared five months ago. What do you think about that? Do you reckon we should tell the police we know where she is?'

'Slow down, Gina. You know the girl in this photo, do you?'

'Well, not exactly. But we were all shown her holographic image. She was going to be in charge of our dormitory team, you see. Team leaders had their own private accommodation and they—'

'Woah! Calm down, you're confusing me. You haven't actually met her then? And what exactly are you going to say to the police? You don't even know where this place is. I think we should keep our noses clean and not get involved.'

But Mary's thoughts weren't about staying clear of the law. It was the other photograph on the page that intrigued her. It was Leon Dabrowski, the nuclear physicist. She recognised him as the man who came to see her a couple of months ago with the picture of his girlfriend – the same woman whose photograph was now next to his. Dr Leon Dabrowski and Professor Magda Tomala – both of them were missing. He was on the run and she was cooped up in one of Rodin's brothels. *What's all that about?* 'Very interesting, sweetheart. But don't concern yourself about this. Trust me – I know what's for the best. So be a good girl and run along.'

Gina scampered away, shaking her bowed head from side to side. Mary waited until she disappeared from sight before picking up the newspaper and reading the whole story. It was beginning to make sense. And what about that other woman in the photo Leon Dabrowski had shown her? She'd been so much like her mother. What if it *was* her? She could still be alive. For the first time in years, she craved a fix. Her confused mind drifted back through its hazy memory banks and she thought back to the days she lived with her brother. He was a bastard like his dad.

It must have been thirty years ago. It was Robert's first visit to the house for weeks as far as she could recall.

'The bitch isn't coming back, you realise? Never.'

'Robert! That's our mother you're talking about. And whose fault is it she's gone? You've no idea how much you took her for granted. Just threw her kindness back in her face, you did.'

'And what about you, little sister? The whore of Hampstead Heath, they call you – did you know that? And what does Mummy think about that, I wonder – proud of her little girl, is she? Don't give me any of that crap, you little slut.'

'Well at least I had the decency to give her some money towards my keep over the last few months. What have *you* ever done for her? I'll tell you what you've done – nothing, sweet FA. You've bled her dry, you have. And now all you can do is moan about her leaving us to our own devices.'

'Yeh, well she's just left us both in the shit. No money to pay the bills, no food, nothing. We're on our own now. But don't worry, sis. I have plans for us both.'

'Plans, you say!' she shouted into his face. 'What plans have you ever had?'

Robert's demeanour changed. He sat down on the sofa and started to reason with her. 'Well, I've been thinking. We have this house to ourselves and it's going to be ages before they think about chucking us out. We'll have months of warnings about not paying the council tax and we could always make do without gas and electricity. Believe me, I'm an expert on all that.'

Mary said nothing. What sort of hare-brained scheme was he dreaming up for them both?

'You see, what I was thinking was that you could work from here. You're more or less doing that anyway, these days. And I could find you your clients. I know plenty of punters who'd prefer to come to a smart house like this one, rather than pay for a quick shag in the park.'

'You mean you're proposing to turn our mother's house into a brothel and you're going to be my pimp?' Mary sneered. 'I reckon you may as well find a few more women on the game and let *them* live here. You'd make a fortune, you would.'

'I hadn't thought of that one. What a good idea – you're not as stupid as you look.'

She couldn't take any more of this nonsense. 'I was taking the piss, you idiot!' she yelled. 'You must think I'm a moron.'

But Robert seemed to be serious about his plans. And over the days that followed he put them into practice. Mary cooperated, but at a price of two black eyes and numerous cut lips. It was over that period that Robert introduced her to heroin. The months that followed

192

became a swirling fog as she spiralled down towards the same oblivion that awaited Robert. Every day became a bad dream. And the dreams were always the same – until the day the police knocked at their door. She expected it to be the bailiffs; they'd already made two visits to the house. It turned out to be a detective inspector with a young uniformed female officer. She could see the distress in their faces.

'Miss Douglas?' the man asked.

'You've found my mother. Is she all right? Where is she?'

'Can we come in? It's bad news, I'm afraid.'

'No, you can't. You can say what you have to say and have done with it.'

The police officers exchanged a look of concern. 'It's about your brother, Robert,' the DI said.

'Oh God, what's he been up to now? Has he been caught dealing?'

'I'm afraid it's more serious than that. He's dead. We found his body on the Heath last night. He'd been stabbed in the throat.'

'Mary, Mary! Are you all right?' Gina was shaking her by the shoulder, her face filled with concern. 'You must have fallen asleep, you've been here for ages.'

Mary rubbed her eyes and sat up on the couch; dazed and clammy, she started to shiver even though it was warm in reception. The clock showed ten o'clock. 'Are there any clients left in the place?'

'No, the last one's just left. I looked after him myself,' Gina proudly proclaimed. 'Shall I lock up?'

'Yes, sweetheart, I think you'd better do that.'

Mary collapsed on to her bed, her head aching at the recollection of Robert's violent death those many years ago. At the time, it shook her so badly that she agreed to have counselling; they even managed to wean her off the heroin and she hadn't relapsed since. Over the years, she'd come to terms with her loss; it was inevitable, she told herself. She thought again about the photograph that triggered her memories and accepted, for the first time in her life, that she'd swept her mother's disappearance under the table. It was finally time to do the right thing. She had to find out what happened to her. But where could she start? She could take a closer look at that photo. *I'm going to have to find Leon Dabrowski.*

CHAPTER 25

The elevator made its upward journey. Magda's heart was racing and her palms were wet with sweat. She was going to see daylight for the first time in months. And there had to be a way out at ground-floor level.

As they entered Sergei's quarters, her immediate impression was that the living space was more palatial than her own. 'Straight ahead,' Sergei said. 'This is the lounge, one bedroom off to either side, each with an en suite bathroom and dressing area.'

'Why two bedrooms?' Magda grinned. 'You have regular guests?'

Sergei returned her smile and opened one of the doors to reveal a large, congested room. 'I use it as my study. I can see you're impressed, but wait till you see my kitchen.'

Unlike his study, Sergei's dining kitchen was clean-lined and uncluttered, but that wasn't what captured Magda's attention. At the end of the kitchen, there it was – the outside world beckoning from beyond a glazed panel. Before Sergei could stop her, she set off across the kitchen floor and headed for daylight. As she bounded over the final few floor tiles, the panel slid open. She threw her arms skyward in a gesture of freedom …

'It's a conservatory?' she said, trying to suppress her disappointment.

'Yes. Beautiful plants, don't you agree?'

She gathered herself. There was a sense of relief after so many months of living underground. The frosted glass made it impossible to discern any detail from the world outside but she could make out a blue-sky day and a lush green garden. There had to be a way out of this glasshouse.

'I can imagine what you're thinking, Ana, but let me explain. You're looking at three inches of bulletproof Perspex. No doors, no openings of any sort – we're in a cocoon.'

Magda wasn't listening; she was too busy walking around the interior garden, studying the possibilities rather than the plants. If she could get hold of a wafer, she could photograph that sheet of brown she could see through the conservatory's glass – it had to be the external elevation of a tall building. A simple Fourier transform routine, a bit of straightforward image processing on her computer … she could bring the building into focus and maybe work out where she was.

'I need to return you to your own quarters. I'm not sure what their attitude would be if they knew I'd brought you to see …'

Might even find a way up there and climb out of a window.

As soon as Sergei left her alone in her quarters, Magda powered up her computer. There had to be many emergency exits in this vast complex but, so far, her predictive model hadn't determined the boundary profile. Her plan was a simple one. Select the preferred exit, memorise the routes towards it and wait for the opportunity to make a run for it. In those few seconds before Sergei realised what was happening, she could be round the first corner and out of sight. With nervous anticipation, she hit the return key.

The modelling routine was doing its job. She rotated the 3-D image on her monitor screen. New rooms, corridors and elevator shafts appeared in red – the result of her programme's probabilistic predictions. The extrapolation was working and the data from Sergei's wafer seemed to be crucial. *But there should be more than this.* The new appendages on the diagram were far fewer than she'd expected and there was so much empty space in the image. That could only mean one thing – Sergei only used this particular wafer when he was with her. *He uses another wafer when he moves about the place alone or when he leaves the main complex – if he ever leaves the complex.* For the first time, Magda realised she would have to abandon her scheme. After all this, her current escape plan was a long shot – wishful thinking, something to occupy her mind and keep her mental capacity in shape until she could think of a *credible* escape plan. She already had such a plan. The thought of it twisted her guts but she'd have to go for it the next time she saw Sergei – that meant tomorrow.

Sergei was more brawn than brain. His physique reminded Magda of Leon, but Leon's beautiful mind shone so brightly against Sergei's dull intellect. She played Sergei like an old Joanna that thought it was a Steinway and even persuaded him that regular visits to his quarters provided her with the psychological therapy she needed as a long-term inmate. Their discussions were becoming more open and Sergei was willing to answer more of her questions, but she had to be careful not to push him too far.

'Tell me more about your time in the navy, my handsome sailor boy. Were the nuclear subs challenging in the technical sense?'

'The technology is old but it wouldn't be feasible to upgrade it. Modern computer installations require years of validation and everything has to be failsafe. This meant we were operating with equipment that was becoming obsolete and we had serious problems regarding spares.'

How boring. Yet what he was telling her showed she was gaining his trust. He clearly had no qualms about divulging his state's secrets to her.

'What about living conditions on board?'

'Cramped and foul-smelling. You only find out how bad the smell really is when you breathe the sea air after docking and when you see the maintenance technicians come on board pinching their noses.'

'You never see a woman for months at a time. Did you have dirty pictures pinned up around the place?'

'No glossy pictures allowed. The interior is covered in wall charts showing system diagrams and instruction sets.'

Magda wanted to laugh at his dryness. 'But all those hot-blooded men must feel randy at times.'

'No time for that. Regular drills and exercises, constant inspection and testing of equipment – at the end of a shift, you just want to return to your bunk. And it's often been slept in by another filthy sailor. Sex is the last thing on your mind.'

'This place must seem like heaven after that. I can see why you were willing to come here to work. Do you have job satisfaction, Sergei?'

'I *had* job satisfaction on the submarines. I was serving my country, making life safer for our citizens. But this job is also pleasurable. I love sport and physical fitness, I take pride in my achievements with ...' He looked sullen.

'With me?' She rested her hand on his thigh. 'Don't worry, Sergei, it's normal. We get on well, don't you think?' She stroked his leg and observed the bulge she was creating in his tracksuit bottoms. 'We could have a proper relationship, you know. But I couldn't give myself to any man who wasn't devoted to me. It would just be lustful animal sex. On the other hand, if we were both free people, outside ... who knows what would happen?'

'I think we need to end this conversation, Ana. I'll take you back to your rooms.'

They made the journey back to her living quarters in silence. Following the familiar routine, Sergei conducted her inside and said his farewells; she smirked to herself as he checked the pocket at the back of his joggers. She gave him a kiss on the cheek, lingering so he'd feel its warmth, and watched with a smile as he backed his way through the door. The seed was planted. Now she had to nurture it so his passion would grow into a love that would drive him to do anything she wanted. She sloped off into the bedroom and sat on the end of the bed. 'Sorry, Leon, I have to do this,' she said, as the tears ran down her face. 'It's for you, my love.' She curled up on her bed and cried herself to sleep.

For Magda, the most sensuous part of making love was the afterglow. Lying motionless on her back, under the single sheet on Sergei's bed, she was aware of him watching her, studying her. But she didn't look back at him. She covered her eyes with her forearm, hoping he wouldn't notice the single tear she could feel running down the side of her cheek. She gave a long soft sigh, hoping he wouldn't sense its falsity. With deep sadness, her thoughts drifted back to the first time she made love with Leon. It was the first time for both of them. Once again, she heard the tumbling piano notes of the Rachmaninov *Rhapsody* playing in the background.

Leon's new apartment was warm and welcoming that cold winter night ten years ago. The music faded, the lights dimmed and Leon stroked her hair. 'I don't need you any more, Magda.'

'I know you don't. You have me forever now.'

'Will you marry me?'

'Yes, Leon. When you become free.'

'You sure you'll turn up?'

'I'll ride to the church in a golden carriage, driven by angels.'

'I thought you might do that.' His kiss was soft on her cheek. 'What we have between us is beautiful.'

'You mean you still love me?'

'Like the arrow of time.'

'That means since before you were born.'

She basked in the glow. Twin spirits back in the womb, she sensed the matching intensity of his feelings coming together with hers like a single strong beat.

And now, for the first time in her life, she'd been fucked. She'd felt the brute strength of the man lying at her side, done her best to move to the rhythm of his pumping torso and let him lure her on to the rocks with his manly pheromones as his long deep thrusts powered them both to a climax within minutes. She was surprised at how they achieved orgasm at the same time, but it pleased her and she was sure he hadn't detected the exaggeration in her orgasmic throes. He'd be happy about his conquest and she'd achieved her first objective.

But he wasn't Leon. Despite the physical satisfaction, the sex left her emotionally flat. Now she must continue to cultivate his love while she sank inexorably into a trough of guilt. The encounter reassured her about her ability to ensnare him, yet she was beset by nagging doubts. *Will all this be worthwhile?*

Magda sprawled on the couch in Sergei's quarters. Her waxed legs protruded from under the silk robe and Sergei was stroking her pedicured feet. She'd been cooped up in this underworld for the best part of six months and when she thought of the amount of time she'd spent honing and pampering her body instead of her mind, she cursed herself. But the cerebral route to freedom was never going to work. She had to continue her seduction of Sergei.

'Tell me about Alexei Rodin.'

'Nothing much to say. We may cross paths once a month, if that.'

'But is he hands on, if you'll excuse the pun … the business, I mean? Or does he just leave you guys to get on with the day-to-day running of this place?'

'Rodin has a considerable say in what goes on, if that's what you're asking. Why are you interested?'

'Just idle thoughts. You took me to meet him, remember? Not a profitable meeting for me, I hasten to add. He's going to get his comeuppance one day.'

Sergei sat up. She could feel the whole of his body stiffening at the remark. *Rodin must have a strong hold over them all.*

'Yes, that's right. He told me that any attempt to escape would be met with severe punishment. He was referring to my loved ones, the bastard.'

'I suggest you don't worry about it,' he said tersely. 'Put your feet back up, relax. I could tell you were enjoying that.'

She lay back and let Sergei continue the foot massage. He was responsive tonight; they'd just had sex and until she raised the subject of Rodin, he was as relaxed as she'd ever seen him.

'How many other girls work here, Sergei?'

'*Other* girls? You don't consider yourself as one of the workers, do you?'

He was priding himself on his wit. But she could see through his delusion and it gave her the confidence to continue.

'This complex is a huge place, but I rarely see anyone during my daily routine. I was just interested to know how many girls lived here. Do you know them all and which teams they belong to? Are they happy and well trained for what they do?'

It was her mention of physical training that captured his interest. Once more, she had him on the hook. He gave her an enthusiastic account of the organisational structure, explaining yet again how the girls were well looked after. They were pampered like royalty – at least, in *his* eyes they were.

'But how much do you know about them? Do you know where they come from? Do you monitor their performance?'

'There *is* a database. It doesn't tell you much but at least they're all accounted for.'

That was what she needed to hear. There could be some vital clues in that database. She pressed on with her line of questioning – squeezing gently so it soothed rather than agitated. According to Sergei, they didn't have much information on her fellow inmates and the records were of variable quality. But from what he told her, it was clear that he had full personal access to this database.

'I'd love to see that, at some stage,' she said, trying to appear indifferent. 'The whole thing fascinates me.' She turned away from him and faked a yawn. 'I'm so tired. Can you take me back to my apartment?'

'Of course.'

She was going to get what she wanted but she'd have to wait until the time was right. *Don't lose him now.*

The opportunity to access the database came within the next week – sooner than she'd hoped. Sergei's computer was so sophisticated compared with the one Jakob had provided. 'I'd forgotten what it's like to use a modern system,' she said, 'yet they don't let you use voice control.'

'I've *never* used voice control, Ana. The computers on the subs were already fifteen years out of date by the time I joined the navy. They still had keyboards and you scanned with a mouse.'

'What! You're telling me you've never had a Melomet voice signature – at your age?'

'That's right. I suppose it's also why I'm a bit slow on this modern equipment – as you've no doubt noticed.'

Was that the blush of embarrassment she could see? 'You're happy for me to go ahead with this?'

'I can't see any harm. I'll log in and leave you to it while I go and shower.' He manipulated the touch screen. 'There we are,' he said as he handed her the control wafer.

She took a deep breath. *OK, let's see what we can find.* She scanned through Sergei's directories – sports science, first aid, physiotherapy … of little value to her. She dug down a couple of levels – plyometrics, creatine phosphate energy systems … *nothing of interest there.* After five more fruitless minutes, she found what she was looking for. The folder was entitled Trainee Database – what else?

Sergei startled her. 'How are you getting on?' Dressed in a towelling robe, his hair wet from the shower, she could smell the masculine peppery odour of his body wash. He wrapped his arms around her and rested his chin on her shoulder. 'Have you found anything of interest?'

'This database,' she said, pointing to the screen, 'it's password protected.'

'Just for you ...' He kissed her on the cheek. 'There we are. I'll go and make some coffee.'

The database comprised a set of personnel records, grouped under the names of PTIs. To her disappointment, she couldn't find Sergei's name among them. *What's this?* A separate directory under the name of Rodin requiring another password – *damn it!* Devoid of any other idea, she entered the name Alexei. It worked. *Can't contain anything of a confidential nature.* The seven sub-directories in Alexei Rodin's personal directory had alphanumeric names and were password protected. She'd seen this subterfuge before in her undergraduate days. She laughed to herself. No doubt Rodin imagined this to be tamper proof, whereas all that was required was a bit of manual decryption – simple for her.

Sergei returned, glanced at the screen and placed her coffee on the desk. Clearly taking no interest in what she was doing, he drifted over to the armchair, out of sight of the computer.

The sub-directories contained detailed records for individuals; perhaps these were the naughty girls, those who caused them trouble? *The team they wanted me to manage?* She cracked the encrypted code of the final directory. There was a rush of adrenalin. This one was about her. But why did it have two folders? She opened the first. The records revealed that her real name was Magda Tomala and that she was from Krakow in Poland. It provided a copy of her academic CV, but that would have been easy to obtain. There was little else. The second folder contained an old-fashioned portable data file – some kind of report, but its date succeeded her incarceration here. *What's this?* She was a competent speed reader but as she scrolled through the report, she found herself slowing down and felt the blood draining from her face. She glanced across the room at Sergei; he was dozing. Just as well – if he looked at her now, he'd probably call for a doctor. She stared again at the screen.

Oh, my God!

PART 3 – 2020

FALLING STARS

CHAPTER 26

The sun cleared the last of the early morning Monaco mist and bathed the magnificent vessel in light. Oleg Malkin shielded his eyes from the glare and looked up from the quayside towards the white-uniformed figure on the yacht's main deck. Surprised to find he could get this far without encountering security, it wasn't until the commissar was halfway down the gangway that he realised he was about to be welcomed to Vladimir Chekhov's home by a lone woman.

'*Bienvenue*, Monsieur Malkin,' she said, before switching to English. 'I hope you had a pleasant journey.' Her French and English sounded perfect, but Malkin wasn't deceived – she was Russian.

'Yes, thank you. The TGV is a most comfortable mode of transport.' Slavic would already be on board, he imagined, flown in by private jet and helicoptered to the yacht. *There's no way I'm ever going to fly again.*

'If you could just hold your Fusion pass up to the scanner please ... Thank you. Welcome to Glasnost.'

The irony of the luxury yacht's name amused him but did nothing to quell his nervousness as he followed the commissar through the upper decks. At every junction, a security officer bowed his head in respect yet followed him with his eyes as if some horrendous fate awaited at the end of the journey. Would this gauntlet ever end? The commissar finally invited him into an empty elevator. As the elevator descended, he leaned back against the side and gave a huge sigh of relief.

The commissar smiled. 'Almost there now, Mr Malkin. Don't worry, most of Mr Chekhov's visitors find his security staff intimidating. Between you and me, he does it deliberately.'

They stepped out into a dimly lit lobby on the lower deck. 'This is where you are to hold your meeting,' the commissar said as she punched in the code to open the cabin door. 'Please go in. Mr Chekhov will be along in a moment.'

The tiny white LCDs scattered around the place were not enough to reveal the room's contents and the silence unnerved him. A movement caught his eye. *What was that?*

'Let me enlighten you,' Vladimir Chekhov said as he appeared from nowhere with Roman Slavic. 'Lights on!'

'Lights on, Mr Chekhov,' replied the Melomet.

Malkin threw his hand over his mouth and gasped with shock. 'Sharks!'

They were everywhere; tiger sharks ranging between six and eight feet in length, their gills and mouths opening and closing in slow graceful rhythms as they glided past – circling him.

'Ah, I see it now. The gap between the annular aquarium's inner and outer walls isn't wide enough to allow them to turn.'

Chekhov laughed. 'Yes, you are correct. Do you like them?'

'It's cruel, isn't it?'

'*They* don't know that. They have a short-term memory, seconds only, and they act purely on instinct.' Chekhov walked slowly around the room's perimeter. He stopped and held his palm flat against the glass as the big fish squeezed by, its predatory black eye staring menacingly towards him. 'Beautiful, aren't they? A perpetual unidirectional roundabout of predators.'

'This is a remarkable place,' said Malkin.

'This is my thinking room. It reminds me that I have enemies and that I must always know who and where they are. They stalk me day and night but my protection is impenetrable and, even if it could be breached, it would mean certain death for them. That is why I don't fear them. But don't panic, gentlemen,' Chekhov said, smiling, 'I'm not going to feed you to the sharks. Now, to business.'

The three men seated themselves around the circular table at the centre of the room. Malkin knew what to expect. Vladimir Chekhov possessed that uncanny ability to switch the mood of a meeting. One minute he was delighted you could be there; you were his lifelong friend. A minute later, you were Corporate Enemy Number One. He'd become accustomed to it over the years, but what was he going to be like today? And why had he been invited to a meeting with Slavic, of all people? There was no possible link between their businesses. *Unless you count …*

'Last week, I had a profitable meeting with my directors of shipping and civil engineering,' Chekhov said indifferently. 'Profitable, that is, because it was face to face. I have regular update meetings with them over our secure video link, as I do with you two gentlemen. But our get-together in this room revealed much more than I'd previously been aware of. I was astounded by the amount of vital information that came out under the most benign questioning from me. So here we are today, gentlemen,' he said, opening his hands in welcome. 'Do you follow what I'm saying?'

They nodded their agreement.

'I will start with you, Slavic.'

Roman Slavic pinned back his shoulders as if he'd received a command from a military general.

'I've read your report. You give the impression that progress on the reactor design is moving forward at an acceptable pace. Just how close are we to our final design safety submission?'

'I'd say we were about two years away from that.'

'And how far are we in front of the rest of the world in coming up with a viable commercial power plant design?'

'Way ahead of anyone else. The Chinese have suspended their fusion research programme and are simply waiting for our franchise. The Americans continue to take an interest in all new forms of nuclear power, of course, but it's a case of heads in the sand with them. They pretend we don't exist, especially as we don't publish our work.'

'Yet I understand the Americans are making good progress on their own research programme into nuclear fusion technology. Am I correct?'

'There are rather a lot of scientific papers coming out of their Lawrenceville Plasma Physics Centre at the moment. All of them are published in the open literature and some may even be of value to us.'

'And they have set up a new design office, I believe?'

'Yes, that's right.'

'You don't think they are breathing down our necks, do you?'

'I doubt it,' Slavic replied, 'but you know what the Americans are like. They'd love to think of it as a race. Their politicians always make out they're doing better than anyone else.'

'And how do you know they aren't winning this race?'

'I'm confident of that. Our experts have analysed every paper they've published. In practice, they're way behind our Greifswald team.'

'You mean to say they would set up a top-secret billion-dollar fusion reactor design programme in Los Alamos on the basis of a few academic papers? What about the reports they *don't* publish in the open literature? What do we know about them?'

'Nothing – by definition.'

The room was air conditioned, yet Slavic was starting to look hot and uncomfortable in his formal suit and institute tie. This would normally be a source of pleasure to Malkin – he'd never liked Slavic – but he was next in the firing line.

'Slavic, at Goldhurst you have an experienced security team at your disposal,' he gestured towards Malkin, 'and you haven't for one minute contemplated using them to find out what the Americans are doing.'

Malkin pursed his mouth and shook his head in mock bewilderment.

'That brings me to my key question. Where is their breakthrough information coming from? They don't even have their own fusion research facility. Who else has the data to back a commercial fusion reactor design?'

'We are the only ones. No one else in the world has such data.'

'Do you think someone is leaking our data to them?'

Slavic looked horrified. 'What, you're not suggesting that—'

Chekhov interjected. 'Who in Fusion has access to this information?'

'Four personnel only. Myself, Dabrowski, Schroeder and Kaminsky. But since the Greifswald breakthrough we've followed your instructions and placed the tightest security around the data from our stellerator runs. We've—'

'That brings me to my next point,' Chekhov interjected again. 'I understand that one of the four you mention has not been seen for weeks. Am I correct?'

'Yes, you're right. Dabrowski left work sick and didn't return. We've been unable to locate him and my team has had to cover for him. I didn't want to bother you with such personnel matters.'

Looking exasperated, Chekhov turned towards Malkin. 'You see what I mean about face-to-face meetings. My chief scientist has gone AWOL and the Americans are coincidentally making remarkable progress on their own reactor design,' he pointed his thumb in Slavic's direction, 'and *he* doesn't think it's important enough to discuss with me.'

At the mention of Leon Dabrowski, Malkin began to share Slavic's discomfort. How did Chekhov find out about this? There was going to be the mother of all searches for Dabrowski – and Malkin knew where to start looking for him in the evenings. He caught a movement from the corner of his eye; the circling sharks were looking at him.

'Slavic, I want to make my position clear, because you don't seem to have any appreciation of the gravity of the situation. The reason I'm investing a billion euros in developing the world's first nuclear fusion-based power station is because I recognised the raw talent in Dabrowski. As a result of his technical leadership, the Wendelstein-7X stellerator can now produce more power from the fusion process than it takes to operate it.'

Slavic closed his eyes and dolefully nodded his head.

Chekhov leaned forward and calmly asked, 'Why do you think I appointed you as my CEO?'

The question obviously surprised Slavic. 'I'm grateful for your confidence in me, Mr Chekhov. I've served you well and the company has thrived under my management, I've supported—'

'No, Slavic, you haven't done any of that. You are a conduit between me and my technical team, as simple as that. As a former public schoolboy, Oxford graduate, president of an academic institution and God knows what else, you provide my London-based company with a suitable figurehead. If I placed one of my compatriots in such a position, he would never command the same respect and credibility. Despite your Russian parentage and your bilingual capability, you are the archetypal English gentleman and, more importantly, you are a yes man. You do not question my instructions or my decisions.'

Malkin chortled to himself as he watched Slavic deflate like a balloon. *Oh, this is really good. I'm enjoying this.*

Chekhov continued. 'I do hope you appreciate my other senior appointments to Fusion. I've provided you with the dream team when it comes to technical specialists. Kaminsky is an outstanding and dedicated IT engineer and Schroeder and Dabrowski are both world class physicists. Dabrowski – ah, yes, the fugitive. Well, he is one of the few people currently alive who you could truly refer to as brilliant. And he works for you, Slavic. For God's sake, man, why didn't you look after him?'

He's going to get the bullet.

'Think yourself lucky I'm not going to sack you on the spot. Believe it or not, I don't wish to dismantle the company's technical lead team while we are on the edge of this precipice. God knows what you would all get up to if I set you loose on the world. Listen carefully, both of you. This is what I intend to do about the unfortunate position we find ourselves in.' To Malkin's surprise, Chekhov turned towards him. 'Malkin, you will arrange for a formal investigation into the efficacy of Fusion's data security procedures.' Turning his attention to Slavic, he said, 'I want you to look into every possibility for accelerating the programme. Finish your design safety reports. When you have them, let me know and I'll see what I can have done regarding corner cutting in the government's safety assessment process. You may leave us now.'

Ignoring Slavic, as if he'd already left the room, Chekhov turned again to Malkin. 'Now, I want to review the overall current security arrangements at Goldhurst …'

Red-faced, Slavic stuffed his papers into his briefcase and skulked off towards the elevator.

'You see, there is a possibility that Dabrowski has defected,' Chekhov continued. 'He may already be working for the Americans, helping them to develop their own design of fusion reactor. Personally, I don't believe he's the sort of person to do such a thing, but we need to find out why he's gone missing at such a crucial stage of the programme. Without Dabrowski, our project could grind to a halt. You have to find him and bring him back in, Malkin. Don't let me down.'

Malkin felt the sweat trickle down the back of his neck. *Oh, God! This is the worst thing that could have happened to me. I'm in charge of tracking down Chekhov's son for the second time in my life.*

Flashing images of Vladimir Chekhov putting a fatherly arm around him, a cold knife sliding into his stomach, a last glimpse of Chekhov's smile … falling. Malkin tried to stand. The seat belt pulled at his waist and claustrophobia overcame him. He started to hyperventilate and the sweat poured from his forehead.

'How did you sleep, Mr Malkin?'

'Whaa …?'

It was coming back. He'd struggled with them until one of them held down his arm while the other administered an injection to the back of his hand. He could see them again, clicking his safety belt into place and reclining his seat before they disappeared into the swirling mist. He must have slept all the way across the Atlantic.

'Mr Malkin?'

There was no choice about this flight. Chekhov had insisted it had to be face to face.

'Mr Malkin, we've landed,' the stewardess said. 'It's a beautiful morning out there.'

'Get me out of this can, for God's sake!'

As he walked away from the airport Arrivals hall, Malkin breathed in the warm dry air with its hint of desert dust. He looked up to the empty sky and embraced its open space as if he'd just left a dark windowless prison cell. The Buick pulled away from the terminal and started to lap up the sixty miles from Albuquerque airport to his destination – distancing him by the minute from that heartless flying tube he'd just stepped out of. He felt a profound sense of relief, yet logic told him he was now travelling at higher risk than on the plane.

The bar on the outskirts of Downtown Los Alamos looked quiet, with only two cars in the parking lot. Malkin gave the chauffeur his instructions to return within thirty minutes and cast a glance in both highway directions before strutting across to the entrance. The front-of-house pool room was almost deserted, as he'd hoped. The main source of light was the canopy over the single pool table, which was occupied by two middle-aged men in corduroys and braces. Focused on their game, they paid him little attention as he headed for the dark corner of the bar towards the only other customer in the room.

He barely recognised Karl Fenner. Early twenties, dressed in jeans and T-shirt and sporting a red baseball cap, it was the first time Malkin had seen Fenner without a suit. 'You fancy a Bud?' he asked.

'No, mine's a Coke.'

The coded greeting confirmed, Malkin ordered from the barmaid and returned to the table with iced water, another signal that meant all was well and the transfer could safely take place.

'OK, Fenner, we have to be quick. We can never be sure if either of us has been followed. Those men at the table?' He tilted his head back over his shoulder without turning.

'I've been watching them. They're not interested and we're out of earshot anyway.'

'OK, give it to me straight.'

Fenner leaned forward across the drinks, his voice hardly above a whisper. 'The data we're getting definitely don't belong to Los Alamos. And I should know cos I'm bang up to date with the input from all the contributing US research teams. This stuff comes from outside the USA and it's potentially shit hot, like the Holy Grail for us fusion scientists – but only if we can see their source data. From my Cambridge days, I know what's generally going on around the world and I'd say this lot comes from Greifswald. I can't be one hundred per cent sure, of course. As you know, their output's now classified as secret.'

'What are the Los Alamos teams doing with this information?'

'The project director partitions the data and sends me what I need for my own work. I have to tell him it's not enough to help our design calcs and he's getting pretty pissed off about it. I've managed to download a section of the data I've been asked to review. Here.' Fenner discreetly palmed a wafer-zip across the table. 'It's the only copy. I'd lose my job if they found out. You can have it checked against Fusion's original data if you know someone who has access. Their physicists would be able to tell if the information belongs to them.'

Malkin turned his head to check that the pool players and the barmaid weren't looking and slipped the button-like object into his jacket pocket.

'You've done well, Fenner. I'm very grateful.'

'I'm the one who has to be grateful, Mr Malkin. The job Mr Chekhov got me is out of this world and it pays twice as much as I would have earned in London.'

'He only just managed to steal you from under the Fusion interview panel's noses, you realise that?' Malkin smirked to himself. *Slavic's loss*. 'Mr Chekhov will no doubt thank you personally one day for what you're doing here.'

'Well, thanks again, Mr Malkin. I hope it's what you want and been worth the trip over. Have a nice flight back to London.'

The meeting had gone well until that moment. Malkin's stomach churned at the prospect of getting back into that tiny jet.

Malkin wiped his sweating palms on his thighs and squirmed in discomfort. Since his return from Los Alamos there'd been little time for him to make progress with his investigations at Goldhurst, and now he faced Chekhov in a video meeting that was rapidly becoming the mother of all reprimands. Chekhov should have been pleased with his progress, shouldn't he? He'd confirmed that the Americans were in possession of Fusion data. Yet Chekhov only seemed to be interested in talking about Leon Dabrowski.

'Still no sign of him? What have you been doing, Malkin?'

'I'm sure Dabrowski is still in the capital, sir. We're trawling London on a daily basis but it looks like he's gone to ground. We're doing our best.'

'Then your best isn't good enough,' Chekhov growled. 'I can wait no longer. I'm sending across a cohort of my own security guards and *they* will find him.'

Malkin shuddered. Chekhov must no longer be interested in restoring Dabrowski to his position in the Fusion technical team. This was about avenging treachery – just like his father used to do. And there was no doubt about the nature of the beast that Chekhov was about to unleash. Trained killers, ex-special forces, they'd track Dabrowski down like hunting dogs and eliminate him. That would solve his own problem, of course, but they weren't chasing the right man. Dabrowski wasn't interested in the project, he was preoccupied with finding his girlfriend.

'Sir, I'll provide your men with whatever support they may need.'

'You do that, Malkin. Chekhov out.'

'Is there anyone else you would like me to call, Mr Malkin?' said the Melomet.

'No!' he shouted, his cheeks burning like hot coals. 'Malkin out.'

He leaned forward on his elbows and cradled his head in despair. If he finds him but doesn't kill him, he'll discover the truth about what happened to his son. He'd have to step up his efforts to find Dabrowski before Chekhov's thugs got to him. And he feared that this race would be over quickly. *Where is Dabrowski hiding?*

CHAPTER 27

The London Metro-tube was at its busiest this time in the evening. To the annoyance of the suited city slicker who'd boarded the train ahead of him, Leon managed to grab the last available seat in the carriage. Although he was exhausted, he'd spent a worthwhile afternoon shadowing one of Schumann's reconnaissance teams and was finally getting to grips with their work at ground level. The data they were gathering on individual brothels would supplement his own satellite surveillance results; he'd start preparing for his weekly briefing with Pavel as soon as he got back to his apartment. He settled back to make the weary return journey, but not before he checked out his fellow travellers. A small group of *Classicos* acknowledged him as they passed down the carriage – no one suspicious among them. He took a final look around, leaned back in his seat and waited for the next stop.

The train left Euston Square station and the new passengers completed their jostling for the vacated seats. As he did at every station, Leon carried out a meticulous survey – could anyone be following him? He noticed a hooded figure at the end of the carriage dressed in black, holding on to an overhead support strap and facing towards the engine – Leon couldn't see his face. Could be a *she*, even? He'd keep an eye on this one.

Passenger exchanges were becoming more frenzied; many had to stand in the aisle where they continually squeezed and shuffled to minimise their personal discomfort. But the figure at the front of the carriage remained rooted to the spot throughout the journey – no discernible movement, part of the carriage's structure, like the Statue of Liberty holding high her torch. *Who is it?* The train was almost at Leon's destination. He should be feeling relieved at this stage of the journey, yet as he waited by the exit door the anxiety wouldn't leave him. And neither did the hooded passenger, who got off the train at the same stop.

Leon reached the station's concourse level. He turned and peered down to the bottom of the escalator where the hooded figure was striding past those who preferred to stand. *No doubt about it, I'm being followed*. He hurried through the turnstiles and out of the station, ran for all he was worth along Melcombe Street and turned into Siddons Lane. He stopped and sneaked a look around the street corner, back towards the station entrance. Satisfied that his pursuer hadn't yet emerged, he took out his wafer.

'Get me Schumann.'

'Schumann for you, Mahler,' said the Melomet, five seconds later.

'Schumann, it's code blue – I'm being followed.'

'Where are you, Mahler?'

'I've just left Baker Street Station. He hasn't come into sight yet, but I'm sure he will – any minute now.'

'OK, I can be there in twenty minutes. You're about fifteen minutes away from your apartment. Try and shake him off. Take a long route back but don't even think about going into the park. And leave the Melomet-link open so I can hear what's going on. If I have to, I'll take him out – you understand that?'

Leon *did* understand what Schumann was telling him. They'd rehearsed this drill several times. The moment Leon felt endangered, he was to summon Schumann who would arrange a rapid response from the *Policja* special unit. Any threat would be removed. But in Leon's mind there was always the concern about one trained assault team coming up against another. And this could be happening now. *Heaven help us.*

Checking over his shoulder at regular intervals, Leon scampered up and down the Marylebone district streets at random until he'd been on the move for twenty-five minutes. *Schumann should be in place by now.* There was no sign of his pursuer – or of Schumann, for that matter. But that didn't mean they weren't there. Either of them could be watching him right now. Time to head home.

At his penthouse apartment, Leon locked the door and waited for fifteen minutes. 'Lost him,' he said aloud. No response from Schumann – he'd keep the line open. Within minutes, there was a knock at the door. Only Schumann and Pavel knew the code for the entrance to this part of the building – this had to be Schumann. At last, he was safe. He opened the door – and took a sharp step back.

Gunther Schroeder, red-faced and dishevelled, pushed back his hood to reveal a tangled mop of hair, wet with perspiration. 'Can I come in?'

'Holy Moses! You've just scared the living daylights out of me, Gunther. What's all this about?' He grabbed Gunther's forearm and pulled him into his apartment. Checking that the corridor was clear in both directions, he locked the door behind them.

'I'm sorry about this, but I had to see you. You need to know that you and I are in the middle of a serious witch hunt that Chekhov's just instigated. And you won't believe how difficult it's been for me to get out here and start looking for you, let alone find you. When I did find you, I had to follow you. I couldn't risk stopping you in the middle of the street. We could have been seen together.'

'Just slow down a minute, will you. I haven't the faintest idea what you're getting at. Try me in a language I might understand. I take it you were on the Bakerloo line an hour ago?'

'Yeh, sure.' Gunther looked embarrassed.

'And how did you get into this building?'

'You'll have to start using more imagination for your entrance code, Leon. Try something a bit more difficult than a prime-number sequence.'

Leon grinned. Same old Gunther – clever dick. 'So, what is it we're both going to be hanged, drawn and quartered for?'

'It's about the stellerator data that we transfer between Greifswald and London. Someone is managing to copy it and they're selling it to the Americans. Would you believe that?'

'I *do* find that hard to believe. Especially as the American fusion teams are likely to be honest and hardworking scientists like we are. Why would they be so unethical as to steal our data? And why would Chekhov imagine that we'd be willing to act against his strict instructions on secrecy? Given that Kaminsky provides the data in the first place, the only other people who have access are you, me and Slavic. Which of us are you suggesting is selling the data to the Americans?'

'Come on, Leon, I'm serious. All four of us are under suspicion. They've stepped up their attempts to track you down. And they've watched the rest of us like hawks these past few weeks.'

'You've come here to warn me, have you? Well, if you're so concerned about my welfare, why have you risked leading the hunt straight to me? They're bound to be following you, aren't they? See who you contact, check whether you're the one passing on the data.'

'Yes, I know that. But I'm not stupid, I've been careful. If I'd been followed, they'd be knocking at the door already, wouldn't they?'

'OK, let's just calm down, shall we?' He took his wafer from his back pocket. 'First of all, I have to call off my *own* hunting pack. You might just get hurt if I don't stand them down. Did you get that, Schumann?'

No answer.

'What did you say?'

'Never mind, Gunther, I'll explain it someday. Like a coffee?'

'No!' Gunther blurted in exasperation. 'We haven't got time. I'm expected back at HQ later today. We need to work out who's doing this. And *you* are going to have to take this seriously – otherwise we're mincemeat.'

The video-wall lit up. Both men snapped their heads to the side. 'Call for you from Schumann, Mahler,' said the Melomet.

'I've been listening to everything you've said, Mahler. I shouldn't have to remind you that your priorities are with us and not with Fusion.'

'OK, point taken, Schumann. My colleague here means no harm. Where are you?'

Schumann laughed. 'Don't worry. My men have had you covered over every inch of ground. Take a look out of the window. Schumann out!'

The video screen went blank. Leon went across to the window and smiled. 'Look here, Gunther. See how well protected I am.'

'Who are they?' Schroeder said, nodding up towards the two men waving from the roof of the building opposite.

'Let's just say they're my guardian angels, so don't worry about me. Anyway, if you want to find Chekhov's thief, you'll just have to remain vigilant. And as you've no doubt gathered, I'm powerless to do anything other than heed your warning. I have my own problems to solve. So, if you're ready to leave, follow me.' He took Schroeder through to the master bedroom. 'Open emergency exit,' he said aloud.

'Emergency exit opening, Mahler,' replied the Melomet. A section of the wall slid upwards, leaving an opening to the side of the bed.

'What the—?'

'The apartment next door is located in a separate quadrant of the building, so you can leave by a different exit. We thought these arrangements might come in handy some day. Go on, you can go straight through. You're the first to use our escape route.'

Schroeder shook his head in blank astonishment. 'It's goodbye, then.' He smiled, '... Mahler.'

Although he'd put on a brave face at the time, the encounter with Gunther three days earlier had left Leon feeling concerned for his own welfare. If a rival consortium was managing to get hold of Fusion's key data, that could ultimately cost Chekhov billions if he failed to establish sole rights to the technology. And worse than that, as far as Leon was concerned, if control of the world's future energy supplies fell into the wrong hands, the whole process of civil nuclear power development could be jeopardised. *Chekhov is bound to think I have something to do with this.* This was seriously worrying. And he had an ominous feeling that Pavel would detect his mood at their weekly exchange. As expected, Pavel queried Leon's gloominess the moment he walked through the door to his apartment and Leon offered the lame excuse that it was due to overwork and sleepless nights. He could see Pavel wasn't convinced, but at least he wasn't going to waste any more of their time on the matter. He started his presentation.

'Here we have a map of the Highgate area, showing the location of Russian-operated brothels. This one and this one ...' Leon pointed to several buildings, 'are *not* operated by Rodin. We're sure of that from the analysis of our reconnaissance data and from the few discreet personal visits I've risked. The rest of them are high-class establishments, attracting affluent punters. What intrigues me is those particular buildings form a distinct geographical cluster with its centre here.' He pointed to the Goldhurst Manor site.

At the end of Leon's presentation, Pavel flopped back in his chair and blew a long whistle. 'Your analysis of movements and accountability suggests these places are physically linked?'

'Almost certainly – underground. As for Goldhurst, well, there's no sign of a brothel being located there. And I should know. I virtually lived there until a few months ago and that wasn't part of the staff benefits.'

Somewhat reticent, they laughed.

'And what about Rodin? Any sighting?'

'Disappointing there. We've found no obvious candidate. One or two remote possibilities, maybe. We track the background of anomalies wherever we can and some of the results are surprising. They appear to have a lot of punters from the medical profession – psychiatrists and psychologists mostly. But who dictates what sort of people use these places? They can all be dirty old men.'

Pavel stood up and patted Leon on the back. 'Keep up the good work, Mahler.' He was in the habit of using Leon's undercover codename by now, his *Classico* name. 'We know so much more than before we recruited you. But, like you, I'm disappointed we have no breakthrough on the identity of Rodin. We have to keep going. It's vital we find him.'

Pavel set off for the door.

'Before you go, there's something of a personal nature I'd like to discuss.'

Pavel came back and sat down.

'My family in Poland, are they OK? My father must be worried sick about the news that I've now disappeared as well as Magda.'

'Your family are fine, don't worry about that. Your mother is still ill, of course, but she's being well looked after.'

Leon's heart sank when he saw the sudden expression of concern in the police officer's face.

'We've had to tell your father what's going on, take him into our confidence so he won't come looking for you and compromise our operation. You see, Chekhov's Goldhurst-based security paid him a visit.' Pavel raised his hand. 'But don't worry, he's not in any danger. He made it obvious to them he didn't know your whereabouts. They know what they're doing, those guys, and they would have detected that his concern was genuine. However, this does mean that they could come after you with a bit more determination from now.'

'I need to tell you something, Pavel. They already *are* coming after me. I reckon Chekhov suspects me of industrial espionage. What do you think I should do?'

Pavel gave a sigh of resignation. 'Ah, so there *is* something wrong? I knew it. But you can't let it distract you from your surveillance work. We'll be watching your back, I promise you. Remember, the sooner we find Rodin the sooner we can resolve this whole mess.'

Pavel's parting words rang in Leon's ears. Rodin had taken away the love of his life. He was the ruin of so many lives and had to be stopped at any cost. With bloodshot eyes, he pored over the data yet again. *He has to be in there somewhere. Why can't we find him?*

CHAPTER 28

I t took weeks of vigilant surveillance for Dimitri
Byelov to work out how to penetrate the security
system around the stately building's grounds. It took
only a few discreet undercover visits from his men to
confirm that the security inside the building was slack.
This really *was* like the gentlemen's club it purported
to be; staffed with only receptionists and waiters, their
defences were almost non-existent. The raid was bound
to be successful.

At last he was inside the grounds. Dressed in black
and out of sight of the cameras, he lay low near the
edge of the shrubbery and trained his night-vision field
glasses on the entrance lobby. He watched the brothel's
punters rolling in, knowing that his own men were
already in place – bona fide clients as far as the gullible
bastards running this place were concerned but ready to
act when he gave the signal. He felt his heart pumping
the adrenalin and smiled at the thought of what must
be going on in there right now. They could have their
fun before the real action, but they had to behave

themselves up to that point. *Whatever you do, don't stand out*, he'd told them, *don't raise any alarms*. Once unleashed, his team would have free rein to create such mayhem that Rodin's clients would be unwilling to use this establishment for a long time. Byelov could already taste the sweetness of revenge for the damage that had been done to his business, and his hatred for a man he'd never met steeled his resolve.

The steady build-up of custom was pleasing – the more the merrier, he thought. This was going to be shock and awe and *what* a shock for those sad bastards. *Tell your friends about this*, he said to himself as he decided that now was the time.

Leon was struggling to contain his enthusiasm as he started his weekly briefing.

'I've got something I want you to look at. You're not going to believe it,' he said, sitting next to Pavel. 'Just watch this – it happened only two days ago at around midnight, at one of Rodin's exclusive brothels.' He dimmed the lights and shook Pavel by the shoulder. *He's going to like this.*

'Video-snap on!'

Leon and Pavel watched the scene play out before their eyes.

In the front grounds of a Highgate dwelling, a small slender girl in a red kimono sits cross-legged on the gravel driveway, her head bowed in meditation, her hands together in prayer; a huge floodlight at her back illuminates the mansion's frontal façade.

A naked man emerges from the house, shielding his eyes from the light. He is flanked by two women wearing sunglasses; they pull him struggling and writhing towards the girl in red, stop a metre short of her and let go of the man's arms. His eyes squinting almost shut, he makes no further attempt to escape while the tiny girl effortlessly eases herself to her feet. For a moment, everyone is still. In a flashing red blur, the girl strikes like a cobra at his groin. He doubles up under the impact from her heel, crumples to the ground and curls into a ball – his mouth gawping like a landed fish. The two women unravel him, drag him by the armpits to a black van at the gate of the drive and throw him like a carcass through the open rear door.

A second naked man, held between two women, is marched calmly down the drive. When they reach the girl, the man makes a sudden attempt to slip the clutches of his escorts but the women manage to hold on to him and lock him firmly upright. The floodlight dims. The girl in red stares trance-like at his groin and he braces himself as if he knows what's coming. This time the girl's fist slams into the man's nose, splattering it over his face and spraying his blood across the white gravel. A strike from her foot follows within a second; the loose bottom half of his fractured shin twists through ninety degrees and his leg gives way. He vomits spasmodically over his chest as the women pick him off the ground and passes out as they haul him to the van.

The carnage continues with three further victims dragged to their brutal fate in front of the blazing floodlight – each of them naked, looking confused and ending up in the makeshift meat-wagon.

Another man, constrained like the others by two women, appears at the entrance of the house. Unlike the others, he is dressed – entirely in black. Black trainers, black jogging suit, black gloves, black balaclava, he walks dejectedly between his two escorts until they reach the girl in the red kimono.

A man in a white jacket emerges from behind the floodlight and stands next to the fighter. He places his arm around the girl's shoulder and whispers into her ear. Arms flared to her sides, she bows to him politely and steps back into the shadows.

The floodlight dims. The man in white pulls the balaclava from the man in black's head, slaps him hard across the face then speaks to him for a few seconds. He slaps him again, then points towards a black limousine with tinted windows and a uniformed chauffeur waiting at its open rear door. The man in black shuffles across to the limousine, stops and turns. He shakes his head in resignation, then gets into the back seat of the car.

'And what do you expect me to say about that?' Pavel asked at the end of the video sequence.

'Well, first of all, I thought you'd be pleased with the quality of that video. It took me two days to combine and edit those satellite and ground-level data files. You have to admit, you could virtually read their thoughts.'

'Yes, yes.' Pavel was clearly becoming irritable. 'Just make your point.'

'We were lucky to pick up that incident. It just happened to coincide with the instructions I'd given your centre for setting the satellite coordinates that evening.

There are two key players in that little scene, conveniently for us, wearing black and white to distinguish them.'

'OK, spare me the witticisms, Mahler.'

'I used my pattern recognition software to correlate the 3-D reconstruction you've just watched with other comings and goings from the establishments that we think are being run by Rodin. The man in black doesn't appear at all within our data. On the other, hand, the man in white is popping up all over the place.'

'What! Then, why haven't we picked him out before now?' Pavel looked like he was about to explode.

Leon felt calm and in full control by now. 'It's because this guy turns out to be an anomaly within Schumann's anomalies. We've recorded him coming out of several of the Highgate brothels, but we've never seen him going in. He's effectively slipped through the coincidence filters in our software algorithms'

'Keep going, I'm getting interested.'

'I've looked for him manually among Schumann's ground-level stills and here he is.' Leon revealed a montage of photographs showing a tall, thin man with blond wavy hair flopping in front of his eyes.

'You're not trying to suggest this is Rodin, are you? Look at him – he looks so effeminate. You've read our psychological profile.'

Leon continued, unfazed. 'Next, I turned to the data I procured from Fusion's security records. 'Sequence forty-eight.'

'Sequence forty-eight, Mahler,' said the Melomet.

'What did I tell you?' said Pavel, sounding exasperated as he watched the video recording of the comings and goings in the Fusion entrance hall. 'Just look at him, mincing along like a pansy. Surely you can't think he's the vicious brute we're looking for?'

Once again, Leon carried on as if Pavel wasn't there. 'I've developed my own mathematical correlation programme to evaluate the likelihood of this character matching the profile of Rodin that you supplied. I constructed an adaptive learning network using parameterised data from the images of every anomalous visitor and by comparing—'

'Just hold it there, Mahler. You're losing me now.'

'Sorry, I got carried away. In simple language, what I'm saying is this. From the look in these punters' eyes and from the way they move around, you can deduce a lot about their characters. My programme digitises the images of their faces. Then it analyses their facial expressions and their movements. I've compared the results for this guy with those I've run for all the other anomalies. It turns out he has a sixty-three per cent probability of matching Rodin's profile. The nearest candidate from the rest of the group comes out at eight per cent.'

'You may be out of my league when it comes to statistical analysis,' Pavel conceded, 'but my cop's instinct tells me you're wrong.'

'There's more to come,' Leon said, smiling. 'The presentation isn't over yet.'

Pavel sat back and sighed. 'OK, go ahead and convince me.'

Leon called up an annotated plan view of the individual brothels in the Highgate area.

'It looks like a wagon wheel,' said Pavel.

'That's because it is. Taking account of our latest personnel movement data, I can now confirm that Goldhurst's situation at the group's geographical centre is not just a fluke. My predictive model shows that each of these buildings is connected directly to Goldhurst and there's no cross linking between them. Everything emanates from Goldhurst. The man who oversaw that human destruction we've just watched has been observed entering Goldhurst on twenty occasions. He's been recorded leaving Goldhurst four times and one of the other Highgate brothels on a total of thirteen occasions. It looks like we've missed at least three of his exits.'

Pavel was sitting upright, slack-jawed.

'The analysis shows that there has to be something big going on in Fusion's headquarters.' He called up a final still photograph that spanned the video-wall from floor to ceiling, the portrait of an intelligent looking forty-year-old man with a feminine complexion and focused ice-blue eyes. 'And, yes. He's our man, all right.'

CHAPTER 29

He could tell that Pavel was dejected the moment he spotted him walking into the opera house refectory. The call earlier that morning, requesting an urgent meeting, was a surprise to Leon. It sounded like bad news so soon after his discovery of Rodin's identity, and the first sight of Pavel left him in no doubt.

'Why are we meeting here?' Pavel asked as he sat down stony faced with his coffee. 'These tickets cost a fortune and I don't even like opera.'

'I told you, I'm getting a bit paranoid these days. Always looking over my shoulder. Besides, it's good to move about. Safety in numbers, mingle with the crowd, just *Classico*s enjoying a night at the opera. Anyway, what news? Have you apprehended him?'

'It's not that easy, Mahler. We can't just go about arresting Russian diplomats. Even politically agnostic people like you must know what that could trigger.'

Leon sat up, rigid with surprise. 'What are you talking about?' He could see that Pavel was angry as well as grumpy.

'Our surveillance teams have been watching out for him over the past week at the exits you specified. We eventually spotted him leaving a Hampstead Lane brothel and followed him across the Heath to Hampstead tube station. He minces along at one hell of a pace, I can tell you – it took all our expertise to stay close to him without being spotted. We managed to get a man into the same train carriage and he followed him as far as Notting Hill Gate where Rodin got off the train. From there, our agent tracked him to Kensington Palace Gardens where he disappeared into Number Thirteen – the Russian Embassy. It was two days before he came out again.'

Leon raised his eyebrows. 'You mean—'

'Yes, I *do* mean – he actually *is* a Russian diplomat.'

'But how can that be? What's he doing getting himself involved in the sex trade?'

'You tell me, clever man. We puzzled over that ourselves. We've done our research, of course. We've discovered that Captain Alexei Rodin is their Defence and Naval Attaché. If you think about it, the Russian embassies were always overstaffed in the days of the Cold War. And their UK embassy is overstaffed again today. God knows what they're up to now and who's sanctioning their activities.'

Pavel's depressive mood was starting to rub off on Leon. 'What do we do next? He's holding Magda somewhere within this string of brothels, I'm sure of that. And I'm going to get her out.'

'But you have to be patient. Don't expect me to burst in there with my men and walk out with her. You know

I can't do that. There's a whole new line of intelligence to be gathered and we just have to get on with it. I'll let you know what I want from you once we've completed our initial analysis.' Pavel got up and without a shred of courtesy left the opera house.

Leon didn't stay to watch Puccini's *Madame Butterfly*, even though he had a ticket for one of the best seats in the house. By the time he completed the long journey home on the Metro and trudged up the stairs to his apartment it was nine o'clock. He slammed the lounge door behind him, summoned the video file containing the violent scenes outside the brothel then sat down with a stiff vodka to watch it all again. *If Pavel isn't going to apprehend Rodin, I'm free to do my own researches.* With no particular strategy or objective in mind, he fast-forwarded to the point where Rodin faced the final adversary in the punishment line. He studied the 3-D images of the man in black. *I wonder who he is and what they're going to do with him.* He hovered the cursor over the aerial view of the victim and called up the pattern recognition software. *Let's see if we can find him elsewhere in the data.* As he waited for the correlation programme to complete its analysis, he picked up his wafer.

'Schumann, I need you over here ASAP.'

Schumann arrived within thirty minutes, impressing on Leon just how passionate these people were about rescuing their compatriots and bringing to justice those responsible for their abduction. *God knows how much money they've thrown at this to date.* But all the money in the world was no compensation for his own loss.

Leon showed Schumann the video sequence of the retribution, as he'd come to call it, and together they scanned the satellite data files for overhead images of the final victim, the man last seen getting into a car.

'He comes and goes from this place,' Leon said, pointing to the wall-map. 'It's not one of our target brothels, but we've picked up data from that location due to its proximity to a couple of Rodin's brothels. In fact, I've visited that one personally.' Leon recalled the evening with clarity – the scatty woman who ran the place, her delusion about her mother when she was shown the photograph. But he said nothing of this to Schumann. 'Did you ever stake it out, Schumann?'

'Let me take a look.' Schumann scanned Leon's copy of his own data. 'Here it is. This file should contain ground-level photographs.' Leon ran the pattern recognition software once again.

'This is him,' Schumann said, as he compiled a montage of photos on the video-wall. 'I recognise him from my own surveillance operations.' He spent five minutes perusing his personal notes among his word files. 'I have it,' he said, showing his delight. 'His name is Dimitri Byelov. He's the director of the brothel you've identified. There must have been some adverse interaction between him and Rodin.'

'You can say that again. But there's something about this that's niggling me. I get the gut feeling that Magda is an ingredient in this inter-brothel conflict. Scientist's intuition, you might say. I think I'll pay Byelov's brothel a visit. Right now, in fact. Let's hope they're still open.'

It was almost midnight by the time Leon arrived at the brothel. The security guard opened the glass entrance door. 'Good evening, sir,' he said in a strong Russian accent. Leon's first impression was that the brothel's security was much less in evidence than on his previous visit, but that made sense. And the brothel's madame was still here, working alone front of house. *Excellent*.

'Yes, sir, how can I help you?'

'It's Mary, isn't it?'

'Yes?' she said with a puzzled expression. 'Do I know you?'

'Mary, I want you to stay calm and listen to me. I'm not here to cause any trouble. We can talk in front of your security guard if you like.' He looked across at the guard who was watching him. 'You don't recognise me, do you? I'm Leon. I was making enquiries about my missing girlfriend when I was last here.'

She gasped. 'I've been looking for you. The photograph. My mother—'

'Shush! We can come to that,' he whispered, 'but first I need to ask you a few of *my* questions. Trust me, Mary. I promise we can discuss your mother once I'm through.'

'OK, but you look so different. We don't get many *Classico*s using this place – they consider themselves better than us, you see. Your up-their-arse colleagues use the more sophisticated houses in Highgate, they do.'

Ignoring her comments, Leon took a deep breath and said, 'Her name is Magda. I have a photograph of her, by herself this time. Take a look.'

'I haven't seen her,' she said, 'but I know someone who might have done.'

Leon's heart was racing. 'Who is it? Who saw her?'

'Wait a minute, I'll be back.'

Mary disappeared down the corridor. The guard's eyes were clamped on him as if he were his prisoner. Leon sat on the couch at the side of the reception desk and nervously tapped his fingers on the arm. To his relief, Mary returned three minutes later.

'This is Gina,' Mary said, introducing a frail little girl.

'Pleased to meet you, sir.' Gina curtseyed and offered her hand.

Leon stood up and shook her hand; her fingers were so tiny that he felt he was meeting a ten-year-old schoolgirl.

'You want to know about Ana?'

'Ana? What are you talking about?' he said, raising his voice. The security guard took a step forward but Mary waved him back.

'Can I see your photo please, sir?' Gina took hold of the wafer-pad. 'Yes, that's Ana, though her hair was shorter. She was so beautiful. She—'

Leon could contain himself no longer. 'You're absolutely sure, are you? This is someone you met and you knew her as Ana? Where did you meet her?'

'In the Fantasyworld.'

'The what? Sit down next to me, Gina. Tell me everything you can remember.'

It took fifteen minutes for Gina to recount her story. It was a garbled and excitable account and Leon only interrupted to stop her from falling over her own words.

'You're saying you didn't actually meet her in the flesh, but you're convinced she was down there at the same time as you and that they were going to make her your team leader?'

'Yes, that's right, sir. The Fantasyworld was my home for months, but I don't know where in London it is.'

'Thank you, Gina. You've been helpful.'

'Can I go now, Mary?'

'You can, my petal. I'm sure the gentleman is pleased with you.' She nodded at Leon with raised eyebrows.

'Thank you, Gina. You've been really helpful.' Gina gave him a clumsy curtsey and skipped away down the corridor.

'Now it's my turn,' Mary said.

'Not quite. First I want to ask you about Byelov.'

Mary looked taken aback. 'You know where he is?'

'Sorry, no. I don't know where he is, Mary. But I'd like to know *who* he is? You told me, when we first met, that he owns this brothel. Is he sometimes known as Alexei Rodin?'

Mary laughed. 'No, he's not Rodin, I can guarantee you that. Byelov actually hates that bastard.'

It was a dummy question. Leon had to cover every possibility. And he also needed an excuse to broach the subject of Rodin. 'You know Alexei Rodin don't you, Mary?'

'I admit, I know of him. He owns the posh places up Highgate, so I'm told. Never met him myself. I've never even seen him. And from what they all say, I never want to. He's a stuck-up ponce, that's all he is. Do you have the photo of my mother?'

That's all I'm going to get out of her. Leon considered this business about Mary's mother to be nothing but nonsense. He'd come here with every intention of avoiding the issue second time round, but it was his bargaining point and he had no option but to placate her. At least he knew that Magda had ended up in London as Pavel had predicted and he'd closed out what to him was the only remaining uncertainty over Rodin's identity. He brought up the photo on his wafer-pad and handed it to Mary. She expanded the image until his mother's face filled the screen.

'Yes, that's definitely her, that's my mother,' she said with tears in her eyes. 'I wasn't sure before but I am now.'

'Mary, the woman you're looking at is *my* mother. I've lived with her for the whole of my life. Her name is Lynne Dabrowski.'

'You think a daughter wouldn't recognise her own mother, do you?'

'OK, Mary. Let's take a logical look at this. My mother *is* English, I'll grant you that. She emigrated to Poland while she was carrying me. I was born over there. Now tell me about *your* mother.' He leaned back into the couch and held out his palms, inviting her to convince him.

'My mother was Jean Douglas, the lady in your photo. Dad left us when I was about fourteen years old, I think. He was a right bastard, he was. Hardly ever there. And when he was, he'd beat the living shit out of me and my brother and Ma. It's him I blame for Robert turning to drugs and setting me up working the streets.'

'Robert's your brother?'

'He's dead now. We didn't really get on but he *was* my brother. What happened to Ma? Well that's a bit of a blur. I was on drugs at the time. It all goes with being on the game, you realise? It's the only way you could stomach all those old drunks who wanted a quick shag in the park. It wasn't my fault she disappeared. I promise you that. *I* didn't ask her to go. But it's all so fuzzy now.' She covered her mouth and nose with one hand, sniffing back the mucous and blinking away the tears that were welling in her eyes. 'What's he like, your father? Is he taking care of my mother?'

Her question came as a surprise, but she *was* rambling. 'Mary, we haven't established yet whether we're talking about the same person. But if it helps, yes. He *is* a good husband and a good father. In fact, my stepfather Szymon is a kind and decent man all round.'

'I'm glad to hear that,' she said, smiling through her wet eyes and sniffing again.

'Tell me what you remember about your mother's disappearance, Mary. Did you just wake up one day to find that she'd gone?'

'That's the problem, I can't remember. I was never clean or sober in those days. The whole of my teenage life is just one big blur with the drugs. It's all gone from my head so I never expected to find out what happened to her – until you came along, that is.'

'But you're clean now, aren't you? Have you ever thought of looking back over old newspaper records from around that time? They do exist.'

'It crossed my mind. But I didn't know where to start. I don't even remember the year all this happened. All I remember is Robert said she'd pissed off and left us. He said she didn't give a shit and we shouldn't worry

248

about her anymore. He reckoned she found another job somewhere. Anyway, someone was paying for the gas and electricity, so what did we care? I decided it would be a waste of time looking at old papers. Besides, she was a nobody. Just another missing person.'

I know where you're coming from. 'Mary, if there's nothing else, you're going to have to accept that the woman in the photo is someone who bears a striking resemblance to your mother. But we're not talking about the same person.'

'I don't accept that. I tell you she's my mother and I have the right to see her. You hear me?'

'Look, Mary, I won't stop you from going over to Poland and seeing *my* mother, if you felt that would provide the close-out you seek. You'd see for yourself she wasn't the person you're talking about.' He paused to collect himself. It was going to be difficult to break it to her. 'But even if you're convinced that the person in the photograph is your mother, it wouldn't do you any good to see her. It would be a waste of time and money. She has dementia and hardly recognises me – her own son. She's dying, Mary.'

At the end of their discussion, Leon felt sorry for Mary. She was so confused. Yet, deep down, she was a good woman who'd strayed from the straight and narrow through no fault of her own. As she recounted her tragic story, he'd seen in her eyes a genuine love for the mother she'd lost. But one thing played on his mind as he left the brothel. He'd also seen his own mother in those sad eyes, lying in her sickbed back in Poland, in the prison that was her mind. He justified not returning to Krakow to see her on the basis that it would be dangerous for all of them. Chekhov would be looking for him there as well as here in the capital. But he would have to return to Poland soon. Like Mary, his own mother was already lost to him. And like Mary, he had to see his mother one last time before she died.

CHAPTER 30

Rodin strapped on the safety belt, tapped the destination into the wafer and sat back. The monopod journey from Goldhurst would take around ten minutes. Ten minutes of relaxation; life was good.

The elevator in the pod reception area glided up three floors to the foyer of the pleasure house where the house manager was waiting. They ran a tight operation here and there was no reason why this weekly progress meeting should take longer than its usual twenty minutes. 'Good morning, Stephan. I presume everything is shipshape. No need to adjourn to your office, is there?'

As anticipated, the meeting was brief, leaving ample time to make the scheduled meeting at the embassy. With no reason to pay attention to the white van parked opposite the gate to the grounds, there was no time to react as two men charged across the road and smashed Rodin to the ground like a bowling pin.

'What the—'

'Shut up and get in the van,' one of them hissed.

'And don't struggle, unless you want to get hurt,' the other said.

They spoke in English but it was obvious they were Eastern European. Blindfolded and bound, the sound of sliding doors slamming shut, frantic instructions from the front of the van – the cold sweat of fear took its grip.

'If you're a good boy and do what we say, you'll come to no harm,' one of the men said as the van drove off.

Good boy? Did they know who they were insulting? They had no idea what serious trouble they were getting themselves into. Concern turned to anger.

'Do you realise who I am?'

The sharp slap to the side of the face felt like a sting from a jellyfish.

'I've told you – shut up!'

'Who are you? Why have you brought me here?'

'We've brought you here to help us with our enquiries. Who we are is of no concern to you.'

'Ah, so you're Russian? Then we can converse in our own language.'

'No, we'll continue in English.'

'Do you know who I am?'

'I do. You are the Russian diplomat Alexei Rodin, and that's the last of your questions I'm going to answer. *I* ask the questions from now.'

'Then you realise you're holding a member of our state's Diplomatic Corps against their will? I'll have you shot for that.'

'Holding you against your will, am I? I see no manacles. There are no guards. The door is open. You may leave as you wish. But if you leave, you have no idea where you are, you have no wafer to call a cab and no money to pay for public transport. The members of the press assembled outside will have a field day with their photographs of a Russian diplomat wandering these streets aimlessly. So, I suggest we continue with our discussion – in English. And you can go when you've agreed to help us.'

'What do you want from me?'

'That's better, I don't mind questions like that. And my first question to you is a simple one, Mr Rodin. We have photographic evidence of you entering and leaving the headquarters of the nuclear power company, Fusion Limited. What were you doing there?'

'None of your business,' Rodin spat out. 'I represent our state and it's a part of my job. Fusion is a Russian-owned company, based in the UK. Our embassy has important matters to discuss with their managers.'

'What you are saying is that you have regular political meetings inside Fusion's London headquarters and that the content of those meetings is sensitive state information?'

'Yes! So, if you could just step to the side.' Rodin got up from the chair.

Pavel patted the air with his hand and Rodin sat back down. 'That's interesting, because you don't appear on their visitor records and I know for a fact that Fusion can't override their own electronic security system. Where exactly do you hold these important meetings?'

'If you must know, I hold my one-to-one discussions in the entrance hall's seating area. Due to the nature of our business, it wouldn't do for MI5 or the like to find out about such meetings from Fusion's visitor records. Are you working for MI5?'

'Our video evidence shows that you're not telling us the truth, Mr Rodin, and I told you – no more questions.'

'Then I assume you represent Fusion's security? Well, you are wrong, Mr security officer. You can't have been doing your job if you haven't observed those meetings.'

Pavel looked up towards the hidden camera and offered the faintest of head shakes.

In the remote viewing suite that the *Policja* had installed in Leon's apartment, Leon recognised from their body language that Pavel had discovered the first chink in the armour. Rodin was bluffing and Pavel knew it. *This crafty old cop has done this before.*

'I think that will be all for the moment, Mr Rodin. I'll have some tea sent up. You see, we're not holding you against your wishes. You're our guest and I'll continue our discussion in ten minutes. I'm sure you won't object if I bring my lie detection equipment back with me.' Before Rodin could protest, Pavel left the room and locked the door behind him.

Pavel returned to the interview room thirty minutes later. The tea hadn't been touched. 'I do hope you enjoyed your tea, Mr Rodin. A fine Russian blend, don't you think?'

'I've had enough of your stupid games. I insist you respect my rights. I have full diplomatic immunity in this country and you're going to have to let me go – right now.'

From the camera view, it became clear that Rodin was clenching a fist and slowly rising from his seated position. Leon stood up involuntarily and leaned against the video-wall with both hands. *My God, he's going to go for him and Pavel hasn't spotted it.*

'Well, if you're going to be like that, I think the rules will have to change,' Pavel said. Leon could see that Pavel was tapping at the wafer behind his back.

'Fuck your diplomatic immunity!'

Before Rodin could make the intended lunge, three of Pavel's *Policja* burst into the room.

'Strap his hands and feet to the chair,' Pavel shouted, 'and wire his head and chest to the lie detector.'

Leon flopped back down in his chair; a wave of relief passed through his skull.

'And who are these goons?' Rodin shouted across to Pavel. 'Untie me at once. I'm a senior attaché to—'

One of the purported goons provided a sturdy slap across the temple.

'I think you should answer our questions, Mr Rodin,' Pavel said, looking towards the door. Two of his three men left the room. Schumann stayed.

Leon watched in horror as the scene played out on the video-wall in front of him. There wasn't supposed to be any form of torture. But the blow to the head he'd just observed confirmed his worst fears. They were moving into heavy mode and he was powerless to stop them. After all, it was *their* operation, not his. Accepting that he was going to have to sit and watch them exert their so-termed justifiable coercion, he turned his attention to the lie detector traces that were reproduced on his monitor.

Pavel continued. 'In addition to your job at the Russian Embassy, you're the director of a string of brothels. Am I correct?'

Rodin offered no response and received a slap from Schumann above the left ear. It seemed to stun him but left no incriminating tell-tale marks.

'You can have as many of those as you like,' Pavel said. 'We have all day. Now, let me ask you once more. Are you operating a string of brothels across the Highgate area?'

'I don't know what you are talking about.'

That was a lie, Leon decided as he interpreted the responses from the transducers. And it should have been crystal clear to Pavel.

'You've been recorded leaving several of these brothels.'

Rodin hesitated – until Schumann raised his hand once again. 'Wait. I'll tell you. Yes, you'll no doubt have evidence of me using a number of brothels, but I'm not ashamed. They're simply gentlemen's clubs. I'm doing no harm.'

'And you don't think your embassy would be concerned over this?' Pavel rubbed his chin in an exaggerated manner. 'I suppose they wouldn't, would they? In fact, you've been operating under their instruction. Is that true?'

'Yes, that's true. I'm doing a job. But I can't say anything more. As a fellow countryman, you have to understand and respect that.'

Can't tell about that one, Leon said to himself as he studied the traces on his monitor.

Pavel continued. 'Why did they send you? After all, it must have been difficult for you to carry out this *job* of yours, being homosexual.'

'That's not true. I'm heterosexual.'

That was the truth.

'Let me see. You must have been trying to get information out of the clients who were using these establishments. But do you expect me to believe that you were just meandering about several different brothels, getting the girls to entice this sensitive information from their clients? How did you know which girls to select as your spies? How could you guarantee that the clients you were interested in would select them? Was it a particular group that formed the subject of your espionage? In short, Mr Rodin, I don't believe you. Then there's the question of your movements between the various brothels. You were never seen entering, only ever leaving. How do you explain that?'

'That must be down to the incompetence of your own people.'

'Oh, come on! You have to give us more credit than that. And what about the many occasions we've recorded you entering Fusion's headquarters, only to emerge some time later from one of the brothels? There are links between the Goldhurst building and the brothels. Admit it.'

Leon could see from the traces that Rodin was nervous. He'd been rumbled. *Go on, finish it.*

'Let me summarise the position. You're running a series of interlinked brothels stocked with Eastern European girls who've been abducted from their countries by sex traffickers. Am I correct?'

'I don't know what you're talking about.'

'But these magic little waveforms tell me otherwise,' Pavel said, pointing to the lie detector. 'Hit him, harder this time.'

'Wait! I'll tell. Yes, the brothels are connected and yes, Goldhurst is at the centre of the estate. But it's just a convenient and discreet way for clients to move around. I use this facility myself.'

'Yes, you would. And as you're so familiar with it all, you'd know who was operating this sordid little empire. It's you, yourself, Mr Rodin. Is that not true?'

'I'm not the manager.'

Schumann must have seen the traces jump. Without any instruction from Pavel, he delivered a blow to the head so hard that Rodin almost passed out. Pavel grabbed Rodin by the hair, picked up the glass of water that was set down next to the lie detector and threw it in Rodin's face. 'If *you* are not the manager, surely you must know who is? I'll ask you once again.'

Schumann raised his hand high, ready to strike again if the lie detector traces told him it was necessary.

'Who is running these brothels?'

'It's me. I admit it. Don't hit me again,' Rodin begged. 'I'm the operator. But I don't know anything about sex trafficking. I don't own these establishments. It's Vladimir Chekhov you need to deal with.'

'He broke down much easier than I imagined,' Pavel said to Leon. 'I can see our psychological profiling was somewhat in error. He's strong when he has his own security at his back but he's as weak as a kitten without

258

them. My God, my granddaughter could have taken more than that. You've done well in your analysis. I must remember not to challenge your judgement next time.'

'But why didn't you push further on Magda? You had Rodin on the rack and you let him go.'

'Sorry, Mahler. It was a judgement I had to make on the spot. Anyway, we're dealing with Chekhov now. He's the *Mr Big* in all of this.'

'I'm not convinced about Chekhov,' Leon said, shaking his head, 'and it's not the lie detector traces. Rodin has just implied that Vladimir Chekhov provides a gateway to a string of brothels from Fusion's London headquarters. Why would he want to do that? He's taking an enormous risk with the future of commercial nuclear power. And I'm no closer to finding Magda.' The tears were welling in his eyes but he had to rid himself of emotion and work out the best way forward. 'You have to agree, there's something not right about what Rodin has told us.'

'I see your point, Mahler, but we're left with only one option. We can't go to the Russian Embassy. We'd risk setting off a serious diplomatic row between our countries. And if the British Government were to get involved – well, it doesn't bear thinking about. We have to arrange a meeting with Chekhov.'

'Are you just going to let Rodin go free? I think Chekhov has been used as a tactical weapon, if you ask me. Rodin wanted to avoid a thrashing and reckoned you'd balk at the prospect of having to face someone of Chekhov's power and influence. It was a gamble and it worked. You've been spooked.'

'Rodin will go back and lick his wounds and I think he'll have more sense than to report this to his ambassador. I feel sure from our interrogation they don't know what he's been getting up to. I agree with you, analysis of the traces was inconclusive. It does cast doubt on Chekhov's role in all this. However, Rodin is clever. And if he *is* telling the truth about Chekhov, the last thing he's going to do is go back crying to him. It's Chekhov or nothing. As for Rodin, I'll have to let him go.'

Where was this uneasy feeling coming from? The door to Leon's apartment closed behind Pavel and Leon returned to the monitoring console. Why had some of the lie detector responses surprised him? He needed to look again at the video records of Rodin's interrogation. He adjusted the phase information from the many cameras in the interview room until he had a near-perfect image – a replay in real time. He walked around the hologram. There was a determined look about Pavel but he was sure it contained no sadism. On the other hand, he could see that Schumann relished this line of work. Schumann's passion was so real that Leon found himself ducking several times to avoid the three-dimensional images of his savage blows to Rodin's head. He observed the intelligence in Rodin's eyes and watched his determination turn to fear as the interrogators carried out their threats. What was it about Rodin that belied their psychological profiling? He walked around the chair and studied Rodin's handsome carved features, his flaxy hair, his elegant neck ... He stopped in front of the life-size image of Alexei Rodin and stared into the effeminate face.

I wonder what Pavel will say when he realises what he's done?

CHAPTER 31

The video conference with Chekhov was set to take place in Schumann's apartment, three weeks after Rodin's interrogation. Pavel didn't seem keen on telling Leon how he'd managed to persuade Chekhov to attend such a meeting, but whatever he said to him in his preliminary video call must have been convincing. Schumann and three of his team were stationed outside the door, ready to resist anything that Chekhov threw at them in the event of him discovering their location, and there was a small army of undercover *Policja* agents in the vicinity.

'Ready for this?' Pavel asked Leon. 'Remember, we have to stay away from the subject of Magda until we know where we stand.'

'I'll stay quiet unless I'm asked to contribute.' They'd been working on this operation for almost seven months and Pavel wasn't about let it slip away as the result of a wild emotional outburst from him.

'Call for you, Pavel,' said the Melomet, 'from Mr Chekhov.' Leon pulled his balaclava down over his face.

The imposing figure of Vladimir Chekhov appeared on the video-wall. His face was lit by a white light from below, making him look like a ghost, and in the background grey shadows drifted across a dark blue surface. *He's projecting these moving shapes to divert our focus?*

Chekhov leaned forward. 'What is this nonsense? Who is that in the balaclava?'

'First of all, thank you for agreeing to this meeting, Mr Chekhov. As you are aware, I represent the Polish police. The department I run deals with sex trafficking crimes. My colleague is Leon Dabrowski, your chief scientist at Fusion, who is assisting me.'

The first signs of confusion swept across Chekhov's floodlit face. 'If he *is* Dabrowski, why the obscuration? How am I expected to know I'm talking to the right person?'

Pavel smiled. 'This is so you can't see what he looks like nowadays. I don't wish to assist your security staff in tracking him down. You no doubt have a voice analyser activated at your end. Once Dr Dabrowski enters the discussion, you'll be able to confirm for yourself.'

Chekhov grunted. 'Pavel, I agreed to this meeting for one reason only. I wish to know why my chief scientist has absconded. You mention he is assisting you. Does that mean the Polish police are paying him to carry out some sort of criminal investigation? Are you wasting his prodigious talent on some futile line of detective work? If that is the case, I will have your career terminated.'

'Mr Chekhov, you seem to underestimate the extent and gravity of these matters. I'll therefore come straight to the point. There are hundreds of Polish nationals who are, as we speak, being coerced into a life of prostitution in the UK. I have reason to believe that you are at the head of this heinous operation and I am going to have it stopped. In your own words, if you are responsible for this, *I* am going to have *your* career terminated.'

Chekhov remained calm in the face of Pavel's blunt accusations. 'And why Dabrowski? Have you had him spying on me from within the position of trust I gave him? What use is he to you now that he no longer comes into my head office each day? That doesn't seem to have worked so well, does it?'

Leon was about to answer but Pavel placed a hand over his forearm.

'It's like this, Mr Chekhov. Dr Dabrowski has a vested interest in that your trafficking gangs seem to have swept up his fiancée, Professor Magda Tomala, into your prostitution empire. I don't think that was such a clever move from an astute businessman.'

Leon was on the edge of his seat. *He's thinking about it?*

'Mr Pavel, I am not denying that I oversee an exclusive adult entertainments business in the UK. If you've done your homework, you will have already ascertained that my directors run a legitimate business which is open to scrutiny by the police, tax inspectorate and any other authority that wishes to investigate our affairs.'

He's definitely the boss. It's not Rodin.

'However,' Chekhov continued, 'I am not interested in listening to this rubbish about sex trafficking and coercion that you accuse me of. Now it's my turn to come to the point. Dabrowski, are you collaborating with the Americans on the design of a nuclear fusion reactor?'

This was bizarre. They were holding a debate at cross purposes. Pavel was only interested in putting a stop to the sex trafficking of his Polish nationals. Chekhov wanted to know if his chief scientist had defected. *And all I want to do is get my darling Magda back.*

'You're wrong,' Leon said. 'I have no interest in the American fusion programme. I absconded for one reason only – I want to be reunited with my girlfriend. We were going to get married before this happened.'

'Ah, Dabrowski. It *is* you, after all. How are you keeping?' Chekhov asked in a sarcastic tone. 'If your girlfriend has gone missing, why did you not ask for help? As you know, I do possess a considerable resource.'

Would Chekhov have really been willing to help him at the time of Magda's disappearance? Or was he the one holding Magda prisoner? Pavel came to his assistance.

'Gentlemen, we appear to have three separate agenda items. Can I suggest we pursue each of these issues in turn? We are all intelligent men around this table and I'm sure we can debate these matters with respect for one another.'

To Leon's surprise, Chekhov decided to go for it. Lips pursed, he nodded. 'I agree. We meet again tomorrow morning at ten. Chekhov out.' The video-wall went blank.

The two men sat in stunned silence. Leon studied Pavel. *He knows I'm not happy.* He could no longer contain himself. 'An interesting meeting.'

Pavel was wringing his hands nervously.

'You're holding back on me, Pavel. You've suspected all along that Chekhov was behind this.'

'Yes,' Pavel replied, lowering his head.

'Why didn't you tell me?'

Pavel looked up with worried eyes. 'I've thought long and hard about it. I decided the best thing for us all was that you didn't know the background. But I'll tell you now – everything I know.' He took a deep breath and gave a long sigh. 'The world sees Vladimir Chekhov as nothing but a ruthless oligarch. But Chekhov is in fact a brilliant man when it comes to commerce and the empire he's building could lead to his supremacy in the world of legitimate business. I don't have to tell *you*, Leon, if Chekhov is successful in retaining the sole rights to commercial nuclear fusion, he would become omnipotent. But none of that interests me. All I care about is the liberation of my fellow citizens. You see, Chekhov recognised the potential in the sex industry many years ago, following the death of his father. He realised that if he could give prostitution an air of respectability, the law enforcers would become tolerant – especially if he paid them off. There have always been high-class call girls to satisfy the needs of so-called respectable clients. But Chekhov has now provided these people with sophisticated brothels on an unprecedented scale. And in doing that he's collared the market.'

'Why did you drag me into this?'

'It's because Chekhov has managed to place an invisible ring of steel around his sex industry, a clandestine protection we need to break down. We needed your brilliant mind to think of a way in. And, in you, we also have bargaining power. We've taken something from Chekhov that he needs back.'

That final statement lit the fuse. Leon exploded. 'You've been using me? That's why you didn't finish the job when Rodin was down. All this time, I've just been a pawn in your game.'

'It's not a game. But if you're going to liken it to chess, I confess you were an essential piece of our strategy. But not a pawn. In terms of chess pieces, you are a queen – the most powerful piece on the board.'

'And what about Magda? Have you had anything to do with her abduction? She was the incentive you provided to ensure my cooperation, wasn't she?'

'No! I swear on my life I had nothing to do with that. Her abduction was the catalyst for our approach to you. Prior to that I was devoid of any sort of plan. You were a godsend to us, a discovered check, you might say. And now we're on the verge of achieving our goals, both of us. We can get them all out of there, Leon – Magda included.'

Leon felt his heart drop to the floor. But he had to stay calm. Once again, he'd have to let Pavel take the lead in their forthcoming meeting and give him whatever support he needed. So, they were to go for Chekhov's jugular. *Never mind chess, we've just set up the world's most momentous poker game.*

The following day, Leon was poised for the showdown of his life. Chekhov opened the proceedings from Monte Carlo. 'I will answer your questions with honesty,' he said, 'but when it comes to my own queries, you must return that respect.'

In London, Pavel scanned his list of prompts on the wafer-board he'd hidden below the table's surface. 'My first question is this – does your adult entertainments business comprise a string of brothels in the Highgate area of London?'

'I prefer to call them pleasure houses,' Chekhov replied. 'They are high-class gentlemen's clubs with additional services. Nobody objects to them as far as I'm aware.'

'Thank you, Mr Chekhov. That's consistent with the testimony we obtained from your estate manager, Alexei Rodin.'

'I don't know any Rodin. My estate manager is Oleg Malkin, formerly my father's bookkeeper. He appoints his own managers.'

'Who is responsible for staffing these establishments?' Pavel asked.

'As I've already indicated, I am not involved in detailed staffing and recruitment issues. I pay my managers to do that. Come to the point, Pavel. What is it you are trying to say?'

'Are you denying knowledge of your own recruitment policy? You abduct and imprison young women. They are being forced into prostitution against their will.'

Leon studied Chekhov's reaction. The image on the screen was becoming softer, the lighting was no longer harsh. For a moment he was sure he saw a huge shark glide past in the background. He shook his head to clear his mind.

'I've told you,' Chekhov responded, 'I don't get involved in the day-to-day running of this business. Besides, Malkin assures me that the girls are content with their living conditions and happy in their work. Now, can we move on?'

Leon could see that Pavel was frustrated. *He's not getting anywhere with this.*

'One final question,' said Pavel wearily. 'Are you aware of the number and disposition of brothels in your estate?'

'Pleasure houses,' Chekhov corrected him once again. 'Of course I am. I have to have an awareness of all my businesses to that extent. But I say again, I don't have time for day-to-day details. Are we finished?'

'Not quite.' Pavel paused.

He'd make a good barrister, Leon thought.

'You *are* aware of the flagship brothel that resides under your Fusion HQ?'

That was unexpected. And he could see Chekhov was puzzled. Leon eased himself upright in his chair. *Go on, push him.*

'I think you are wrong about that, Pavel. There could be no such facility. You can confirm that, Dabrowski?'

Pavel's line of questioning made Leon think about the results from his modelling. Goldhurst was without a doubt at the geographical centre of Rodin's estate. But he'd never seriously considered the prospect of a brothel within Fusion's headquarters. 'I expect you're right. But sometimes you have to look beyond the logic. There's no physical reason why you couldn't install a pleasure house, as you call it, under Goldhurst. But why would you ever want to do that?'

'There you are, Pavel. I would never do such a thing.'

Pavel came back in. 'But there *is* something going on under there. We have evidence to show that the rest of your establishments are linked to that building.'

The meeting was taking them nowhere – and at a painfully slow pace. Fired up with frustration, Leon ploughed in like a raging bull.

'Are you willing to take us under Goldhurst? I for one would love to see it.' He thought back to the time he watched the Arab delegation disappearing into thin air. There must be some way of getting into the basement.

'Don't be ridiculous. You more than anyone should appreciate that I can't have casual visitors wandering around my company HQ. And with respect, Dabrowski, that is what you are. You are suspended on account of your own actions and you no longer have freedom of movement within Fusion. As for the Polish police, Pavel, you will get a search warrant over my dead body.'

Pavel had an expression of defeat across his face. Leon cursed himself – he'd just given Chekhov the upper hand. Chekhov was perfectly entitled to stop them going into a classified area in a company that he owned. There was little point in raising the subject of Magda now.

As if this dead end to their enquiries wasn't enough, Chekhov reminded them of his next agenda item. 'We are yet to talk about my security issue. Dr Dabrowski, can you please tell me why you went absent without leave from Fusion Limited?'

'I've already told you, I needed to take time out to look for my girlfriend, Professor Magda Tomala. The Polish police showed no interest when she went missing

– until my colleague here offered to help in return for my assistance with his investigations. I did nothing wrong. Any man among us would sacrifice his career to find a lost loved one.'

Chekhov's head drooped; the movement was barely discernible but Leon knew he'd struck a raw nerve.

'Mr Chekhov, will you please help me to find Magda? I love her and I want her back. I'll give you anything I have within my power if you can find her for me.' Leon was sure he could see a tear running down Chekhov's cheek. It must have been a trick of the light. He spotted a movement in the background. *My God, that really was a shark*. The stress was getting to him now. In desperation he'd played all his cards in one go. *Why should he help me? I'm a fugitive on the run – from him.*

Chekhov rubbed his face and his composure returned. 'I will try to help. I'll make some enquiries of my own but from what you've told me, I wouldn't raise your hopes. Now, I have a request to put to you.' He continued in dismissive fashion. 'Dabrowski, I want you to come and see me in Monte Carlo. Are you willing to meet face to face on my yacht?'

Pavel covered the side of his face with his hand and offered Leon the slightest shake of his head. *No*, he was saying, *don't do it*.

'No.'

'What is your concern? Don't you trust me?'

Leon sympathised with Chekhov. Without him, Chekhov would struggle to maintain the pace in Fusion's programme and stay ahead of the Americans. If he returned to his job, he could even get to the bottom of this data theft

271

and put a stop to it. The security of this planet's future energy supplies was in his hands. But so was Magda's safety. He looked down at the table and gave a slow and wide shake of the head. Pavel confirmed Leon's response with a single discreet nod of agreement and a half smile.

'If that is your position, I can make no further contribution to this meeting. Good day, gentlemen. Chekhov out.'

'You know you were out of order there, Leon?' Pavel said, pacing the room after the video-wall went blank.

Leon said nothing. There was little point in arguing among themselves.

Pavel opened the door and invited Schumann to join them. 'I think you can stand your men down, Schumann.' He brought his officer up to date with the outcome of their meeting. 'That's where we are, I'm afraid. But we're not going to give up. We have to regroup and redouble our efforts. I'm not going to give in to a man like that. He thinks he—'

The Melomet cut in, 'Call for you, Pavel, from Mr Chekhov.'

The three men stared at each other in surprise. The video-wall came back to life. Pavel was the first to express his astonishment. 'What the devil—?'

The three men gawped at the huge tiger sharks swimming around behind Chekhov. 'Where the hell is he?' Schumann blurted out.

Chekhov's face was a picture of despair. Leon could tell he hadn't called to gloat or to challenge him further on his commercial espionage problem.

'Gentlemen,' Chekhov said in a downcast voice, 'I do apologise for the intrusion on your debriefing, but I've just been given some information which you, Dabrowski, should be made aware of.'

The goose-pimples sprang to life on Leon's neck.

'I've just received some sad news.'

Please God, not Magda.

'I've been informed of the demise of Dr Pawel Kaminsky. He has been murdered.'

Leon's first reaction was to suppress his relief. Then the shock took hold. 'Kaminsky was an unassuming and courteous man. Who would want to kill him?'

'I don't know. The Metropolitan Police homicide team are pursuing their inquiries. All I know is they found his body in a toilet at Gatwick Airport. He was returning to Germany after delivering the data from the latest stellerator runs. The coroner has just informed me that he died as a result of an administered toxic agent.'

'Was he found with a wafer-zip on his person?' Leon asked impulsively.

'The police are revealing no further details at the moment.' Chekhov's demeanour turned. 'I'll find out who did this and I will also find *you*, Dabrowski, now that I know what you look like.'

Leon broke into a cold sweat as he realised what Chekhov meant. Following their meeting, he'd removed his balaclava.

CHAPTER 32

Magda was becoming more tired and listless by the day. *There must be a syndrome like this for every prisoner who's been incarcerated for this length of time*, she told herself. Hopefully the depression will lift. In the meantime, she would put the bad feelings to one side and continue to work on Sergei. As she waited for him to come out of the dressing room, she began her warm-up stretching, though she found it hard to muster any enthusiasm. Why did he bring her to his quarters before this particular training session? *Why the change in routine?*

Sergei came into the lounge looking more serious than usual.

'What, no smile? You feeling OK, Sergei?'

'Yes, Ana. I'm feeling fine. Sit down, I have something important to say.'

This sounded like bad news. 'I don't think I'm going to like this.'

'But you will,' he said. 'I've thought about our recent discussions and I have to admit you're right.

This is no life for either of us. I'm going to take you out of here.'

She couldn't believe what she was hearing. *Just like that?* This was her dream. Her thoughts of escape and seeing Leon again kept her going through months of meaningless days and the lonely nights. Why was he offering this on a plate after all this time?

'You have no thoughts on that? I did imagine you'd be pleased.'

'I'm delighted, Sergei. But I need to know one thing before I agree to what you're proposing. You *are* doing this for us, aren't you? You're going to take this huge risk so we can have our freedom and start a new life together.' She mentally crossed her fingers in hope that he was telling the truth, rather than nullifying her own blatant lie.

'Of course, I'm doing it for us. Why else would I suggest this?'

He kissed her cheek and her doubts became stronger. *It's another ruse, but I have no choice.* 'When do we go?'

'Tonight. We wait until it becomes dark outside and everyone is back in their rooms. Most of the complex will be on emergency lighting by then and the alarms and cameras will be inactive.'

Tonight! This was a shock. And why would their security systems be disarmed tonight? Surely this was the time of day when they were needed most – unsupervised inmates, opportunities to move about the place in silence – none of this made sense. *I have to take my chance – I may never get another.*

'I suggest you get some rest, Ana. Try and sleep. I'll wake you when the time comes.'

She got up and kissed Sergei on the lips. 'I'll be ready.'

Sleep? How could she sleep? *I'm coming, Leon. Please be there for me, my love – whoever you are.*

CHAPTER 33

Gunther Schroeder and Roman Slavic sat stony faced in Fusion's main conference room. Kaminsky was dead. Slavic's secretary closed the door behind her and both men tried to speak at the same time.

'You first, Gunther,' Slavic conceded. 'What do you think we should do?'

'I think we should try and get Leon back in. We've been struggling ever since he left and now that Kaminsky has gone, we can't run the show ourselves.'

'But Chekhov wouldn't stand for that. He still thinks Leon is responsible for passing the data to the Americans.'

'And what about you, Roman? Who do *you* think is responsible?'

'I have to agree with Chekhov.' Slavic looked down at the table. 'Why else would Leon just disappear like that?'

'It couldn't have been him. How could he get the data out? We're going to have to work together on this. In the meantime, I'll have to move back to Greifswald and take over Kaminsky's data transfer role.'

'But that would leave me here as the only remaining member of the lead team.'

'What else do you suggest we do? Chekhov isn't going to want to suspend the project, is he?'

'I suppose you're right. We have to—'

The conference room door burst open. A team of armed security staff charged in, followed by Ivan Kuzmin. Schroeder jumped up.

'What the—?'

Before Schroeder could get the words out, he found himself handcuffed. Two of Kuzmin's men eased Slavic out of his chair. 'Mr Chekhov has instructed me to apprehend you both while he completes his investigations into the disclosure of Fusion's classified research information to a third-party organisation. You are under house arrest until he has the opportunity to question you. I would ask you to come with me, gentlemen,' announced the stern faced Kuzmin, as if reading their criminal rights.

The two men looked at each other in dismay. 'I've heard a rumour that there are old prison cells somewhere in this building's basement,' Slavic said. 'God help us both.'

The nurse left the cell. Roman Slavic flopped back on his tiny mattress, gazed up at the flaked and dirty ceiling and began to construct images in his head from the amorphous patterns of shadows and smudges. It was like the game he used to play as a schoolboy during his summer holidays, lying back on the grass and creating one magical scene after another from the evolving cloudscape. But there was no movement in this tableau, just the static demonic shapes of those who were about to torment him.

The sedative, or whatever it was they gave him, seemed to kick in as soon as the syringe was drawn back from his forearm. It would make him feel relaxed and dreamy. This morning was no different but in the back of his mind there lurked more sinister emotions. He thought about the other members of the technical lead team. *He* was the boss, but *they* were seen as the brains behind the operation. And that had always hurt him. He was forever having to let the clever young upstarts take the credit for Fusion's technical progress. Why hadn't God made him a super-brain like Leon Dabrowski? *He* was a bloody genius. It wasn't fair. *Yes, I have a doctorate in natural philosophy and from a good university at that –* but so what? *The pay at Fusion is good –* but that meant nothing to him either. The only silver lining to this dark cloud was his position of authority within the company – that allowed him to retain his status within the academic institutions. His fellow academics tolerated him though none of them respected him for his intellectual capacity, he was sure of that. And where had his ambitions taken him after all these years? They'd taken him nowhere. He'd fallen short of his goals by a long way. He was an old fossil, a figurehead, an administrator, a suit, a bloody laughing stock.

My team, my team. How I've let them down. They worked so hard to secure the future of nuclear energy. They entrusted me with their data. And now he'd shown that vile man Vitaliev how to operate the crypto-key. *Poor*

Pawel, he didn't deserve to die. Would these people kill the others? Should I have warned Gunther? He shuddered at the thought of a gifted scientist like Leon Dabrowski being mercilessly killed for someone's commercial gain.

Slavic started to sob, rolled over and stared at the wall a foot away from his eyes. Like the ceiling, it hadn't been decorated for years, decades even. Why did Chekhov maintain such a godforsaken place as this? The thought of Vladimir Chekhov filled his stomach with the sick taste of fear. What was to become of him? How long would it be before they came for him? He sat up on the rickety old bed, took off his shirt and surveyed every inch of material until he found a weak spot. He began to pick at it with his bare fingers.

Ivan Kuzmin carried the breakfast tray down the dusty wooden steps. It was so different from the rest of the building down here – a place so incongruous that he felt he was entering a different era, a different world even. Every morning he followed this same routine. He could have arranged for one of his men to do it, but he preferred to carry out the task himself; the old man deserved some respect, didn't he? In Kuzmin's eyes, Slavic was a loyal and dignified company man who shouldn't be treated like a criminal, and these disgusting cells should have been converted to something useful years ago. God only knew what heinous acts they committed in this cell when Anatoly Chekhov was alive. Was Vladimir Chekhov aware of its existence?

He set the tray down on the table outside the door to Slavic's cell, unlocked the door with the ancient gaoler's key and pushed it ajar. 'Your breakfast, Dr Slavic,' he said courteously. He opened the door a little further, conscious of the need to preserve the old director's dignity. 'Dr Slavic, are you awake?' It was unusual for Slavic to be asleep at this time and, when there was no response, Kuzmin fumbled at the light switch. But the light didn't come on. His eyes adjusted and through the gloom he made out the shape of a bare arm dangling towards the floor. He threw the cell door wide open to make best use of the feeble lighting in the corridor, took a single step into the room and stopped. A kneeling figure leaned forward at an angle of forty-five degrees. 'Oh God, Slavic!' he shouted as he swiped the alarm icon on his wafer.

The two duty security officers arrived within a minute, switched on their magno-torches and illuminated the cell with brilliant white light. All three men stood frozen at the entrance and gawped at the purple-necked naked body of Dr Roman Slavic, held rigidly in place by a taut ribbon of twisted cloth that was tied to the bed's metal headboard. Kuzmin was first to speak. 'God, he must have calculated that to perfection.'

CHAPTER 34

'Wake up, Ana. Time to go.'

Magda was already awake. Filled with anxiety, she'd been unable to sleep. Throughout the restless hours, she'd occupied her mind with her partially constructed computer model – every room she'd been in, every corridor, every predicted appendage to the subterranean complex. The waiting was over. She was ready to go.

The entrance door to Sergei's quarters closed behind them. 'Follow me and question nothing I say.' They set off down the corridor into the gloom; only the pale blue emergency lighting illuminated the way forward. After ten minutes and two downward elevator journeys, Magda found herself in a corridor that she recognised. *Surely, we're not going into the Drum Room?* She said nothing and followed Sergei into the pitch-black silence of the cylindrical room. A few steps in, the LEDs came to life and the surface became soft under her feet. Sergei tapped his wafer and a section of the room's wall slid back to reveal what to Magda looked like a bank of ATM slots. Fascinated, she watched him insert his wafer into one of the slots and, from the slot above, another wafer emerged. Taking the replacement wafer, Sergei spoke for the first time since they'd left his quarters.

'Initiate exit route.'

The floor beneath Magda's feet took on a solid feel. 'You told me you'd never had a Melomet signature. You lied to me.'

'I also told you to keep quiet. Follow me.'

They walked to the centre of the room. Sergei stopped her dead with his hand. 'Activate plinth.' The cylindrical section of floor under their feet started to rise. Soon the rest of the floor was twenty metres below them and they were still accelerating – they were going to pile into the roof. Magda grabbed hold of Sergei and pulled herself into his chest. Impact was only metres away. At the last moment, the ceiling slid to the side and they glided through the aperture. Magda breathed a sigh of relief as the plinth settled to a steady speed. After a further minute, they slowed to a halt.

'Open exit door.' A door slid open in the wall to reveal a long tunnel curving away into the distance.

This is it, the way out. Her model hadn't predicted that the Drum Room doubled up as a hidden elevator shaft. Why should it have done? She'd been plotting her way out through a multi-channel maze. She chastised herself. *Why didn't I have the foresight to develop parallel models?*

Sergei took her hand. 'Are you ready for this, Ana?' They stepped forward on to the aluminium floor. 'Start!'

'A travellator?'

'It *is* safe for you to speak again now,' Sergei said with a hint of annoyance in his voice.

'Sorry, I forgot myself again.'

The moving walkway soon reached its operating speed. Magda felt the thrill of its rapid pace around the circular tunnel. *At last, I'm getting out.* But escapades such as this had a habit of ending up in strange places. And Sergei was more unpredictable than normal tonight.

The walkway decelerated. 'What happens next?' she asked, but no answer came back. She looked across at Sergei and realised he wasn't listening. The travellator had slowed to a crawl and his eyes were glued in the forward direction. 'Sergei, are you OK?' He didn't move. She followed his gaze and saw what had grabbed his attention. There was a junction ahead. 'Who are they, Sergei?'

'This wasn't meant to happen.'

'But who are they?'

'Reverse!'

The travellator accelerated away from the junction. Sergei snapped out of his trance. 'The junction we were approaching is a carousel roundabout. It links both complexes to the exit. But it shouldn't be occupied by those people.' He pointed back up the tunnel. Magda caught a last glimpse of the group in the distance. It was a steady stream of pedestrian traffic by now.

'It looked like a fire drill,' Magda said. 'You're telling me there's another complex? What's going on, Sergei?'

'We don't have fire drills down here. But I agree, it looks like some sort of evacuation. We mustn't get mixed up in that. I know of one more emergency route. We're here now. Stop at EJ One.'

The travellator stopped. Magda noticed a thin red line around the circumference of the tunnel's otherwise white wall; next to the line was a small label: 'Emergency Junction 1'.

'Open EJ One!'

A door slid back to reveal another tunnel. This one was straight with a rectangular cross section. 'We walk from here but be careful.' Sergei pointed up to the tunnel's roof. 'Those alarm sensors have narrow detection beams – we have to keep to the edges. And don't touch the walls.'

They set off down the tunnel, taking care not to drift into the middle. Magda couldn't prevent her thoughts from being diverted to her model. *A second complex? It has its own secret exit route and the two routes meet at a single junction? Got it, two parallel complexes integrated into the same three-dimensional space. Two independent worlds with minimal cross-linkage. How clever.* For the first time, she understood why her model had predicted so much unused space.

Sergei stopped. 'Here it is.'

Magda could see no indication of their next junction. He looked at her and smiled. It was a glimpse of the old Sergei.

'Look up. See how the sensors in the roof are missing at this point. You're safe to cross to my side now. Open exit!'

The hidden door revealed itself by moving back a couple of centimetres before flashing to one side. But it wasn't the outside world that Magda was looking at. She peered down yet another corridor, just like those she saw on a daily basis. The weight of dismay pressed on her shoulders. She felt like bursting into tears. 'Sergei, you've been deceiving me. It's just another one of your cruel jokes. You—'

Sergei placed his finger over her lips. 'One final leg, I promise. But you must remain silent once more.'

As they approached the end of the corridor, Magda could make out a sign through the gloom: 'Emergency Exit'. *The door to the world outside?* She jumped as he called out, 'Exit!' and grabbed her by the elbow. They dashed for the closed door. 'Don't stop,' Sergei shouted. Ten metres from the door, Magda felt herself being tugged forward as Sergei stepped up the pace. The solid-looking door hadn't budged. They were going to slam into it. 'Now!' Sergei yelled at the top of his voice. The door slid open. They burst into a vast hall and the door zipped shut behind them.

The hall was teeming, people wandering everywhere in a maelstrom. 'Quick,' Sergei said, 'keep you head down and don't show your face till we get out.' They weaved and pushed their way through the throng. Magda tucked into Sergei's armpit as he hustled her along the hall. A pale white light shone from above but she knew better than to look up. Her freedom was approaching. *Please God, don't take it away now.* They reached the glazed entrance door to the building's ground floor.

'Please form lines and stay calm,' someone shouted above the purling din.

Sergei glanced back over his shoulder. 'Goodbye,' she heard him whisper as he held up his wafer to the reader. The door opened. 'We're out!' he cried as the door closed behind them. 'Let's go!' Heads down and holding hands, they ran down the gravel drive and through the open wrought-iron gate – the gate to freedom.

The early morning silence in the park was enticing. *Her turn to drag him*. She grabbed Sergei by the hand. 'Come on, PTI, let's go.' The cold air battered her cheeks as she ran and the delicate scrunch of frosted grass under her feet was exhilarating. She shouted out loud. 'We're free, Sergei, free at last!'

They stopped under a leafless old oak tree that peered over a sea of white turning green in the heat of the rising sun. Hands on knees, Magda panted deep breaths of fresh cold air and felt the lifeblood surging through her body. *It's all so beautiful*.

'Look, Sergei, look at the sunrise.' She tilted her head up to the pale blue sky and spun around with her hands in the air. 'It's the sun we can see over there, with nothing but empty space separating us from it. None of your frosted glass. And look at the grass down there. Real growing grass, not gym matting.' The joy of freedom overwhelmed her. She flung her arms around him and sank into his heaving chest. 'Oh, Sergei,' she sobbed, 'we've done it.'

But Sergei wasn't holding her like he normally did. He removed her arms from his waist and eased her away. 'Yes, Ana, we are free.'

Why was he handling her like this, with a total lack of emotion? With the break of dawn, the full realisation of what they'd done flooded her body like an urn filling with water. 'Sergei, what's wrong?'

He didn't answer. He looked at her in a way she didn't recognise. She'd used him and he knew it. She'd slept in his bed and it was as if he'd forgotten. He'd been her minder, trained her body to the peak of fitness and smiled at her while he did it. She was looking at the same handsome face and impressive body, but the Sergei she knew and pretended to love was no longer with her. This was someone different standing in his place. And she was afraid of this man.

'Sergei, I have to go.'

'Ana, you always had to go. And I wish you well.'

She kissed his cheek and remembered the first time. It was another peace offering but this time it was also a goodbye. 'I'll miss you, Sergei.'

Sergei said nothing but offered his hand. It was so impersonal, so businesslike. It seemed wrong to part like this. Ladylike, she shook his hand but couldn't look at his face. In the knowledge that these were her final moments with Sergei, she turned away and walked across the open expanse of grass. She could feel his eyes following her. Had she hurt him? Did he despise her for what she'd done?

Compelled to look at him for one last time, she stopped and turned back. There was nothing but fields surrounding the old tree, and the nearest park feature was a copse over a hundred metres away. As if everything she'd experienced was a dream, PTI Sergei disappeared. Magda stood alone wondering what to do next. Then she realised – *Ana is gone too.*

CHAPTER 35

Malkin had an uneasy feeling that something was going on around him today. As usual, he was shut away in his private viewing room, busy reviewing old recordings, looking for potential improvements to feed back to Rodin and the sexual fantasy designers. And as usual, he spotted few opportunities for enhancing the fantasies. The close-up shots of his clients showed them to be delighted with their experiences in Eight Over Nine. Rodin was doing a fine job.

Thinking about it, he hadn't seen Rodin for days. The other job had to take priority at times, of course, and the benefits outweighed the risks as far as links to the Russian Embassy were concerned. And what about the strange noises he'd heard earlier that morning? He instructed the Melomet to reduce the soundtrack volume and listened again. The rumblings were still there but sounded as if they were coming from further away. He'd investigate this later. Perhaps it was a test run for one of Rodin's new fantasies. *Where the hell is Rodin?*

He turned his attention back to the video-wall. The screen went blank. *What the …?*

'Call for you, Mr Malkin,' said the Melomet, 'from Mr Chekhov.'

Malkin jumped as the imposing figure of Vladimir Chekhov snapped at him, 'I will see you in the *pakhan*'s office, Malkin. Chekhov out.' The screen went blank.

Chekhov? Here at Goldhurst, waiting for him down in the lower levels. A hot wave of panic surged inside him. He must have already seen what's been going on in his father's old domain and he'd have gone ballistic. What was he going to tell him after all this time? *Oh, and by the way, Vladimir old chap, I meant to mention my flagship brothel, Eight Over Nine. It just slipped my memory.* He hurried to the elevator.

He left the security compound by the emergency exit and made his way through Goldhurst's entrance hall. The Fusion Ltd reception desk was deserted. What was going on? He found the wall panel at the end of the hall, checked that nobody was watching and pushed the large brown wood-knot at the panel's bottom corner. The panel slid back and, for the first time since the old *pakhan* was alive, he slipped into the entrance lobby of the secret route into the underground complex. Which route had Chekhov taken to the old *pakhan*'s office? *Oh, God, what's going on?*

The lower corridor hadn't changed since Vladimir Chekhov's last visit to Goldhurst thirty years ago. *Thank God I didn't sell the paintings.* Brushing back his hair with his fingers and straightening his jacket, Malkin hurried towards the door at the end of the corridor. With closed eyes, he took a deep breath and drifted back to that first meeting many years ago. He knocked on the door and heard again the penetrating voice of Vladimir Chekhov. He entered the room and walked towards the desk behind which Chekhov and Ivan Kuzmin sat. *What's he doing here?*

'Do take a seat, Malkin.'

No first-name terms today, but Chekhov's calm demeanour made him feel at ease. Malkin took his seat and realised he was sitting in the wooden captain's chair which Anatoly Chekhov always used for his one-to-one meetings. *Where has that reappeared from? Oh God, he's going to ask me where the pakhan's chair has gone.* His face must be glowing red by now.

'I've asked our head of security, Mr Kuzmin, to attend this meeting,' Chekhov said in a matter-of-fact manner. Kuzmin raised his eyebrows as if to say *I knew nothing about this.* Chekhov studied Malkin for a while before getting down to business.

'Following my investigation into our prostitution operation and into the background of the estate manager you appointed, Alexei Rodin is to be dismissed from my organisation with immediate effect. I will subsequently make sure she is discredited at the Russian Embassy. Do you have anything to say?'

What *could* he say? *God, how did he find out about Rodin?*

'Good, that is agreed. Next item, the whole fleet of London brothels is to be closed down and the liberated … inmates … are to be sent for rehabilitation before their repatriation, where that is applicable. Do you understand that, Malkin?'

Although Chekhov remained calm, Malkin could tell his anger was building and that there was worse to come.

'Sir, can I say I agree with your decision about Rodin. I was going to—'

'Be quiet, man!' Chekhov picked a thick sheaf of paper from out of a briefcase and dropped it on the desk. It hit the surface with a dull slap. 'This is a printout of a database which my security staff found on the brothel's computers. I still prefer paper records, myself. I don't like working with electronic files.'

Kuzmin raised his eyebrows again and slowly shook his head, as much as to say it was nothing to do with him. *Kuzmin is loyal. He wouldn't split on me.*

'It will give me great pleasure to hand this file over to the Polish *Policja* in person. Have you anything to say?'

'I'm sorry, sir. I did my best to make money for you. I realise I should have kept you informed. I—'

'You stole most of my money, Malkin. Is that what you're going to tell me? Well, I can save you the bother. I know about your special accounts and I've taken back what is mine – that is, all of it. Impressive, I must say. If ever I decide to restore the prostitution business, I may well consider using your excellent business model. Now get out of my sight, you little moron, while you still have your legs.' He turned towards Ivan Kuzmin. 'Would you please see Mr Malkin off the premises?'

Malkin was in a state of complete shock as he stumbled into the elevator with Kuzmin. He looked with the eyes of a pleading puppy at his former security man, but realised he'd get no sympathy. Kuzmin was now Chekhov's man. It went without saying that he would no longer figure in Chekhov's will but at least he'd escaped with his life. And thank God Chekhov had no idea of his role in his baby son's abduction all those years ago. He'd lost his current fortune – except for the few hundred thousand he'd placed in a contingency account; he'd have to make do with that for now. It was time to disappear into the sunset while he still had the chance – and his legs.

CHAPTER 36

'm in Poland. What city is this?

Magda's sense of freedom was beginning to subside. Abandoned and shivering in an open field, she'd head towards the sunrise until a man-made feature appeared – there was bound to be a path. Follow the path to a junction, a road perhaps. Follow the road to a hamlet, but always in a direction away from that vile prison. Children – what were they doing out here by themselves, so early in the morning? *They're teenagers.*

'What city is this?

'You been drinking, miss?'

'She's on the game. How about me, darling? Any chance of a freebie?'

Laughter – all four of them. *They're English.*

'Look, guys, I'm lost. Just tell me where I am or I'll tell your teachers you're kerb crawling on those toy bikes of yours.'

'She's a nutter. Come on, boys, leave the bitch alone before her pimp turns up.'

Follow the path to a junction. Magda walked at a brisk pace until she came to a boundary. *A gate – with houses beyond*. She ran for the gate and the sense of freedom returned. *You're free, Ana*. No, not Ana – Ana was gone. The houses were distinctly English; a large park like this, cars driven on the left – from the whole ambience, it had to be London. She was in London, the home of Fusion's headquarters. She walked along the empty street, relishing the feel of the pavement beneath her feet. An electric car swished by. The traffic was building a mile or so away; the shrill sound of distant horns intermingled with the cooing of pigeons – it was a Mozart symphony to her. *A road sign – Highgate three miles to the left*. That's what she'd do, she'd find the Fusion building – *Goldhurst, they call it?* She followed the road for a mile, turned left at the next signpost and made her way through the suburbs. The sight of fine English houses with their long drives was reassuring. Yet with every step, a weight was building on her shoulders and her legs began to buckle under the strain. *This is going back to where I started*. They'd drugged her again. This was all a dream – she'd wake up in her private quarters. Sergei would arrive any time now and whisk her off to the gym. She sat down at the roadside and wept.

'Are you all right, ma'am?'

Magda looked up at the police officer. 'What?'

'I think you'd better come with us.'

Midday – the sun burned in cold air. *Please don't let it disappear*. The gravel crackled under the wheels of the police car. Magda's heart was beating so fast that she felt it would slip its gear and stop.

'You *will* stay with me?' she asked the young police officer who was driving.

'If you want me to.'

'I don't want you to leave me for one second.'

Through the glazed entrance door, she could make out a tall and well-built man with short hair, standing at a reception desk on the other side of a large hall. 'The scan will take a few seconds,' the officer said. The door slid open. Magda and the officer walked into a vast hall with light pouring in from above.

'Professor Tomala, I believe? I am Vladimir Chekhov. Please come this way.'

Her escape with Sergei earlier that morning was all so hazy, but her sense of direction during the short journey from the police station told her this was the place. Her heart told her this was the place. This *was* the place. She took hold of the police officer's hand and he smiled at her. Tightening her grip, she followed Chekhov past the reception desk, surprised at the rude manner in which he left them trailing behind. He was already sitting at the desk by the time they entered the large ground-floor office. 'Do please take a seat, professor.'

A chilling thought dawned on her – beneath her feet was that crazy metropolis in which she'd spent months of her life against her will. All this time she'd lived under Fusion's headquarters. *Thank God they didn't take me to an elevator.*

'The officer can stay if that makes you feel better,' Chekhov said. 'I can't begin to imagine what you've been through these past months and you have my profound apologies. I have only recently discovered for myself what is going on.'

The police officer – he was familiar with the building entry protocol. 'I don't know who to trust anymore. If this is some ruse, I'll commit a murder, I promise you.' She let go of the officer's hand.

'Professor, you have my word – you are safe now. In fact, I'm delighted that you've come back to my company's headquarters. It must have taken a lot of nerve, given the traumatic experience you've been through in that place below. I myself am devastated. When I arrived two days ago, I was appalled to discover what was going on in the complex I built for my family. The place even had its own name – Eight Over Nine, they called it.'

Magda could see how they derived the name but was in no mood to appreciate it. 'That place down there is just one huge nightmare. How could you have let that happen? Surely, you must have known what they were up to. You condoned this Eight Over Nine, didn't you?'

'Please, professor,' Chekhov threw up both hands, 'calm down.' He patted the air in front of him. 'For personal reasons, I conducted all my Fusion business via video link. I had no reason to visit Goldhurst. I really had no idea—'

'Where is Leon?' She could see that Chekhov was galled at being interrupted. Yet he remained so calm.

'Ah, I'm glad you ask me that question because I would like to know myself.'

'You mean he's not here? Is he looking for me?'

'One presumes that to be the case. However, *I've* been looking for *him* for months and come up with nothing. He's well hidden in this large city and has obviously migrated within Melomet-space. I suggest you and I put our heads together and see if we can solve this problem.'

'Surely someone in Fusion would know of his whereabouts? How about Gunther Schroeder? Leon and Gunther were inseparable.' Chekhov wasn't going to answer. The mist inside her head cleared and she analysed every word he'd just said – there was a lot happening here. She spotted Chekhov's glance towards the man at her side. *The police officer – he knows him.* She had to get out before they grabbed her and dragged her back down into that infernal underworld.

Chekhov was looking at her as if he could read her thoughts. From out of his desk drawer, he took a small piece of paper and a pen, scribbled a name and number and handed the paper to her.

'This man works for the Polish police force. He probably knows where Dr Dabrowski is but he refuses to speak with me. You may have better luck with him.'

'Thank you. I'll restore my wafer-set and feed the code for this Mr ...' she looked at the note '... Pavel, through the Melomet pi-protocol.'

Chekhov pursed his lips and shrugged his shoulders.

'I need to go.'

'You are free to go any time, professor. Please keep in touch.'

'I can make my own way out,' she said, scowling at the police officer.

Chekhov and the police officer exchanged glances once more, then Chekhov nodded to her. 'I'll give you some money,' he said. 'Good luck, Magda.'

Leonid Pavel proved to be about as easy to contact as a member of the UK monarchy. Three days after Magda's meeting with Chekhov, Pavel's office finally called her to say he was back in Warsaw and acknowledged her message. Now she waited patiently in a Soho bar for him to return her call. She smiled to herself as the strains of Grieg's *Morning Mood* filled her private booth. How she hated this piece; it was the first sound she heard when she woke up in Eight Over Nine and it had haunted her dreams ever since. But not anymore. It meant nothing to her now, she could dismiss the effects of their brainwashing at will – well, most of the time. Would Pavel call, she wondered? His secretary had suggested he'd be back in the office within the hour but that was two hours ago. She started people watching to kill time.

These new music cafés were fascinating but what bizarre customers they had, all of them looking the same. She must stick out like a sore thumb in this place. Yet most of the customers were ignoring her, like you'd ignore someone wearing a casual suit at a formal gathering. There were mostly couples occupying the booths opposite. One booth at a time, she studied their body language; they were happy – with the music and with each other. She was drawn towards a man of about her age. The lighting was dim but from what she could see of him, *he* didn't look happy. He reminded her a bit of Leon. *I imagine he's pretty miserable at the moment too. I've missed you so much, Leon. Where are you, my darling?* But Leon would never have his hair cut like that. Besides, this guy's body was distinctly scrawny in comparison to Leon's athletic frame.

'Call for you Miss Tom,' said the Melomet, 'Mr Pavel.'

'Miss Tom, I presume. What can I do for you?'

'I explained to your secretary that Vladimir Chekhov gave me your Melomet code. He said you might know the whereabouts of my boyfriend, Leon Dabrowski.'

'He would do that, wouldn't he?'

'Sorry?'

'Miss Tom, I presume you're claiming to be Dabrowski's fiancée, Magda Tomala. As you must be aware by now, I'm a senior officer in the Warsaw *Policja* and you have to credit me with *some* intelligence.'

'What are you talking about? I *am* Magda Tomala. And I'm desperate to find Leon. I'll have you know that over these past months I've been—'

'Miss Tom,' Pavel interrupted, 'do you take me for a fool? You can tell your boss that, although I'm eternally grateful for what he's done for my compatriots, I have my principles. I'm not going to help him track down a loyal colleague of mine.'

'Look, Pavel, if you know where Leon is, you have to tell me. You can see me on the screen. What makes you think I'm a fake?'

'You're one of Chekhov's agents. My policeman's intuition tells me. The crafty old sod is trying to con me into revealing Dabrowski's whereabouts.'

'And how do I know that *you* aren't one of Chekhov's agents trying to home in on my wafer signal so you can follow me to Leon. Why do you think I re-registered under a different name?' *This is getting us nowhere.* The man opposite left his booth and walked towards the exit. *God, he does look like Leon.*

'I can see your location as we speak. You're in Café Classico in the Soho area of London. Chekhov is killing two birds with one stone here. He has you trying to trick me and, at the same time, you continue your search for Dabrowski in the *Classico* bars …'

Oh, damn! What have I done? Magda pocketed her wafer, burst out of the booth and ran for the exit. The street outside the café was crowded. *Try right.* She shot off down the road and the cars coming towards her blasted their horns. After a hundred metres she stopped and turned. Back – past the café, towards the end of the street. *Run faster, for God's sake.* At the junction there was no *Classico* to be seen in either direction. *Lost him.* She put her head in her hands and started screaming. People were looking at her as if she was a lunatic. She collapsed to the pavement, sobbing. *Leon, Leon.*

CHAPTER 37

The days crawled by. These were the darkest days of Leon's life. He'd spend his time moping about his London apartment and thinking of nothing but Magda. Had she been abused, tortured, killed even? There were occasional visits to one of the many *Classico* hangouts in the West End – the atmosphere cleared his head and helped him think. It was risky now that Chekhov knew of his disguise – his security officers would no doubt have his latest photo on their wafers. But what did he care? He cared about nothing to do with Chekhov – his security team, his nuclear data, his nuclear power company even. He'd do anything to find Magda, even if it meant throwing caution to the wind. He needed Pavel to help him – but where *was* Pavel? Without him and Schumann, there was little point in continuing surveillance of the brothels. If Magda was still locked away in one of them, the only way of finding her would be by personal visits.

'Video call for you, Mahler, from Pavel in Poland. Will you take it now?'

'I'll take it in the lounge.'

Let's hope he has some news for me.

'It's over,' Pavel said. He looked like he'd lost ten years overnight. His face no longer gaunt, he even managed a smile. 'We were right about Fusion's headquarters. There's a huge brothel down there the size of a town.'

'It's over?' quizzed Leon.

'Leon, it's marvellous. They've let my people go,' he said in biblical fashion. 'Chekhov has gone in there himself and opened the gates to freedom for them all. He's even arranged to start their psychological rehabilitation.'

'Magda? Have they found Magda?'

Pavel's expression darkened. Once again, he became the embattled old police officer he'd worked alongside throughout this past year. It was bad news.

'Chekhov's evacuation team checked every individual in an attempt to find her among the brothel's residents. They obtained a copy of her photograph from the university and showed it to everyone they interviewed. A few confirmed she was down there among them but none of them knew her current whereabouts. I'm sorry, Leon, she's gone missing. I need to go. Pavel out.'

A churning sickness filled Leon's stomach. In the bathroom, he swilled his head and face with cold water, shook his head vigorously and swilled his face again. *Think, Leon. Get that brain of yours working.* Where could Magda have gone? *They've taken her away?* No, she wouldn't have let them do that. She wouldn't have waited in a line while they carried out a census, she'd have found a way to slip away from them. What would she have done next, he wondered? She must surely have realised he was over here looking for her and she'd have soon found out he was no longer welcome at Fusion. *She's found her bearings and she's looking for me.* So, where would she look? Magda was extremely bright, she'd think like he did. She'd ask herself what was the best way of keeping out of sight while searching for a lost person? *She's going to look for me among the Classicos.*

The Classico Calypso club just off Soho's Dean Street was dark inside, even on this sunniest of days. As always, the club swayed to the rhythm of calypso and Bob Marley and the air was thick with exhaled vapour. Until Chekhov had caught sight of him in disguise, Leon felt secure in this place. Why would Chekhov's security team think of looking for him among a set of Rastafarians who'd latched on to the *Classico* philosophy for mixing intellectual socialising and music? And even if they were to start enquiring about a missing scientist in here, as far as the club's staff and clientele were concerned, he was just one of the many casual visitors to this place from the *Classico* fraternity. The risks of him being tracked down had now increased, but at least these people knew *nothing about nothing*, as they put it, if they suspected the authorities to be in their midst.

A group of middle-aged men were laughing and drinking at the corner of the bar. Among them he spotted a tall, slim man who wore a seventies-style flared velvet suit and had an Afro haircut that looked like it was connected to an electrical generator. He was scowling at him. The man tapped one of his colleagues on the back, pointed across the room then strode menacingly towards him. As he approached, his mouth opened into the broadest of grins to reveal a perfect set of shiny white teeth; he slapped Leon heartily on his shoulder and bellowed with laughter.

'Yo, Mahler. Here to listen to some real music?'

'Hi, Marley. How are tricks?' Leon greeted his acquaintance with a high five. 'Listen, friend. I was wondering if there'd been any enquiries about someone who fitted my description.'

'Always people asking about other people in this joint. Who ya expecting, man? Not in any trouble, I hope?'

'No trouble. There's a good friend of mine who could be in London at the moment. Take a look at this photo.' Leon handed his wafer to Marley.

'No offence, man, but these white women all look the same to me. That one could have been in here, I suppose. In fact, churning the old grey matter, someone a bit like that was asking after a Polish dude a couple of hours ago. Wouldn't be you, would it?'

Leon felt his heart racing. This could be Magda. She was looking for him as he'd hoped. 'Can you tell me about her? Did she give a name? Did she say where she was going?'

'Whoa, steady on, my man. Here, let me have another look at that photo.' Marley pursed his lips and slowly shook his head. 'Can't be sure, hmm – maybe. Your woman did mention a name, though – Chekhov, I think it was. Yeah, that's right. Chekhov.'

Magda? Or one of Chekhov's agents? 'Did she say anything else, anything at all?'

'Nothing that made sense. The woman did say something really odd, though – "pawn to e4," she said. It's an opening chess move, isn't it?'

'I have to go. Call me immediately if you see her again. But don't let on you know me.'

'You can always count on big Marley.'

'Thanks for your help, Marley. You're the man.'

As he set off towards the exit, Marley laughed loudly. 'Hey. Not staying for a drink, Mahler?'

'Some other time, my friend.'

Leon left the club, took a quick look at his surroundings and summoned up an image of the London Metro map in his head. *It's either Piccadilly Circus or Leicester Square. Which one? They're about the same distance from here.* He looked at his watch; it was 4.10 p.m. There wasn't time to get to both stations – he'd go for Piccadilly. *Get running, Leon.*

He arrived at the forecourt of Piccadilly Circus Metro station with five minutes to spare, found the Metro map and, still panting hard, stared at it in anguish. He'd got it wrong. Leicester Square was the nearest station to the Classico Calypso club – just. *Damn it!* Magda would have waited there for the agreed half hour in accordance with the rules of the childish game they played when they were dating. She'd be leaving there this very moment – to go who knew where. But she was in London looking for him and she wouldn't give up. *I won't give up either, Magda. I'll find you.*

CHAPTER 38

The powerful marching beat of Holst's *The Planets* suite was almost deafening as Magda entered the Classico Philharmonic bar. This was her tenth *Classico* bar of the day and, looking around, it wasn't one she'd expect Leon to frequent. But she'd leave her coded message anyway.

The interior was filled with a life-size hologram of a symphony orchestra and the booths around the edge of the room were stuffed with young people, laughing and chatting away in silence – standing room only. She studied the customers as they percolated through the image, making their way to and from the bar. Most of them were likely to be regulars but, with no obvious top-bananas, Magda decided that the receptionist would have to do.

Beyond the acoustic limiter, the stifled strains of 'Mars, Bringer of War' became instantly tolerable – relaxing even. Sitting behind the desk in the anechoic booth was a young girl whose natural feminine looks were ruined by her stubby short hair and jeans held up with braces. She spoke in an echo-free voice.

'Yes, madam, what can I do for you? Are you planning to join one of our groups today?'

'No, I'm just looking for someone. I'd like to take a walk around and see if he's here, but first I'd like to leave a message in case he comes in later.'

'How would I know him? You can see how busy we get.'

'Simple. He'll ask if anyone has left a message. Tell him "knight to f6." Can you remember that?'

'And who shall I say was enquiring about him?'

'He won't ask.'

After a single tour of the premises, Magda stepped out into the street and took a deep breath of city air to purge the oppressive atmosphere she'd absorbed inside the bar. *I can't believe Leon would go into a place like that.* She glanced at her watch; it was three thirty. *Have to move on. Can probably do four or five more venues before I start making my way to the Shard.*

Magda stopped at the open doors of Classico Choral and listened to Mahler's eighth symphony playing inside the bar. One of Leon's favourites – redemption through the power of love. *He's been here. I feel it.* With less than forty minutes to lodge the coded message and make her way to the city's tallest structure, she'd make this her last visit of the day.

The bar was sparsely populated, despite the fact that office workers would be pouring out by now; she may even have time to speak to every customer. Before she could make up her mind where to start, a giant of a woman emerged from one of the booths and minced her way across the floor in a farcical attempt to gyrate and twirl in time to the music. Magda was struggling to suppress her laughter. When was the last time she found anything funny? *My God! Who's this?*

'Hello, darling,' the woman said in a deep, manly voice. 'You have a message for me?'

'What? How do you know that?'

'So, I'm right. I thought you looked his type. Pity really, I fancied him myself.'

Careful not to mention any names. This could be a trap. 'Who are you?'

'I'm Didi. I come here every day. It's the only gay *Classico* bar around these parts. Not sure what your boyfriend was doing in a place like this but he did seem keen on finding you. He *is* your boyfriend, I take it?'

'OK, I'm going to leave a message. If he comes back in, tell him "knight to f6." He'll know what I mean.'

'Well, your luck's in, sweetie. Now that you've told me that, I can give you *his* message. I must admit, these queer games you play are beyond me.'

Magda left the bar trembling with excitement. *Knight takes queen. No specified time. Where's the nearest hotel?*

The Bloomsbury Hotel was lavishly decorated and furnished in the deep reds and blues of the Art Deco period, with polished brass everywhere. Magda walked through the open-plan lounge and reception area and made her way to the bar. Leon would have left his message here, she decided as she took her seat.

'Yes, madam, what can I get you?' said the tuxedo-clad barman.

'Fresh orange with ice, please.' *OK. Need to tread carefully here.* 'I'm a visitor to London. Over here for a mathematics seminar and one of my colleagues should have left a message for me?'

'I'll go and see. Your drink, madam.'

A minute later, a smart-suited middle-aged woman came across with a folded note. 'Yes, your colleague was in earlier. He explained that you would need this before your conference. This mathematical stuff looks gibberish to me.'

'Thank you.' *And thank you, Leon Dabrowski. You're so predictable. I wonder how many other hotels you've left a note like this in.* She took the note and her drink to a table in the corner of the lounge. On the sheet of paper was a long alphanumeric string. *You're certainly going to lengths to cover your tracks, Leon. They must have you scared rigid.* Magda mentally split the string into chess moves. *I see it. It's a set of directions. Very clever, physics boy.*

CHAPTER 39

L eon still wasn't sleeping, yet he felt positive for the first time in weeks. He would set off for Soho within the hour and continue to drop his covert messages around the place. There were hundreds of *Classico* bars if you included those outside the Soho area and he'd have to consider extending his searches. In the meantime, he'd try and contact Pavel and, with his department's help, restore the surveillance activities. *Come on, Schumann. You haven't finished the job yet.*

The doorbell chimed.

Schumann. Thank God. He crossed the floor and opened the door.

'Still using prime numbers as your entry code?' she said to him with a straight face.

'Magda!'

Magda flopped into his arms. The tiny shudders from her sobbing spread from the back of her head to her shoulders. He guided her towards the couch, sat her down and eased himself alongside. She'd lost weight but her arms felt firm, like iron. Magda rested her hand on his knee and started to speak, but she didn't look him in the eye. 'Leon, I've …' She covered her eyes with her free hand.

'Don't try to tell me now, my love. We have plenty of time for that.' He held her in silence for a few moments. 'How did you find me?'

'Chekhov. I went to see Chekhov. It was all I could think of.' Leon stroked the back of her hand. 'He gave me the name of your colleague, Pavel. I managed to contact him in Poland – something Chekhov wasn't able to do himself, by all accounts. Pavel didn't believe my story or even who I was, but he did let on that you frequented *Classico* bars. I've been scouring them for days. What have you been up to, Leon? You look so ridiculous.'

'You have to believe me, Magda, I've searched for you every waking minute, with the help of some serious people and some incredible technology. They had you so well hidden.'

'Chekhov told me …' She started to weep. 'It was there, beneath my feet. That's where they kept me all this time. Underneath Fusion headquarters. Underneath where I was sitting with Chekhov and where you were working.'

'But I *wasn't* working there. I *don't* work there anymore. I'm a fugitive from Chekhov. He must have also told you that. The important thing is we're back together. And we need to go home – to Poland.'

'Chekhov desperately wants to find you, Leon.'

'I know.'

'There's a lot I don't understand. And there are things we need to talk about.'

'Shush. Let's go through to the bedroom.'

312

'I want that, Leon. But we can't make love just yet. Not until we've talked.'

'I know that too, Magda.'

Over the days that followed, Leon listened to Magda's account of her life in Eight Over Nine. She explained how the brothel's name related to the largest fraction of an iceberg lying below the surface of the sea. Living below the surface, she didn't see daylight for months. He began to understand how she could come out of this ordeal with such fitness and yet be a psychological wreck. He almost collapsed with relief when she told him she hadn't been used as a prostitute.

Magda seemed just as keen to hear about Leon's experiences.

'How is your mother, Leon? You haven't mentioned her.'

'She's stable, from what I've been told. But I haven't seen her since that night you were taken from me.'

'That's appalling. How could you be so callous?'

'I know. I'm not proud of it. But we'll be going home soon. She won't even know how long it's been since we were last with her.'

With an air of duty, Magda returned to her story – the black drum, her race ... But Leon needed to know more about this PTI Sergei character and his assistance with her escape from the brothel. 'Why did he do it?' he asked. Why would he turn his back on his employers, renege on his duties and help her to escape?

'All in good time,' she told him – and there was something about that turn of phrase that wasn't Magda.

The rain thrashed against the windows, driven by a force six. The sort of evening when one of them would have said we don't have to go out tonight. The sort of evening when they would turn on the music and curl up on the couch, exchange views on the world they lived in and end up in love-talk. Magda's abduction had destroyed all that; their relationship wasn't the same. He'd have to make sure it didn't destroy the rest of their lives.

'There's a matter I want to discuss with you about Eight Over Nine.'

At last she's going to tell me the truth about Sergei.

'Sergei helped me in a way that took me by surprise.' Leon braced himself. 'He let me have access to a confidential database.'

This wasn't what he was expecting.

'A database that contained details on every girl in the brothel, including me. And do you know what my file contained? It contained a report, Leon. Written by one of their security officers. A report on *you*.'

'What on earth do you mean? Are you suggesting I had something to do with all this? Your capture and incarceration were down to me in some perverse way?'

'I'm not sure *what* it means. I just know from what they're saying in that report, there's some issue about the identity of your parents – your mother Lynne and your biological father. They're saying you aren't who you claim to be. What do *you* think it means?'

Her disclosure did nothing to quell his curiosity about Sergei. To the contrary, he was desperate to know the truth. He couldn't hold back his frustration any longer. He turned on Magda for the first time since they'd been reunited – for the first time in their lives.

'Look, Magda. I realise this doesn't stack up and I'll look into it when I get the chance. In the meantime, I'm more interested in getting to the bottom of this business with your PTI, Sergei, or whatever he calls himself. Don't think I'm jealous, but from what you've been telling me, there's been something going on there. I can see the guilt in your eyes every time you mention his name.'

'Guilt? Jealousy? These are new words for our dictionary, aren't they?' Magda screwed up her face. 'Yes, Leon, there *was* something going on between us,' she yelled. 'If you must know, he had sex with me. But there was a reason I had to let him. And in your present frame of mind I'm not willing to discuss that. To hell with you, Leon Dabrowski, I'm going to bed!' She stormed out of the room and into the bedroom, slamming the door behind her.

Make a drink and have another go tomorrow. They would both have calmed down by then. Maybe that would give him the chance to tell her about Mary and the visits to all those brothels?

There was a new air of tranquillity about the place in the morning. They could behave as reasonable human beings, without arguing.

'You select the music, Magda. Order something serene and relaxing. I'll get the coffee,' he shouted through from the kitchen. 'I've booked our flights to Krakow, by the way. We're flying from Manchester.' Chekhov wouldn't be expecting that; he'd be checking passenger lists at the London airports. He tried to tell himself they were safe but if Magda could have seen his face, she would have realised he was terrified.

The revelations continued. Leon suppressed a grimace as frank and full details unfurled about Magda's seduction of Sergei. He tried to understand and accept what she'd done. But it cut him like a sharp knife. He listened with contrived indifference to what she had to say, refusing to give any reaction. But inside he was simmering with hurt. It became obvious that Magda couldn't wait to finish her confession and move on to a different subject. He told her about his encounters with the prostitute, Mary.

'If Mary is right, that makes her your half-sister.'

'She's *not* right. As I've already said, I'll get around to carrying out the research that she hasn't bothered to do. I'm a scientist, am I not?' He looked up and mentally kicked himself when he saw the sadness in her eyes. She was only trying to help. And if truth be told he *was* jealous of Sergei, even though his instinct told him this hadn't been infidelity. What Magda did was so brave. She'd risked everything for their love. As their eyes locked together, he knew that *he* was the one looking guilty now. 'I *do* appreciate what you've told me and I'll do as you suggest. I'll go back through the historical records and find out how the statements in their report could have arisen. And you must want some answers yourself.'

'I just want our love back, Leon.'

CHAPTER 40

The London apartment provided a safe house in which they could spend twenty-four hours a day together after months of separation; a place where they could lock themselves away and pour out their stories and their feelings in private. But it was becoming claustrophobic and their relationship was strained. After a week spent in their little piece of Earth between heaven and hell, Leon and Magda returned to Poland. Leon's Krakow apartment was to provide a peaceful haven in which they could recover from their respective traumas, settle down and learn to relax once more. At least that was the idea. Magda was watching the European business news when the entrance door crashed open.

'TV off!'

'TV closing down, Mahler,' replied the Melomet.

'Must remember to restore my old wafer-set. Don't want to be a *Classico* fugitive for the rest of my life.'

'I was watching that,' Magda said indignantly. 'It's all about Fusion Limited and progress in developing nuclear fusion power. I take it you're still interested in that?'

'Later, maybe? You and I have some serious detective work to do.'

'What are you talking about?'

'I'm talking about getting to the bottom of why we've lost almost a year of our lives through no fault of our own and why our relationship is now like a cotton thread under tension. You were swept up at random into an Eastern European sex trafficking operation and ended up in one of Alexei Rodin's brothels. It just happened to be located under the headquarters of the world's leading private nuclear power company where I worked. What's the probability of that happening?'

'Why are you raising your voice, Leon? Vanishingly small, I would say.'

He'd irritated her but he didn't seem to care. 'Agreed. It wasn't random at all. You must have been targeted. The next question is why? I'll tell you my own thoughts on that. Whoever arranged your abduction and incarceration did it to get *me* out of the way. If they could arrange for me to become preoccupied with finding you, it would divert me from my role within Fusion and provide them with the opportunity to help themselves to the data we'd accumulated from months of research at Greifswald. The data on the Goldhurst computers would be worth a fortune to any would-be hackers.'

'But how did they know you wouldn't go to Chekhov and ask for his help? They must have taken an enormous gamble.'

'I did consider speaking with him but it was a non-starter. Don't forget, I was involved with the Polish police by the time I came over to London. Imagine Chekhov's reaction if he'd discovered that? Whoever set this up must have carefully thought through the risks and rewards.'

Magda nodded. 'I think you're right. That had to be their motive for abducting me.'

'So, who arranged your abduction?' Leon asked.

'It could only have been Alexei Rodin. But if I was a specific target for him, then it means ...'

'Yes, you're thinking along the right lines. Rodin must have been involved in the data smuggling operation and she was the one who wanted me out of the way.'

'She?'

'Yes, Rodin is a woman. If we could gain access to the Russian Embassy's records, I think we'd find her name is spelt A–L–E–X–I. She dressed as a man while she was at Eight Over Nine to avoid detection by any vice squad. She must have realised that MI5 would be looking for a sophisticated madame who was capable of running a chain of high-class London brothels, whereas the Polish police would be looking for a brute of an overlord who controlled Eastern European sex trafficking gangs. Her disguise would throw them both.'

'But Rodin wouldn't be short of money. So, what was her motive for stealing the data?'

'Well, if you ask me, it *was* money,' Leon said confidently. 'Rodin must be a ruthless chancer and she must have realised that the rewards would be astronomical. But she couldn't have accessed the data herself. Someone had to be doing it for her.'

Magda looked at Leon with a wry smile. 'And it obviously wasn't you. How about Gunther? Would he have a motive?'

'I know Gunther and I trust my own judgement. I'm sure he wouldn't do anything like that, and they'd have watched Kaminsky like hawks while he physically handled the stellerator data. I reckon Kaminsky was murdered because whoever was responsible for the data theft must have discovered that he was getting close to rumbling them. That means someone inside Goldhurst with a high level of security clearance.'

'What about your CEO, Roman Slavic?'

'Slavic craves prestige and fame but isn't driven by money. And he appreciates that any Nobel Prize is likely to go to me and Gunther.'

'Oh, modesty, I must say.' Magda laughed at her own quip but she could see that Leon was in no mood for humour. 'You know these people better than I do, Leon. So, all we have is Alexei Rodin as the mole. What are we going to do about it?'

'Nothing – at the moment. We have our theory, that's all. We need to get proof and work out how she did it. That won't be easy now I no longer work for Fusion.'

Magda threw up her arms. 'What? You physicists and your damned theories.' She shook her head in dismay.

'Don't worry, Magda. I'll find the answers. Then we can start to rebuild our lives.'

It took Leon the best part of a week to persuade Magda to go back to the Stare Miasto in the centre of Krakow. 'I don't want to wake up in Eight Over Nine,' she kept telling him, and it hurt him to see someone with such a fine rational mind talking like that. They entered the main underground bar area of the Keller Klub. Leon pointed to the bar. 'Look, the seats we had that night – they're free. Let's sit there.'

Magda froze. 'Do you think this is such a good idea?'

'We have to face it,' Leon said, squeezing her hand. 'It's the only way we can unravel this torment in your head. Somehow, we have to wipe the slate clean, get back to where we were.'

Magda placed her hands flat on the bar. *She's trying to prevent me from seeing that she's trembling.* He touched her fingers as he had that fateful evening and she withdrew her hand. 'Leon, I don't think—'

He placed his finger over her lips. 'Don't talk. Just close your eyes and drift back. Remember how you felt. Remember our touches—'

'It's not going to work,' came a voice.

'What the—' Leon looked up. The man who'd taken the seat next to them was tall and well built; his penetrating eyes shone out from behind steel-framed spectacles.

'I said it isn't going to work. The damage is psycho-subliminal. It's burned into your psyche.'

'You just look here,' Leon snapped. He was standing now. 'You can mind your own business. And do it somewhere outside this bar.' He squared up to the big man who remained seated.

'Hold on, Leon. How does he know this?' Magda turned her attention to the stranger. 'You know what they did to me? You're one of them, aren't you?'

'In a sense I am. I work for Vladimir Chekhov.'

The throb of fear buzzed in Leon's ears. He turned towards Magda. Her mouth was open and her face was white. She must have realised it too. *Chekhov has finally tracked me down.*

'Forgive me,' the stranger said. 'Let me introduce myself. I am Ivan Kuzmin.'

'Kuzmin?' Magda sat up straight. 'I recognise that name. You're the one who wrote the report. What are *you* doing here?'

'I'm here to help you. I can get your mind straightened out. It requires a psychological procedure, a form of neuro-version.'

'You mean you're suggesting I let them zap my brain again? You can forget that.'

'Professor Tomala, believe me when I tell you I'm your only hope. What I'm offering is to arrange a reversal of the process known as n-flash. It would be the same neurosurgeon who applied the initial procedure. But don't worry, he no longer works for the Eight Over Nine management. He reports to Mr Chekhov without the pressures he encountered from the organisation at that time.'

'You make him sound like a Nazi death doctor,' said Leon.

'I can tell you don't trust me. And I can also see that you're afraid of what I represent.'

'I'm afraid of Chekhov, if that's what you mean. He wants to kill me.'

Kuzmin smiled and shook his head. 'You're wrong. Why would he kill you? He needs you. And this is what I seek in return for helping Professor Tomala. I want you to agree to a meeting with Vladimir Chekhov.'

'Why would I want to do that?'

322

'I'll explain. But first I must inform you of the current situation within Fusion Limited – *your* company, Dr Dabrowski. You've recently convened meetings with Mr Chekhov and you're therefore aware that results from research being carried out in Germany are being copied to American research teams.' Leon nodded. 'I must also inform you that this embezzlement of data has continued, despite the deaths of Drs Kaminsky and Slavic.'

A surge of cold electricity shook Leon's body. 'Slavic? He's dead too?'

'Yes. It was suicide, I found him myself. This means that you and your colleague Dr Gunther Schroeder are the only personnel who retain access to the data in question. Dr Schroeder is in custody.'

'You've imprisoned Gunther Schroeder? I can guarantee he wouldn't do anything like this. And *I'm* not involved. It has to be more complicated than you imagine.'

'Forget the data security issue for a moment. What's more important to Mr Chekhov is Fusion's research programme. Following the disruption to his senior management team, he's going to have to rely on *you* for the continuation of the programme. Without you, there would be no more data.'

Leon's mind shifted into overdrive – he had to be careful. Chekhov was astute; he desperately needed him back in charge of his programme and would probably pay anything for the privilege. But you never declare your hand early to a poker player like Chekhov. 'You mean Chekhov wants me to give his project a boost? Well, there'd be terms associated with that – his guarantee of my ongoing health for a start.'

'I'm afraid I can't provide guarantees on Mr Chekhov's behalf. In fact, he doesn't know I'm here. All I'm saying is that a meeting could be of great benefit to you both.'

'It sounds like you're not sure whether either of us would agree to such a meeting. What is it that's driving you?'

'Let's just say I'm doing my job. And in return for your cooperation I'm offering to help Professor Tomala.' He smiled at them in turn. 'I think it could be good for your relationship. Perhaps I should leave you now so you can think about my proposals?'

'Just a minute,' Magda said, 'I still have one more issue to resolve.'

'And which issue is that?'

'Your report, Kuzmin. Why did you investigate Leon's background, why all those questions about his parentage?'

'All in good time, Professor Tomala. I wish you a good evening. A pleasure to meet you both.' Kuzmin disappeared up the staircase. Leon and Magda were left looking at each other in astonishment.

The day was filled with a sparkling freshness and bright sunshine. Arms linked, they made their way along Kacik Street, pulling up close for warmth.

'You seem remarkably positive today, Leon,' Magda said, 'especially considering where we've just been.'

'What did you think of the museum?'

'It was more or less what I expected. Rewarding in its own way. Good for the soul.' She leaned her head on his shoulder. 'You've never visited Schindler's factory before. Why now?'

'I did it to put my life into context, Magda. Did you know that Szymon's father worked in there?'

'I didn't realise Szymon's family were Jewish.'

'They weren't. They were Christian. But his father married a Jewish girl. It was unusual around here at the time and for reasons I don't need to go into it turned out to be their nemesis. He and his first wife were taken to Auschwitz by the Germans. She was never seen again, but Mandek Dabrowski survived the holocaust, thanks to Oscar Schindler arranging for him to work in his factory.'

When they reached the bridge, Magda suggested that instead of going straight home they should continue down to the riverbank. 'Remember when we used to come here as students?' she said as they walked along the path at the side of the Vistula.

'I remember it well.'

'Leon, I recognise that look of determination in your eyes. But there's another programme running in that computer inside your skull. You're concerned about Chekhov, aren't you? Worried he's going to find out where we are and come for us?'

'Chekhov already knows where we are. He could be watching us as we speak.'

'He couldn't find you in London and since we no longer register our addresses in Melomet-space, he wouldn't be able to find you here.'

'Kuzmin found us, didn't he? Pavel has promised us round-the-clock protection and I believe him. But if Chekhov wanted us killed, we'd already be dead, believe me. No, it's not Chekhov that worries me. It's Gunther Schroeder.'

'What?'

'Poor Gunther is festering away in a cell while I'm doing nothing about it. He's innocent, I know he is. But how do I prove it? Oscar Schindler put his life on the line to save those hapless concentration camp inmates. He helped individuals he'd never even met. What am I doing to save my best friend?'

'You're going to agree to Kuzmin's request?'

'I have no choice. I have to meet Vladimir Chekhov.'

PART 4 – 2021

DAWN OF THE NUCLEAR FUSION AGE

CHAPTER 41

I t seemed like years since Leon was last inside Goldhurst. The receptionists were cheerful as usual, yet he sensed they'd been briefed on the reason behind his absence.

'Welcome home, Leon, we've missed you,' said the head receptionist. 'I'll let Mr Kuzmin know you're here.'

'Thank you, ladies. All is well, I hope.'

Their lack of response told him it wasn't. However, Kuzmin arrived within a minute, which was reassuring.

'Ah, Dr Dabrowski. So glad to have you back. Mr Chekhov is delighted with your decision to return to work and looks forward to meeting you in Monte Carlo. Here, I've renewed your pass.' Kuzmin placed the lanyard around Leon's neck. 'We can go straight up to the viewing room. Dr Schroeder is waiting for us.'

'Gunther's up there?'

Kuzmin waited until they were inside the elevator before he answered. 'I persuaded Mr Chekhov to move Schroeder from the old cells. I don't think he appreciates what poor conditions exist down there. It was like one of your old Victorian prisons – a legacy from his father's era. However, you can be assured that Dr Schroeder is now occupying more salubrious surroundings. He's still under house arrest, of course, until we get to the bottom of this commercial espionage matter.'

'You mean Chekhov still suspects him?'

'I'm afraid so.'

'But he *is* fit and well, isn't he? You haven't—'

'No, Dr Dabrowski, we haven't tortured him. We've even provided him with food and water. You're about to see for yourself.' The elevator door opened.

'Gunther!' Leon embraced his colleague, took a step back and shook him by the shoulders. 'Are you OK, my friend? You look terrible.'

'I'm all right. You look a bit drawn yourself.'

They embraced again.

'Ahem, gentlemen,' Kuzmin interrupted, 'can we proceed with the entry protocol?'

'Sorry, Kuzmin. You have to appreciate how glad we are to be here.'

Kuzmin ignored his sarcasm. 'Request access.'

The door to the data viewing room slid open and the three men entered. 'That's your seat on the extreme right,' Leon said, to Kuzmin's obvious annoyance. He took his own seat in the middle of the row of five stools, the room lights dimmed and the three occupied stools lit up in blue.

'Members *beta*, *gamma* and *epsilon* present,' said the Melomet. 'Members *alpha* and *delta* absent. Can the validator please confirm?'

Absent friends, thought Leon as he exchanged a sad glance with Schroeder. He nodded to Kuzmin.

'*Epsilon* confirms,' said Kuzmin, taking his cue.

'View latest upload,' Schroeder commanded.

A twisted loop of brilliant white ribbon sprang to life in front of the video-wall and the holographic image rotated about its vertical axis. 'It's looking good, Gunther. You've done a fine job since I've been away.'

'I'd hoped to be further on than this,' Schroeder replied, 'but you know the circumstances. Things would have been so different if you'd been here with us.'

'What does it all mean?' Kuzmin asked.

'This holographic image depicts the behaviour of the plasma within the stellerator during our latest tests. The process is the same one that powers the stars – the forced fusion of low-mass isotopes which releases enormous energy. You're looking at an image of man-made starlight.'

'You'll have to spare me the physics lesson, Dr Dabrowski. I'm more interested in security breaches at the moment. Can you determine what we've leaked and the implications?'

'I can. After all, this is why Chekhov let me back in, I presume. Can you provide the data status file, Gunther?' The hologram disappeared and a vast array of zeros and ones covered the video-wall. 'This doesn't represent the actual stellerator data, it merely shows the key dates for this particular test run, including when the initial upload took place, when the partitioned data were subsequently downloaded for use by individual engineering teams and so on. We can interpret this array to find out if a whole dataset has ever been copied in one go – a situation we wouldn't normally expect. How's your memory functioning, Gunther?'

'Let me see. This particular dataset is a month old and I can tell it hasn't been copied.' A glaze of sadness appeared in Schroeder's eyes.

'That means the Americans don't have the data from our most recent test run,' Leon said, trying to rid himself of the thought of Pawel Kaminsky's demise. 'Go back about six months, will you?'

'This one *has* been downloaded on to a zip,' Schroeder said, sounding dismayed.

Kuzmin was beginning to look alarmed. 'Can you tell who requested the download?'

'No, there's no electronic signature as such,' Leon replied. 'But we could perhaps infer who it was from the date. Who had access to the central computer system that day, which system technologist had clearance? It would require someone to trawl through the security records and it would take time. A job for your boys, Kuzmin.'

'Let me know what we need to do and I'll arrange it at once. What I don't understand is if the Americans have the data from a recent stellerator run, that's all they need, isn't it? They could use that to carry out their own research and continue to design a commercial reactor in parallel with us.'

'I can put you at ease there,' Leon said. 'The data in the file whose status we've just checked are incremental. In other words, only the *changes* since the previous run are recorded, not the absolute values. The Americans will be clever enough to back-extrapolate, of course. But if they don't have the stellerator settings from the breakthrough runs, they can't relate the data to the actual plant configuration at the time.'

'Do you want us to continue?' Schroeder asked.

'Yes, for a while. But as far as I can see, we're already in a position to start our security investigations.'

The binary digits scrolled slowly upwards. Leon only took his eyes off the video-wall for a few seconds at a time between datasets. It looked as if Kuzmin was struggling to stay awake. After fifteen minutes, the display froze. Schroeder turned towards Leon and stared with the hollow eyes of someone who'd just seen a gory murder. Leon shook his head, *say nothing*. 'Well, I reckon we have enough information to make our report to Chekhov next week,' he said, trying to mask the concern in his voice. 'What do you say, Gunther?' He turned towards Kuzmin. 'We need to go somewhere private to hold a detailed technical discussion. Can I suggest Dr Schroeder's latest prison cell?'

Kuzmin frowned at Leon's sarcasm. 'I'm glad to see your enthusiasm for continuing with the project but don't forget, security matters come first with Mr Chekhov.'

Leon shook his head cynically. *That's not what you told me in Krakow.*

The three men rose from their seats. The seat lights extinguished and a pale white light flooded the data viewing room.

They descended to Level G in the secondary elevator. Kuzmin left them with the two security guards posted outside Schroeder's ground-floor apartment. Leon showed the guards his pass and one of them opened the door.

'What do you reckon, Gunther? They downloaded those critical datasets only six weeks ago. That means someone has managed to bypass or decipher the crypto-key.'

'It's a tricky one. If the Americans have the data from those runs, they're in a strong position. Best of luck to them, I'd say. If we're going to provide the world with unlimited energy, we should have been collaborating with them in the first place.'

'I see where you're coming from but you haven't thought this through. We are just the scientists who solve the problems. If we don't keep it under wraps until it's fully developed, this technology could get into the hands of politicians, ruthless business magnates, megalomaniacs even – who knows what they'd do with it? At least we know where we stand with Chekhov. He's out to make money, as simple as that. Look, Gunther, I'm going to have to ask you this – and it will be once only.' Leon steeled himself. 'Are you stealing the data?'

Gunther clenched and unlocked his fists. 'No! It isn't me.'

They locked eyes for a while. 'That's good enough for me. We'll say no more about it.' But Leon could tell that Gunther wasn't going to leave it there.

'Leon, you know my views on Chekhov depriving the rest of the world of this technology. But they'll get it one day, even if they have to pay the devil in royalties. The real problem arises if a third party gets hold of our data *now*. That could result in years of litigation on intellectual property rights and we could end up with a debilitating drag on technical progress. Like you, I'm on Chekhov's side.'

'OK, I apologise. But *someone* is pilfering our key foundation data.'

'But do they appreciate the significance of their last download? And even if the Americans worked out what we'd done, they'd still have to find someone capable of fabricating the high precision super-conducting magnets, like we did. Then what would they do? Because what they haven't got is *you*. Your technical insight is so brilliant that it opens up enormous possibilities for whoever has that technology. Without you, they're going to take years to complete the task. Even *I* fail to understand how you manage to determine the parameter changes between our test runs. You provide us with a clear set of instructions, but there's no documented logic.'

'Just put it down to maverick intuition, Gunther. Like the chess grand master who holds a hundred scenarios in his head before he moves a single piece.' He smiled. 'Well, perhaps a bit more complex than that. And a lot of pieces to be moved.'

Schroeder returned a resigned laugh. 'I suppose you haven't made any serious mistakes so far. But you do realise that because we aren't allowed to publish our work, you're not even an internationally renowned scientist. If the Americans knew of your personal contribution to this project, it would be *you* they'd be stealing, never mind the data. I can see why Chekhov was keen to track you down. Anyway, as things stand, we're going to have to inform him of the significance of what the Americans now have in their back pocket.'

'*Might* have in their back pocket. We don't know whether they've done the deal yet. Listen, Gunther, I have a pretty good idea who is dealing with the Americans. But what I don't know is how they're getting hold of the data in the first place. We need to find out and stop this.'

'I may be able to help. What I didn't say in front of Kuzmin is that the data status files we looked at show some strange activity. Old data have been recently reviewed – as opposed to copied. Why would anyone want to do that? I'm going to take it up with the sys-techs.'

'OK, it's worth a shot. Keep me informed.' Leon rubbed his cupped hands down his face then ruefully shook his head. 'Fix us both a drink, will you? I'm going to give myself a tour of your new premises. Not a bad gaff, I have to admit.'

'Better than my last apartment,' Schroeder said, with a broad grin.

The accommodation was palatial and there was comfort in the fact that Chekhov must have sanctioned Gunther's relocation. But a disturbing thought took hold. What if today was just a ruse to get him to come here, what if he was now a prisoner too? He forced it to the back of his mind. Kuzmin had to be trustworthy, didn't he?

He wandered into the conservatory and was drawn towards the massive building façade he could see through the semi-opaque glass. The blurred view of the red brick wall to the side of the garden sent an icy prickle up his spine and a cold sweat enveloped him.

He pictured Magda, talking to him about her ideas for photographing and analysing the building's exterior – her sole view of the outside world in her time as a captive. But that could only mean … he slipped away from the living area, back into the apartment's private lobby. Kitchen, bathroom, that door had to be … he entered the bedroom. The king-size bed was unmade and hand-scribbled notes were scattered everywhere. He stood, mesmerised, in a sea of excruciating thoughts. This could even be where …

Schroeder came back from the kitchen with two steaming cups, just as Leon arrived back from his nosing about. 'You OK, Leon? You look like you've seen a ghost.'

'That's exactly what I *have* seen.'

CHAPTER 42

The first rays of dawn were filtering into the bedroom when Leon woke up from his shallow sleep. He'd hardly slept overnight – too much on his mind. Despite the mountain of work that confronted them in London and Greifswald, he needed this weekend break in Poland. Gunther's investigations were completed within days and the outcome was shocking. And he still had to work out what to tell Chekhov in a week's time. For a few moments he studied Magda, sleeping peacefully next to him, then slipped out of bed and crept into the kitchen. When the door behind him slid shut he ordered coffee.

'One black coffee ready, Leon,' said the Melomet.

He listened at the kitchen door. Satisfied that the Melomet's melodic-metallic voice hadn't stirred Magda, he crept into the lounge and sat down with his morning drink.

'You're up early,' Magda said, surprising him. She pecked him on his cheek then yawned and ruffled her hair as if this was her way of shaking the tiredness from her head.

'Good morning, my love. I couldn't sleep.'

'You're not feeling troubled, are you?'

'Well, actually, there was just one final matter I wanted to discuss with you. About Sergei.'

'Leon! I really *am* getting tired of this. It's a misplaced jealousy.' She was fully awake by now. 'How many times have I told you, I didn't love him, I didn't enjoy sex with him, I didn't want to do it, full stop. There was nothing else I could do, I saw it as my only way out. Sometimes I could—'

Leon put his arm around her. 'You're wrong, Magda. I don't hold anything against you. Or him, for that matter. I accept that what you did was for us. But I need to ask you one more question. It's the last one, I promise.'

She sat down, fury in her eyes. 'OK, what is it?'

'I don't mean to goad you. Trust me and just try to answer the question.' He paused and looked deep into her eyes. 'Did you see Sergei every day?'

'Leon, you're at it again. You—'

'Magda, please.' He was speaking in a soft voice. 'Did he take you training all day every day?'

'No, he didn't actually. There were days when he'd disappear after lunch and I'd be left in my room for the rest of the day. Sometimes he didn't come for me for days. Why do you ask?'

Leon walked to the rear window and breathed a deep sigh. He looked pensively towards the Krakow ghetto then walked back to the sofa and sat next to Magda.

'Leon, what is it?'

'Do you remember the long philosophical discussions we used to have when we were students?'

'I remember them well,' she replied, looking relieved. 'It was up with maths, down with physics. I used to love our debates, especially as I always won them.'

'Yes, you probably did.' He laughed. 'And I always had to concede that you mathematicians came up with solutions that were perfect. QED, as you would say. We physicists, on the other hand, would come up with some staggering theories that explained everything. Yet we could never be absolutely sure they were right. There was always some new phenomenon that would spring from nowhere and punch a hole in your theory. No theory is perfect, as they say.'

Magda smiled and hugged him. 'I do love you, Leon.'

'Which is why,' he continued, without responding to her cosseting, 'I've had to revisit my theory about your abduction and the smuggling of stellerator data to the Americans.'

'What are you talking about? I thought you and Gunther decided that Slavic was providing the data to Rodin. So, what exactly are you revisiting?'

'It's the loose ends that bother me, Magda. I need to fill the gaps in the theory.' He stood up and paced in front of her. 'You remember how you told me you were surprised they hadn't had you killed? Well, that means someone was reluctant to do that. And from what I've learned about Rodin, it wouldn't have been her. She would have snuffed you out as soon as look at you. Next dilemma, how did Slavic get the data past Fusion's security scanners? He may have had the highest security clearance and direct access to the data, but even *he* wouldn't have been able to stroll past the scanners with a wafer-zip full of top-secret data in his back pocket.'

'Do you have any ideas?'

'As it happens, I do.' Once again, he took his seat next to Magda. 'Since Chekhov added Slavic's former role to my own, I've had clearance to go anywhere on the Goldhurst site, unchallenged. And you'd be amazed at what I've found.'

Magda sat up straight.

'At the far end of the entrance hall, there's a corridor off to the left. At the end of that corridor there's a hidden entrance to a ground-floor complex that was under the control of Oleg Malkin. The complex is out of bounds for Fusion staff and it includes both Malkin's and Rodin's personal quarters and a control base for their respective security teams. As these security teams serve both Fusion and Eight Over Nine, this common control base is physically linked to both operations. And, as I've discovered, Fusion's security scanning system doesn't apply to the link between their main offices and the security control centre. They rely entirely on manual intervention to prevent unauthorised personnel access. You can see their logic in designing the place like that. It allows rapid deployment of security personnel in the event of an emergency.'

'That means there's a hole in Fusion's security boundary which in principle would let a wafer-zip pass through,' Magda said.

'Exactly. But Malkin recognised this at some point and had scanners fitted between the living quarters and his security control centre. The rest of his private complex had no physical links to Fusion.'

'Except, of course the security centre.'

'Right again. Then we have the administrative security barrier. Let me show you.' Leon grabbed his wafer-board and started to sketch.

Magda pointed to the obvious flaw in Fusion's security system on Leon's scribbled map. 'The security personnel would come and go to work via that corridor, which forms part of the living quarters in which Malkin had electronic detectors installed. But for health and safety reasons, they have their own separate emergency exit here,' she dotted her finger on to the diagram, 'leading straight into Fusion's entrance hall and bypassing the scanners. God, how did he miss that?'

'I agree, it's a howler. Unless of course he left Rodin to design the details. After all, Rodin *did* design Eight Over Nine itself.'

'You mean Rodin set this up so she could have simply gone into Fusion, collected the wafer-zip from Slavic and walked out with it, undetected?'

'Aha! You're getting there. But it's not quite as simple as that. Rodin didn't have security clearance to go inside Fusion. I presume that's because it would have been too contentious for a Russian diplomat to be seen wandering around a highly sensitive nuclear power company. Although the two security teams shared the same control base, they in fact operated as independent units with mutually exclusive personnel. Except, that is, for Rodin's mole.'

Magda looked at Leon. Her face went white as if she'd come over sick.

'I can see it in your eyes, Magda. You now realise what's been going on. Yes, it *was* Sergei. He was the mole who carried the data through for Rodin. Sergei Vitaliev was initially employed as a Fusion security officer to work under Oleg Malkin. When Rodin incarcerated you, she persuaded Malkin to assign Vitaliev to special duties inside Eight Over Nine – as your trainer. Rodin now has a man with a foot in both camps. Vitaliev could keep an eye on you while he flitted between his two jobs as he saw fit. That's why I pressed you about his schedule. It was nothing to do with jealousy.' Leon could see the effect this was having on Magda; she was shocked and angry with herself.

'OK, your logic seems sound. But tell me this, physics boy. How could Slavic have been persuaded to pass over the data and why would Sergei have been willing to carry the zip through? They'd have both been acutely aware of the consequences of being found out. How did Rodin persuade them to do it?'

'Well, the first part of your question is easy. As you discovered yourself, Sergei Vitaliev was in the navy. I've since found out that he was known to Rodin when he took on the Fusion security job. That's because between his military service and his job at Fusion he was used by Rodin as a hitman. It's almost certain that he was responsible for Kaminsky's murder. As a trained killer, it was easy for Vitaliev to persuade Slavic to part with the data. He probably just threatened to cut his gonads off. Slavic would have been completely out of his depth and no doubt petrified. As for Vitaliev, he simply did whatever Rodin asked of him.'

'You mean I've been sleeping with an assassin? You seem to delight in telling me this, Leon. If you're so sure, what was Sergei's incentive? How can someone be persuaded to do something as vile as kill another person? And if Sergei was that evil, why didn't he just kill me and have done with it?'

'I don't know the answer to that last question. You must have had a guardian angel who prevented him from doing it. As for the incentive, Rodin coerced Vitaliev using the most powerful force she had at her disposal – the power of love. Rodin and Vitaliev are lovers.'

Magda's pallid face turned red. She stood up and prodded Leon in the chest. 'We're going to get the bastards,' she said, then stormed off to the bedroom. Leon heard the anticipated slamming of the door. He hated himself for doing this but there would have to be no lingering secrets between them before their wedding. Sergei Vitaliev may have disappeared, but they both had to know the truth about him so they could move on from beneath his shadow. And in his own case, this was now becoming personal in more than one way. *I could be his next target.*

CHAPTER 43

The big fish glided silently past. Sharks were lone predators unless they gathered at a feeding frenzy. Here they had no choice. *Fascinating.* This meeting was going to be about sorting out their differences, working together and getting Fusion up and running again. Kuzmin was right – Chekhov was never going to punish him.

'Good morning, Dabrowski. I wasn't aware that your scientific interests extended to marine biology.' Vladimir Chekhov and Ivan Kuzmin marched into the room.

Their handshakes were warm and genuine. Chekhov kept hold of Leon's hand for what seemed like a full minute. 'Intriguing place to hold a meeting,' Leon said.

'Playing on home territory, as the English would say. We have much to discuss. Please take a seat and I'll have coffee sent down. I hope you don't mind Mr Kuzmin joining us. As you know, he's my security specialist.'

This was a good start. The table's circular shape represented strength and symmetry; it avoided the *us and them* syndrome. In this together and safe from the sharks.

'Why do you think I've brought you over, Dabrowski? Tell me.'

Interesting opening gambit. 'You want to know whether I think someone is trying to reconstruct our reactor design using our proprietary data,' Leon replied.

'You are right, of course. Data security is one of the items on my agenda. Hence Kuzmin's presence. More importantly, I've brought you here to meet you face to face. You've worked for my company for almost four years and during that time you've led my technical team through one of mankind's most significant scientific steps forward. Work which I have funded. Yet only now do we appear in the same room together.'

'Not my fault. You never came over to Germany to observe our work. You haven't even visited the London design office that *you* set up – your own company HQ. Until recently, of course.'

'And *you* were always too busy to travel to Monte Carlo. We always had to communicate by video link. Well, things have changed during your absence. I now hold meetings with my directors *here*, at my home. And *you* are one of my directors, Dabrowski. Think of it as a project progress meeting, if you like. An extremely important one on this occasion, I might say.'

'You have my full attention. Where's the agenda?'

Chekhov gave a mocking laugh. 'How many other directors would speak to their president like that? They would be sacked on the spot for insolence. However, in your case your intellect saves you. You are vital to the future of my company. Hence, I must continue to tolerate your tantrums. Because that is what I see you as,

346

Dabrowski – a spoilt child. Did your father have to put up with such behaviour?'

Leon was boiling inside but he wasn't going to let the steam escape. 'I didn't know my father, he died when I was a baby. But in answer to your question, I had a perfectly good relationship with my stepfather. The man who brought me up as a child was a fine father to me.' He felt regret as soon as the words left his mouth. Chekhov was clearly offended by his remark. And why did Kuzmin look so uncomfortable? *Not such a good start, after all.*

'Back to business,' Chekhov said, restoring order to the meeting. 'We have evidence of Wendelstein-7X design information being available to scientists at the Los Alamos laboratory. I was hoping you would have some idea of who provided them with this information and how they managed to extract it from computers that are supposed to be protected with the highest levels of data security.'

'I have proof that Dr Slavic was responsible. He managed to get hold of software that ports our system's artificial intelligence-based protection interface to a zip at the time of the illegal download. Sorry, Kuzmin, I've only just confirmed this for myself.'

'Slavic?' Chekhov said with surprise.

'Yes. But you need to know he wasn't stealing data for financial gain or even for altruism's sake, so the rest of the world could have this technology. He was doing it because his life was being threatened – by Alexei Rodin.'

Chekhov and Kuzmin sat up straight.

Now they were really shocked. 'Yes, Rodin is your real culprit and she disappeared before you could sack

347

her. I suggest we don't waste any more time discussing how and why and start to look at the significance of the data the Americans have already obtained.'

Chekhov nodded. Leon could see that Kuzmin was smiling his approval across the table. *I'm beginning to like this guy.* 'Kuzmin and I have sat down with Gunther Schroeder and the three of us have identified the data files that have been copied. I have to say, it's pretty serious. The latest datasets they copied contain the key foundation data. If the Americans get hold of the data from those particular runs, they effectively have our fundamental design.'

Chekhov went rigid. 'What do you mean *if* they get hold of the data? You've just told me they have a copy.'

'I told you *someone* has a copy. But we can't be sure the Americans have it yet.'

'Why wouldn't they?'

'The crypto-keys for the foundation datasets are significantly more complex than those of the latest runs. This is because our artificial intelligence software progressively increases the complexity of the protection algorithms with time. Slavic would have had to explain that to Rodin to make sure she didn't embarrass herself with the Americans. On one hand the Americans would be close to their pot of gold. On the other hand, they'd have to overcome a significant barrier to get to it. My guess is that Rodin, wherever she is at the moment, is engaged in a complex set of negotiations with Los Alamos.'

'We have to recover their latest pirated wafer-zip,' Kuzmin said. 'Let's hope Rodin is still in the UK.'

Chekhov turned towards Kuzmin. 'You must start your enquiries at once. Find out where Rodin is hiding and retrieve the vital data. And bring back Rodin – I wish to speak with her. Dabrowski, come with me. I have other matters to discuss.'

'Why have we moved? I was enjoying your shark aquarium.'

'Here in my private quarters, I discuss only the most sensitive aspects of my business, Leon. Only the most senior members of my service staff and security team ever see the inside of these rooms. Consider yourself to be privileged. Please be seated, I have a few more questions for you.'

Leon was intrigued. Not only about the privilege he'd been afforded but the fact that Chekhov addressed him by his first name.

'If you are right about Rodin, and I believe you are, why did she do it? If her colleagues at the embassy planted her at Goldhurst specifically to steal this information for the Russian State, why would she become a traitor to her country?'

'Money – as simple as that. Once she discovered the true fiscal value of the data, she decided to defect and run off with any money she could bleed out of the Americans.'

'I agree to the release of Dr Schroeder.'

Leon was taken aback. After all his pleading, Gunther would at last be set free – just like that.

Chekhov fired in the next question. 'If we can't stop Rodin, what are the ultimate consequences of the

Americans having access to our fundamental fusion reactor design?'

Leon felt like he was in an interview to preserve his own job. 'Commercially, they'd be snapping at our heels. But I'm afraid that would be your problem, not mine. Your lawyers against theirs, patents and intellectual property rights, proof of ownership, that sort of thing. I can't help you.'

'So, it would be winner take all?' Chekhov smiled. 'I assure you, we don't have a problem on that account. However, once the Americans have this pot of gold you refer to, what is to stop them from developing the technology in an alternative direction and offering certain unscrupulous states around the globe a better and cheaper energy option than ours?'

'There's *nothing* to stop them.' It was now Leon's turn to smile. 'But technically they'd never be ahead of us – as long as you have me and Gunther on your side.' The smile left Leon's face. *Or unless they took us out of the equation.*

'I was hoping you would say that. Your relationship with Professor Tomala. Are you expecting to become married in the near future? If so, is it likely to affect your focus on the job in hand?'

My God, he's so hard to keep up with. 'The answer to your first question is yes. I intend to marry her. But there are personal issues to resolve before that can happen. Regarding my performance in the job you've just given me, I won't let you down. Magda has always been interested in my work from a theoretical point of view. I occasionally find it helpful to seek her opinion on the mathematical aspects.'

'Perhaps we could use her as a consultant? Do you think she would be of benefit to us as a company employee?'

Leon laughed. 'Nice try. I've even suggested that myself. But she just switches off at the hint of any suggestion she should move into the commercial world. She's a dyed-in-the-wool academic and wild horses can't change that.' He looked Chekhov in the eye. 'If we're going to consider personal relationships in this discussion, may I ask *you* a question?'

'Go ahead.'

'You reinstated me in my job. In fact, you promoted me to the top job in the company. Yet you had concerns over my potential involvement in data smuggling. What gave you the confidence to reappoint me?'

'You are quite right, I wasn't one hundred per cent convinced by your story before today. But I always realised that *you* were. I saw it in your eyes, even though I was looking at a video screen. The way you appealed for the release of your friend. Your whole demeanour was one of sincerity.'

'I could always tell that you were studying me – watching me more than listening to me.'

Chekhov smiled. 'How perceptive you are. And the moment I met you face to face I knew you were honest.'

'Thank you.'

'Yes, I've always considered myself to be a fine judge of character. It serves me well in my business dealings. Take Oleg Malkin, for example. I gave him complete freedom over my father's former business empire, yet I knew from day one he was swindling me and even mocking me behind my back. The British have a vulgar expression for it, something to do with the removal of urine. But I refuse to imitate their gutter-level behaviour with the use of such terms.'

'Why did you tolerate him?'

Chekhov smiled sardonically. 'Oh, I have my reasons for that. Think of the sharks in my tank. In their simple minds they think they're in charge of their own destinies. But in reality, they're helpless. I have them trapped where I can see what they are up to. I can even decide whether they live or die. And that is where I had Oleg Malkin – in an inescapable tank. You see, Malkin's treachery came as no surprise to me. My initial character judgement was vindicated. He was a fool but he was useful to me, he was generating a valuable income stream. And even though he was helping himself to the lion's share of the rewards, all the time I was taking back what was rightfully mine.

'How did you manage that?'

'Simple, I hacked into his bank accounts.' Chekhov looked down at the framed photograph on his desk. 'But I *have* made mistakes. There is one significant misjudgement of character I made many years ago. And it proved to be a costly one. Although it had little effect on my business at the time, it had devastating implications for me personally.'

Leon looked at the photograph. 'I did hear about your late wife. I understand she died in childbirth. And I can see it still affects you. Would it help to tell me about it?' He winced. He shouldn't have asked such a personal question about the death of Chekhov's wife and child.

He felt as if he'd just undone all the positives they'd cultivated over this past hour. 'I'm sorry, I didn't mean—'

'Don't be sorry, young man. You may just be right. I've not spoken of this since I was a young man myself. Yet it haunts me every day of my life.' He picked up the frame and rubbed his thumbs down its edges as he studied the fading photograph of Natalia Chekhov. 'She left me with a beautiful young son after her death. He was to be my sole heir and the world would have been his oyster.'

The child didn't die?

Chekhov continued. 'But he was taken from me when he was only a few months old. Kidnapped. And to this day, I've failed to discover what their demands were to be. I hunted them for ten years and I still don't know why they did it. But I do know *who* was at the heart of this plot.' He squeezed the frame with shaking hands. 'It was Abram's nanny. Would you believe that? I will never forget that evil woman. Her name was Jean Douglas.'

Leon felt as if a sledgehammer had smashed into his chest. He fought for breath, praying that Chekhov wouldn't look up and see his distress. He was no longer listening. He could see Mary Douglas sitting in the chair at the other side of the desk, her sad eyes pleading for the truth about the whereabouts of her mother, beseeching him to admit that it was *her* mother in the photograph. Her image evaporated. Still in shock, he found himself listening once more to Vladimir Chekhov.

'I have to accept that Abram is dead. They would no doubt have killed him many years ago. But I will continue to hunt down the nanny until I find her.' He was still looking at Natalia Chekhov's photograph. 'I don't even have a photograph of Abram. Nothing whatsoever to remember him by.'

The room filled with an unnerving silence.

'Oh, but you do,' Leon said at last. He took off his security pass and slowly pushed it across the desk towards Chekhov.

'What is this?' Chekhov snapped as he inspected Leon's photographic ID.

'It's a photograph of your son.'

'Is this some kind of sick joke?'

'It's no joke. Look at me. Then look again at the photograph on your desk. Can you have any doubt? She's my mother.' He swallowed hard to prevent himself from bursting into tears. 'And I've only just found out.'

Leon faced his biological father in stony silence. They met for the first time today – in every sense. Who would ask the first question? How would they feel about each other?

The knock at the door wasn't enough to wrench them from their tense contemplations. A few moments later, Ivan Kuzmin let himself into the private office.

'Sorry to intrude, sir. I propose to travel back to London this afternoon and continue my investigations from there. I've already been in touch with the Metropolitan Police.'

Chekhov snapped out of his trance. 'Just get on with it, Kuzmin. Get the duty helicopter pilot to take you to the airport.'

'Would Dr Dabrowski like to accompany me? Have you finished your business?'

Leon could see that Chekhov was about to say no – but changed his mind.

'Yes, I think we have,' Chekhov said, giving Leon a stern look, 'for now.' He turned to Kuzmin. 'On your way out, would you please take Dr Dabrowski to my surgery and ask the phlebotomist to take a sample of his blood. I want the results from his DNA analysis reported to me by this evening.'

Leon felt numb. It was going to take the rest of his lifetime for this to sink in. And why was Kuzmin looking so pleased? *Of course – his report.*

CHAPTER 44

Leon and Kuzmin arrived in London early evening and went straight to Goldhurst.

'Rodin must be aware of the value of those datasets,' Leon said, as Kuzmin finished installing the schedule of risks on the video screen. 'She'll hang in for millions.' They were in the private annexe of the security complex, getting ready to brainstorm for all they were worth.

'But she's had the data for weeks. How can we be sure it's not already too late?'

'We can't. But if you want the data back, you have to be optimistic and assume that Rodin is still bartering.'

'She *is* still bartering,' said Chekhov.

Leon and Kuzmin looked at each other in surprise, then turned towards the video-wall.

'I've listened to everything you've said over these past few minutes. And I can reliably inform you that the Americans don't yet have the breakthrough data.'

Leon smiled to himself. *No Melomet, the crafty old sod.*

'Sir, how do we know that, if you don't mind me asking?' Kuzmin said.

'I thought you could have worked that out for yourself, Kuzmin? We have our own mole inside the Los Alamos centre. Remember?'

'Ah yes, Karl Fenner.'

This was fascinating. 'The name sounds familiar. I recall Gunther telling me of an outstanding candidate he'd interviewed during our recruitment drive. We need to get him back. He could be a significant asset. You also need to let me meet the designer of the shark tank I can see behind you. He's made huge advances in holographic imaging technology. He could help us with—'

'Later,' growled Chekhov. 'For now, all you need to know is that Rodin is still negotiating. Press on with your endeavours. In the meantime, I have my own contacts to pursue. Be assured I'm working as hard as you are on these matters. Chekhov out.'

'How did you know the aquarium was a hologram?' asked Kuzmin.

'I agree, it looks real. But there's no obvious video screen in that room. I decided he had to switch one segment of the tank between functions when his meetings included external members.'

'You're such a clever—'

Kuzmin was interrupted by the Melomet. 'Call for you, Mr Kuzmin. It's Mr Chekhov.'

Leon raised his eyebrows to Kuzmin. *That was quick.*

'We've found Rodin!' There was an excitement in Chekhov's voice that Leon hadn't heard before. 'I should have told you – my enquiries inside the Russian Embassy uncovered more details of Rodin's henchman, Sergei Vitaliev. I contacted the Metropolitan Police and convinced them he was their prime suspect in the murder of Pawel Kaminsky. They've been searching for him for days and at last they have a sighting at the Paddington Hilton Hotel. And would you believe it, Rodin is with him? We have them trapped in their hotel room. I want you to get over there right away, Kuzmin. The police are expecting you. You'll have to let them take Rodin into custody but make sure you retrieve the wafer-zip before they do. Vitaliev may be armed so take a couple of your best men with you.'

'I'll go with him.'

'No, Leon! I forbid it. It would be too dangerous.' Chekhov stared out of the screen with pleading eyes. 'And you are very precious to me.'

The black cab rolled into the forecourt of the Paddington Hilton. This was some big hit – half a dozen police vehicles, two ambulances, blue lights flashing. The dog handlers were getting their dogs back into the vans and it looked like the armed police officers were retiring. *Job done.* Leon showed his Fusion pass to the uniformed officer at the entrance and breezed past him into the hotel's reception. Ivan Kuzmin and his two security officers were standing at the reception desk; Kuzmin was speaking into his wafer – reporting the good news to Chekhov, no doubt.

'Leon? What are you doing here?' Kuzmin slapped the wafer on to the desk.

First-name terms, he must be happy. Leon gave Fusion's head of security the broadest of smiles. 'I couldn't resist—'

'This is no laughing matter. Mr Chekhov is going to be angry.'

'He needn't be. I only followed you to catch the final curtain. I knew you'd do a fine job. I'm just a member of the public, don't forget. And the police wouldn't put the public at risk—'

'The police bungled it!' Kuzmin snapped. 'Their observers failed to do their jobs. Look!' He pointed. Two paramedics were each wheeling a stretcher with a body bag perched on top. 'Rodin and Vitaliev slipped through the net and that's what they've left behind – both shot between the eyes.'

'What?'

'Yes. We've lost them thanks to police incompetence. That's what he's going to be angry about. Not your disobedience. Who knows where they are now? They've probably arranged a new rendezvous with their contact. The airport is close. All those terminals, scores of shops and restaurants – it's going to be impossible to find them.'

'You're right, they have to be heading for the airport. And there *is* no contact. The zip is so valuable that Rodin has to be carrying it over personally – with Vitaliev riding shotgun. Quick! Get on to the flight scheduling sites. Find the most direct route to Los Alamos and forget the police. From now, we're taking over the chase.'

'Screen on!' Kuzmin frantically worked the reception's touch screen. 'Here they are. Terminals 3 or 5. Los Alamos via Dallas Fort Worth. Which one?'

'Flight times. Look them up.'

'Let me see. Dallas Fort Worth – Terminal 5, British Airways four hours from now.'

'Any more flights? Hurry!'

'Yes, there's another – Terminal 3, Delta Airlines just under two hours' time.'

'That has to be the one. Let's get a move on. There's a new Metro-link that takes only ten minutes.'

'How did you know about—'

'Come on. We're wasting time.' *The last few months of my life have burned the Metro map into my brain. That's how.*

Kuzmin and his men regrouped. After searching the whole of the Terminal 3 Departures area, there was no sign of Rodin or Vitaliev. 'They're not here,' Kuzmin said.

Leon clenched his fists like a boxer and tapped them against his temples. 'Let me think. OK, let's check the Arrivals area.'

'What? Are you sure they won't have already gone through to the Departures lounge?'

'Call it a hunch. Why would they pass through security so early? And they wouldn't just hang about here. Come on, follow me.'

The Arrivals hall was teeming. 'We're never going to find them among this crowd,' Kuzmin said, sounding dismayed.

Leon was beginning to think Kuzmin was right. They were chasing a lost cause. He peered towards the throng of passengers pouring out through Customs. A young man in baggy jeans, Dallas Cowboys football top and a baseball cap caught his attention. Nothing unusual about being dressed like that if he'd just got off an American flight, but why did he carry no luggage?

'Leon, what are you looking at?'

'I've seen that guy before. Got it. The photograph Gunther Schroeder showed me of his interview candidate. It's Karl Fenner, our man at Los Alamos.'

'That's impressive. You must have a photographic memory.'

'Yes, I have,' Leon casually replied. 'Don't you see? I was wrong. They were never going to fly over to New Mexico themselves. The deal was probably finalised days ago and Fenner has come over to collect the data. He has to be a double agent. Come on, let's follow him. You and I will stay a few paces back, Kuzmin. He may just recognise our faces.'

'Kobra, Gaduka – get after him!' Kuzmin yelled, 'Melomet-links on open.' The four men followed Karl Fenner out of the terminal building. 'He's heading for the car park. Once he reaches it, spread and stay well back until we identify the car he's making for.'

'I'll stay right with you, Kuzmin.'

'Make yourself scarce, Leon. If Vitaliev is here, I don't want you anywhere near him. We'll sort it out. These guys are trained in tactical assault.'

'I'll be careful.'

'Just get out of here.' Kuzmin broke into a trot.

Leon watched Kuzmin until he was three car ranks ahead. A thought struck him. *He's going to recognise Vitaliev. They worked in the same security centre.* Disobeying orders yet again, he followed Kuzmin. Within thirty seconds, the wafer traffic went into overdrive.

'Red Mercedes saloon on Row M.'

'Got it. One male, one female inside. It has to be them. Kobra, get to the back of Row N and wait until I give the signal. Gaduka, back of Row M. Start moving towards the target, but keep low.'

'Directly behind target. The mark is at the driver's side now.'

'Stay low, Kobra. And don't budge.'

'Ready.'

'Can you see the mark, Gaduka?'

'Yes.'

'Wait.'

Leon watched their adroit manoeuvres from Row K. As if part of Kuzmin's team, he crouched behind a Mini and peered across its bonnet towards the Mercedes. Fenner was speaking to Rodin through the open car window. Kuzmin was walking slowly towards the car. *What's he playing at? They must be able to see him by now.*

'Go!'

Kuzmin's men sprang from their positions and bounded towards the vehicle like leopards. Kuzmin went full tilt at Fenner and downed him with an American-football-style tackle. Alexei Rodin's mouth gawped open. The security officer code-named Kobra dragged her out of the driver's seat and held her in a rear arm lock. Rodin cut a sleek figure in her silk blouse and short skirt. *At least they had the decency not to beat up a woman.*

A man wearing jeans and a tight sweater leapt from the passenger's side of the car. *So that's Sergei Vitaliev.* Leon jumped up, whistled and waved his arms in an attempt to distract him. It worked. For a second their eyes met across the rows of parked cars. The second security officer charged in from the side. *Gaduka has him.* Vitaliev moved like lightning. Before Gaduka could take him out, he caught him by the arm and twisted it up his back. Gaduka's arm broke at the elbow joint with a loud snap. He screamed like a banshee. Vitaliev let him drop to the ground and bolted off like a sprinter. With no idea of what he was going to do next, Leon set off after him.

'When does the next flight leave?' Leon asked, panting as he arrived at the Delta Airlines Terminal 3 check-in desk.

'Thirty minutes,' said the girl behind the desk. 'You still have time to get to the gate, sir.'

Leon produced his Fusion security pass. 'I have no passport. Can I use this? First class if possible.'

'Of course, Dr Dabrowski. A director of Fusion can travel on almost any airline in the world. Let me see, I'll just scan it through. Yes, that's fine. Fusion's account is now debited. Will there be anything else?'

'No thanks. Have to run.'

'Call for you, Leon,' said the Melomet, from the wafer in his pocket. 'Mr Chekhov.'

Leon was taken aback. Attractive though the voice might be, the trouble with the Melomet was it didn't convey the caller's emotion. *He's going to be mad, I know it.*

'Leon, you've just booked a flight to St Petersburg. What are you doing?'

'Vitaliev. I'm going after him.'

'I've already told you. No! We have Rodin and that traitor, Fenner. Leave Vitaliev to the police. I don't wish to lose you a second time.'

'Sorry, Father. It's important to me.' *Father? Just doesn't sound right. And he made no mention of the zip.* Decision made, he scurried towards the Departures lounge. Still running, he flashed his Fusion pass across the scanner at Gate 7. *Made it.*

The gate was open and the economy class passengers were beginning to scan their boarding passes. No sign of him. According to Magda, Vitaliev was planning to go back to St Petersburg once he finished his contract at Eight Over Nine. With Rodin and Fenner arrested, surely it was time for him to implement his retirement plan? *I've blown it.* Vitaliev wasn't taking this flight after all. *He has the zip and he's on a plane to the States right now.* He rubbed his hands across his eyes and looked up towards the gate as the final passengers filed through. And there at the back of the line was Sergei Vitaliev. *Game on.*

Leon settled back into the seat in his private corral. 'Welcome to first class, sir,' said the hostess. 'Can I get you a news-wafer?'

'No, thanks. I'd like a blindfold, though.'

'Certainly, sir. Would you like me to wake you up before we land?'

'Don't worry, I won't be sleeping.'

Let's just think about this. If they've searched and interrogated Rodin and Fenner, Chekhov would know by now that Vitaliev has his precious data. The zip in Vitaliev's pocket contains key information that would assist the Americans in developing their own commercial fusion reactor and he's well aware of its value. He's going to hold out for megabucks. And if Vitaliev realises who I am, he'd be doing the Americans a favour by killing me. How have I got myself mixed up in all this? He lifted the blindfold and rubbed his tired eyes. Gunther Schroeder was standing in front of him.

'If the Americans knew of your personal contribution to this project, it would be *you* they'd be stealing.'

Have they lured me on to this plane?

Schroeder faded away and Chekhov took his place. 'You are very precious to me.'

He tried to stop me getting this flight. Is it because he doesn't want the Americans to have me?

Magda, is that you?

'Guilt? Jealousy? These are new words for our dictionary, aren't they?'

Is it about Magda and Vitaliev … or me and Vitaliev … or me and Magda?

A long and stressful afternoon was drawing to its close; the emotions flooded in and Leon let out the tears in silence.

Thirty minutes into the flight. *It's time. There can't be many passengers back there in economy class. Let's hope the seats next to him are unoccupied.* Leon was halfway down the aisle when he spotted him. *Window seat, alone. Perfect.* With his heart in his mouth, he sat down next to Sergei Vitaliev.

'Mind if I join you?'

Vitaliev's face was a picture of surprise. 'I saw you in the car park,' he said, wide-eyed. 'Who are you? Ah, don't tell me. You work for Vladimir Chekhov. You're a Chekhov boy.'

'Yes, to both assertions.'

'You have no business with me. What do you want?'

'I want the zip you're carrying. It doesn't belong to you.'

Sergei sneered at him. 'You're not one of his security team – I can tell. Besides, I'd recognise you if you were. You want your data back? Go ahead, take it from me if you can. I'm waiting.'

It was Vitaliev who made the move. Like an expert pickpocket, his hand darted inside Leon's jacket and emerged with his wafer. 'You won't need this,' he said, switching it off. 'Now what are you going to do?'

Leon now had no way of alerting the authorities. He cursed his own stubbornness. His jealousy had driven him to this showdown, with no available backup. He was at the mercy of a killer and looking him straight in the eyes. Should he tell him who he was? *That would only give him the opportunity to gloat over his conquest of Magda.* He shook his head to clear the thought. Vitaliev wouldn't give a damn about Magda.

He knew who he was and he'd be deciding whether to kill him.

'Ladies and gentlemen, this is your captain speaking. We are about to enter a zone of high turbulence. For your own comfort, I would ask you to remain seated with your seat belts fastened. In the event of an emergency, please carry out the actions shown in the hologram. Thank you.'

Leon kept his eyes fixed on Vitaliev throughout the captain's announcement. It was almost like looking in a mirror. Did Magda use him as a substitute to satisfy her womanly needs? Would she have closed her eyes and pretended it was him every time they made love? Surely, it had to feel different for her? Was it better?

The plane lurched to the side as it dropped into the air pocket. Involuntary yelps of surprise rang around the cabin. Leon instinctively turned in his seat and clicked the buckle of his seatbelt. He realised his blunder too late – it provided his adversary with the chink of opportunity he needed. He felt a sudden pressure on his throat as Vitaliev's forearm pinned him back in his seat. His first reaction was to raise his right arm to defend himself but it felt limp and useless. He felt a sharp icy pain on the wrist of his free arm. A heavy weight pressed down on his legs and shoulders and the cabin lights swirled above his head. His mouth sagged open as his head collapsed on to his shoulder and he felt a warm liquid running off the fingertips of both hands. *I'm dying.* His whole body was numb and his eyes were closing. With his last shred of energy, he raised his eyes and stared through the haze. Vitaliev was smiling, brandishing his gleaming white teeth. 'Goodbye, Chekhov boy.'

CHAPTER 45

Leon's eyes focused. *Another gleaming smile.* 'Magda, is that you?'

Vladimir Chekhov welcomed Leon back into the world with a squeeze of his hand. 'We were all worried about you.'

'Where am I?'

'St Petersburg. You are in hospital, my son.'

'What happened?'

'It was Pentothal, a barbiturate that induces general anaesthesia within thirty seconds. Vitaliev used a specially adapted wafer with an edge honed to razor-blade sharpness. It would have been undetectable to the airport security scanners. He also tried to kill you by slitting your wrists. What sort of person carries such vile and covert weaponry?'

Leon looked down at his bandaged wrists. On the opposite side of the bed to his father, a peristaltic pump squeezed fresh blood through his veins. 'But, how did—'

'How did we stop him? It was Ivan Kuzmin who did that. On my instruction, he followed you on to that flight.

He was a few rows back in the main cabin. For my part, I arranged a brief delay in your take-off to make sure he boarded. And your next question is what happened to Vitaliev?'

Leon tried to smile but he felt like one of the old Metro-tube trains was rattling through his head.

'Kuzmin is good at his job, Leon.'

'But Vitaliev is a trained killer.'

'Even trained killers go down like a sack of stones if they receive an old-fashioned uppercut to the chin. Vitaliev wouldn't have been expecting it and as Kuzmin was familiar with him from their Goldhurst security training programmes, he knew exactly what style of assault would work best. All Kuzmin then had to do was identify the flight's shotgun rider and borrow his handcuffs. That wasn't difficult – the undercover antiterrorist agent came across to investigate the disturbance within seconds. Kuzmin simply showed him his Fusion pass and the agent assisted with the arrest.'

'The wafer-zip?'

'While Vitaliev was out cold, Kuzmin searched him and retrieved the wafer-zip. I had it destroyed. The whole process of securing this planet's future energy resources is back under control.'

'Magda, is she OK?'

'She's on her way, my son.'

CHAPTER 46

The old *pakhan*'s office was empty. From the smell of beeswax and linseed, Leon could tell the floor had recently been polished.

'Why have you invited me here, Leon? Don't you understand how I feel about Eight Over Nine after all I've been through?'

'This room is beautiful, don't you think? Can you feel the spirits? I wanted us to be together in this place.'

'Before you convert the whole subterranean complex, you mean? You can't imagine how much that pleases me. What will you do with this room?'

'I haven't decided. Perhaps I'll make it my office?'

Magda raised an eyebrow and gave him a wry smile. 'And those magnificent paintings in the corridor?'

'Fake. Just like everything else in Eight Over Nine. Music!'

'What would you like to listen to, Leon?' said the Melomet.

'Shostakovich. Second piano concerto.'

The sound of piano music echoed around the panelled room.

'Would you like to dance?'

'You can't possibly dance to this.'

'You can dance to any music, if you try.' He took Magda in his arms. 'You see, it's easy. If you want something so badly, you can have it. Like I want you and you want me. I've rid myself of the spectre of Sergei, by the way.'

'Just like that? We can't turn the clock back, Leon.'

'Why not? The arrow of time goes in both directions. I thought you knew that?'

'Why is it constrained to only two directions?'

He looked into her eyes and laughed. That sense of humour would never fade. 'You'd make a good physicist, Magda Tomala.'

'Talking about physicists, one thing puzzles me. We spent all that time and effort on our predictive models – you trying to find a way in, me trying to find a way out. I'm a mathematician, I was developing a mathematical algorithm to provide me with an answer. You were following a similar process. Yet as a physicist, you can design a nuclear reactor in your head. Why did you need a formal model?'

He laughed again. 'You mathematicians can be so serious at times. For me, it's like this. I get this amazing feel for what's going on at the quantum physics level. I knew in my heart the adjustments we made between stellerator runs were going to work. But when it came to finding you, there was a cloud of emotion fogging my thinking. It's called love. And no physicist will ever be capable of analysing love.' She continued to sway in response to his steps but he knew they were both out of time with the music.

'This movement is so beautiful, Leon. It makes me want to cry. I feel as if we're together as one again.'

'What did I tell you? We can always go back and recover what belongs to us. I can tell you're fully recovered from your brainwashing without undergoing the reversal process. And I have you back. There are no longer any obstacles along our path through space-time. We've just proved that.'

'Oh, Leon. I do love you.'

The lace curtains of Glasnost's grand ballroom fluttered in the warm spring breeze. With the string quartet permitted to play nothing but cheerful music and the champagne flowing, Vladimir Chekhov's guests were bound in a heartfelt happiness.

'Ah, the blushing bride. You look a picture. It reminds me of my own wedding.'

Magda raised her eyebrows. 'Vladimir, you promised.'

'Don't worry, my dear. There is no sadness in my heart today. Only love. I can't begin to explain what it means to me to see my only son marry such a beautiful, intelligent girl as yourself. His mother would have been so proud of him. In fact, I feel happy for the first time this century.' He beckoned across the room. 'Leon, come and join us for a toast.'

Leon strode across the dance floor, wearing the beaming grin he'd displayed since the moment the registrar pronounced him and Magda man and wife.

'I haven't had the chance to thank you, Vladimir. Oh, sorry.'

'No, don't be sorry, Leon. I realise how difficult it must be for you to call me Father. And you don't have to. I want you to know that I've had a long discussion with Szymon. What a delightful chap. And we agreed you should retain his name. After all, he's done a wonderful job in bringing you up.'

'And my stepmother, Lynne?'

'Leon!' Magda had her arms folded. 'It's our wedding day.'

Chekhov was quick to answer. 'What she did was wrong. Yet, despite what people say, I can be a good listener. And believe it or not, I can even forgive. But this is all for another day. Today we have a party to start. Not only is it your wedding day, but we are celebrating the future of nuclear fusion power. The world will no longer have to rely on fossil fuels or inefficient natural resources. Soon we will be generating most of our power from man-made starlight. Fusion will make sure it is all done responsibly and that everyone gets their fair share of the benefit. And it's all down to you, Leon.'

'Yes, we're well on our way. And I understand the US government departments are having success in weeding out the bad apples at the top of their organisation. What a situation we were in. American Tycoons versus Russian Oligarchs ... Oh, sorry, I didn't mean—'

Chekhov's scowl turned into a wry smile. 'I know, Leon. It must have been terrible for you and your colleagues. And your technical counterparts at Los Alamos, of course – devout and trustworthy scientists, all of them. We'll find an acceptable commercial way forward one day, I promise you that.'

'But there is one issue I need to resolve.'

'Which is?'

'Ivan Kuzmin. Why didn't he come to the wedding?'

Chekhov looked puzzled. 'He has urgent security matters to attend to. You knew that.'

'That's what I was coming to – security matters. What concerns me is if Kuzmin is so sharp, how come he didn't spot that huge security hole in the boundary of the mansion.'

'What do you mean?'

'I mean, why didn't he install a wafer-zip detector at the main exit – stop anyone leaving the building with a zip in their pocket? The main security systems would have detected a zip at reception, of course. But for the sake of a ten-minute job, we would have had defence in depth. There has to be a good reason for him not doing it and, if I didn't know better, I'd even say Kuzmin could have been in on this data heist. Do you want me to have a word with him?'

Vladimir Chekhov laughed out loud. The room went quiet and the guests stared with incredulity. He'd obviously never been heard to laugh like this before. He wrapped his arm around Leon and hugged him close.

'Just for once, young man, you are so wrong.'

CHAPTER 47

Oleg Malkin stepped out of the Chevrolet cab and followed the sidewalk along Daytona Beach. He abhorred the flashy beaches in this part of the world, yet he always recognised the financial potential of tourist areas such as Florida's east coast. The Americans could do more with this, he thought as he looked out at the tide of beach dwellers cavorting at the water's foaming edge. It was a sweltering day and he found the dry air stifling. But there was a lucrative deal on offer; why else would he leave his air-conditioned pad in Kissimmee and suffer Florida's oppressive summer climate? He was to meet with Jake Howard, a big player in these parts who had plans for a new super-brothel in Downtown Orlando. He'd been impressed by Jake's ideas during their preliminary video chat, they matched his own – and Jake had big backers. He'd even managed to convince Jake that his own experience would be invaluable and the word *partnership* was mentioned more than once. For the first time since arriving by transatlantic liner three months earlier, Malkin was excited by his financial prospects.

The Rip-Tide beach bar was everything Malkin feared. The fierce sun burned down on its glitzy open areas and the regimented rows of sun worshippers left scant space for anyone to walk along the bar's private beach. The bar itself was jammed with bikini-clad American beauties sipping at fluorescent cocktails served by bronzed and muscled waiters. How could they drink so much alcohol in heat like this? Why would Jake Howard choose such a venue to outline his proposals? *At least there's recruiting potential here.*

'Ah, there you are.' Jake Howard smiled down at Malkin as he offered him a long scrawny hand, toasted brown from years under the Florida sun.

He hadn't expected Jake to be as tall as this. He looked up into his wizened old face, shielding his eyes with his hand and squinting as the bright sunlight shone from behind Jake's head. 'Nice to meet you in the flesh, Jake.'

'Glad you could come along, Oleg. We're over the other side. It's more pleasant round there in the shade. Come and join us for a drink.'

'You've invited others to the meeting?'

'Only one. He's one of your compatriots, living in England. Already thinking of setting up a similar operation in London, I believe. And when I described your experience, he seemed keen on joining us.'

I should know the main players back there. Maybe he's someone new?

The other side of the bar was, as Jake promised, cooler and more comfortable. He was beginning to feel good about this meeting, confident he could start up again and rebuild the empire he'd lost. He was going to enjoy life once more. *I'll show Chekhov what he's missing.*

'There he is. The table in the far corner,' Jake said, giving Malkin a friendly nudge forward. 'Go and introduce yourself. I'll bring over a jug of iced orange and we can make a start.'

Jake Howard's guest was sitting with his back to him. There was something familiar about this figure. *Perhaps I do know him after all?* Malkin was within a metre of the table when Ivan Kuzmin stood and turned.

'Good to see you again, Mr Malkin. Mr Chekhov is keen to talk to you about his son. We have a private jet waiting for us at Orlando International.'

EPILOGUE

'You have visitors, Lynne. I'll leave you in peace, my love.'

The lights in the bedroom were dim, making it almost impossible to see the man who fed her and tended to her daily needs. He seemed a good sort, but who had he brought along to see her?

'Leon? Magda? Is that you? Come and sit down, I have a chair to either side. Though I don't get many visitors. Sit close to me. I don't see too well nowadays – everything seems so foggy.'

A tender kiss on the cheek. When was the last time?

'How are you feeling, Mum?'

'Leon. So nice of you to come. How is your work going? Are you doing well?'

'Yes, it's going well. I've spent a lot of time in London. But I'm here now.'

'I hope you've been looking after this good lady. Has she been in London with you?'

She felt her hand being squeezed. The soft caressing

378

of her bedraggled hair made her smile. She couldn't remember the last time she smiled.

'You're very affectionate today, Magda. Tell me what you've been doing. What's the matter, dear? I can tell you're upset. I've never seen you cry before.'

'I love you, Ma. I've always loved you.'

'Mary, my precious.'

ACKNOWLEDGEMENTS

My sincere thanks go to Dr John Coffey, Zoe Fearnley and Janet Hutchins for their feedback and support throughout the drafting of this novel.

I am particularly indebted to Dea Parkin and her brilliant team of editors at Fiction Feedback. Thank you, Dea, for your invaluable advice, mentoring and patience.

Printed in July 2019
by Rotomail Italia S.p.A., Vignate (MI) - Italy